Prais

"Delacroix brin... ...re with her stunning talent for storytelling."
—*Literary Times*

"When you open a book by Claire Delacroix, you open a treasure chest of words, rare and exquisite!"
—*Rendezvous*

"Delacroix only gets better and better all the time."
—RomanceReviewsMag.com

THE ROSE RED BRIDE

"Perfect . . . intriguing . . . full of historical detail that draws you into the time era . . . I highly recommend this book."
—RomanceJunkies.com

"Fun . . . Fans will enjoy [this novel]."
—**Harriet Klausner**

THE BEAUTY BRIDE

"Lyrical . . . one of Delacroix's stronger novels in recent years."
—*Publishers Weekly*

"What a hero and heroine! An intricate plot and strong characters . . . This is another shining example of the expertise of Ms. Delacroix's writing . . . I could not put it down."
—TheBestReviews.com

more . . .

"FOUR STARS! As beautiful as a fairytale . . . Heralds the beginning of a captivating series."
—*Romantic Times BOOKclub Magazine*

"Delacroix proves once again that she is the master at creating strong, likable characters and a satisfying romance."
—*Booklist*

"A most entertaining read . . . I highly recommend *The Beauty Bride* as a historical with a flair for the unusual and a delightful cast of characters."
—RomanceJunkies.com

THE WARRIOR

"Delacroix's satisfying tale leaves the reader hungry for the next offering."
—*Booklist*

"An enchanting and exciting story . . . Delacroix is one of today's leading historical romance writers, and *The Warrior* demonstrates that."
—*Chronicle Herald*

"Exemplary . . . Delacroix has saved the best for last in her final book of this trilogy . . . A great read!"
—*Old Book Barn Gazette*

"Enchanting and sensual . . . [with] marvelous paranormal touches . . . Wonderfully romantic and action packed."
—*Romantic Times BOOKclub Magazine*

THE SCOUNDREL

"Four stars! . . . Thrilling . . . fast-paced . . . sensual . . . original and cleverly plotted, with many twists and turns. Kudos to Delacroix for being an original!"
—Romantic Times BOOKclub Magazine

"Enthralling and compelling . . . I was captivated and couldn't wait for the plot's resolution."
—Old Book Barn Gazette

THE ROGUE

"A beguiling medieval romance . . . engrossing . . . Readers will treasure this rich and compulsively readable tale."
—Publishers Weekly

"A marvelous . . . intriguing medieval romance . . . Delacroix demonstrates a remarkable creative flair . . . Her vividly realized characters create a fabulous world . . . The Rogue comes highly recommended."
—Midwest Book Review

"Four stars! . . . Intriguing . . . Merlyn is a delightfully charming rogue . . . Delacroix evokes the era, providing us with an accurate portrait and an enchanting tale—just what readers expect from this talented author."
—Romantic Times BOOKclub Magazine

The Snow White Bride

CLAIRE DELACROIX

WARNER BOOKS

NEW YORK   BOSTON

Cover design by Tony Russo
Book design by Giorgetta Bell McRee

Warner Books

Time Warner Book Group
1271 Avenue of the Americas
New York, NY 10020
Visit our Web site at www.twbookmark.com

Printed in the United States of America

First Paperback Printing: November 2005

10 9 8 7 6 5 4 3 2 1

This trilogy is dedicated to my readers,
with heartfelt thanks for your loyalty and support.
May you enjoy reading about the Jewels of Kinfairlie
as much as I have enjoyed recounting their tales.

The
Snow White
Bride

Chapter One

~

Kinfairlie, Scotland—December 24, 1421

THE SNOW WAS FALLING FAST AND THICK, the starless sky was darker than indigo, and it was well past midnight when Eleanor knew that she could flee no farther. The small village that rose before her seemed heaven-sent: it was devoid of tall walls and barred gates. She did not believe that it truly could be this peaceful anywhere in Christendom, but the town's tranquillity was seductive all the same.

She did not know its name and she did not care. She spied the church and decided immediately that this sleeping town, with its quiet surety that the world was good, would be the place she chose to rest.

The night would not last much longer, for darkness already gave way to dawn's light. Eleanor did not know where she would go from here, but knew she could make no decision when she was so exhausted.

The church portal was unlocked, and Eleanor sighed with relief as one last fear was proved groundless. She stepped into its embracing shadows and let the door close heavily behind her. She waited, half-expecting the illusion of tranquillity to be shattered, but only silence reached her ears. She stood on the threshold and inhaled deeply of the scent of beeswax candles, the air of prayer and devotion, the aura of a holy place.

Sanctuary.

There was a single small glass pane over the altar, and the light cast by the snow illuminated it and the chapel's bare interior. It was a humble church, to be sure, for she could see its emptiness even in the shadows. The altar was devoid of chalice and monstrance, evidence that even this community believed that treasures should be locked away.

Eleanor spied the bench near the altar, perhaps one used by the priest, and eased herself onto it. She sat down and stopped running for the first time in what seemed an eternity.

Then she listened, fearing the worst.

There was no sound at all beyond the pounding of her heart. No hoofbeats echoed in pursuit. No hounds bayed as they found her scent. No men shouted that they had spied her footprints.

The rapidly falling snow might prove a blessing, for it would quickly hide her path and disguise her scent. She sat, intending to wait the necessary interval until she knew that she was safe.

Eleanor felt every ache in her exhausted body, and she realized only now how cold she had become. She could not feel her fingertips, so she crossed her arms and pressed her hands into her underarms. She supposed that her belly must be empty, but she was too numb to be certain. She had a keen thirst, to be sure.

Had it only been three days and nights since everything had changed, and changed irrevocably? She shied away from considering what would happen to her now, was too tired to speculate beyond the nigh impossible goal of escape.

Instead, she sat and marveled that she could hear only the faint roll of the sea. It was a gentle sound, its effect not unlike a lullaby. Was it possible that Ewen's kin had abandoned the hunt for her?

Eleanor could not believe as much. She sat vigilant and she listened, but slowly she began to feel warmer. That warmth betrayed her, undermined her resolve to remain awake, coaxed her to succumb to exhaustion. She fought against slumber, but she had endured too much of late. It was not long before she gathered her booted feet beneath her, wrapped her ermine-lined cloak more tightly about herself, and dared to consider sleeping for the first time since Ewen had died.

Although she murmured a prayer, Eleanor did not pray for her husband's recently departed soul. She knew that Ewen was lost beyond redemption, she knew that he roasted in hell.

Worst of all, Eleanor knew that, deep in her heart, she was glad. She was also sufficiently wicked to believe that he deserved no less.

With the dawn, she would begin to atone for her sins of thought and deed. In this moment, she managed only to draw her hood over her hair before her eyes closed and she welcomed the bliss of sleep.

～

THE FIRST MORNING SERVICES in Kinfairlie's chapel were attended mostly by the women, both from the keep and from the village, and though it was the day of Christmas Eve, this morning was no different.

Madeline arrived with her sisters: Vivienne, Annelise, Isabella, and Elizabeth. Both Madeline and Vivienne were ripening with child, though the other sisters were yet maidens. They were a noisy party, for Madeline and Vivienne had not been home to Kinfairlie since their nuptials earlier in the year, and all five sisters chattered even as they arrived in the village chapel.

The woman kneeling before the altar started at the sound of their arrival. She caught her breath and glanced over her shoulder, fear etched on her features.

She was so beautiful that Madeline gaped in astonishment.

And she was a stranger. There were few strangers in Kinfairlie, particularly at this time of the year. Madeline was intrigued, as was probably every other soul who followed the Lammergeier sisters into the chapel.

This woman was no maiden, for she wore a gossamer veil and circlet over her hair. What Madeline could spy of the woman's hair was more golden of hue than flaxen. In that moment that she stared at the sisters, Madeline noted skin so fair that the woman might have been carved of alabaster. Her eyes were a startlingly vivid green and her lips as red as rubies. She might have been of an age with Madeline.

But the stranger's fear was almost palpable. She pivoted abruptly after scanning the arrivals. She drew the hood of her sapphire cloak over her hair to hide her features, and bent to her prayers once more. Madeline wondered what horrors this woman had faced that she should be so fearful of strangers.

The woman's cloak was remarkable in itself, of wool spun finer than fine, and trimmed with a king's ransom in ermine. The stranger was noble, then, for no common person could have afforded such a garment.

Yet she was unattended, and there was no fine horse outside the chapel. Surely such a woman would not travel on foot, or alone?

Not unless she was in dire peril. Madeline caught her breath at the simple truth of it, and immediately she yearned to be of aid. Indeed, any other noblewoman would have rapped on the gates of the keep and demanded hospitality of a fellow Christian.

But this woman had no steed. Her boots were mired, there was dirt on the hem of her cloak. She must have been afraid to ask for help, which said little good about her circumstance.

Father Malachy granted the praying woman a benign smile, then frowned at the boisterous sisters. Madeline and her sisters meekly genuflected and became silent as mice as they took their places at the front of the chapel, alongside the stranger. Madeline could fairly feel the questions of her sisters, and was not surprised to find herself eased closest to the stranger by mutual and silent consent.

As eldest, she had been appointed to learn more.

The service seemed impossibly long, and Madeline found herself thinking more about the stranger beside her than her prayers. Finally the priest was done and the woman tried to leave the chapel immediately behind him.

The sisters had other ideas. The stranger jumped when

Madeline touched her elbow, even with the barrier of that cloak between them. When the stranger paused, Annelise and Isabella slipped around her to block her exit from the chapel.

"You are unknown here," Madeline said.

The woman's eyes widened at the realization that she had been surrounded, though she nodded acknowledgment. "I mean no harm to any soul. I halted only to pray." She tried to leave, but the sisters stood resolute.

"Someone means harm to you, though," Vivienne said with conviction. "You would not have sought sanctuary in the house of God otherwise."

The woman's eyes narrowed with suspicion. "Who are you, and with whom are you allied?"

"Do you not know where you have come?" Madeline asked.

The woman shook her head.

That in itself was intriguing. She must be far from home indeed. What would compel her to flee into the night without a clear destination? Madeline herself had done as much once and felt a certain kinship with this woman as a result.

"I am Madeline FitzHenry, once of Kinfairlie and now Lady of Caerwyn," she said, softening her words with a smile. "These are my sisters. We are gathered to celebrate the Yule together in our ancestral home of Kinfairlie and mean no harm to any guest of our hall."

"Kinfairlie." The woman's gaze flicked between them. "You must be kin with the Lammergeier then. I have heard tales of them."

"Lammergeier is our family name," Vivienne agreed.

The woman took a deep breath as if to steady herself,

as if the news of where she stood was unwelcome. "The Lammergeier are said to ally long with no man."

"That is a somewhat harsh charge from one who does not know us . . . ," Isabella began, but Madeline laid a hand upon her arm to silence her.

"Of what import is our alliance? Have you need of aid?" Madeline asked. "Do you fear someone who might have allies in these parts?"

The woman gathered her skirts and made again to leave. "I thank you for your concern, but it would be safer for you to know no more of me." She pivoted and Isabella and Annelise, faced with her determination, stepped out of her path. The chapel had emptied now, save for the sisters and this woman who strode away from them with the grace of a queen.

"And what would be safer for you?" Madeline asked quietly, her words carrying through the chapel.

"Tell us who you flee and why," Isabella said, always unafraid of such details.

The woman paused, seemingly tempted. "How do I know that I can trust you?"

"Who else can you trust?" Madeline asked. "You have not so much as a steed, let alone a maid, to accompany you. I would wager that you cannot run much farther than you already have. I would further wager that you are in peril. We offer aid to you."

The woman's strength seemed to falter then, and she looked at the stone floor. Madeline stretched a consoling hand toward her, but then the stranger straightened and tossed back her hood.

She spoke with a regal resolve. "My tale is not that uncommon. My father wed me to a man of his choice, a man far, far older than myself. When I was widowed some years later, my father wed me to another man."

"Who also died," Vivienne said, guessing the next part of the story as she was inclined to do.

"But not before my father himself died. I have no other kin than my husband's family: my mother died long ago and neither of my husbands granted me a child."

"Surely your dowry once again becomes your own?" Isabella asked.

The woman's smile was wry. "Surely not." Something flashed in her eyes then, a determination that was greater than any fear, and Madeline guessed that the woman did not like her husband's kin. Her dislike must have been potent for her to abandon her dowry.

"It has long been said that a woman weds once for duty and once for love," Vivienne said. "To be wed twice for duty is beyond expectation."

"And against my every desire!" the woman said, her eyes flashing. "I have done all that I can to avoid such a fate. I have left my old abode with only the garb upon my back, I have abandoned what should be my own, but it is not sufficient for them. They pursue me, like hounds at the hunt. Indeed, I dare not confess the name of that holding to any soul, lest they find me again." Her lips tightened with a quiver that rent Madeline's heart.

"You have need of protection, not further flight," Madeline said.

"Who would be so foolish as to protect me?"

"A new husband would defend you," Vivienne said.

"One of your own choice!" Elizabeth interjected.

"Impossible." The woman shook her head. "I am sorry. I should not have burdened you with my woes."

"But where will you go?" Elizabeth asked.

"As far as I must," she said, and gathered her cloak about herself as she hastened down the aisle. "I dare not linger here longer. Only as far as Kinfairlie," she whispered, almost to herself. "They will be fast behind me." She drew up her hood and reached for the handle upon the heavy wood door.

"We cannot let her go," Madeline said, and her sisters nodded agreement. "She will never flee farther than they can follow."

"Surely her fears are overwrought," Vivienne said. "Her husband's kin might have threatened her, and they might even follow her, but as soon as she wed another man, they would abandon the chase. It would not be reasonable to do otherwise, especially if they already hold her dowry."

"Doubtless she has had little chance to muster her thoughts," Madeline mused, feeling sympathy for the woman. "I wonder when last she ate a meal."

"Or slept, without fearing that her avaricious kin would pounce upon her in the night." Vivienne shivered at the prospect.

"She has need of a stalwart defender," Elizabeth said with gusto. "Like a valiant knight in an old tale, one who will vanquish all of her enemies."

"It will be a rare and honorable man who takes her cause," Annelise agreed.

"It will be a bold man, unafraid to face any foe to see his lady's safety assured," Elizabeth said, her love of tales evident. "He will slaughter dragons for her, and send evil flying from the gates!"

"There are no dragons to be bested," Isabella said wryly. "Only greedy kin."

Madeline exchanged a smile with Vivienne as an idea apparently came to them both of one accord. "Hmmm," Madeline mused. "A brave knight, unwed but in possession of his inheritance, so entitled to wed."

"A man with a reputation for ensuring justice is served," Vivienne said as her smile broadened.

"A man who would court the lady's favor, and treat her with the honor she is due," Annelise contributed, for she clearly discerned Madeline's thoughts.

"Would it not be perfect if we knew such a man?" Madeline said.

"Especially if the nuptial vows of such a man would ensure that his debt against his own sisters is paid in full?" Vivienne said.

Elizabeth began to laugh, though Isabella still appeared to be confused.

"Alexander found husbands for us when we had no desire of them," Madeline explained. "I say we return the favor, and aid this beleaguered noblewoman at the same time."

"It would serve Alexander well to taste his own dish," Elizabeth said with some heat. "Though I think her too fine for him."

"The lady herself must agree," Vivienne said, ignoring this. Elizabeth had become quite vexed with Alexander of late, and was increasingly inclined to voice her unflattering opinion of him.

"Lady!" Madeline cried, and the sisters gave chase as one. "Stay your flight!"

They burst out of the chapel in pursuit. The woman paused in the bailey, the fresh snow as high as her ankles. She glanced back, as if afraid to hope that any soul might assist her.

"My brother, Laird of Kinfairlie, has need of a bride," Madeline said. The sisters surrounded the woman once again, their eyes alight with the perfection of their scheme.

"He is a man of honor," Vivienne said, "and one who will see you protected. He is not so hard upon the eyes, and can be charming."

"He is a bit mischievous," Isabella warned the woman.

"But he takes his responsibilities most seriously and serves Kinfairlie well as its laird," Annelise said.

"But you cannot expect him to wed me. You scarce know me and he does not know me at all."

"Marriages are arranged all the time," Vivienne said with a smile, and Elizabeth laughed. The woman looked between them, not understanding the reference. Vivienne stepped forward and looped her arm through the other woman's elbow. "Come and look upon him. If he meets with your favor and wedding him seems to you a suitable scheme . . ."

Madeline took the woman's other arm. "Then you may rely upon us to arrange the details."

"There will be guests aplenty in the hall this night," Vivienne said. "No one will note another, and if you decide against this course, you can travel onward on the morrow."

The stranger nodded at this plan, but Madeline was not fooled by her apparent reserve. There was new vigor in her step, just for having a choice, and Madeline knew that Alexander would be at his amiable best this night. Her brother might try to delay his duty to wed, he might even protest the sisters' interference, but once this beauty was in his bed, once he had a child to bounce upon his own knee, he would thank her and Vivienne for their aid in finding him such a bride.

Madeline was certain of it.

ALEXANDER LAMMERGEIER, Laird of Kinfairlie, had had his fill of responsibility. The accounts for Kinfairlie would never balance, not without a massive financial gain from some unanticipated source. He had seen two sisters married this year, on the counsel of those who knew more of running an estate than he, and could not for the life of him see what fiscal benefit had been derived from having two less mouths to feed. There were dozens yet residing within his walls, after all.

The sound of merrymaking rose from Kinfairlie's hall below. It was Christmas Eve, and he was laboring over Kinfairlie's books, trying to find a stray denier.

There were no stray deniers. Alexander knew it well. And further, he despised being Laird of Kinfairlie. He wanted his parents back, hale and hearty; he wanted to ask his father how that man had managed the burden of responsibility; he wanted to know what he should do when the seed was washed away and the peasants who relied upon him were left hungry.

Further, he wanted his uncle Tynan, upon whom he had heavily relied after his parents' demise, to walk out of the grotto beneath Ravensmuir and explain that he was not dead, after all. He wanted his aunt Rosamunde, also lost in the rubble that had been Ravensmuir, to leap from beneath the stones, to explain that tales of her death were mere exaggeration, and to present an ancient relic along with its tale. Though Rosamunde was not their aunt in truth, Alexander and his siblings continued to regard her as such, even after the revelation that she had been adopted as an infant.

Alexander wanted answers; he wanted counsel, he wanted the merriment of his former life back.

Yet all Alexander had were burdens. His sisters were no longer foils for his teasing or even victims of his jests, but maidens for whom suitable husbands had to be found. He had seen the two eldest of his sisters wed, but did not for a moment deny that Fortune had smiled upon him in those two circumstances. He had not handled those nuptial arrangements well and it was good luck alone that had seen Madeline and Vivienne happily wed.

His two brothers had been dispatched to Inverfyre and Ravensmuir to train, at Uncle Tynan's suggestion, which had relieved Alexander of the cost of supporting them, but also of the merriment of their company. Worse, Malcolm stood heir to Ravensmuir, though he was younger and less knowledgeable than Alexander—and he came to Alexander for counsel the older brother could seldom give. Ross was at Inverfyre for the foreseeable future, training to earn his spurs, and though Alexander thought this a great favor by their uncle, the Hawk of Inverfyre, still he missed Ross's companionship. It was beyond disappointing that Ross would not be home for Christmas after all.

Alexander was lonely, he was frustrated and saw no promise for change in his future. He had failed on all accounts, when once he had been able to do nothing wrong. He scowled at the cursed books, listened to the music being wrought by musicians he had no notion of how he might pay, and swore with vigor.

It was Christmas. He had seen fit to entertain Kinfairlie's peasants, as was traditional, despite the dearth of coins in his treasury. He might as well enjoy the festivities himself.

It might be the last merry Christmas at Kinfairlie.

Alexander slammed the ledgers of his abode with a vengeance, then dropped them back into the trunk where they were stored. He savored their resounding thump, then dropped the lid on the trunk so that it slammed. He locked it and only just stopped himself from hurling the key out the window into the snow, which had not ceased falling for an entire day.

Indeed, he had lifted his fist when his castellan's discreet cough halted his gesture.

Alexander pivoted smoothly, slid the key into his purse, and smiled at Anthony as if that man had not interrupted a healthy impulse. "Good evening, Anthony. I trust all is well in the hall?"

Anthony surveyed the chamber, his white brows bristling in disapproval. "Well enough, my lord. Might I conclude that you have balanced Kinfairlie's accounts for the year?"

"You might," Alexander said with a cheer he had not felt in considerable time. "But you would be in error."

Anthony scowled. "Your father would never have left his chamber until his labor was done."

"My father is dead, and though his habits were exemplary, they will not necessarily be mine." Alexander swept past the older man and sniffed appreciatively. "Venison! What a marvel you are, Anthony."

"The miller felled two bucks, supposedly by accident, my lord." Anthony frowned more deeply. "There is certainly more to the tale than what we were told, for all know that common people have no right to hunt deer, and it is difficult to mistake a deer for anything other than what it is. I would suggest that we delve to the bottom of the tale lest all think they can hunt without repercussions. . . ."

"I suggest that we enjoy the meat and the season and leave the matter be," Alexander said with resolve.

"But . . ."

"But they are hungry, Anthony. The harvest has been poor and most gardens have not prospered, either. It is to their merit that they share the spoil with all."

The older man straightened with disapproval. "Your father would never have allowed such a transgression against his rights. . . ."

"Nor would he have allowed those beneath his hand to starve." Alexander softened his tone and laid a hand upon the older man's shoulder. "This year has been most uncommon, Anthony, and I will not punish my guests for ensuring that the board groans this night. Christmas is a season of celebration and forgiveness. Let us welcome the year with hope."

Anthony took a deep breath, but Alexander did not want to argue about his breach of convention again. Instead of choosing a select few peasants from Kinfairlie village to feast in the laird's hall, Alexander had invited them all. The population of the village had dwindled in the past year due to the poor conditions and he wanted every man, woman, and child to share in whatever largesse he could offer. They had been arriving steadily since morning mass, bringing their napkins and their spoons and undoubtedly their appetites. Many had brought the chickens and candles they owed to the laird for this feast.

Alexander had given his villagers what he could—he had ensured that they had justice, he had tried to supply seed for the fields, and no matter what it cost, he would see their bellies filled this night.

It was Christmas. Let Anthony say what he might.

Alexander's brother-in-law Rhys FitzHenry and sister Madeline had arrived the day before and, at Alexander's request, Rhys had ridden to hunt with two of Kinfairlie's falcons and the men in his party. He had returned with four dozen rabbits.

Five baskets of eels had been collected at Inverfyre by Alexander's sister Vivienne and her husband, Erik Sinclair, on their journey south to Kinfairlie, and Vivienne had brought half-a-dozen goats heavy with milk to swell the ranks of livestock at Kinfairlie.

Alexander himself had sent to York for six cured hams, and the peasant children had foraged for the eggs of wild fowl. The musicians had arrived this very day with the hams and requested accommodation and alms for the season, which Alexander had not been able to protest.

The most startling facet of all was that Alexander even found himself *thinking* in inventories. He tallied and calculated, concluding that there was food enough for the considerable company for perhaps four days, at which point, he would have a problem.

At least the problem was four days away.

Alexander marched past his astonished castellan, then paused at the top of the stairs. He snapped his fingers and pivoted to face Anthony, whose silvery brows had formed a single line of bushy reproach. "There are two casks of wine yet in the cellar, Anthony, according to the ledgers. Please have them brought to the hall and opened this night."

Those brows shot skyward. "My lord . . ."

"Do as I bid you immediately, Anthony," Alexander interjected crisply, knowing that his castellan was as surprised by his command as his tone. "And be sure to taste the wine yourself before allowing it to be poured."

The wine would do his proper castellan good, in Alexander's opinion. He strode down the stairs, the music lightening his heart, and resolved to have a measure of that wine himself.

ALEXANDER WAS PLEASED to note how his sisters had brought greens into the hall, for he had been so immersed in his books that he had forgotten about this ritual. Hundreds of candles burned and the Yule log, a particularly massive specimen that would surely last for the entire fortnight, burned on the hearth. Mercifully, some soul had recalled this ritual as well.

The hall was warm and golden, filled to bursting with trestle tables and chattering people. He could smell the roasted meat, and the musicians led the assembly in a merry tune. His sisters were adorned in their best and laughing at the high table. Even the sight of the unbound tresses of his three maiden sisters failed to trouble him on this night.

Alexander might have paused there on the stairs to savor the sight, but to his surprise, the detection of his presence in his own hall was greeted with a rowdy cheer. The peasants of Kinfairlie rose to their feet, then turned and lifted their cups of ale in salute. "My lord!" they cried as one.

They saluted him. Tears pricked Alexander's eyes at this unexpected tribute. What had he done to deserve their respect? He had tried, to be sure, but the Fates had conspired against any success. Ever one for a jest, he turned and looked behind himself, summoning a hearty laugh from the assembly.

"God bless the laird of Kinfairlie!" cried the miller, who had evidently been appointed spokesman. "The fairest laird that ever there was." There was another ripple of laughter and the miller flushed. "I mean, of course, that his courts are fair and that justice is found in his courts." The miller grinned. "Though my wife tells me that he is not hard upon the eyes, either."

The assembly laughed. "A wife is what our laird needs," cried one bold soul.

"Nay, a dozen bairns is what he needs," shouted another, but the miller held his hand up for silence.

He sobered as he held Alexander's gaze. "It has been a year of challenges unexpected at Kinfairlie. Though none of us would have wished for the sudden loss of our former laird and his lady"—many in the company crossed themselves in reference to the deaths of Alexander's parents—"I have been chosen of all of us to thank you for so boldly taking on your duties, sir."

Alexander inclined his head. "I was raised to assume this duty, as well you know."

The miller shook his head. "Few men could have faced this past year with such courage, my lord, no less with such grace and generosity. You serve your father's memory well, Alexander Lammergeier, and may you prosper at Kinfairlie for years untold." With that, the miller lifted his cup higher.

"Long live the laird of Kinfairlie!" cried one soul, and the company echoed the blessing. They lifted their cups in salute, then drank heartily.

Alexander was deeply touched, though he characteristically hid his response with a jest. "I thank you kindly," he said, then bowed deeply to the company. "But you should know that I called for the wine to be opened *before* I knew that you meant to greet me thus."

The assembly laughed and the musicians sang a ditty on the merits of wine, a comparative rarity in these parts. Alexander made his way through the company, welcoming peasants by name and exchanging Christmas blessings. He found himself laughing at one tale and pinching a child's plump cheek, enjoying himself despite the odds.

He glanced up, feeling the weight of someone's gaze upon him, and met the steady stare of a woman he did not know. She must have been among the entourages of Madeline or Vivienne, perhaps a friend of one of his sisters. Alexander was intrigued by the very sight of her. She watched him from the high table, her eyes the clearest green he had ever seen.

But there was a sadness in her eyes and a downward curve to her lips that snared Alexander's attention. She averted her glance as soon as their gazes met and eased herself into the shadows. She was veiled as a married woman, but no man attended her. Worse, she was not merry on this night of festivity, and Alexander decided then what his mission would be.

He would make this lady smile. Once, he had been good at coaxing women's laughter. Once, he had savored feminine companionship. His pulse quickened at the challenge, for he had not lingered overmuch with women this past year. It would be good to prove—if only to himself—that he had not sacrificed all of himself to his duties as laird.

The castellan brought him a goblet of ruby red wine, that man's lips still taut. "I thank you, Anthony." Alexander raised the cup to his guests assembled in Kinfairlie's hall. "And I thank you not only for your kind salute, but for joining me on this night of nights. I bid you be merry in Kinfairlie's hall, one and all, and may this Christmas Eve feast be but the first of many we share."

The assembly roared agreement and raised their cups, then drank of Alexander's ale and wine. Alexander raised his cup to the beauteous lady at his board, who feigned ignorance of his salute. She sipped his toast and her cheeks pinkened slightly, though, which was progress of a kind.

Alexander Lammergeier would not be so easily defeated as that.

Indeed, he purposefully made his way to sit at her very side, not caring a whit for changing the arrangements Anthony had carefully made at the head table.

This lady's smile would be won, regardless of the cost.

ELEANOR WAS NOT A FICKLE WOMAN, but a single glimpse of Alexander Lammergeier utterly changed her thinking. She had erred when she had accepted the sisters' offer. She merely spied the man in question and knew she could not wed him.

For the laird of Kinfairlie was not what Eleanor had expected. She had assumed him to be a portly curmudgeon of an elder brother, perhaps one from an earlier marriage of the women's father, a man vastly older and less eligible than his pretty sisters.

But Alexander possessed none of those traits. He was young, for one thing, a mere half-dozen years older than herself. He was also cursedly handsome, which Eleanor distrusted to her very marrow, and worse, he was clearly aware of his own merit. Like Kinfairlie itself, he presented an allure that must be only skin deep. No man could be handsome and kind and unwed; no holding could be fully peaceful. Both laird and estate were illusions and thus untrustworthy.

Indeed, Alexander's peasants held him in such uncommon regard that Eleanor concluded that they feigned their affection. They must be fawning, out of fear of some caprice of his nature.

Further, there was no reason, from the look of him, that the laird of Kinfairlie would have any trouble finding a spouse for himself. What did his sisters know of him that Eleanor did not? She could imagine a thousand ugly liabilities.

Which particular weakness was his curse was not that important. She would break the wager, here and now, and to seal her decision, she would leave Kinfairlie. No one would pursue her when there was a banquet to be savored in a warm hall.

"I have made my choice," she whispered to Madeline, who regarded her with optimism. "I will not wed your brother."

Madeline's smile disappeared. "But you cannot do so!"

"I most certainly can." Eleanor rose to her feet.

"At least remain for the meal," Vivienne protested.

"But you know nothing of him," Madeline said, sounding so pragmatic that Eleanor might have been persuaded under other circumstances. "At least, meet him before you decide."

Eleanor shook her head and seized her cloak. "It was a poor idea, though well-intentioned," she said, forcing a polite smile for the sisters. "I appreciate your courtesy and wish you both well." She pivoted then, and would have fled, but Alexander himself stood directly before her.

He did not look inclined to move. He was a formidable obstacle, tall and broad as he was, though it was his charming smile that made Eleanor reluctant to show herself rude. She felt flushed and flustered beneath his attention, as he must know. "Surely you cannot depart when we have yet to be introduced?"

Had his sisters notified him of their scheme? Was she the one to be cornered into marriage, instead of Alexander? Terror claimed Eleanor that she was sought yet again for the wealth she might bring a spouse.

"I apologize for my haste, but it is later than I had believed. I must leave immediately," she said.

"Do you seek your spouse? We can send for him," he said with a courtesy she did not trust.

"I have no spouse. I am widowed," she said, and made to step past him.

But Alexander claimed Eleanor's elbow. She flinched at his touch, though his grip was gentle, and he lifted his hand away immediately. "I apologize. It is not my intent to harm you," he said, his words so contrite that another woman might have believed him.

But Eleanor had heard such apologies before, and she had been trapped by ambitious men before. Her thoughts whirled. How could the sisters have known of her inheritance? She had not even told them her name. The news of a fortune to be won traveled on fleet feet, however, as Eleanor had learned.

Surely, even if Ewen's kin had come this way while she slept in Kinfairlie's chapel, they would never reveal the true reason they sought her? Her fortune could easily be claimed by any man with a prick and a barren left hand.

Eleanor did not know. She did not truly care. She felt hot and cornered beneath this man's steady gaze, discomfited that he had noted her aversion to being touched. She wished to flee as far as she could.

"I thank you for your hospitality," she said, hearing the fear in her own words. "But I must leave immediately."

"Then I shall escort you to the stables," Alexander said in a tone that brooked no argument.

"You cannot leave before the meal is served," Vivienne said.

"No one should journey on Christmas Eve!" Madeline protested.

"The lady shall do as she desires," Alexander said with resolve, and Eleanor was surprised to have him defend her decision. He winked at her most unexpectedly and her heart skipped. When had a man ever flirted with her?

"And I shall ensure that she has her choice," Alexander said, his tone firm. He offered his elbow to Eleanor, who found herself shocked that any man would so cede to her.

She took his arm, though did not allow herself to become less wary, and Alexander led her from the hall. She did not feel more at ease, curiously, once they were alone in the corridor beyond the hall, once there was only shadows and the distant clatter of the feast being served.

For the laird himself accompanied her, of course, and his attention was fixed fully upon her.

"I have a boon to ask of you before you leave Kinfairlie," Alexander said, sparing her a glance.

He had blue eyes, Eleanor noted, eyes filled with a thousand sparkles, as if his good humor could not be contained. His hair was as black as a raven's wing, the black of his lashes making his eyes appear yet a more unholy blue. There were faint lines beside his eyes, as if he oft smiled, and he was tanned, as if he was oft outdoors. His manners were perfect, his grace unrivaled. She braced herself against his allure, reminding herself to trust no one. Who knew what lies a man might tell to ensnare her?

"I have little to grant and less inclination to surrender whatsoever I do possess," she said, and glanced away.

Alexander chuckled, a beguiling sound if ever there was one. "I ask only for your name," he said. "I am Alexander Lammergeier, Laird of Kinfairlie, and I bid you welcome to my hall, however short your visit might prove to be."

"I was solely here on your sisters' sufferance, but do thank you for your hospitality." Eleanor said no more, though she felt him waiting, felt his gaze upon her, felt her color rising ever so slightly.

"Have you not a name?" he asked with some amusement.

"Why would you have need of it?" They took measured steps together, despite Eleanor's attempt to hasten. "I intend to leave and never return."

"Then perhaps I shall seek you out, like a knight upon a quest. It would be far simpler to succeed in that feat if I knew your name."

Eleanor was certain that he jested at her expense and stole a glance at him. She found his eyes sparkling yet, but he watched her avidly, as if truly interested in her answer. She recalled the sum of her father's fortune and reminded herself that many a man would find that worthy of fascination. "You have no good reason to seek me out," she said primly.

"Ah, but I do."

He spoke with such conviction that Eleanor had to look his way again. The corner of his mouth was tugging into a smile. He had a dimple beneath one corner of his mouth, and looked the very image of mischief.

He shook a finger at her. "You would have me think that you are not curious, but I can see that you are. Perhaps you do not wish to encourage me, knowing as you do that the ogre appointed as your guardian would savor the chance to devour me."

"There is no such ogre!"

Alexander nodded sagely. "Perhaps you show your interest in me by fearing for my hide in undertaking such a quest. It shows a kindness of nature that is yet more enticing than your beauty."

"Perhaps I show no such concern."

He laughed, undeterred, and Eleanor found herself tempted to smile. "But surely you are not devoid of curiosity," he teased. "You do not even ask after the details of my quest, although it concerns you alone."

"I suspect it is the same as most men's quests, when they ride in pursuit of women," Eleanor said. She dared to give him a stern glance. "A coupling, either willing or nay, and a son, either legitimate or nay."

The sparkle left his eyes, though she felt no triumph

that she had insulted him. "You have a grim view of my fellows."

"I have been taught to expect no more and no less than that."

He considered her before he spoke. "How uncommon for a demoiselle. How unfortunate."

"I am no maiden," Eleanor retorted. "But a woman twice widowed." She lifted her chin and regarded him steadily. "There are many who would consider me well-sampled for that. As for Fortune, she is a fickle companion."

"I know that well enough," he said so wryly that she dared to glance his way again. He smiled at her. "But surely the merit of a woman is not measured by her innocence?" He spoke with such soft conviction that Eleanor was tempted to believe he thought as much.

But men lied. Not a one of them was to be believed, especially one so certain of his own charm as this Alexander.

She said nothing, and they stepped through the last portal, into the bailey. Eleanor took a deep breath of bracingly cold air. The snow still fell, though not as thickly as it had the night before, and it was dark. Snow gleamed on the roofs of Kinfairlie village. The land seemed shrouded in silence, and though she listened with care, she heard no approaching hoofbeats.

"So you assume me to be of the ilk as those men you have known, though I am not. How might I persuade you otherwise?"

At his words, Eleanor realized that Alexander had been watching her. She wondered how much he had guessed of her thoughts and feared his intent anew. "You will not."

He smiled then, a smile of such confidence that she

knew she had not deterred him. Indeed, she seemed to have done the opposite. "Then my quest shall prove interesting, indeed."

"If you pursue me, you will not bed me."

"That is not my intent."

She could not contain her curiosity then. "I do not understand. What then is your quest?"

"To see you smile, no more and no less."

Eleanor stared at Alexander, so shocked was she. He smiled at her, his very expression beguiling her, tempting her, teasing her with the prospect of fulfilling his sisters' scheme. He had firm lips and a steady gaze.

He would not be so fearsome to meet abed. Eleanor's heart leapt in a most uncharacteristic manner.

She scoffed then, seeing the trick in his words. "Ah, but you would demand a tribute upon your success, to be sure."

Alexander shook his head. "If you were inclined to grant one, I would accept it, but it is not my manner to force myself upon unwilling women."

She had forgotten that she had been holding Alexander's arm, but she became aware of it now, beneath his sure regard. His arm was warm and strong beneath her fingertips, and Eleanor thought she could feel the pulse of his blood beneath the flesh, even through the barrier of cloth. He was no ancient man, but one young and virile and intrigued by her. She looked at him, noted the mischievous curve of his lips, and knew that she would have surrendered her heart to Alexander Lammergeier a dozen years earlier without a murmur of protest.

But she was no innocent maiden any longer. She would have been happy to have never learned the lessons she had learned, but that did not change how they had shaped her life.

Eleanor pulled her hand from the crook of Alexander's elbow and stepped away, half-certain that he mocked her. "You are light of heart for a man so burdened with responsibility as a laird should be." She folded her arms across her chest, feeling the cold now that she was two paces away from his heat. "Perhaps you are not laird at all."

Alexander sobered then, his gaze flicking over the village before them. When he met her gaze again, though, his smile was less mischievous and his words came low. "Perhaps for this night, I have decided to forget my obligations."

If his jesting manner was enticing, his thoughtfulness was more so. Eleanor had never been able to resist a man with his wits about him. She had to depart and do so immediately.

Eleanor forced a smile, though it was a sad one, then shrugged. "There is your quest fulfilled, Alexander Lammergeier, and now I will depart. You may disregard your obligations, but I will never forget mine."

"Not even for one night?"

"Not even for one moment." With that, Eleanor turned away from this intriguing man, gathered her cloak about herself, and began to walk away.

Kinfairlie was no sanctuary, not with a man such as Alexander as its laird, a man who could make her doubt even for a moment all she knew to be true.

She was best away from this false haven; the farther away and the sooner, the better.

Chapter Two

ALEXANDER'S INNATE SKILLS had clearly withered in the past year. Indeed, his ability to beguile a woman had eroded to nothing at all. Never had he watched a woman turn her back upon him, never had he seen a woman dismiss his presence so readily.

But this lady strode resolutely away, choosing a night in the snow over him and the pleasures of his hall.

It was little consolation that she was the most intriguing woman that he had ever encountered. Not only was she lovely, but also her wits were quick, and she had already surprised him more than once.

He wanted to know more of her, not have her walk away and disappear forever.

Alexander shoved a hand through his hair. He might have seized her arm and forcibly halted her, but he recalled how she had cringed from his touch.

So, he was loathsome as well. His charm was lacking, to be sure.

"Have you no horse?" he called after her.

She did not turn, as if she thought the answer evident.

Nor did she slow her pace, much less halt. He might never have spoken.

Alexander cursed that he was apparently so forgettable, then strode after her. He swung his cloak from his own back and dropped it over her shoulders. She was finely wrought and even her luxuriant cloak could not be sufficient against this night's cold.

She glanced up at this slight courtesy, the surprise in her expression telling him that she had not lied.

Twice wed and poorly served both times, he would wager. His determination to show her that all men did not fit her experience redoubled.

"You cannot walk away from Kinfairlie on Christmas Eve," he said with false cheer. "As laird of this holding, I forbid it."

"You were the one who chose to put your obligations aside. If you are not laird this night, then you cannot command my doings."

Alexander smiled. "True enough. Then I argue on grounds of concern for your welfare. You will not find a hearth to welcome you on this night."

"On Christmas Eve? You have a low opinion of the charity of your fellows!"

"They are all at my board, not home to answer your knock. It is but the truth of the situation."

She bit her lip to consider that. Then a shadow touched her features, as if she recalled some matter of urgency, and she quickened her pace. "All the same, I dare not linger."

"Am I so fearsome as that?" Alexander demanded. "I will ensure that no man plagues you in my hall."

Her sidelong glance was wry. "What of you?"

"But I seek only a smile. It will cost you little to entertain my quest for a single night."

She hesitated before she replied, then spoke with care. "Surely your lady wife will take exception to you seeking such a favor from another woman."

"Surely not, as I have no lady wife."

"Whyever not?" Her tone revealed that she was not surprised. "You possess a holding, thus can wed. You are of an age to marry and clearly possess some increment of charm."

Alexander grinned at that, but when she did not share his delight, he shook his head. "The matter is not so simple as it might appear. I have three sisters yet to see married happily and much to learn yet about managing my estate. My uncle counseled that I wait to wed until I had ensured stability for Kinfairlie, though I fear that goal may not be readily won."

He granted her a glance, fearful that he bored her, but caught her watching him, assessment in her eyes. "But why do I burden you with such details? My worries are not yours." He shook a playful finger at her and she abruptly returned her attention to the snow. "You are of little aid in my scheme to forget my obligations this night."

"Perhaps then you should let me depart."

"Ah, but there will be insufficient time to seek you out before the burden of my responsibilities returns in the morning," he argued genially. "Indeed, it would be best for both of us if you returned to my hall for one night, the better that I might succeed in my quest, and you might be warm and safe. Can you not be tempted to taste the wine from my cellars?"

"You must be affluent indeed to have wine in your cellars, no less to share it with your peasants."

Alexander laughed. "I am as impoverished as ever a man could be," he admitted. "But I have had family in Sicily and more family who traded in goods, and thus have the good fortune to have been given several casks of wine, which are yet in my cellar." He granted her a quick wink. "It is better drunk than left to ruin."

"And many a man is better drunk, though that might lead him to ruin," she retorted, prompting his laughter again.

"Only a man quick to temper is better drunk than sober, for then he has not the ability to act upon his whims," Alexander said. "Though I assure you that I am not in their number."

"Is that the truth of it," she said mildly, as if unpersuaded.

Alexander did not know whether she was doubtful of his notion of drunken men or his own merit.

He shivered elaborately. "Though I am reluctant to end our conversation, truly, it is too cold to jest thus in the bailey. Surely we might proceed so far as an introduction by this point? What is your name, lady fair? You must have one, though you are reluctant to surrender it."

"Eleanor," she admitted, to his astonishment.

"Eleanor." Alexander rolled the name across his tongue as he considered how to proceed. He marveled that she had surrendered her name, noted that she had not included an estate—though she was clearly noble—and wondered whether it was her name in truth. He had little to lose by teasing her, he reasoned. "Perhaps it is not truly your name."

She looked so outraged at his suggestion that he knew

it must be her name, or at least a part of it. "What mockery is this?"

"Surely it is uncommon for a lady to grant so little of her name when most would surrender all of it? You admit to no title and no house. Perhaps you have another name."

"Perhaps I am not noble."

She was troubled by his perceptiveness, Alexander noted, so he made a jest. "Then whence came your gown?" he teased. "You did not find garb such as this abandoned in a gutter."

She bit her lip, seemingly without a response.

Alexander touched the trailing end of her sleeve, rubbing the cloth between finger and thumb. He was tempted to touch her wrist, so close was her flesh, but dared not press her overmuch.

Indeed, she pulled her hand away from him, and put a step between them. Alexander did not comment, nor did he miss her response.

She liked her secrets, to be sure, but he tired of her low estimation of his nature. He decided to press her slightly.

"Such finely woven cloth can only be from the Lowlands," he mused, "so rich a hue could only have been dyed in France. And the embroidery is lavish indeed. This is not a gown from one of my sisters, for I should recall the cost well enough. And the cloak . . ." He whistled through his teeth. "Ermine would beggar a king in these days." He met her gaze again. "No common woman could buy such garb, thus you must be noble. I would wager that your husbands were not petty lords, either."

She caught her breath and quickened her step. "I might be a thief," she said.

Alexander grinned and easily matched his pace to

hers. "From whom would you steal? You would have to have traveled far with your ill-gotten gains to have found yourself in my hall."

She lifted her chin and he saw her lips set stubbornly. "Perhaps I am a rich man's consort."

Alexander pretended to consider this, then shook his head. "Bereft of your benefactor, but so afraid of a man's caress as you are?" he said softly. "I think not."

She turned upon him with flashing eyes. "I am not afraid!"

Alexander shrugged, though truly he was beguiled by her response. "A courtesan would seek another patron, and I am the best proposition in this vicinity." He spread his hands and smiled at her. "I invite you, Eleanor, to seduce me."

But she did not share his merriment. "Oh! You are so certain of yourself, even knowing so few details as you do," she fumed. She faced him, hands on her hips, eyes flashing like the sea in sunlight. "Perhaps my patron is possessive. Perhaps I but wisely ensure that I am a faithful consort." A challenge lit her eyes. "Perhaps I hasten to meet my lover."

"Where?" Alexander glanced pointedly back at his hall. "In my experience, rich men do not hide themselves so well that they pass unnoticed, even as guests."

"Nor do they welcome their mistresses at the board when their family gathers for a religious feast."

"Nor do they fail to provide a mount for any soul they hold in regard. Why do you avoid my stables? You cannot mean to abandon the horse provided by your patron?"

She pursed her lips and folded her arms more tightly about herself. "You are a persistent foe," she said through gritted teeth.

Alexander laughed. "True enough. Think of how vexing it would be to have me in pursuit of you." She made a sound of annoyance and he clucked his tongue as if pitying her that ordeal. She met his gaze, appearing sufficiently amused that he was encouraged. "I am cold and I would make you a wager, fair Eleanor."

"One that will cost me dear, from the look of you."

He laughed again. "Not so dear as that. Grant me one night to win your smile."

"Between the sheets?"

"In the hall, at the table, in the company of others."

"In some places, those conditions would not preclude an attempt to be between a woman's thighs."

Alexander grinned. "They do in my abode. I would try to win your smile this night with words and gallantry, no more than that." He put his hand over his heart. "I grant you my word of honor."

She arched a brow. "Though I know not its worth."

Irked, he leaned closer and lowered his voice, sober as he had not yet been. "Had I desired a rape, it could have been done by now, with nary a witness of the deed."

Eleanor took a step back and he cursed himself for making her cautious once again. "Many a man feigns honor to win a lady's trust."

Alexander shrugged. "There is but one way you might know my merit in truth." He offered his hand.

She stared at his upturned palm, then squared her shoulders and met his gaze steadily. Her chin lifted, as if she would challenge him—and truly, she did. She looked as regal as a queen and as indomitable as a warrior and Alexander was utterly charmed. "I daresay your price would be higher than a mere smile if you succeed."

"I desire no more than to see you smile," he insisted. "If I win, that sight will be reward enough. Your wealthy man has not granted you much in truth, if he has not made you merry."

Eleanor did not comment upon that. "You will not touch me."

"I would offer you aid in walking so that you do not slip," he said with some annoyance. "Whether you take my arm or not is your choice, as is that of a hot meal, a cup of wine, and a warm pallet this night."

Eleanor took a quick breath, then put her hand in his. Her hand was small and cold, and Alexander's urge to gather her close was nigh overwhelming. He restrained himself, though, and merely tucked her hand into his elbow. He turned immediately back toward the keep, concern for her welfare lending speed to his steps. "Be warned, fair Eleanor, that I do not intend to fail."

"You put more stake upon this than a smile would merit."

He placed his hand over his heart, knowing she would think he made a jest, but there was truth in his words. "I stake all upon it. If I cannot coax your smile this night, then I have lost far more than I have gained this past year." He winked at her, noting her surprise at his manner. "And truly, if you chose to surrender more than a smile to me in my triumph, I would not protest overmuch."

She snorted, though a reluctant twinkle lit her eye. "No woman could be as charmed with you as you are with yourself."

"Let us see if we can amend that situation," he said with newfound resolve, and he was nigh certain that she fought against her answering smile.

IT MUST BE EXHAUSTION AT ROOT, Eleanor decided.

That could be the sole reason she had succumbed to Alexander's plea. She did not change her mind upon a whim, not she, much less because of a man's attempt to persuade her to do so.

After all, she did not believe that Alexander possessed any allure. Eleanor stole a sidelong glance and corrected herself.

Perhaps he had a small increment of allure.

She liked how tall Alexander was, how determined he was, how resoundingly he laughed. She liked his wit and his whimsy; she liked how his eyes sparkled. She liked that he had already noted her aversion to a man's touch, however casual it might be; she liked better that he acted upon that observation and did not touch her.

And she had been charmed by his rueful acknowledgment of his lack of coin, for he had dismissed the matter instead of turning an expectant eye upon her. Eleanor had been persuaded then that Alexander knew nothing of her true identity, that he knew even less of the fortune she could bring to a spouse, and her fears had faded. He had not seen her as the solution to his woes, and that had proved to be seductive indeed.

What was even more astonishing was the fact that Alexander thought *she* had allure.

That was novel in Eleanor's experience. No man had ever looked at her without seeing the fortune she could bring him, no man had ever courted her favor for its own merit. Certainly no one had sought only her smile.

Eleanor had wondered, as they bantered, what it would be like to be the sole focus of this handsome and charming man.

Perhaps curiosity was as much the root of her choice as exhaustion, for Eleanor had decided then to indulge herself. She had borne much in her days and she would undoubtedly endure much more. But on this one night, she would be as carefree as her host. She would let him try to coax her smile, as if neither of them had any matter more pressing before them than his whimsical quest.

The warmth of the hall embraced them when they crossed the threshold, and the golden light was the most welcoming Eleanor had ever seen. She could smell the roasted meat and the beeswax candles and the press of several hundred people. The music was joyous and loud, the laughter raucous.

Indeed, a cheer rent the hall when Alexander was spied and he winked for Eleanor, then bowed deeply to his guests. Clearly, the wine was finding favor, for many in the hall applauded him with gusto.

"Did you leave a morsel for me?" he demanded in mock indignation, and a fulsome wench at the closest table held up her own trencher for him.

"The meat is toothsome, my lord," she said, boldly smiling at him. Eleanor did not doubt that she offered a good deal more than the meat piled on her bread.

Alexander leaned closer, making a show of examining the meat. "Is this the venison, Anna?"

"In pepper sauce, my lord," the wench agreed. "Spicy yet savory all the same. It lingers upon the tongue with a delightful heat."

Eleanor nigh choked upon the woman's audacity, but

Alexander chose a morsel with solemnity. She noted that he picked the finest piece on the trencher. She had only a heartbeat to consider the poor measure of his manners before he pivoted and held the meat before her own lips.

"My lady fair?" he murmured, inviting her to partake of the bite.

Eleanor momentarily did not know what to do. It was beyond intimate for a man to feed a woman, and for him to do so in such a crowded hall when every eye was upon them shocked her to her marrow. She liked that the wench was so displeased by the failure of her ploy, and she knew her manners well enough to know that she should accept his gift. All the same, she did not wish to show herself as common as the woman who had offered the meat in the first place.

Her tutors had not prepared her for this moment, to be sure.

It was the daring glimmer in Alexander's blue eyes that resolved her dilemma. He thought she would decline, and that was sufficient for Eleanor.

After all, she had argued that she was a courtesan. And she had decided to indulge herself this night.

"I thank you, my lord," she murmured, letting her expression show pleasure, though she did not smile. She took the meat from his fingertips in one languorous bite, holding his gaze. She ensured that her tongue caressed his flesh when she claimed the last measure of gravy from his knuckle. She chewed it slowly, rolling the meat around in her mouth, then ran the tip of her tongue over her lips.

Alexander swallowed visibly.

"Delicious!" she said, lowering her voice to a purr. "It must have been a most robust buck."

"And have you a taste for such virile beasts?" he asked, his eyes dancing.

"On occasion, I have found them amusing," she allowed. "Indeed, I find my appetite for such virile meat mustered with that morsel."

"Then we must hasten to the board," Alexander said, smiling so that the bold wench could not be insulted, then sweeping Eleanor to the high table. "You tempt me apurpose," he muttered.

"While you did not intend to tempt me?" Eleanor whispered, then preceded him to the high table. "I am a courtesan, as you were warned. I know no other game."

A spark lit in Alexander's eyes then, one so filled with mischief that Eleanor's heart skipped. "Is that the truth of it?" he mused in an undertone. "How would a man make a courtesan smile, without some intimate tickle abed? I shall have to ponder the matter."

Eleanor did not doubt that he would do more than ponder it. Indeed, she felt a tingle of anticipation, for she could not guess what he might do.

His sisters nudged each other, probably thinking that their scheme held promise once again. Eleanor did not tell them otherwise. She was introduced to all of them formally—Madeline, Vivienne, Annelise, Isabella, and Elizabeth—then to Rhys and Erik, the spouses of Madeline and Vivienne, respectively. Two young girls, the daughters of Erik from his first marriage, peeked around Vivienne's skirts as they were introduced. They were Megan and Astrid, though Eleanor was not certain which was which, and they looked to be thrilled with the promise of the feast.

She let Alexander seat her upon his left hand, not caring what any person in his hall thought of that, and accepted the goblet of wine that he filled with his own hand.

He touched his cup to hers, some wickedness making his eyes dance anew, then raised his voice. "To laughter," he cried, and sipped of his cup's contents.

Eleanor drank the toast with caution, assuming the wine would be passing fair at best; then her eyes widened. It was a fine French wine, much to her astonishment, one that would have earned praise in a king's hall.

"You smiled!" Alexander whispered in triumph.

"For the wine, not for you," she said, sobering immediately. "Your quest is not fulfilled, sir."

"That is not fair," he argued so good-naturedly that she knew he was not truly offended. "I will not be bested by a mere beverage!"

"This wine has a considerable charm," Eleanor admitted, then sipped of it again.

"You have scarce seen the full measure of mine," he retorted, and she stifled the urge to chuckle.

But she could not let a man with such cursed confidence win his way as readily as that.

THE WOMAN WOULD HAVE HIM believe her to be a courtesan. The very notion was absurd, given her reluctance to be touched, but Alexander was prepared to agree with it, if it meant the lady would remain in his hall for this evening.

It did not, however, preclude his teasing her over the matter.

"Is it true," he asked when venison was promptly laid upon the trencher they would share, "that a woman of pleasure oft feeds her patron his every morsel with her fingertips?" He held another piece of meat for Eleanor, ensuring that it did not drip upon her garb.

This bite she accepted more hastily, granting him a warning glance. "There are those who do, or so I hear. My own favor is for my own spoon." She lifted another piece of meat with that utensil, but Alexander bent and ate it himself, before she realized his intent. She was delightfully startled, her ruddy lips rounding in a circle of astonishment.

He claimed her spoon and laid it out of her reach, along with his own. "I confess to preferring fingertips. Will you not see my own hunger sated?" He looked pointedly to the trencher before them.

Eleanor grasped the largest piece of meat between finger and thumb, and offered it to him. Alexander made to bite it, but she pushed it all between his lips. "That will ensure your silence for a few moments," she said, her tone surprisingly teasing. She ate then at leisure while he fought to chew his way through the piece of meat.

His sisters smirked on either side.

"You have a drop of wine upon your lip," he murmured to Eleanor when he could do so, though in truth she did not. Eleanor licked her lips hastily, the sight of the tip of her tongue sending a spark through Alexander.

"The other side," he lied, wanting only to see her repeat her gesture. She did so, then met his gaze again.

"No," he said, shaking his head with solemnity. "You missed it. A bit more to your right." She ducked her head this time and wiped her mouth with her napkin.

"It proves to be elusive, indeed," he said softly. "Let me do you this courtesy." Before she could argue the matter, he slid his own fingertip across her bottom lip. He began at one corner of her mouth, holding her gaze all the while, then eased his finger to the other corner with excruciating slowness.

The ruby fullness of her lip tugged beneath his fingertip, its softness tempting him to linger. Eleanor stared at him, her eyes wide, and did not seem to breathe. Alexander was tempted to kiss her, though guessed that she feared he would do as much.

And that would certainly not prompt her smile.

Instead, he licked his own fingertip, as if savoring the drop of wine he had claimed from her lip. "Sweet," he said, then arched a brow, "though it might seem tart when it first falls upon the tongue. An unobservant man might miss its value."

Eleanor flushed, her face turning absolutely crimson, then looked down at her side of their trencher. She ate half-a-dozen pieces of meat so quickly that she could not have tasted them and Alexander sipped his wine, knowing that she was not so immune to him as she would prefer he believe.

Still, he had to make her smile.

On impulse, he decided just how the deed might be done.

ALEXANDER STOOD AND CLAPPED his hands, mercifully turning his gaze away from Eleanor. She had wondered whether it had been prudent to wish for his attention, after he had fixed it so resolutely upon her. The man was discomfiting, to be certain, and she was flustered.

Yet curiously, she felt more alive than she had in years. Every fiber of her being tingled. She was aware of the muscled heat of his thigh so close to her own, the low rumble of his voice even when he spoke to others, and she swore she could feel his very gaze land upon her.

The man roused unwelcome questions in her thoughts—or perhaps he roused only one. Was it possible that there was more pleasure to be found abed than she had experienced? It was not hard to believe as much, and Eleanor found herself possessed of an uncommon passion to know the truth. She did not doubt that the man by her side would be delighted to exhaust her curiosity.

How would Alexander beguile a woman abed? The very notion lit an unfamiliar fire deep within Eleanor. She watched his hands, lean and strong and tanned, and her mouth went dry at the thought of them upon her flesh. His touch was gentle, she knew as much already, and he was observant beyond men she had known. But doubtless, there would be little difference between him and the others in the end, little difference once his lust was sated, little difference once she failed him in some expectation.

Meanwhile, the hall fell silent at Alexander's summons and every eye fixed upon him. He smiled at the company and spoke so that his words carried across the hall. "Again I welcome you to my board, and I hope that you have eaten heartily this night."

The company roared, more than one pair of crockery cups clunking together. There was a hoot from the back of the hall, as if some table of merry souls had imbibed overmuch; then feet were stamped.

Alexander clapped his hands again, even as he laughed. "I shall take that as assent," he said, though few could have heard him over the ruckus.

He shook his head when quiet did not ensue, then let loose a piercing whistle of fearsome volume. His sisters clapped their hands over their ears and protested the noise, though the hall fell silent once more.

Alexander bowed slightly. "Though it is clear that you all enjoy yourselves already, I would propose an entertainment this evening." The musicians began to play a tune, but he waved them to silence. "There is a tradition common in other halls but new to our own, at least on Christmas Eve. In the past, we have saved our folly for Twelfth Night alone."

"Tell us your scheme!" roared some intrepid soul.

Eleanor noted that all three of Alexander's younger sisters looked wary. "He savors this moment overmuch," muttered Elizabeth, the youngest. "It is a poor omen for us."

And truly, Alexander's eyes danced so wickedly that even Eleanor half-feared what he would suggest. "What say you all to the appointment of a Lord of Misrule?" he cried.

"So long as he cannot make marriages," Isabella replied.

Alexander feigned insult. "Do not be absurd! My sisters shall all choose their own spouses, for my lesson has been learned."

"Do not trust him for a moment," Elizabeth growled, though she was ignored.

The company bellowed approval of Alexander's suggestion, and feet were stamped with deafening vigor.

Alexander whistled again. "I reserve the right to appoint each person in this hall to his or her new position. We shall play our parts for all this evening, and revert to normal manners in the morning. No soul may injure another, no person may be cruel. This is folly and amusement, no more. Are we understood?" The company grunted agreement, and more than one man nodded approval of this sentiment.

"Now we begin." Alexander spun and surveyed the company, as mischievous as a pixie. "Marjorie, the ale maker, shall trade places with my sister Madeline and be Lady of Caerwyn this night."

An older woman with a kindly face rose to her feet, clearly embarrassed to be the focus of attention, yet excited as well. She flushed scarlet when her companions cheered. Madeline smiled and rose with grace to exchange places with the woman. Marjorie might have bowed to Madeline, but Madeline bowed first, then kissed Marjorie's hand. The woman's mouth fell open and she fairly gaped in delight when Madeline put her own silken veil and circlet on Marjorie's head. Madeline then sat at the board with Marjorie's kin as if she had been there all along.

"Go sit in my place at the high table," Madeline bade Marjorie when that woman hesitated. Marjorie's eyes lit with excitement as she crossed the hall and she giggled as she fit herself into the space on the bench that Madeline had vacated. Madeline's husband kissed Marjorie's hand with gallantry and the woman giggled.

"Rose, the cook's wife, you will take the place of my sister Vivienne and be Lady of Blackleith this night," Alexander said. Another matron fairly dashed to the high table in her enthusiasm; then Vivienne surrendered her veil and circlet in her turn. Rose sat beside Erik and spared him a coquettish glance.

"Do not be so quick to think the lord of Blackleith will be the same man in moments as he is now," Rose's husband, the cook, teased, and the company laughed. That man then gave Vivienne a hearty buss on the cheek as she arrived at the place Rose had vacated. Rose appeared so indignant that the company laughed.

"Indeed, you speak aright," Alexander agreed. He quickly named two men to take the places of his brothers-in-law, one elderly and the other a young boy who was pushed forward by an older man.

"The tanner and his apprentice," Isabella confided to Eleanor.

Alexander worked his way down the high table, replacing his siblings with peasants with such speed that the hall became chaotic. "Elizabeth will trade with the blacksmith's eldest daughter; Annelise will trade with Ellen, the spinner; Isabella will become the shepherd's wife. Father Malachy will trade with the miller, and Owen, the ostler, with Siobhan, the baker's wife."

The ostler, a burly man with a formidable mustache, donned the apron of the baker's wife, who was not a small woman herself. He then seized two round loaves of bread from a table, slipping them beneath his shirt. He fluttered his lashes and the company howled.

The baker's wife poked Owen in the shoulder in gentle reprimand, clearly accustomed to his antics. She then tucked her skirts into her boots, quaffed an entire mug of ale, wiped her mouth upon her sleeve, and belched fit to rattle the rafters.

This must have been an accurate mimicry of the ostler, for even that man found it amusing.

Then Alexander winked at Eleanor. "My lady fair professes a desire to be a courtesan this night." He paused while the company shouted approval of this notion and Eleanor found herself blushing anew.

Alexander lowered his voice, his manner so somber that none would doubt his words. "Though you may be assured that any discourtesy visited upon her this night will be recalled by me on the morrow when my customary duties are regained"—he held up a hand for the good-natured protest that followed his threat—"thus Anna will take my lady's place."

Eleanor watched as the maiden who had made to tempt Alexander earlier got to her feet and straightened her bodice, a knowing gleam in her eye. Eleanor made to exchange places with the woman, knowing that she would not have taken even a subtle suggestion that she was a courtesan so coolly in that woman's place.

Unless it was not only the truth, but known to all.

The two women passed on the floor, though Eleanor spared the woman no trinket to play her role. Their shoulders brushed as they passed each other.

Just then, Anna whispered beneath her breath for Eleanor's ears alone, her tone triumphant. "You see that he is mine, after all. Any man likes fire better than ice."

Anna had no chance to gloat, though, for Alexander raised his voice once again. "And I would surrender my place, until the stroke of midnight, to the new Laird of Kinfairlie and Lord of Misrule." The company held its breath as one, and Eleanor turned back to find Alexander grinning. "Matthew, the miller's son!" he cried. "Come take my place this night!"

Anna's expression of horror made more than one soul in the hall laugh aloud.

A lanky young man stood up, his eyes wide in disbelief. "Me, my lord?"

"Yes, you, Matthew," Alexander beckoned. "Hasten yourself to the high table."

Matthew looked to the older couple who shared his table, and the miller—who now wore the priest's cassock—nodded encouragement. Matthew was crimson to find himself the center of attention and did not look as if he would summon the resolve to walk to the high table. Father Malachy patted Matthew on the shoulder in encouragement.

The woman wiped away a tear as she smiled. "Go on, then, Matthew," she said. "Be a good lad and do as the laird bids you."

"But I cannot be laird," Matthew said with a stubbornness that made Eleanor wonder if the boy was slow of wit.

"Only for one night, Matthew," Alexander said, his tone cajoling. "The burden will not flatten you so fast as that! I have need of a laird to ensure that all is well in Kinfairlie, a man with a good heart, and you, I know, are the one best suited for the task."

The miller rose when Matthew still did not move and took his hand, whispered something into his son's ear, then urged him toward the dais.

Matthew's wonder was evident to all when he reached Alexander's side. Alexander tugged his tabard over his head; then he and the miller saw Matthew garbed in the colors of Kinfairlie.

"I will not fail your trust, my lord," he said, his reverence for Alexander clear.

Alexander smiled. "I expect no less." Then he feigned a whisper as if confiding some detail, though it was yet loud enough for the company to hear. "Mind no man hunts the deer upon your land, my lord, for it is forbidden by the king's own law." At this counsel, the miller turned as red as a beet and several men guffawed in the company. Alexander grinned at the miller, and Eleanor knew that this was some old tale between them.

"For this night and this night alone, Kinfairlie is beneath the command of Matthew, Lord of Misrule!" Alexander cried, then lowered his voice. "I beg you to ensure that all are entertained well." He winked at Matthew, pushed his signet ring onto Matthew's finger, then bowed low and kissed the boy's hand. Matthew gaped at the gold ring on his own calloused hand.

The castellan caught his breath in disapproval. "My lord! You should not surrender such a prize so readily as that!"

"It is merely for one night," Alexander said, putting his hand upon Matthew's shoulder. "Matthew can be trusted to hold it fast."

There was affection between the two of them, an affection that surprised Eleanor. She had not often seen lairds take much interest in those who labored upon their lands. But Matthew's father beamed and she knew that this warmth was not feigned.

"I can have more wine?" Matthew asked, hope in his eyes.

"Even better, you can command all to do your will for this one night," the miller explained.

"And they must do it?"

"Just for this one night," his father counseled, clearly foreseeing trouble from this. He and Alexander laughed.

Matthew's eyes lit with sudden resolve. "But if I am laird, then I must have a lady."

Alexander turned to the wench he had appointed in Eleanor's place. "But Anna . . ."

"I will not be his lady," Anna snapped, and turned away.

"So long as she has not kissed Matthew, the miller's son, she has not welcomed every man in Kinfairlie," shouted some bold soul. The company laughed, even as a furious Anna sought the man who had so commented.

Matthew was untroubled by this. "I would have a lady by my side," he said, then looked anew to Alexander. "Could Ceara be my lady fair?"

A plump young girl at the back of the hall gasped and became redder than red when the entire company turned her way. She stood up, then sat down, then hunkered low as if she would hide herself. She was not a beauty, but she was fair of face. The way she kept her eyes downcast suggested to Eleanor that Ceara was shy.

And that perhaps Matthew's admiration was returned.

"A man of merit must ask a lady's favor," Alexander suggested.

"Ceara, will you be my lady?" Matthew shouted across the hall. Helpful hands urged shy Ceara from her hiding place and she nodded assent, apparently struck mute by the honor.

Meanwhile, Elizabeth had woven a pair of crowns from the greenery in the hall, and she presented them now with a flourish. The new lord and lady were crowned to the delight of all. The pair smiled shyly at each other. Matthew swallowed, then took his lady's hand. That intimacy seemed to overwhelm them, so shy were they, and they looked away from each other, blushing furiously. Alexander and the miller exchanged knowing glances.

Eleanor was touched that Alexander had granted the boy his heartfelt desire. She had never known a laird to care about the happiness of his peasants.

Matthew took a deep breath, then pointed to the priest. "Father Malachy, you said that you wished you could dance, but that it was not fitting for a priest."

"True enough, Matthew, though on this night, I am a miller."

"Then you must dance, Father Malachy! You must dance all the night long!" Matthew looked around, avidly seeking someone to command. His gaze fell upon Eleanor. "And you must dance with the lord's lady."

"Ceara?"

"No, my lord Alexander's lady."

Father Malachy, in good humor, came to Eleanor and bowed low. "As you command, Lord Matthew." He winked at Eleanor. "To dance with a courtesan will be a rare treat for me, indeed." Doubtless he assumed that he would lead her in some courtly dance, but the minstrels immediately struck a bawdy tune.

"Everyone must dance!" Matthew cried. "It is Christmas, after all!"

The musicians sang a playful ditty about a sailor and a mermaid, a tune evidently well-known in these parts with words that left little to the imagination about the state of the happy couple's intimate bliss. The priest was an artful dancer and Eleanor found herself enjoying the quick steps and merry music. He turned her gracefully, as courteous as a man could be, and her worries eased yet more. Alexander's hall was warm, his people were happy, his wine was good, and this was a night to celebrate.

They did not fear him. They trusted him. And so would she—for a single night.

More than one couple joined them in the dance, and one tune spilled into another. Soon the hall was rollicking. Eleanor found herself out of breath, but with no shortage of partners. Every man evidently wanted to dance with the courtesan—even the ostler in his apron. She caught only brief glimpses of Alexander as he circled the hall.

Eleanor danced as she had seldom danced, for the tunes were vigorous and the clapping of the company was infectious. She had no obligations, no man kept a censorious eye upon her, no one would later demand an accounting of her every step. Her cup was filled with wine at every opportunity, and the minstrels seemed to know a hundred tunes.

Matthew called commands from the high table all the while. In every direction, Eleanor could spy some folly. One man tried to balance a spoon upon his nose at the Lord of Misrule's bidding, a feat complicated by his earlier consumption of ale. Another man tried to drink three tankards of ale in quick succession, his companions noisily trying to cheer him on. A plain maiden collected her due of a kiss from every man in the hall, blushing furiously all the while. It was harmless amusement, no malice in it at all, and Eleanor decided that Alexander had chosen his replacement well.

"A KISS!" Matthew cried suddenly. "Every man must collect a kiss from his partner!" The ostler, in his apron, happened to be Eleanor's partner in that moment, and truly, Eleanor had never kissed a man with both a thick mustache and two considerable loaves of bread as breasts.

In the end, it was not Anna's comeuppance that made Eleanor smile, nor was it the dozens of acts of foolery being committed in Kinfairlie's hall. It was not the ostler's errant "breast," not even when he had to crawl under the tables in pursuit of the one that had leapt free when he feigned a faint after her buss upon his cheek.

It was the expression of rapture upon Matthew's face when Ceara gave him a quick kiss, full on the lips, that made Eleanor's lips curve. The young man appeared to be stunned by this honor, while Ceara herself looked astonished at her own boldness. The pair regarded each other so ardently that Eleanor did not doubt that a courtship would soon begin.

"God bless my lord Alexander," a woman said from close proximity. Eleanor spied Matthew's mother not a trio of steps away, her gaze fixed upon her son. "There be a man with eyes in his head and the will to do something about what he sees. I thought Matthew would never so much as speak to that girl, so smitten is he with her, but my lord has seen the matter resolved."

Eleanor felt her smile broaden. What a Christmas gift Alexander had given the miller's son! She turned, seeking the man responsible, but did not need to look far. She felt his hand upon the back of her waist, heard his low voice behind her.

"If you will pardon my interruption, lady baker," Alexander said to the ostler, who snorted with laughter. "I would claim your partner for her next dance."

"By all means, my lord," the ostler said in falsetto. "Though I have already collected her kiss."

"Ah, it is a richer prize I seek," Alexander said as he swung Eleanor into his arms and the dance began. "Is it true that you smile?"

"Indeed, your quest is won." Eleanor studied him, for he looked both younger and more dangerous with his tabard gone and his hair rumpled. His chemise was of fine linen, but he might have been any charming rogue, not a man with a holding beneath his hand. Truly, it was a marvel how the man's eyes sparkled.

"And the evening is yet young," he mused with a wicked smile. "Do you imagine that your smile can be coaxed again?"

"On this night, in this hall, I would not wager against it."

He grinned. "I will take that as a compliment to my hospitality."

"It is Matthew's hospitality on this night, I believe," Eleanor corrected, and Alexander laughed. She sobered. "You granted him a fine gift this night. It was kind of you."

Alexander shrugged. "His is a good heart, and one deserving of good fortune. I merely hastened his inevitable success."

Eleanor liked that he did not insist upon gratitude for his deed. She liked that he had concern for his people, and that they trusted him as they did. His hand was not heavy upon them, and they relied upon his judgment, it was clear. She had erred when earlier she had suspected that they feared him, just as she had erred when she had assumed Alexander to be a man concerned with his own pleasures alone. She found herself less anxious to flee Kinfairlie's hall in the morning.

"More wine?" one of Alexander's sisters demanded suddenly from their side.

"Doubtless you recall Isabella," he said, courteously and subtly reminding Eleanor which sister was which. She found herself smiling for him again. She had met his sisters so quickly that she did not doubt she would have confused their names.

"The next sister but one that Alexander must see wed," Isabella said with a grimace.

"Not this night, at least," he agreed amiably, ignoring her dark glance. "You could find yourself a suitable match in your time and I would be all the more merry for that."

"Take your wine," Isabella said, urging the cups upon them. "There is more in this one, Alexander, for you."

"Ah, but Eleanor favors a good wine and has found this one amiable." Alexander gallantly offered the glass that was more full to her, but Eleanor saw Isabella's eyes light with alarm. The younger woman shook her head while her brother's attention was diverted, and Eleanor guessed that the full glass was intended for him for some reason.

"I have indulged too much this night," she said, and accepted the less full cup. "Take it, Alexander, lest it be wasted."

"If you insist."

"I do." Eleanor watched Isabella as that girl nodded with relief. She wondered then what had been put in Alexander's cup, but she did not have to wonder long.

Within three dances, the man was stumbling over his own feet in a most alarming manner.

Chapter Three

Eleanor FOLLOWED THE PARTY that wound its way upward to the laird's chamber of Kinfairlie, the sound of the festivities below carrying through the floor. Erik and Rhys fairly carried Alexander, the two men ensuring that the laird successfully made the climb to his bed. Madeline and Vivienne followed Eleanor and the other sisters trailed behind. Eleanor was more upset about the trick played upon Alexander than she might have expected.

"You could be of some aid," Rhys grumbled to Alexander, who seemingly could not put one foot before the other.

Alexander made no reply.

"I doubt that he could be," Eleanor noted, wondering at this potion they had come by. She hoped that no error had been made in its formulation.

"I hope whatsoever you gave him wears off quickly enough," Erik said. "It felled him more quickly than might have been thought possible."

"I, too, hope that you have not injured him," Eleanor said.

"It is harmless enough," Isabella said crisply. "Jeannie said as much."

"A potion of any kind can be unreliable," Rhys growled. "I have learned my lesson well enough in this."

"But Jeannie is well-known to us and her skills with herbs are of wide repute." Madeline laid a hand upon his arm. "Fear not, Rhys, for she can be trusted."

Eleanor guessed that there had been some potion of dubious merit in their past, for Rhys was uncomfortable, indeed. It did not reassure her, for she shared his distrust of such elixirs.

"We could have ensured he slept some other way," Rhys muttered.

"Aye, he is owed a blow or two from me," Erik agreed, and the two warriors grinned at each other. Eleanor could not imagine that such a man as Alexander could be due any such thing. She hoped the pair made a jest, for they were formidable, indeed.

"Do not look so fearful," Elizabeth bade Eleanor. "Alexander is hale enough."

"And the potion will only make him sleep deeply through the morning," Isabella added. "Jeannie assured me as much."

They halted on a landing and Vivienne pushed past the trio of men, producing a key from within her skirts. She unlocked the portal and pushed open the door, standing aside so that Alexander could be carried into his chamber.

"I cannot rest," Alexander mumbled, though his voice was so slurred that it was difficult to discern his words. "I have guests. I have a quest; I must ride the breadth of Christendom to conquer ogres. . . ."

Eleanor caught her breath, fearful of the way Alexander's thoughts wandered. The men cast the laird of Kinfairlie none-too-gently into his own bed.

"Your guests will leave soon enough," Rhys said.

"And you can pursue your quest on the morrow," Erik added, but Alexander had fallen asleep.

His long limbs were sprawled across his own bed, his hair tousled and his face flushed ruddy from whatever had been in the wine. He looked young to Eleanor, yet alluring all the same. She could not keep herself from the side of the bed, could not resist the urge to lift his eyelid. He twitched when she did as much and with some effort she discerned that his pupil was small indeed.

The sight stilled her heart. Perhaps he had need of protection from his own kin.

"What was in your potion?" she demanded, but Isabella merely shrugged.

"Only Jeannie knows the secrets to her elixirs."

Eleanor laid her fingertips upon Alexander's throat and was not reassured by the wild race of his pulse.

"I have never seen him so merry as he was this night," Rhys noted.

"He was always thus, *before*," Elizabeth said. She folded her arms across her chest and stared at her sleeping brother. "Alexander was amusing once, before he became laird. This is the first time we have glimpsed him in a year."

Erik laid a hand upon her shoulder. "He has many obligations in these days. You should have compassion for him, for the death of your parents was most difficult for him."

Elizabeth grimaced. "I would have compassion if he were not so solemn all the time, and if he were not so determined to be rid of all of us. He wants Kinfairlie all to himself, it seems!"

"You are old enough to wed," Rhys dared to suggest, and the youngest of the Lammergeier family turned upon him in a fury.

"Maman and Papa waited to be wed!" Elizabeth cried. "They waited until they found each other, until they found a love that could not be denied! Maman was not auctioned, and she was not abducted, and she was not treated with indignity."

Rhys captured Madeline's hand when that sister made to speak. "But an auction can end well enough," he said.

Madeline smiled at him and eased closer. "Indeed, it can."

Vivienne stepped to Erik's side and he slipped his arm around her waist. "As can an abduction," he said, sparing a smile for his spouse.

Vivienne leaned her cheek upon his chest. "That it can."

Eleanor was touched by the obvious affection between the two couples. Alexander had not done so badly in seeing these sisters married. Both of their spouses had holdings, both men were young and hale, and both sisters looked happy, indeed. She spared a glance for the man in the bed, who now had settled into a deep sleep, and thought he saw a poor reward for his efforts.

Elizabeth was clearly not so inclined to grant credit to her brother. "Just because the matches Alexander made for you ended fortuitously does not mean that the others will!" she argued. The heat of her anger revealed her fear. It was a fear with which Eleanor could sympathize, though she felt it misplaced in this instance.

"One might expect Fortune to turn against him," Annelise suggested softly.

"Twice he has succeeded, against all reckoning," Isabella contributed. The three younger sisters stood together, as unified in their posture as their attitude. "It defies belief that such a trend could continue."

"Which is why we would see him wed himself," Madeline said, her manner authoritative.

Vivienne grinned, the same mischief in her expression that Eleanor had glimpsed earlier in Alexander's. "Marriage will keep him too occupied to force his will upon you three."

Elizabeth nodded vigorously. "It will give him a taste of what he has rendered unto others." She looked at Eleanor and nibbled at her lip with newfound doubt. "That is, if you still wish to wed him, after all you have witnessed this day."

The entire group turned to Eleanor. She keenly understood their fears, for she had survived two poor marriages and feared that they were more common than happy ones.

But in truth, her sympathies lay with Alexander, a realization that made her doubt her own judgment. She had known the man but an evening, and already his charm and good looks persuaded her to take his side. Did he not appear to be too good to be true?

"Can you see their ribbons?" Madeline asked abruptly. She smiled at Eleanor's evident confusion. "Elizabeth predicted the happy state of our marriages. She could see ribbons emanating from each of us, entwined with those of our spouses."

"Elizabeth can see the fey," Rhys said so solemnly that it could not be mockery. "She has a rare gift."

Elizabeth snorted. "I can see nothing uncommon, not since Darg disappeared." She met Eleanor's inquiring gaze. "Darg was a spriggan, a fairy who abided with us for a while."

"But she returned to Ravensmuir with Rosamunde," Annelise said quietly, and a pall settled over the small group.

"Neither of them returned from Ravensmuir," Isabella told Eleanor.

"Ah," she said, not knowing what else she should say. This was an uncommon family, to be sure. Perhaps there was a measure of madness in their veins.

"But that is not of import this night," Madeline said with mustered cheer. "You have seen that Alexander is not so foul as you might have feared."

"And you need not fear that he is frivolous. He is not usually as he was this night," Annelise assured Eleanor.

"He is usually most sober and responsible," Isabella added.

"*Too* sober and responsible," Elizabeth complained, though no one paid her much heed.

"He is courteous to women," Vivienne said, "for our father would have suffered no less."

"Kinfairlie, as you can see, is a fine holding," Madeline contributed. "Though not as rich as many others, it is well-endowed."

Eleanor started at this assurance. She studied again the faces of those who regarded her so expectantly and she saw that they had no inkling of how dire matters were for their family abode.

They did not know that Kinfairlie's coffers were empty.

There was only one soul who could have protected them from that fact. Eleanor crossed the chamber to the bed and stared down at Alexander. This man who would have all believe that he was concerned with his own desires alone had shielded his siblings from a truth that would have shaken them all.

He had kept his secret for an entire year, even while struggling with the newfound burden of managing an estate and the grief of losing both parents suddenly. She again felt an admiration for Alexander Lammergeier—this man who had provided the nudge to begin a courtship between two shy souls in his village, out of kindness alone. There was more to him than a merry jest. He was protective of those reliant upon him, and she liked that.

Truly, he had a dangerous ability to soften her formidable defenses against all men. She bent and touched her fingertips to his throat, reassured that his pulse began to settle into a more normal rhythm already. Though Kinfairlie had not been her destination, she wondered whether some divine force had ensured that she come to Kinfairlie's gates.

For against all expectation, Eleanor held the key to Kinfairlie's salvation, though neither Alexander nor his kin knew it. That they had asked so little of her, even in ignorance that she could grant them so much, that they offered her this place in their family simply on the basis of her gender and compassion for a plight they knew little about, was astonishing. But they were a family. She had seen the affection between them, the comfort they had with each other, the ease with which each expressed fears and joys.

Eleanor had never belonged to such a family. She

looked at the watchful group again and found the younger sisters' fear undisguised. They regarded her with a mix of hope and uncertainty. She knew that she could ensure that they wed well, as well as their sisters had.

But there was only one way she could manage as much, and that was as Alexander's wife.

"I will stay at Kinfairlie and wed Alexander," she said with sudden resolve, finding her voice more hoarse than she knew it to be. "I will keep our wager."

To Eleanor's astonishment, the three younger sisters cheered and spontaneously embraced her. She was momentarily disoriented by such a show of affection.

"This will end well, you can be certain of it," Isabella said. "He likes you, we can see as much."

"And you bring out the best in him," Elizabeth added, squeezing Eleanor's hand heartily. "He has not been so merry in a year."

"We will do whatsoever we can to ensure that you are happy," Annelise whispered against her shoulder, and Eleanor found tears rising to her eyes. They were virtual strangers to her, yet had shown her compassion and understanding.

And they had granted her a haven, with no understanding of how precious it was. She would not fail their trust.

"You must leave," she said with resolve. "And take all of our garb, to ensure that Alexander has no doubts as to what has occurred this night."

Madeline frowned. "But there will be no consummation this night. There cannot be. . . ." Rhys and Erik laughed and the younger maidens blushed.

"Give me a sharp knife," Eleanor said. "To cut one's

finger is an old trick, but no less effective for all of that."
It was true that she had confessed to being twice widowed, but there was no guarantee that she was not still
virginal. She guessed from what she had witnessed of
Alexander that he would wed her promptly if he believed
he had claimed her maidenhead.

She eased him aside, cut her finger, and let the blood
drip onto the linens in the middle of the mattress.

The three younger sisters were dispatched then, and
the men disrobed Alexander. Madeline and Vivienne
shielded Eleanor from the men's view as she discarded
her own garb. The men left the chamber with averted
gazes; then Eleanor was alone with the two elder sisters.

"He is a good man," Madeline assured her, then kissed
her cheek.

"So long as you do not deceive him, he will strive to
make you happy," Vivienne said, then kissed her other
cheek.

Eleanor did not think it prudent to note that cutting her
finger was a deceptive beginning to their match from any
perspective.

"He will be fine on the morrow?" she asked.

Madeline chuckled. "He is as hale as an ox. This sleeping draft will leave him with no more than an aching
head."

"As if he had savored too much of the wine," Vivienne
agreed. "Do not fear for him."

Alexander snorted and rolled over to his back, then
began to snore with gusto. The sisters laughed, then scurried from the chamber with Eleanor's garb, closing the
door behind them.

The key turned in the lock and Eleanor folded her arms

across her chest. Their footfalls and whispers faded from earshot, but she stood long in the same place.

Once alone in a locked chamber with a man, she could not help wondering at the folly of what she had done.

THE SNOW HAD STOPPED and the sky was clear outside the window of Kinfairlie's laird, the stars shining brilliantly. The air was icy, prompting Eleanor to shiver. She crossed the floor with measured steps, the wood cold beneath her feet, lured by the temptation of a warm bed.

Alexander slept like a dead man, and Eleanor knew there was no chance of her awakening him soon. The red of her own blood glistened against the white of the linens, taunting her with the import of her deed.

By this time on the morrow, Alexander would be her wedded spouse. They would meet abed in truth. She would be his possession and she would have many years to learn whether her glimpse of his nature this night showed the truth or not.

It was, in many ways, a fearsome prospect.

Eleanor pulled back the coverlet and looked more boldly upon Alexander than she would have the audacity to do when he was awake. He was, as she had suspected, finely wrought, and something deep within her thrilled at the prospect of coupling with a man who was neither aged nor fat.

Alexander was muscled, evidence that he actively trained at arms. The last vestige of a tan faded from his hands and face. There was a dark tangle of hair upon his chest and a darker one somewhat lower, a finer smattering of dark hair on his forearms and legs. His thick ebony lashes would have served any woman proudly, but there was no doubting his gender. She studied his firm lips, still slightly curved in sleep as if he dreamed of some hilarious jest. It was his merriment that beguiled her, his humor in contrast with his thoughtfulness.

She stood a long time and gazed upon him. Reassured that he did not waken or move or expire, she stretched out on the bed alongside him. She ensured that she did not touch him at any point despite the chill in her limbs.

But no sooner had she pulled up the coverlet than Alexander curled up behind her. Eleanor stiffened in shock as he slipped an arm around her waist, her eyes flying open. He grunted and pulled her closer, coaxing her back against his chest, her buttocks against his thighs.

She stiffened, startled, and waited for the amorous assault that would surely come. But the moments passed, and Alexander did not seize her breast or force his erection against her.

Indeed, he did not seem to have an erection. His breath stirred her hair, his breathing slow and deep. And he was warm, blessedly warm. His lips were against her shoulder, his brow at the back of her neck, as if he had fallen asleep while pressing a kiss to her nape.

He was asleep. Of course. The elixir had ensured that he would not be otherwise. They lay together, like two spoons on a shelf, an intimate yet not sexual embrace.

Eleanor had never been embraced, not without a specific sexual goal in her partner's thoughts. She dared to place her hand over Alexander's hand, which rested on the mattress before her belly.

He immediately, instinctively, entwined their fingers,

then nestled his knees more closely behind hers. Again she caught her breath, but their interlocked fingers were the sum of his objective. She marveled at this. She felt cosseted, surrounded by his warmth, protected.

Safe. She felt his pulse, letting its regular pace soothe her like a lullaby. She closed her eyes, the sanctuary Alexander offered to her welcome beyond belief.

Fortune had finally smiled upon Eleanor and she was not so foolish as to spurn that lady's offerings.

ALEXANDER AWAKENED the following morning with a groan.

He rolled to his back, then grimaced at the clamor in his head. He opened his eyes warily, intending to seek the rat that had apparently slept in his mouth, and was assaulted by a rogue beam of sunlight. He fell back against the linens, stunned.

He might have lingered abed, but it became imperative that he hasten to the bucket beneath the window. His belly churned, then settled, leaving him dizzy and disoriented. At least he had not emptied his belly's contents. A bead of sweat coursed down his back and he felt unwell.

Alexander leaned against the wall, wondering at his state. How much had he drunk the night before? Indeed, what had happened the night before? His thoughts were an uncommon muddle.

He kept his eyes closed as he considered his course. Morning had clearly come, but he was exhausted. How long had he slept? He recalled little of the night before, so little that he was leery of the truth. There had been wine, he remembered that, and he had spurned responsibility.

Wine and music and himself carefree—and a beauteous woman named Eleanor. Alexander groaned, certain he must have offended her beyond expectation. His tongue felt thick and foul, unfamiliar in his mouth. His head hurt; indeed, his very marrow ached.

What had he done?

His signet ring was gone, its familiar weight absent from his finger. He recalled his appointment of a Lord of Misrule and was relieved that Matthew would yet have the ring.

"And a merry Christmas to you," a woman said at startling proximity.

Alexander yelped and straightened, his eyes wide open now. Mercifully, the wall did not show any inclination to move, as he was compelled to hold fast to it to keep his balance.

He gaped at Eleanor, who reclined upon his bed wearing no more than one of his sheets. Her hair hung loose, the golden tresses cascading over her bare shoulders and pooling upon the mattress. Her pose was stiff, as if she knew not what to expect from him, and her gaze was wary if not condemning.

Suddenly there were a number of pertinent details about the previous night that Alexander would have paid his soul to recall. How had Eleanor come to be in his bed? And what had happened once she had arrived there?

He, too, was nude, which might have been promising, had the lady looked more pleased. Alexander had never been so intoxicated that he had disappointed a lady— much less that he could not recall having done so—and this morning, with this lady, was, in his estimation, a poor place to begin such a habit.

Nonetheless, he could not remember.

He washed, taking elaborate care with his toilet, even as he tried to muster his thoughts. There was a cup of ale left for him, perhaps by a thoughtful Anthony, who knew he would need ale to spurn ale's effects. He rinsed his mouth thrice, then quaffed a goodly swallow of the ale, reassured that his belly welcomed it.

Alexander returned to the bed and eased his weight to his elbow as he stretched out beside Eleanor, endeavoring to look unsurprised by her presence. He doubted, however, that her keen gaze had missed his astonishment.

He sighed in mock dismay. "I see that you do not smile as yet."

"Would you abandon your quest then?"

Alexander watched Eleanor, unable to understand her hard tone. What had he forgotten? Something of import, he would wager. It was unlike him to forget anything, but there were great gaps in his recollection of the night before.

"I am nothing if not persistent in pursuit of my goals," he said, then reached across the expanse of the bed to touch her. "We must still try to coax your smile. After all, the most lofty goal is not won by a man who abandons the quest too soon."

His hand very nearly landed upon her waist; then his fingers closed upon empty air. Eleanor had slipped from the far side of the bed, eluding his caress in the last moment. She even took the linens with her and wrapped them about herself with a fierce gesture, ensuring that he did not win the barest glimpse of her nudity.

What had he done to insult her? For she was insulted, of that he could have no doubt. Her lips were set in a thin line and her eyes snapped with a fire that would have been more beguiling, had it been born of ardor instead of anger.

"Perhaps you would prefer to meet the bold wench who offered you a morsel from her trencher."

Alexander fought to recall this detail. "Anna, the ostler's daughter?" He scratched his head, and even that hurt. "I should think she would have found another suitor by this time."

"But she is ambitious all the same, to try to tempt the laird himself. We might well find her outside the door, awaiting your favor."

Alexander grinned. "Hardly that! Anthony would not endure it."

"Anthony?"

"My castellan. All must slumber in their place, by his reckoning. He does not rest until all is as it should be."

"Which explains, of course, my presence here. Does he oft indulge your whimsy in taking women to your bed?"

"I do not take women to my bed. . . ."

Eleanor coughed, politely correcting him.

"Perhaps you seduced me," he teased. "Perhaps you evaded Anthony's keen eye to join me abed. You said you were a courtesan, after all."

"Perhaps not." And she gestured then with a single finger to the mattress.

Alexander frowned and looked downward in confusion, the vivid red stain upon the linens silencing any clever comment he might have made. He gaped. He blinked. He shook his head, but there was the mark of a broken maidenhead upon his linens all the same.

No wonder she was vexed. Indeed, he was vexed himself that he did not recall this particular mating.

When he glanced up, wordless for once in his life, Eleanor regarded him coolly. She was wrapped fully in that linen sheet, one end cast over her shoulder, her arms folded across her chest.

"You are not a courtesan," he said.

"You were right in that."

Alexander shook his head, still fighting to make sense of the blood. "You said you were twice widowed."

"And without a child from either match," she said quietly, then arched a brow, as if daring him to calculate how that circumstance might have come to be.

Alexander fell back across the mattress, perplexed beyond belief. Eleanor, the most enticing woman he had met in years, had been wed twice and two different men had failed to consummate their match with her. They might have been elderly men or sickly men, but Alexander could not imagine forgoing a consummation with Eleanor if he were dead.

Perhaps the lady had been the one to decline.

Then why would she have surrendered her all to him, on the first night of their acquaintance, and that when he was drunk? He glanced her way, finding her as impassive as previously.

Oh, he had erred beyond belief.

"Why? Why me?"

Eleanor shrugged. "I was curious."

"I was drunk!"

"Yet, amorous all the same."

"But I remember nothing of it!" He sat up and looked around the chamber. He resisted the urge to protest the unfairness of it all. "I do not even recall returning here."

She watched him, her expression turning shrewd. "Perhaps that was part of your allure."

"What is this?" Alexander rose from the bed in one bound, casting the linens aside and pursuing her across the chamber. The floor was cold, but he did not care.

Eleanor's eyes widened, and perhaps her grip upon the linens tightened somewhat, but she did not retreat. They stood toe to toe and he could smell the sweet sleepy scent of her flesh, see the myriad hues of green in her eyes.

"You chose me because I would be oblivious?" he demanded, incredulous when she nodded minutely. "What manner of woman wishes an insensible lover? What manner of woman uses a man for her own pleasure and grants nothing in return?"

She tilted her head to regard him. "Have you not known men to do as much?"

"No! Yes!" Alexander shoved a hand through his hair and paced the width of the chamber. "It is not of import."

"Have you not done as much yourself?"

He flushed, then glared at her. "If so, it was different."

Eleanor folded her arms more tightly across her chest. "As was this. It matters little what I have done, much less why. What is done is done."

"What has been done is but begun," Alexander retorted. Before she could retreat, he caught her chin in his hand and kissed her. His was not a forceful embrace, but it clearly surprised her. She stiffened, but Alexander slanted his mouth across hers.

He would have a kiss to remember, if not more.

She kissed like a virgin, breathless and tentative and frightened of what he might do. It was as if she had never embraced a man before. Alexander saw that red stain in his mind's eye. Perhaps she was sore this morning. Perhaps he had not been as gentle as he might have been. Perhaps he had injured her.

He wished he could have recalled. He felt a surge of compassion for her and lifted his lips from hers. She regarded him in astonishment for a moment, then stepped back.

"I trust that will suffice to sate you," she said, her words hoarse.

Alexander felt a cur, but he was determined not to let this matter be. "It will not begin to suffice," he murmured, savoring her quick glance of confusion.

"What do you mean?" She was uncertain, so uncertain that she was not able to hide her thoughts from him. Could it be that the lady was unaware of her many charms?

Alexander knew how he would become better acquainted with this lady. He would disarm her with his caress. It might take years, but he would show her the pleasure that could be found abed, he would court her and cajole her, and he would win the conquest of that smile.

There was but one way to do that honorably, for he had already taken more than had been his to claim.

Alexander smiled with a confidence he did not quite feel. "We will be wed this morn," he said with resolve, fully anticipating that she would spurn him. "It will never be said that the laird of Kinfairlie does not finish what he has begun."

Eleanor's eyes narrowed but she gave no other hint that she was surprised, though surely she must be. She glanced toward the bed, swallowed, and then nodded with a meekness he had not known she possessed. "So it shall be," she agreed quietly.

Alexander hesitated for a heartbeat. From any of his sisters, such complacency would have been a sign of conspiracy, but Eleanor regarded him, her eyes wide with innocence. He smiled and closed the distance between them once more.

"Such an agreement should be sealed with a kiss," he murmured.

"Surely one will do?" she said, her words breathless.

"Surely not. Your kiss is most restorative, my lady fair. Perhaps it will even restore my recollection of our first night abed together." Her eyes widened at that prospect. "Surely you cannot fear as much," he teased. Alexander winked when she said nothing, then claimed her lips anew.

HIS WAS A KISS that changed all.

Eleanor had never been courted with a kiss. She had been bussed, she had been used for a man's pleasure, she had been bedded for duty and treated like property.

She had never been seduced.

She had never been granted the gift of time. Alexander kissed as if he did not care how long it took her to become accustomed to his touch, as if he did not care how long it took to rouse her ardor. He kissed as if he expected to both give and receive pleasure.

It was wondrous, this kiss of his, and she indulged herself in a newfound pleasure. Something thawed within her, something opened like a blossom touched by the sun's heat.

Eleanor closed her eyes, for it was but a kiss, and lost herself in sensation. She parted her lips, inviting him closer, and caught her breath when he deepened his kiss. Still, he cajoled; still, she suspected that she could halt him with a fingertip; still, she surrendered more.

His kiss was pure sorcery. There was no unbridled violence in his embrace, to be sure, and conviction of that dissolved Eleanor's resistance. He did not judge her and find her wanting; he did not desire only one deed of her.

He courted her for her own self. Eleanor found her hands sliding across his shoulders, her fingers kneading the muscled strength of him, then twining in the thick waves of his hair. She found herself welcoming his embrace like the courtesan she had professed to be; she found herself meeting him, touch for touch, and yearning for more.

His hand rose to her breast, cupping its weight, his thumb sliding across her nipple, teasing it to a point. Eleanor arched her back, fairly pressing herself against him, and he made a sound of pleasure that thrilled her. She wanted only to coax him closer. She could not think sensibly. She could not remain angry that he had forgotten his own victory in his quest. She could not consider anything of import beyond the persuasive pressure of Alexander's kiss.

And that was dangerous, indeed. She had never known a man determined to court her favor, for its own merit. Eleanor wished heartily that they *had* met abed the night before, that he had claimed her maidenhead, that she was not deceiving him.

The recollection of her trick was sobering. Eleanor

broke their kiss with an effort. She pushed Alexander away, so that there was a step between them, as well as a great deal else.

He watched her, his gaze simmering, then leaned his fists on the wall on either side of her shoulders. Though he did not touch her, she was trapped within the circle of his arms. To be trapped, to see his determination, to note his fists upon the wall, all combined to awaken an old fear. Eleanor caught her breath.

Did his sweet kiss make her forget all that she knew?

"I am yet sore," she lied hastily. She ducked under his arm and quickly put the width of the chamber between them.

Alexander let her go, much to her relief.

When she dared to glance back, he stood with feet braced against the floor, arms folded across his chest, splendidly nude. His expression was difficult to read and he was uncommonly still.

"Did I injure you last evening?" His softly uttered question seemed to echo in the chamber, seemed to hang in the air and demand a reply.

He had not, of course, though the suggestion offered an easy means of keeping his caresses to a minimum. Eleanor shrugged. "No more than most men would have done, I assume." She turned away, as if unable to look upon him, but not so quickly that she did not see him wince.

She felt bad then, for he did not recall the truth and she used his ignorance against him. But encouragement would undoubtedly see her back in his arms, and the truth would see him rescind his proposal. Eleanor had never been so caught between truth and her own objectives, and she knew not what to say.

Worse, her lips burned in recollection of Alexander's caress, making her think of matters more earthy. It was not like her to yearn for a man's caress. She needed a moment to collect her wits, to think clearly.

"I am sorry," Alexander said, and she heard his footsteps as he crossed the floor. "Grant me this chance, Eleanor, to win your regard. Wed me and let me court you abed anew. Let me show you that our nights abed together do not have to repeat our first one." He offered his hand then and she liked his resolve. "Put your hand in mine, Eleanor, wed me and let us put a poor beginning behind us. It can be done."

She straightened. "I had thought you a man to put value in a quest."

"And so I am." He tilted his head to regard her, his eyes dancing with those delightful twinkles again. "Surely it will not be so onerous to have a knight laboring for your favor, all of each day and all of each night."

"But you won my smile already. Do not tell me that you have forgotten even your own triumph?"

He stared at her, aghast, and she knew that he did not recall. Had the potion stolen away his recollection, or was he so careless about winning the favor of women that he would have forgotten even without the potion?

Eleanor wished she could know the truth.

She also wished she did not feel so shrewish for having stolen the laughter from his eyes.

Alexander shoved a hand through his hair. "I am doubly indebted to you then, and must labor stridently to win your favor. I apologize, Eleanor. I do not know what happened to me last night."

Eleanor glanced away, awkward in her own knowledge.

"Allow me the chance to win your favor again." He bowed deeply over her hand, and should have looked comical in his nudity. Instead, Eleanor was aware of the breadth of him, the strength of him, and the masculinity of him. She desired him with such sudden vigor that she could not catch her breath. "Trust that I am at your service, as all men of merit should be at the service of ladies in peril."

"I am not in peril," she corrected hastily.

Alexander granted her a stern glance. "Of course you are. You are in peril of losing your heart, for I intend to win that prize next." He touched his finger to the bare skin revealed above the sheet, touching her just above the place where her heart beat wildly in response to his very presence. "You may be certain that I will never surrender that prize, once it is securely within my grasp."

Eleanor felt her eyes widen. She could smell his skin. Warmth emanated from that small point of contact and she saw how Alexander's eyes darkened to indigo. She licked her lips, unable to not do so, and he watched the tip of her tongue greedily. He whispered her name and stepped closer. She felt his erection against her hip, felt only the smooth barrier of cloth between them, but curiously she had no desire to flee.

"But why?" she asked, her voice sounding so husky that it might not have been her own.

He smiled. "Because it is right and proper for a man to hold his lady wife's heart, just as she should so possess his."

Eleanor stared up at him, astonished by his whimsical endorsement of love. She had never been so aware of a man, had never lusted for a man's touch as she did in this moment. She wanted to meet Alexander abed, this very morning, though she was astonished by the power of her own desire.

Alexander bent his head and touched his lips to hers. This kiss was tentative, as if he asked her permission to continue, and its effect was more heady than that of the finest wine.

Eleanor closed her eyes and lifted her lips more resolutely to his. Alexander's mouth closed over hers with possessive ease, his hands locked around her waist. He lifted her against his chest and kissed her thoroughly this time.

Marvel of marvels, Eleanor was not afraid. She opened her mouth, she echoed his every gesture, she tasted of him as he feasted upon her. She forgot herself, her past, her fears, and knew only that she wanted the heat of Alexander Lammergeier within her.

Immediately.

In that moment, the key was suddenly and noisily turned in the lock of the door to the solar.

"MERRY CHRISTMAS!" shouted Alexander's family. Five sisters and two brothers-in-law poured over the threshold. Their anticipation of what they would find was nigh tangible.

What they did find made them gasp aloud in astonishment.

Alexander swore. He shoved Eleanor behind him and she felt her face burn. She dropped her brow to the back of his shoulder, savoring the shield he made, though she was the one who had the linens. He stood nude before his blushing sisters and stared down the chuckles of his brothers-in-law. Those men hastily barricaded the view of the younger sisters while their wives laughed aloud.

"Alexander!" Madeline gasped. "You rogue!"

"He is more the rogue than ever we imagined," Vivienne agreed.

"I suppose," Alexander said, even as he seized the end of Eleanor's sheet and wound it around his hips, "that you all find it amusing to interrupt me abed with my intended bride."

"Bride!" Madeline and Vivienne declared in unison and mock astonishment, then exchanged a conspiratorial glance that Eleanor was certain would reveal their involvement to Alexander.

"Yes, *bride*," he said, apparently oblivious to this exchange. "Elizabeth, please inform Anthony that there will be nuptials celebrated this very morning. Isabella, please tell Father Malachy as well. . . ."

"But the banns . . . ," that sister protested.

"Will be waived," Alexander said with resolve. "If he wishes to argue the matter, we can do so when my lady and I reach the chapel." He claimed Eleanor's hand and granted her a glance that she did not doubt was supposed to be reassuring. "It will be a short argument."

"You have evidence upon your side," she said, reminding him of the linens, and Alexander nodded crisply.

"Indeed, I do. Madeline, would you gather the bed linens and Annelise can ensure that the priest and the household see them." Eleanor noted that he had dispatched his maidenly sisters from the solar with haste. "And I would beg the aid of all of my enchanting sisters in seeing Eleanor fittingly attired. It would be a good portent if she wore some new garb for our nuptials."

"Oho, he flatters us," Vivienne said with a smile. "Surely that means trouble ahead for all of us."

"Have you brothers, Eleanor?" Isabella asked with mock innocence; then Alexander roared and sent them all scattering.

"I should find some garb more fitting than the linens," he said to Eleanor when they were alone. She had only the warning of his mischievous wink before he flicked the sheet away from her, leaving her nude before him. Eleanor covered her breasts with her hands before she realized the folly of what she did.

Oblivious to her gesture, Alexander marched across the floor, then claimed the key. He frowned for a moment that it was on the outside of the door and Eleanor was certain he would realize that they had been locked in, not that they had locked the others out. He then shook his head and locked the portal with a flourish before turning to face Eleanor anew. Her heart fairly stopped, so familiar was this circumstance.

A nude man with an erection, a formidable man with a determined gleam in his eye, had locked her in his chamber and taken away her sole garb. Despite what Eleanor thought she knew of Alexander, a raw panic seized her.

The situation was too familiar, its ending all too sure. A trio of kisses and she was as much a fool as once she had been. A trio of kisses and she forgot what a man could do when his merest whim was denied.

"And what were we doing before we were so rudely interrupted?" he mused, his confident manner and his nudity feeding her terror.

"Nothing!" Eleanor cried, to his obvious astonishment. She lunged for the portal, uncaring that she had not a thread with which to cover herself. Alexander made to catch her about the waist, but Eleanor tripped him.

Alexander cursed as he fell. "What ails you?" he cried, then cursed as he hit his knee on the floor. The key loosed from his grip and danced across the floor.

Eleanor fairly fell upon the key, then raced to the door.

"Eleanor! You kissed me readily enough a moment past!"

Eleanor shoved the key into the lock with shaking fingers and ran into the corridor, leaving an astonished man behind her.

"What have I done?" Alexander bellowed, but Eleanor paid him no heed. He cursed audibly, but did not immediately pursue her.

Eleanor fled down the stairs. She managed to descend only one flight before the sisters surrounded her, all achatter with what she might wear, and coaxed her into their chambers. She stood quivering amid them, willing her wild heartbeat to slow. Silks and samites were spilled across the floor, slippers mingled in disarray and stockings piled before trunks. A plump maid shouted for order, to no avail.

Eleanor sat down heavily upon a trunk and heaved a sigh of relief when the door was barred against men. Her breathing slowed and she calmed enough to realize that Alexander probably had only desired to finish his kiss.

And then she felt seven kinds of fool for having fled his side.

The man would certainly think her witless. And indeed, Eleanor would not have argued that view, for her own deeds might well cost her the respite at Kinfairlie that she so ardently desired.

THERE WAS A PARTICULAR KIND of insanity loose in Alexander's hall, and he did not know what to make of it. He could not fathom Eleanor's sudden fear of him, nor could he satisfactorily explain his determination to ease her fear. She was an enigma and a conundrum, a woman determined to keep her secrets, and he should have been content to let her have them.

Instead, he wanted to aid her.

And truly, he wanted to meet her abed again; for this time, he would be certain to recall the deed. He certainly would not forget the sight of her smile, should she ever grace him with another. He needed time to name and exorcise the many demons that plagued her, and marriage would grant the gift of time.

Indeed, the more he thought about the matter, the more Alexander was convinced that his fascination with the lady was a good omen for their future together—although that argument might have been more persuasive if the woman had not fled him in terror.

Surely he had not lifted a hand against her the night before? The prospect stilled his steps. He could not imagine so doing. Surely he had not destroyed any chance of winning the lady's trust? Alexander wished he could have been certain.

How strange that he had slept so deeply. He did not think that he had drunk that much of the wine. He had been too concerned in winning Eleanor's smile. It was doubly curious that the key to the lock on his chamber door had been on the outside of the door. Had he heard the key turn before his family had interrupted Eleanor's delightful kiss?

And why had they come to his chamber, as if they expected something of him? It was most uncommon. Usually he met them in the hall, though he supposed that habits were broken during the holidays.

Perhaps they had witnessed more of his courtship of Eleanor than he recalled. Perhaps they had guessed what—or whom—they might find in his chamber.

If that were not sufficient to puzzle a man—never mind one whose head ached as Alexander's did—there was other oddity in his hall. It seemed to him—and admittedly, he was less than his usual self on this morn—that everyone knew of his nuptials before being told of them. Alexander was well aware that gossip was fleet of foot, but truly, it seemed that everyone at Kinfairlie had known of his intent to wed on this day before Alexander had guessed as much himself.

Anthony had already made preparations for a feast and the kitchens were redolent of meat being roasted and stewed. There was bread baking and eggs cooking and vegetables boiling, and all this by the time Alexander left his chamber, mere moments after persuading Eleanor to accept his suit. The tables were being set in the hall and there were peasants clustering around the portal already, spoons and bowls and napkins expectantly in hand.

It was Christmas Day, to be certain, but at Kinfairlie there was usually a feast on Christmas Eve in the laird's hall and then not until Twelfth Night.

But everyone appeared to know that tradition was to

be broken this year, no less that it was being broken for a wedding.

Alexander supposed that he must have courted Eleanor amorously, indeed, the night before, for his intentions to have been read so clearly by even his vassals.

Or was there another explanation?

The way his sisters giggled together certainly had a way of making a man suspicious that all might not be as it appeared. Perhaps this was all an elaborate prank, in which Eleanor participated, and she had no intention, in truth, of wedding him.

Perhaps Eleanor's flight from his kiss had been a hint of what was to come. Alexander would not put it past his sisters to play a jest upon him. As he put his hall in order and issued commands for his wedding day, Alexander braced himself for the worst. Aye, he could imagine Vivienne and Madeline thinking that a public embarrassment at the altar would be fitting retribution for his matchmaking for them.

Perhaps they did not know—or had not anticipated—that the lady felt a measure of attraction to him. Alexander knew a thing or two about women, and although Eleanor was more mysterious than most, there was no doubting that she welcomed his kiss.

Perhaps she could be persuaded to accept him truly, in defiance of whatever scheme his sisters had. The prospect of that put a spring in Alexander's step as he went about his morning duties.

Chapter Four

Eleanor indulged herself with a dream.

She stood on the threshold of Kinfairlie's chapel on Christmas morning, the warmth of sunlight on her head and shoulders, the sparkle of fresh snow all around her. The air was crisp, and the rumble of the sea carried from the cliffs beyond Kinfairlie's shores.

She was dressed in vivid crimson, a gossamer veil of golden silk wound over her head and gloriously gilded red leather slippers upon her feet. Alexander's sisters had raided their own stores of garments to dress her appropriately for her nuptials and she felt resplendent in red and gold. She had been surrounded by five laughing women, as intent upon seeing her look her best as if they had been her own blood sisters.

She knew they had accomplished their goal, for Alexander's eyes had glowed when she had first stepped into his hall. He had claimed her hand, kissed her knuckles, and not allowed her to be parted from his side since. It was intoxicating to be the focus of his attention and Eleanor dared to dream that this day would not end.

Alexander had not pressed her about her flight from his side, though he seemed determined to keep her close, and for this, she was grateful. He had even refused to hear her apology, insisting instead upon offering his own.

Eleanor's heart pounded in a most unfamiliar way and she knew that her cheeks were rosy. She wondered whether a measure of the starlight in Alexander's eyes had entered her own. She took a chance in defiance of all she had learned, but hope for a better future was a potent lure, indeed.

Alexander gave her hope, a rare gift for one who had seen and experienced as much as Eleanor had.

Alexander held her hand fast within his own even now as Father Malachy raised his hand in blessing. Alexander's siblings were gathered behind them, and the peasants of Kinfairlie clustered behind them, the entire company smiling. Alexander slid his thumb across Eleanor's hand, a leisurely caress that made her mouth go dry.

She risked a glance in his direction and found his gaze upon her, his eyes dancing with that barely contained merriment that she found so enticing. He looked pleased to be standing beside her, pleased to be exchanging vows with her.

As if he had chosen her himself to be his bride.

As if they had chosen each other. Eleanor added that element to her dream. He was finely wrought, this man intent upon taking her to wife, this man she had tricked. And he was honorable, so honorable that Eleanor felt remorse for having deceived him.

Eleanor chose to believe for a moment that this was a match that would endure, that Alexander would not prove to be a brute, that this sunny Christmas morning might bode well for her future. And she indulged herself with the impossibility of this being her first match, perhaps her only match. What if she *had* been a virgin the night before? The lie with which she had snared Alexander was more appealing than the truth, and she wished fervently that it could be the truth.

Her hand rose, seemingly of its own volition, to caress the crucifix that she always wore beneath her kirtle, the crucifix that should grace her garb at her nuptial vows, but found nothing.

Of course, the gem was no longer there. Eleanor had worn it for so long that she still forgot that it was gone. She caught her breath, knowing that the presence of her heirloom would have blessed this match as it could not have blessed her last two. She told herself that the loss of the gem was a small price to pay in exchange for her life.

"What is amiss?" Alexander whispered. In truth, he looked concerned, so concerned that she felt the need to grant him a reply.

"I lost a gem of my mother's and miss it still." Eleanor shrugged, as if the matter were not of import.

"What manner of gem?"

"A crucifix. It was merely a sentimental piece," she lied, not wanting him to realize that she had possessed any heirloom of such value as the ruby-studded golden crucifix that Ewen had seized.

To her dismay, Alexander was not deterred. The priest cleared his throat pointedly, but Alexander continued their conversation all the same. "You do not seem the manner of woman to lose things, especially items of sentimental value," he murmured, his gaze assessing. "Should we seek it?"

"Nonetheless, I did lose it and lost it long ago." Eleanor looked back at the priest, willing him to continue. "It is gone, gone beyond reclamation." The priest's gaze flicked between the pair of them, and his lips tightened in displeasure. Eleanor bowed her head deeply as if contrite.

Alexander tightened his grip upon her fingers. "You must describe it to me and I will seek another," he said as he bowed his head in turn.

Eleanor caught her breath. She was touched that he would make such an offer purely to see her pleased, before she recalled that he could not do as much. "Surely you should not waste whatsoever lurks in your coffers upon such a frippery?" she said quietly, and he inhaled sharply. She felt rude then for reminding Alexander of the truth of his financial situation.

Father Malachy crossed himself and said "Amen" before he glowered at the inattentive pair before him. Alexander granted the man such a smile that his scowl immediately began to soften. The company echoed the blessing with gusto; then Alexander slid a heavy ring onto the ring finger of Eleanor's left hand.

She looked down at it, surprised by its weight, and was more surprised by the ring itself. A large, round emerald fairly filled her knuckle, its green depths gleaming, its circumference marked with a plethora of small white pearls. It was a substantial piece and one no man without means could have acquired.

Had Alexander lied about his lack of coin? Or were the Lammergeier truly the thieves they were reputed to be?

Her astonishment must have shown when she met his gaze, for Alexander grinned.

"It was my mother's wedding ring," he said. "My father accepted it as his sole claim from Ravensmuir's hoard of treasures, and my mother left it in the treasury for safekeeping before they undertook the journey that proved to be their last." He touched a fingertip to her chin. "I could scarce bear to look upon it before this morning, but now the gem reminds me of the hue of your eyes."

"You could sell it, if you lack for coin."

"Never," he said with ferocity. "There are treasures with value beyond their price."

"You should keep it, then, in case you might have need of it."

His lips tightened and he spoke with vigor. "I should surrender it to my lady wife, as my parents doubtless intended I should do, that it might gleam from its rightful place upon her hand."

Eleanor blinked, for she knew not what to say in the face of such generosity. She was honored beyond belief by this gift and ashamed anew that she had tricked him. Words eluded her.

Eleanor had little chance to speak, though, for Alexander bestowed yet another of his bewildering kisses upon her. Appreciative of his thoughtfulness, she leaned into his embrace after only the barest hesitation. She savored his heat and the crisp scent of him, welcomed his caress with a remarkable confidence that he would not press her too far.

She would do her best to serve him well as his wife.

The company cheered at this public show of affection and Eleanor's cheeks heated, but Alexander continued his languorous kiss. One of his hands cupped her nape, the other held fast to her left hand, enclosing the ring that she now bore. Once again, Eleanor felt cosseted and safe. Heat spread to her very toes and her flesh tingled, her hand rose to his shoulder and she eased to her toes, wanting more of whatsoever he offered.

Alexander broke their kiss all too soon, his smile warm as he gazed upon her. Eleanor smiled in return and liked how his eyes lit.

"This is a finer beginning," he said, for her ears alone, and Eleanor felt herself flush. Her heart was light, lighter than she could ever recall it being.

Father Malachy tutted at Alexander with little censure, then turned and led the company into the chapel to celebrate the mass. Alexander gallantly offered his elbow to Eleanor, and his sisters beamed at what they had wrought.

It was perfect. This was as Eleanor had dreamed her nuptials would be and the truth of it put a lump in her throat. If this was illusion, it was not only artful but also one she ardently desired.

The candles had been lit and the priest had just lifted the Eucharist when destriers came galloping into Kinfairlie's village. Eleanor knew in that instant that her fledgling dream was to be shattered. She braced herself for the worst, even as she bitterly regretted that her past should prove to be so fleet of foot.

ALEXANDER HEARD THE HORSES and would have thought little of it, had Eleanor not started in such alarm. She glanced over her shoulder, her eyes wide, and her fingers tightened upon his. He looked at her just as the portal opened, heard her catch her breath, and saw the color drain from her face.

Then she pivoted to face Father Malachy anew. Alexander knew he did not imagine that her hand trembled within his, though she stood tall and straight.

He glanced back then and his own lips thinned at the new arrivals. It was the Black Douglas clan, the oddly fair Alan at the fore of the party. There was something uncanny about Alan, more than the pallor of his eyes or the strange fair blond of his hair. Just the sight of him made people awkward.

Alan's party marched noisily into the chapel, sparing no respect for the service in progress. Alan smiled at the sight of Eleanor, though his was not a kind smile. It was a smile that put Alexander in mind of hungry wolves and he pulled Eleanor closer to his side. Rhys and Erik followed Alexander's gaze and eased their wives away from the center of the chapel.

Alan cast his helm and gloves to a squire, then made his way through the chapel. The peasants fell out of his path, and muttering followed in his wake. He pushed his way between Erik and Rhys, neither of whom granted him any quarter, then reached for Eleanor's elbow. How did he know her?

Eleanor never glanced up, but she pulled her arm abruptly out of his reach.

"Well met, sister," Alan said, interrupting the priest.

"Is that the truth of it?" Eleanor murmured.

"Hardly well met at all," Alexander said, wondering at the link between these two. Were they siblings? "Have you no respect for the divine offices?"

"Earthly matters are of greater import in this moment,"

Alan said, then seized Eleanor's left hand, lifting it so that the light played in the gem Alexander had just placed upon her finger. "Ah, I see that I interrupt nuptial pledges." His smile turned cruel as he studied Eleanor. "I always knew that you were a shrewd bitch, but this is cunning beyond expectation."

Alexander's sisters gasped as one. Rhys and Erik stepped forward at the insult offered to Alexander's lady. Father Malachy caught his breath that such language would be used in church, but none had a chance to respond.

Alexander had already struck Alan. His fist landed solidly upon Alan's nose. Alexander was not dissatisfied to hear a bone crack beneath his blow. Alan fell back, blood erupting from one nostril, and no one stepped forward to aid him.

Alan steadied himself and glanced over the watchful company. Eleanor said nothing, though her gaze flicked between the men, seemingly missing no nuance of response. Alan's men made to move forward, but Alexander's men blocked their progress.

Alan fingered his nose, which was swelling even as it reddened. He glared at Alexander. "I had always thought that you were not overly keen of wit."

"And I have always found you to be devoid of chivalry, although this incident is far beyond anticipation," Alexander retorted. "No one speaks to a noblewoman so coarsely upon my lands, much less in a chapel reliant upon my protection."

"Amen," said Father Malachy.

Alan only smirked. He straightened, then eyed Alexander anew. "Let me grant you some counsel, neighbor, and save you from your own error before it is fully made."

"I do not welcome your counsel."

"You should." Alan snatched at Eleanor's hand. He pulled the ring from her finger, even as she gasped in outrage, then cast it at Alexander. Alexander caught the ring, and in that same moment, Alan hauled Eleanor to his side so quickly that she stumbled. "Keep your bauble, neighbor. This bride is fatal to claim."

"No!" Eleanor protested, and pulled her hand from Alan's grasp.

"The choice is not yours to make," Alan said with a snarl. He grasped her hand again and Eleanor winced as his grip was clearly harsh.

"Is Eleanor your sister?"

"Nay."

"Is she your niece or daughter?"

Alan granted Eleanor that unpleasant smile. "She is the widow of my brother, Ewen."

Alexander blinked at this morsel of news, then glared at Alan. "Then the choice most certainly *is* the lady's to make," he said. He seized Alan's wrist even as that man glared at him in defiance. Alexander was younger than Alan and he did not doubt that he was stronger. Indeed, he tightened his grip steadily upon the other man's wrist until Alan's grasp upon Eleanor was released.

Alan swore.

Eleanor pulled herself free with haste and the red mark upon her flesh made Alexander angry.

"There is no cause to handle a woman thus!" Alexander urged the lady behind him. "You have no claim upon her, and less claim to give insult in my abode. Begone, Alan, before worse is said this day."

Alan's eyes narrowed. "You know little of the matter, it

is clear. As my brother's widow, and a widow whose own kin is dead, Eleanor's future is mine to determine. I do have claim upon her, and I do intend to see justice served."

"I owe you nothing!" Eleanor said with heat.

"The lady declines your kindly interest in her future," Alexander said coldly. "And truly, there is no need for your involvement, as she has already wedded me."

"Is this true?" Alan demanded of Eleanor.

"Indeed, it is," she said.

"And you wed him willingly, without coercion?"

Alexander felt Eleanor straighten behind him, and her words revealed that some of her determination had been restored. "That is an intriguing query from a man who would see me wed by force."

To whom would Alan see Eleanor wed?

Alexander noted the avarice in Alan's expression and thought he could guess the answer to that query. He assumed that Alan had a fancy for his late brother's wife, one that was not reciprocated by that lady and one that was unacceptable by the church's law. The realization made him doubly determined to defend her. His sisters had oft expressed fear of Alan Douglas and he could well understand why Eleanor might have fled that man.

"I but seek to ensure your welfare, sister," Alan said.

"It is assured," Alexander and Eleanor said in unison.

"You are far from your abode, neighbor," Alexander added with pointed politeness. "And surely must make haste to see yourself at your own board this night."

"We rest at Tivotdale this Yule, which is not so distant." Alan nodded to Eleanor. "Though your bride could have told you as much, had she so chosen. She walked here from that hall, after all."

That Eleanor had walked so far in the snow to evade Alan and his scheme told Alexander all he needed to know.

Alan sneered at Eleanor. "Did you walk to Kinfairlie specifically because you had heard tell that its laird was unwed?"

"No!" Eleanor retorted so hotly that Alexander believed it to be true. "I but fled, and knew not where I ran. The direction was of less intent than flight itself!"

Alan smiled and might have said more, but Alexander had heard sufficient. "Your presence is unwelcome upon these lands, Alan," he said with resolve. "For you show yourself to be a poor guest. Leave now, and we may meet again in good cheer. If you remain, and continue to cause insult, that circumstance is less certain."

"It is my intention merely to be a good neighbor and ally," Alan said smoothly, bowing to Eleanor with a charm that only fed Alexander's distrust. "I would simply warn you of the merit of the woman you would take to wife, before it is too late."

"I know the lady's merit," Alexander said, recapturing Eleanor's hand within his own. Her fingers were cold. He could well understand her fear of men if she had been wed to Ewen Douglas. That man had been a loud and violent drunkard, by Alexander's reckoning.

"Do you?" Alan smiled that wolfish smile again. "Surely a man of sense would think twice afore taking a murderess to his bed?"

The company recoiled in shock, as clearly Alan had anticipated they would. He turned to his rapt audience and nodded as if confiding a secret in them. "It is true. We have hunted this viper for four days and nights, ever since in fact, we found my brother, Ewen, her legally wedded spouse, murdered in his own bed at Tivotdale. There was no sign of his wife, save the trail of her departing footprints in the snow."

The company gasped, but Alan held up a finger. Alexander noted that the only person unsurprised by this revelation was Eleanor. She glared at Alan, her hatred undisguised.

It must be a filthy lie Alan told, and Alexander did not blame Eleanor for despising him for it.

"You make charges without proof," Alexander said.

Alan held up a finger. "The only soul who had been in Ewen's company was his lady wife, none other than the lady your laird would wed this morning. She had fled her own chamber in the middle of the night, with only the garb upon her back, and this upon the same night that my brother was killed."

He regarded the company. "My brother, Ewen, disregarded the tales that were told of the demise of the lady's first husband and the lady's rumored part in that demise, and that to his own loss."

He turned to Alexander, the cunning in his eyes doing little to persuade Alexander to believe him. "Save yourself now, neighbor, and spurn this woman before your match is consummated. She can only bring you grief."

"And if Alexander spurns her, what then will be her fate?" Madeline demanded. Alexander did not doubt that his sister meant to make the full result of any such choice clear to him, but he had no intent of spurning Eleanor.

How could he surrender her to the custody of a man who would so willingly defame her? Alexander did not doubt that worse than cruel words would await Eleanor beneath Alan's hand.

Alan smiled his chilling smile. "She will return to our abode and face justice as she deserves."

Alexander watched Eleanor, whose expression was impossible to read. She arched a brow, as if anticipating what he might ask. "Do whatsoever you will, my lord," she said to Alexander, her tone tart. "It is not a woman's place to choose, after all."

Alexander saw that Eleanor expected little from him, and knew that her expectation had been learned. Doubtless, Ewen had taught her to expect nothing, not even courtesy, from a spouse. That must have compounded the lessons of her first spouse.

Alexander would teach her to expect otherwise from her husband.

"It is, however, my wife's place to remain at my side in Kinfairlie," he said, and knew he did not imagine the surprise that lit Eleanor's eyes.

"What folly is this?" Alan said.

"No folly at all. I thank you, neighbor, for your counsel, but the lady and I have already consummated our match." He drew Eleanor to his left side, where she rightly belonged, and bestowed a smile upon her. "I fear that we celebrated the nuptial night afore our nuptial vows were made. It matters little in the end, so long as both are completed in timely manner and neither of us is desirous of an annulment."

"But this cannot be . . . ," Alan protested.

Alexander snapped his fingers and beckoned. Vera, his sisters' maid, came through the company, proudly bearing the stained linens from his own bed. The priest blessed the bloodstain and prayed for the favor of sons, while Alan's brow darkened yet more.

"This is impossible," he said with fury. "It proves nothing."

"It proves that Ewen did not have blood in his veins," Alexander said quietly, "if he was never tempted to claim his bride. It seems the lady's two former husbands had much in common, though little of merit to be sure."

The other man looked as if he would make a hot reply, but Alexander allowed him no chance to speak. "Has it not long been said that Ewen favored his ale above all else? Perhaps he fell in his chamber, being too besotted to find his own bed."

"You know nothing of my brother or his nature!" Alan began, but Alexander shook his head.

"And you seem to know nothing of his demise. You offer only accusations. You offer no evidence against my wife, save her absence from your hall, and no proof of her guilt. There are those who must marvel that Ewen was not dead of his excesses years ago."

"But . . ."

"In fact, your behavior shows the lady's good sense in leaving Tivotdale once her spouse was dead. No woman of wit would expect justice from you."

"You cannot argue with me! You have no right to harbor a murderess!"

"Your accusation is a poor gift to bring a neighbor on Christmas morn, no less upon his wedding day," Alexander said, not acknowledging Alan's interruption. "Further, you interrupt our celebration of this day's miracle." He met the older man's gaze. "Join us or leave."

"You cannot compel me. . . ."

"Mine is Kinfairlie, and mine is the command of those upon its lands." Alexander laid his hand upon the hilt of his sword. "Make your choice." He saw in the periphery of his vision that his two brothers-in-law had also dropped their hands to the hilts of their blades.

The chapel was silent for a moment; then Alan swore.

He pivoted and marched back to his men, snatching his gloves from the squire, then glared at Alexander. "This matter is not resolved between us," he warned, but Alexander smiled.

"I say that it is ended, and rightly so."

With that, Alexander turned his back upon the unwelcome visitor, fairly daring Alan to act upon his threat.

The other man left with a curse, as Alexander had guessed he would. The portal slammed and the sound of the horses carried through the chapel, the echo of hoofbeats gradually fading from earshot. The company heaved a collective sigh of relief, then began to chatter.

Alexander lifted the ring between himself and Eleanor once more, holding it between his finger and thumb. He held it before her hand, and met her gaze, letting her decide whether to don it or not.

She studied him for a moment, marvel in her eyes. It was clear that the lady had not been defended from innuendo and rumor before, but Alexander meant to show her that marriage could be better than what she had known.

Without a word, she solemnly pushed her finger through the ring's circle. He saw her blink back her tears and was heartened that she could grant him a chance, after whatever she had endured.

Ewen Douglas had been a brute and would not be mourned by many.

"It looks right upon your finger," he whispered to her

when its weight had slipped over her knuckle. "As if it was left to me, so I would have it to give to you."

"I thank you," she whispered. Then Eleanor smiled, a smile so brilliant as to leave Alexander dazed, a smile that he knew he would never cease to seek, much less that he would forget. "Your gift to me is beyond expectation," she whispered, then tightened her fingers around his.

Alexander attended Father Malachy's words only partly then, a lump in his throat and his bride's hand fast within his. Against all odds, he had been granted a bride who made his blood simmer, and between them both, Alexander knew, they would make a marriage worth all the gold in Christendom. They might have had an unconventional beginning to their match, but that had not stopped his sisters from finding happiness.

So it would not halt him.

MOIRA GOODALL HAD A TALENT for taking whatever pittance God had granted her and making the most of it. She had been granted a nature best for service, and she had served Lady Yolanda faithfully until that lady died.

Further, she had undertaken the pledge that Lady Yolanda had demanded of her, upon that lady's deathbed in the birthing chamber. She had served the lady's daughter, Eleanor, from the moment that child made her first wail, and this despite the protests of Lady Yolanda's husband and Lady Eleanor's husbands. Moira had not always been made welcome in her mistress's new households, but she had a talent for making herself useful and she had managed each time to remain by Eleanor's side.

God knew that the child had had need of her.

Moira also was plain of face, but she had offered that burden to God and had found usefulness in it as well. A man's eye would pass over her so readily that she could join any company and her presence would neither be noted nor remembered. So it was that she had joined the company of Alan Douglas, mingling with the whores who followed any campaign, when he set out in pursuit of his brother's widow. Moira guessed that avarice would ensure that Alan found Eleanor and she knew that he would never take note of her presence among those who trailed his company.

And so it was that Moira found her errant lady, albeit in happier circumstance than she might have hoped. Her loyal heart fairly burst to find her lady in Kinfairlie's chapel, the laird himself looking upon her with the respect she deserved.

Moira left Tivotdale's whores while Alan Douglas argued with the laird of Kinfairlie. She eased herself amid the merrymakers from Kinfairlie village as if she had been in their company all along. Even the whores, so fascinated by events before themselves, never noted her departure from their midst.

So it was that Alan Douglas left Kinfairlie with one less soul in his party, none the wiser for Moira's presence or her absence. No one would ever miss her at Tivotdale, this Moira knew well, and she could now serve her lady faithfully once more. There was but one soul in Kinfairlie who would recognize Moira, and Moira wished to be certain of her lady's circumstance before she revealed herself.

Moira drew up her hood, remained within the com-

pany, and listened to every morsel that came to her ears.
One never knew what detail one would have need of, especially in service to this ill-fated lady.

CHOICE.

How sweet it was that Alexander granted Eleanor the
choice. He defended her, but then left it to her to decide
to don his ring again. Eleanor had never been granted a
choice, not by any man, and on this morning, she prayed
with rare fervor, giving thanks that her footsteps had
brought her to Kinfairlie's gate.

She would give Alexander a son.

The notion came to her so suddenly that it might not
have been Eleanor's own, but she knew the rightness of it
immediately. She would grant Alexander a son, for in so
doing she would inherit her legacy and the survival of this
precious sanctuary would be ensured. This was the gift
she could give to him in exchange for the gift of choice
he had granted to her.

This was what she could do to repay the debt she owed
to him.

No sooner had she made her decision, no sooner had
her heart begun to thump with the prospect of meeting
Alexander abed, than Father Malachy raised his hands
and the company sang the end to the mass in unison.
Then the assembly cheered and exchanged the kiss of
peace, the chapel erupting in happy chatter.

Alexander seized Eleanor's hand, doubtless intending
to kiss her soundly, but in so doing, inadvertently pinched
the cut upon her thumb. Eleanor winced and caught her

breath at the stab of pain. The cut she had inflicted upon herself the night before was barely healed and began to bleed again.

Alexander looked down at her hand. He frowned at the clean cut, obviously guessing that it had been wrought by a blade. "You have injured yourself," he said in some confusion.

"It was nothing," she said so hastily that his gaze flew to meet hers.

"But it is a wound of considerable length," he said, shaking his head. "I do not recall you being so injured this morn, though it is fresh."

"It happened last night."

"Surely I did not so injure you?"

"No, no. I did it myself. Foolishly. With my eating knife. At the board."

He studied her, a suspicion dawning in his eyes. "But I recall the end of the feast, and you did not use your knife throughout the meal."

Eleanor licked her lips, remembering all too well how he had fed her morsels so seductively. She dropped her voice, her thoughts upon what they might do abed this night. "I had no need of one, as I recall, for you saw me sated."

But Alexander frowned. "Indeed, I did not think you carried a knife." He looked to her belt, which was, in fact, barren of a small blade, for Ewen had forbidden her to possess one.

"I must have left it in your sisters' chamber," Eleanor lied.

Alexander turned her hand and studied the cut, undeterred. Eleanor pulled her hand from his, but she knew he did not cease to think about the matter.

"We should adjourn to the hall," she said, hoping to distract him.

But Alexander glanced over the company with a frown. "They all knew of the nuptials before I did," he mused, and Eleanor feared he was overclose to the truth.

"But you were amorous last night," she said with haste.

Alexander met her gaze. "I never have forgotten a lady abed," he said with a slight shake of his head. "I heartily doubt that you would be the first."

"Can there not be a first for every matter?" Eleanor heard the fear in her voice and knew she did herself no favors by answering him. Still, it seemed that she could not hold her tongue.

"There is an old trick," he said quietly. His gaze fixed upon her, those stars notably absent from his eyes, and her heart began to pound. "When a woman wishes to be thought a maiden."

"What would I know of such tricks?" Eleanor spoke too quickly, she saw, for Alexander's eyes narrowed.

"What jest do you and my sisters play upon me?"

"None!"

"Tell me the truth of this cut. Tell me the truth of what occurred between us last night." He straightened, looking so grim that Eleanor feared his judgment. "Tell me the truth of what I have done. Did I strike you? Did I give offense?"

"Of course not."

"Then what occurred?"

Eleanor glanced about herself, but Alexander's sisters had left the chapel, abandoning her to their brother's difficult questions. She, cursedly, was a poor liar and, even worse, Alexander was dangerously perceptive.

"I see no need for such confessions," she said with a shrug. "We are wed and happily so." She leaned forward, initiating a kiss for the first time in her life, though it was but a peck upon his cheek. "Let us retire to our chamber, my lord, and leave the others to feast in our stead."

Alexander stepped away. "What is at the root of Alan's false accusations? Why do you fear him so?"

"That is hardly of import."

"I think it is."

"He means to wed me, in his brother's stead," she admitted, hoping it would deter his curiosity.

It did not. Alexander's frown only deepened. "Why does he anticipate that you would do as much? Such a match would be most uncommon; indeed, it would be against the church's law."

"Which was why I would evade it, of course."

"It makes little sense." Alexander paced the width of the now-empty chapel, shoving a hand through his hair. "Why did you not confess to being Ewen's widow? Do you not think it of import which of my neighbors I offend? I am scarce in a position to defend myself against them all."

"It is but a cut!" Eleanor cried in frustration.

"Had you merely surrendered your name to me, I would have known the truth," he retorted. "Why did you hide it from me?"

Eleanor flung out her hands. "How did a single wound upon my thumb awaken such doubts within you?"

"They must have been there all along," he said, his manner grim. "But your beauty distracted me from their importance."

It was impossible to be flattered by his comment in

such context. "But these questions are not important, not to our match. Alan's scheme is not relevant, not now!"

He folded his arms across his chest and regarded her. "Then answer my queries for me. If the truth matters so little, then your answers should not delay us overmuch."

Eleanor took a deep breath, disliking the corner in which she found herself. Oh, for a child in her belly already!

But she had no child, and indeed they had not even met abed yet. She dared not confess as much to Alexander, though, for he could spurn her all too readily with that morsel of information.

And Alan was still dangerously close at hand.

"You are churlish to demand such confessions so soon after our nuptials," she said, her tone light. "Surely we can discuss such matters at our leisure?"

Alexander glowered at her. "Answer but one question and I shall leave the matter be."

Eleanor straightened, praying that he would not ask the one question that could send all awry. "Fair enough," she said with a confidence she did not feel.

"Explain the cut to me."

Eleanor felt her lips part, though no words erupted for a moment. "Your sisters saw me injure myself," she said in sudden inspiration. "I am certain that they will recall how inadvertent it was." She forced a laugh. "Truly, Alexander, you make much of little."

He watched her, his expression inscrutable. "Understand this, my lady fair. I will endeavor to build a marriage from a poor beginning, but I will not tolerate one based upon a lie. Honesty must be the cornerstone of our match, Eleanor, for without honesty, we can build nothing at all. Trust rests upon honesty's foundation, as does affection and even love. All are undermined by deception and, truly, there is nothing so capable of infuriating me as a lie."

She did not like how his voice lowered. "And without honesty?" she dared to ask.

Alexander shook his head. "Then, in truth, we have no match and it is but a formality to see such a false marriage annulled." His sudden glance was piercing and she feared he would see her many secrets. "Did we meet abed last night? Did I claim your maidenhead in truth? Do not lie to me, Eleanor."

Eleanor held his regard, for in this moment, she had no choice but to tell a falsehood. "Of course we did," she lied, hoping against hope that Alexander never learned the truth.

And she was a poor liar, as poor a liar as she had feared. He studied her for a long moment and she knew she did not imagine either his delay in offering his hand to her or the formality of his posture.

He did not believe her.

She had lied to ensure this match, but in so doing had condemned it. There was a barrier between them, one that had not been there before. Just as he had said, her lie undermined all they might possess together.

As Eleanor put her hand within Alexander's, she wondered what she could do to make this matter come aright.

ALEXANDER WAS LIVID.

Eleanor lied. Despite his warning, despite his insistence that she provide him with the truth, despite his appeal for honesty between them, Eleanor lied. The blood upon his linens was from her thumb, he would have wagered his soul upon it.

Her husbands had not failed to consummate their matches. He had not assaulted the lady himself, much less bedded her. He had not forgotten what had occurred between them, for nothing had occurred. Eleanor had tricked him, undoubtedly with the aid of his conniving sisters, and they most assuredly all found it a merry jest.

He had not lied in declaring that nothing infuriated him more than a falsehood, unless perhaps it was a falsehood that could prove expensive for all beneath his hand.

His sisters and new wife knew nothing of the realities confronting him. His father had always allied with the Black Douglas family and now Alexander had alienated Alan. It would only be a matter of time before an army came to his gates and Kinfairlie would not be able to withstand a major assault. Alexander had no coin in his treasury to prepare for that inevitability. The prospect that those dependent upon him would suffer because his sisters sought to see themselves amused infuriated him beyond all belief.

Alexander entered the hall in a foul mood, escorted Eleanor to the high table, and left her there without a word. He spied Matthew and strode to that young man's side.

"Matthew, you must still have my signet ring," he said, his manner yet terse. "I would have it returned this morn." Alexander put out his hand, and Matthew colored.

"I do not have it, my lord," the younger man said.

"What is this?" Matthew's father demanded. "You

cannot have lost the laird's signet ring!" Those seated at other tables turned at the miller's raised voice.

"Where is the ring, Matthew?" Alexander asked, his patience nigh expired.

"I returned it to you, my lord," Matthew said, his gaze darting along the floor. He seemed uncommonly shy this day.

Alexander feared that Matthew lied to him as well, but he strove to be fair. "When?"

"When—when you retired, my lord. I returned it to you then."

Alexander exchanged a glance with the miller. "Are you certain of this? The ring does not grace my finger this morn."

"Perhaps you did not don it this day, my lord."

"Perhaps you did not return it, Matthew."

"Do you call my son a liar, my lord?" the miller asked softly, and Alexander knew that his frustration with Eleanor had affected his manner.

"No, of course not," he said, forcing a smile. "I am merely vexed because I cannot find the ring. As you know, it is the mark of my authority and not an item one would wish to misplace."

Matthew stared stubbornly at the floor, his ears a vivid hue of red, and said no more.

The miller cleared his throat. "Perhaps you put it in a different place than is your custom, my lord," he suggested. "You were not, after all, your usual self last night."

"So I understand," Alexander said. He nodded to miller and son, then strode back to the high table. It was strange how the evening ended so abruptly in his recollection, for he knew he had not drunk that much of the wine. Of course, he had not eaten much either, so the wine might have had a more potent effect upon him.

"Where is the ring?" Eleanor asked when he took his place beside her, for she clearly guessed his mission.

Alexander shrugged. "Matthew says he returned it to me when I made to retire."

"Liar!" she muttered.

Alexander spared her a glance, intrigued by her charge.

"I remember every step betwixt high table and solar," she said with such resolve that he believed her. "And Matthew did not return your ring."

"I can scarce call him a liar when I do not recall events myself," Alexander said.

"Then perhaps you should not have drunk so much wine," Elizabeth teased.

"I did not drink much wine. That is what is so curious." Alexander caught the guilty expression upon Isabella's face, then noted the glance she exchanged with Madeline and Vivienne.

The odd manner spread down the high table. Rhys was suddenly grim. Eleanor had developed a fascination with her soup, though she only filled the spoon and let the soup dribble back into her bowl. Elizabeth seemed to savor a private joke while Annelise was crimson from hair to throat.

Alexander surveyed his siblings and pushed back slightly from the board. "In fact, the last thing I recall was you, Isabella, bringing Eleanor and me each a cup of wine."

Isabella flushed scarlet in her turn. "I wished only to

ensure that you had some of it," she said so brightly that he knew she concocted a tale. "People drank it with such gusto that I feared you would be left without a taste at all."

"And you insisted which cup I should take." Alexander felt taut with the certainty that he had been the butt of a jest that was not amusing in the least. "What was in the wine, Isabella?"

She fidgeted. "Nothing. Nothing at all, save the wine itself."

"You are a less adept liar than my wife," Alexander said with heat. He cast down his napkin and raised his voice. "What was in the wine?"

Isabella granted him a mutinous glance. "You have need of a wife. We cannot trust you to not marry us against our wills, as you did with Vivienne and Madeline."

"Perhaps a woman will take our sides more readily," Annelise suggested.

"Perhaps you are fortunate that there was not more added to your wine," Elizabeth said. "For the weight of your authority is onerous indeed, Alexander."

"Aha!" Alexander roared. "So it *was* tainted."

"I told you that naught good would come of this," Rhys informed Madeline.

"He is hale enough," that woman said. "Alexander, you make much of little. We wished only to give you a measure of your own treatment in return, and see Eleanor's safety assured as well."

"So you see me sedated, you see that my allies are turned against me"—he turned to Eleanor, who had the grace to look discomfited—"you lie to me, and you expect me to greet this revelation with good cheer."

He cast a glance over the hall and found the old midwife grinning at him. She was half-mad, was Jeannie, but
her expression told him that she knew something of the
matter. He gestured to her. "Jeannie, did you mix a potion
last evening?"

"Aye, I did, my lord, the better to ensure that you slumbered deeply. I trust the taste was favorable enough."

"I never guessed the wine was tainted, if that is your
meaning."

Jeannie nodded with pride and whispered to herself.

"Jeannie, since you know what you mixed, tell me
this," Alexander demanded. The entire company was rapt.
"Could a man have lain with a woman, could he have
planted his seed within her, after drinking of that potion?"

Jeannie laughed. She slapped her thighs and laughed
so hard that none could doubt the answer. "He would
have neither the will nor the means, my lord, after that
cup's contents. All of him would slumber, if you understand my import. All of him would be so limp as to be
without life."

Alexander lowered his voice, addressing only his kin
at the high table. He spoke through gritted teeth and there
was heat in his words. "But there was blood in my bed.
The blood seemingly of a lady's maidenhead, yet apparently shed by a woman twice widowed."

Alexander lifted Eleanor's hand, displaying the cut
upon her thumb to the entire table. It confirmed his suspicions when not one of his siblings was surprised by the
sight. "But it was blood from her thumb and I would
wager that you all knew it well."

"Alexander," Madeline began to protest, but Alexander
had no interest in her side of matters.

Intriguingly, Eleanor said nothing in her own defense. She was pale and sat with her hands clenched tightly together, her head bowed.

"You tricked me," Alexander said to his sisters, his words hot. "So fair enough, you have had your jest. The amusement ends immediately, however."

"But, Alexander . . . ," Vivienne protested.

"You cannot . . . ," Madeline began.

But Alexander had risen to his feet, anger burning hot in his chest. They had lied, they had deceived him, they had seen one of his allies alienated, and they had put every soul in Kinfairlie at risk. Alexander Lammergeier did not find humor in the situation.

"Be merry, all of you," he shouted to the company. "Partake of the hospitality of Kinfairlie, but know that you celebrate no nuptials this day."

The assembly stared at him in astonishment.

"My wedding was but a jest, contrived by the lady and my sisters, in honor of our evening of misrule. Surely you are all entertained." Alexander halted, but no one smiled. "So, feast, all of you, eat your fill and savor the tale of my own folly. Father Malachy, I would ask you to strike the entry in your ledger this day, as if no wedding had been performed."

The priest stood and visibly took a deep breath. He shook his head. "I cannot undo what has been done, my lord. The banns were waived, at your insistence and over my protest, and thus I would counsel you to stand by what you have done. Many a match begins inauspiciously and proceeds well."

Alexander granted the priest a stony glare, displeased at yet more defiance. "No match of merit is based upon a lie," he said with resolve, "for affection cannot take root in deceit."

"I beg your pardon," Madeline began to protest.

"I have a thought upon that matter," Vivienne said, both sisters rising to their feet in indignation.

Alexander ignored them both, for the priest did not waver in his conviction. "I leave you all to the meat, then, for I have a letter to write to the bishop. When all is said and done, the lady and I will annul our match as if it never had been pledged, upon that you can all rely."

With that, Alexander left the board, fuming.

He glanced back but once from the foot of the stairs, and saw Eleanor staring fixedly across the hall, her chin high and her shoulders squared. He knew a moment's doubt then, for he should not have embarrassed her so. It was not seemly.

She had lied to him, though, despite his granting her the chance to surrender the truth. Alexander told himself not to let her beauty or her spirit weaken his resolve. She had participated in the deceit against him, and even given a chance to explain herself, she had persisted in the lie.

He had no need of such an untrustworthy wife, no matter that every soul in his hall thought otherwise.

The sooner he wrote to the bishop, the better.

Chapter Five

WHAT WAS IN THE POTION, Jeannie?" Eleanor demanded once Alexander was gone and the hall had descended into pandemonium.

"I have no need to confess my secrets to you," the old crone said with a cackle.

Eleanor fixed her with a stern eye. "You could be tried for attempting to murder the laird to whom your fealty is sworn," she said, seeing the ripple of shock that roiled through the company. She stood and walked toward the old midwife, whose bravery faded with every step Eleanor took.

"I did no such deed. Every soul knows that I hold no malice against the laird."

Eleanor began to count effects on her fingers as every soul in the hall listened attentively. "His pulse was wild last evening, and his skin was flushed."

"That is not uncommon for a man in his nuptial bed," jested one stalwart soul, but Eleanor did not spare him so much as a glance.

She continued to count, her gaze fixed on old Jeannie.

"He was uncertain of his whereabouts; his thoughts wandered; his pupils were as tiny as the head of a pin." Eleanor halted beside the midwife, who fidgeted. "His belly heaved this morn with some gusto, after he slept deeply indeed. You and I both know these to be the marks of a poison in a man's blood." She leaned closer. "What would we have seen if we had put a drop of his urine in the eye of a cat?"

The harridan started, then stared at Eleanor with fear. "You cannot know what I used. You cannot guess!"

"It was nightshade," Eleanor said, and saw acknowledgment in the old woman's expression before she turned away.

"You should not reveal my secrets," Jeannie complained.

"You should not try to kill your laird," Eleanor snapped, and pivoted to face the high table. She cursed herself, for she should have guessed the herb sooner. Only nightshade could affect a man with such haste.

But nightshade could easily kill a man, howsoever hale he might be. Alexander had eaten precious little the night before, far less than any soul might have anticipated. That he had done so because he had escorted her outside, the better to persuade her to stay, was terrifying, indeed. His pursuit of her could have led to his demise—and the way his very presence addled her wits had kept her from thinking so clearly as to be of aid to him.

She was a fool, indeed!

But she was not the only fool in this matter. Eleanor glared at Isabella. "What folly was in your head that you granted Alexander nightshade?" Every person at the high table started at her tone, save Madeline's spouse, Rhys. He regarded her with wary respect.

"Jeannie said she knew the right potion to mix," Isabella said, clearly not realizing the potency of this plant.

"And you trust her word, so readily as that?" The entire company watched Eleanor, but she was too angry to care. "Nightshade can kill a man. Merely three berries will kill a child. Three!"

"It makes a man sleep," Jeannie declared with a shake of her head. "You respect it overmuch."

"While you do not respect it enough. A man will awaken from a sleep induced by nightshade, but only if the measure is correct. And the difference between a measure to make a man sleep for a night and the measure that will make him slumber for all eternity is slight indeed." Eleanor shook a finger at Isabella. "You may have meant well, but there was dangerous folly in this. Your brother could have been found dead this morn."

"I know the measure," Jeannie insisted.

That the woman could believe herself so certain of what could not be known with certitude only made Eleanor more furious. She turned on the woman with such anger that the harridan cringed.

"You of all souls should know the folly of that declaration! Each plant has its own strength, and the differences must be respected. Every handful of soil will vary in the potency it grants such a plant. And even from year to year, even plants growing in the same place, will vary in their strength due to sun and rain and heat. It is not for nothing that the goddess Atropos was said by the Greeks to use nightshade to cut the thread of life." Eleanor took a shaking breath. "I was taught that only fools and murderers use nightshade. Which, Jeannie, are you?"

The assembly was silent for a long moment, then

erupted in excited chatter. Eleanor did not doubt that they speculated upon the sisters' ploy, but she held the old healer's gaze determinedly. The madness seemed to ebb in old Jeannie's eyes, and was replaced by a kind of cunning.

"You know much of poisons for a lady," Jeannie said coyly, and the hall fell silent. "Perhaps your intent is of greater import than mine."

Eleanor would not endure any such insinuation, not when it was without cause, not in this place that was already so precious to her. "Hardly that!" she replied. "You mixed the potion that was surrendered to your laird, not I, and it was not mixed at my dictate. I knew nothing of it until now. Solely the intent of those who knew of it is in question, and truly, Jeannie, I suspect that you alone knew the potency of what you concocted."

The harridan's eyes narrowed, but Eleanor did not allow her to speak further. She looked again at Alexander's sisters. Isabella, to her credit, could not hold Eleanor's gaze. "Though I appreciate that you did not mean harm, harm could easily have come of this. You owe my husband an apology."

"He is not your husband any longer, not by his own accounting," Elizabeth noted.

"No letter has been dispatched to the bishop as yet," Eleanor retorted. "Alexander is my husband until word comes from the bishop, and perhaps even after that."

The company gasped, but Eleanor had given them sufficient to consider. She turned to leave the hall, her crimson skirts rustling, chin held high.

"Now I suppose that she will ensure our matches are loathsome ones, simply for spite," Elizabeth muttered, her words carrying from the high table to Eleanor's ears.

Eleanor pivoted, letting the silk swirl around her ankles, letting the girl see that her comment was unwelcome. "I am appalled to hear that the laird of this holding, a man who has treated me with uncommon kindness for little reason beyond his own goodness, should be shown such a lack of respect in his own hall."

"Hear, hear," declared a villager at a table beside her.

Elizabeth colored, but she did not look away from Eleanor. Indeed, she rose to her feet, defiance making her eyes glitter. "Alexander would see us wed against our will, as he did with our two eldest sisters."

"And where would be the harm in that example?" Eleanor demanded. "Your sisters are wed to men of honor, men with holdings to their names, men who are young and virile and treat their wives with courtesy."

"But . . ."

"Tell me the flaw in either of these men," Eleanor invited, and Elizabeth's defiance slipped.

"Alexander has been fortunate, to be sure. . . ."

"Or perhaps he has an astute eye for character."

Vivienne lifted a finger to argue. "You cannot protest that Elizabeth does not have a viable concern."

"I can and I do," Eleanor replied hotly. "Does your husband beat you? Does he share your favors with his men? Does he leave you undefended? Does he insult you at your own board? Does he ensure that none in his household show you a measure of respect?"

The company murmured at this litany of foul prospects and the sisters exchanged glances of horror. "Of course not!" Vivienne and Madeline declared in unison.

"Then you know little of how poor a marriage can be,"

Eleanor said. "Indeed, you will find little sympathy from me in this matter, Elizabeth. How many summers have you seen?"

"Twelve."

"And yet still you sit at your brother's board, a maiden well-fed, well-adorned, and well-protected." Eleanor lifted a hand and indicated the next eldest sister, intent upon letting Alexander's siblings know how indulged they had been. That they did not appreciate his concern, that they disparaged him when he fought to keep the truth of Kinfairlie's finances from them, infuriated her beyond belief. "As does your elder sister, Isabella. How many summers have you seen, Isabella?"

The tallest sister—she with the glorious red tresses, the fine garb, and the affection for Jeannie's potions—shrugged. "Fourteen."

"And Annelise?"

This sister was more soft-spoken, a shy maiden with auburn hair unbound over her shoulders. She alone seemed chastised by Eleanor's anger. "Sixteen, my lady."

"And yet here you all sit, certain that your fate is yours to command; indeed, certain that you have the right to make demands of your brother. Here you all sit, content in the surety that there will be meat to fill your bellies, fripperies to trim your hems, and armed men to guarantee your chastity. I am certain that you think little of how these marvels come to be."

The sisters exchanged glances, the two eldest nodding in quiet agreement. Eleanor found understanding in the gazes of those two husbands.

But not from Elizabeth. That girl opened her mouth to argue, but Eleanor had lost her patience. "You think yourself poorly served, Elizabeth, that much is clear. I invite you to speculate upon what fate you would have found, had you truly managed to see Alexander dead this morn." The girl might have spoken, but Eleanor was not done. "Indeed, let me tell you what it is to be poorly served. I was wed at twelve summers of age, against my will, to a friend of my father's who had seen more than sixty summers himself."

The sisters looked up as one, their eyes wide, but Eleanor continued with heat. "To have called him cruel would have been to overstate his compassion for any creature other than himself. And when I complained of what I endured in his household, my father told me that I was as good as my husband's chattel." She straightened and held Elizabeth's gaze. "He told me, mine own father, that if my husband showed disfavor with me, then I must surely have deserved his rebuke."

Elizabeth averted her gaze. It was not half of the story, though Eleanor would share no more. She knew the more clever among them would link her earlier questions with her tale of her first spouse, and rightly so. Her first husband, Millard, had been a cur beyond compare; a charming cur possessed of a cunning cruelty.

The company was silent, staring at Eleanor. She found herself shaking in rage at what she had endured, at the audacity of Alexander's sisters in expecting more to be their due.

"From where I stand," she said, "you have no complaint with your brother's intent, for he has shown greater care than many a man would do in ridding his hall of mouths to feed. Women can be wedded as soon as their courses begin, so give thanks for every month since that day that you have not been compelled to wed a man against your choice, no less an unfitting one."

Madeline stood then and laid a hand upon Elizabeth's shoulder. "You go too far in this. Our matches are good ones because we made them so, not because of any care taken on Alexander's part."

Eleanor would not even cede this. "Every marriage is wrought of chance, but in choosing men of merit to take your hand, Alexander ensured that Fortune rode in your company. Did I not hear that you had the opportunity yourselves to choose your spouses, an opportunity you both declined to take?" Madeline and Vivienne colored slightly when they nodded. "Grant credit where it is due, all of you. My lord husband has served you well, far better than most men would have done. You should have the wits to recognize as much, no less to appreciate the blessings you have gained."

With that, Eleanor spun and left the hall, even as she heard them begin to chatter behind her. No sooner had she gained the corridor than she heard a man begin to applaud.

"Hear, hear," he cried, and Eleanor halted in the shadows to listen. She smiled in relief as another joined him, then another and another, then the hall was filled with applause.

She had confessed far more of her own history than she had intended to do, but she was fiercely glad that she had defended Alexander. She had behaved as a good wife should, and for once in all her days, she was glad of it. The duty had not been forced upon her and she was pleased to have done it so well.

All she had to do was persuade Alexander to keep her as his wife.

Yet, there was one deed she had to complete before she sought out Alexander. It would not hurt that her errand would allow his temper time to cool, and grant her time to concoct a plan.

The sorry truth was that she had no idea what she might offer this man to convince him to keep her by his side.

ALEXANDER DRUMMED HIS FINGERS upon the table. His letter sat before him, an appeal couched in the most polite terms, the wax seal drying as he watched. He frowned at the missive, disliking that he had had to write it.

At the root of his disquietude was not that requesting an annulment a half a day after wedding a woman made him look like an impulsive fool. It was not that Father Malachy had refused simply to eliminate the entry for the wedding from his books, though defiance was never a good sign. It was not even that the red wax was unadorned with the imprint of the seal of Kinfairlie—because Alexander's signet ring was lost, due to his own foolish trust and his sisters' potion—that irked him.

It was the memory of Alan Douglas and that man's determination to provide so-called justice for Eleanor that made Alexander reluctant to dispatch the missive. No matter how the lady had deceived him, no matter how right it was to put her aside, it was impossible to think her deserving of a day in Alan's courts.

It would take a witless man, indeed, to believe that Alan did not mean harm to Eleanor. Alan lied to blame Eleanor for his brother's death and no good could come to Eleanor of that. Was Alexander a fool to care what happened to her, when she had tricked him on a matter of such import? Alexander pushed to his feet and paced the chamber, pausing to look over the rolling sea.

If ever he had desired the counsel of his father and uncle, he desired it more in this moment.

He started at a slight rap on his door, then looked back at the sea. "Enter, Anthony," he said, knowing that the castellan would delight in enumerating his many failings. He might well agree with Anthony on this day.

"If I am not Anthony, may I still enter?"

Alexander glanced over his shoulder at the familiar feminine voice, and was still surprised to find Eleanor on the threshold. She had opened the door only an increment, and stood with one hand on the latch, as if poised to flee. Her cautious manner made him regret his public display of anger again, though he still did not trust her.

"I did not think to see you again," he said, and turned his back once more.

"I expected as much." There was no inflection in her voice, no way by which he could guess whether she thought that good or poor.

But she had sought him out. That must be of some import.

"If you have come to tell me that I am a knave beyond compare, then have your say and be done with it. I do not dispute that my manners were poor. You can quickly tell me that I am sour to find no humor in my sisters' jest, then leave me be."

"They could have killed you with that potion," she said with heat. "There is nothing amusing about their deed and, truly, I would think you witless if you found humor in it."

He glanced back with surprise at the passion in her tone, and found her eyes flashing.

"I have told them that you are owed an apology," she said, her manner fierce. "That Jeannie is a fool, indeed, if she imagines that she can readily assess the potency of a nightshade plant. You had virtually no meat in your belly last night—either a pinch more herb or a mouthful less food would have ensured that you never awakened this day."

Alexander blinked. It was rare for any soul to defend him. "I did not finish the wine that Isabella brought to me," he said, for he could think of little else to say.

"And there is the truth of it. That harridan *would* have seen you dead, had you consumed it all. The worst of it is that she does not even know what she very nearly saw done!"

Eleanor was transformed by her fury, as if the ice in her had suddenly melted away. That her appearance should be so vitalized out of indignation on his account was remarkable, indeed.

"And here I thought you came to tell me that my sisters were right, after all."

Eleanor smiled wryly and entered the room, apparently taking his lack of protest as an invitation. "To their credit, I have oft thought that what was sauce for the gander could be sauce for the goose."

"I did not try to harm either of my sisters, merely to see them wed and wed happily."

"But it seems that harm could have been done in both cases, despite your intent otherwise. Perhaps there is not so much difference between the three situations."

"Perhaps there is." Alexander held her gaze. "An error served in return does not make other errors come aright."

"Fair enough, but you cannot blame them for trying to ensure that you wed as well."

"I can blame them for failing to understand what is at stake. For my sisters' matches, there is no more and no less at stake than their happiness and security."

"You cannot blame them for not knowing what you did not tell them," she noted, and he glanced to her in confusion. "About your barren treasury."

"No, but that is of less import in the matter of my own marriage than my status as laird. The suzerainty and security of Kinfairlie and those sworn to it must be assured, even if the price is my own happiness."

Eleanor looked at her slippers.

Alexander took a breath, then said what had to be said. In truth, it was a relief to have some person with whom he could speak bluntly. "You must know that I would not have alienated the Black Douglas clan of my own volition. Had you told me your allegiance last night, I might well have let you depart."

Eleanor's lips set as she regarded him, and he felt obliged to qualify his statement. "I would have done so in ignorance of Alan's intent, to be sure, for I would never willingly endanger a lady. Traditionally, though, we have allied with them and this feat annuls that old agreement. Such a choice should be made deliberately, not by accident, for it could endanger every soul who has sworn fealty to me. The risk of retaliation is not small."

She dropped her gaze, apparently disappointed in his reply. "You would prefer to ally with them."

"It was my father's preference and that of my uncle as well." Alexander watched her, then decided to continue his blunt speech. "Perhaps you will appreciate their conviction that it was preferable to have a Black Douglas beside you than behind you."

Eleanor laughed then, as if surprised by his candor, then regarded him with some amusement. "I can indeed understand such a sentiment. They are men who stop at nothing to see their aims achieved." She arched a brow and sobered. "There is no wickedness beneath them, to be sure."

He was tempted then, to ask about the kind of marriage she had had with Ewen, to ask what she knew of that man's death, but she spoke before he could do so.

Later he would wonder if her choice was deliberate.

"So, you wed your sisters in haste, though by unconventional means, wanting only to ensure their happiness and security. And they resent your choices, though they have found good marriages, indeed. Perhaps it is not Fortune who smiled upon them. Perhaps you have a sense for making a good match." She met his gaze. "Perhaps you saw the truth of these men, despite the circumstances that cast them in poor light."

"I would not claim such a gift," Alexander said with a shake of his head.

"I guessed as much," she said with soft vigor. "Which was why I claimed it for you."

Alexander looked up to find her eyes gleaming. His heart leapt at the sight of her. "What is this?"

Eleanor smiled in a most captivating way. "I told them that they had no cause for complaint, for much worse marriages could be arranged for them than those you arranged with Rhys and Erik."

"Except that I did not arrange those matches," Alexander felt obliged to note. "Both men deceived me and I hunted them both once their truth was revealed. I would have killed them without a qualm, had my sisters been injured."

"So you are protective of those beneath your hand, but still they do not understand the reason you were so anxious to see them wed in haste. Not a one of them knows that Kinfairlie's coffers are empty, do they?"

"How could I tell them such a thing?"

"How could you keep every burden for yourself?" she demanded with some impatience. "You had to guess that without knowing your reason, they would fear your intent. You had to know that they would disparage you!"

Alexander sighed again. "And if I told them, one might choose a suitor with undue haste, perhaps condemning herself to unhappiness. There are no good choices in this." His gaze strayed out the window, to the fields that had yielded so little this year, and considered the elements, so seemingly benign this day, that had seen the seed rotted in those fields.

"So they fear you, instead of fearing for Kinfairlie's prosperity," Eleanor said, her hand landing upon his arm. "That fear led them to deceive you, which put your own life in peril."

Alexander shrugged. "I do not doubt that you speak aright. Indeed, I will not argue with any soul who protests that I have done poorly at this responsibility of lairdship." He thought she might criticize him, so spoke in haste before she could do so. "What of you? Do you despise your father for choosing your spouses for you?"

It was Eleanor's turn to study her shoes. She frowned slightly and he yearned to ease the furrow from between her brows with a fingertip.

"I did," she admitted, then looked up. Her gaze was clear. "There were years when I hated him with all my heart and soul, when I could not believe that a man who loved me as I had believed he did could have consigned me to such wretched marriages."

"You sound as if you have changed your thinking."

She studied him now. "In talking with you, I wonder whether I knew all of what confronted him. I wonder what choices he had, if he had fewer such choices than I believed he did. I wonder what was in our coffers and who mustered on our borders." She smiled and shook her head. "He was my father, the sole parent I knew, and I confess that I believed he had hung both the sun and the moon." She heaved a sigh and her voice softened. "I wonder if he had responsibilities to weigh against his own desires, if he only had me with which to wager."

"You never asked him?"

"He was not a man who spoke of such intimate matters," she said quietly. "As were all who held his confidence." Eleanor looked out the window in her turn. "And my guardian would tell me nothing of my father's thoughts, even if he knew them. He would regard that deed as a betrayal, to be sure."

Alexander frowned at this unlikely morsel. "You have a guardian? But why?"

Eleanor spoke quickly. "I speak of him thus, though his duties are surely fulfilled. I have been wedded twice, after all."

"But . . ."

"Look." She lifted her hand, apparently hiding something in her fist. "I came to give you something."

Curious, Alexander put out his hand. Eleanor held his

gaze as she pushed something cold and hard into his palm, then folded his fingers over the item. Her eyes danced, so pleased was she with her gift, and he felt his mouth fall open in astonishment.

It was his signet ring! Alexander knew as much without opening his fingers. He stared at her, no less amazed when she smiled. Her eyes shone at the surprise she had given him.

"But how did you find it?" Alexander opened his hand and gazed at the ring resting in his palm. "*You* had it all this time?"

She laughed. "No. I merely guessed where it was, and persuaded its keeper to surrender it to me." Her fair brow arched. "She was mightily frightened by your anger at the board, so you unwittingly made my task easier."

Alexander pushed the ring back onto his finger with relief, then shook his head. "But I do not understand. She? Surely you coaxed it from Matthew's grasp?"

Eleanor shook her head. "He did not return it to you last evening. I remember as much, though you cannot. But he could not surrender it to you today, because he did not hold it any longer."

"Ceara!" Alexander guessed, and Eleanor's smile flashed again.

She shook a finger at him. "No matter what your sisters say, you would seem to have a talent for matchmaking. Matthew and Ceara pledged their troth last night, though would have kept the matter secret until Ceara's parents granted their permission."

"And so he gave her the ring, my ring, to seal their agreement?"

Eleanor laughed, a captivating sound. "You are shocked!"

"It is hardly a trinket to be so used." Alexander found himself smiling in turn.

"They do not know its value, save that it is a handsome piece." She lifted his hand and turned the ring so that his insignia caught the light. Her touch was light and her eyes sparkled in the most alluring way. "And they respect the man whose hand it usually graces." Her smile turned mischievous as she leaned closer, and Alexander was charmed. "She had it hidden beneath her chemise, snared upon a piece of string. I doubt your ring has ever been more tightly cosseted than it was between Ceara's breasts."

Alexander laughed. It was uncommon to feel that any soul in this household was allied with him, that his burdens were shared, and he liked this sense well. "Surely they do not think their pledge undone now?"

Eleanor shook her head. "Isabella offered them a silver ring to replace this one. In truth, I think they liked it better, for it fits Ceara's finger."

Alexander frowned in suspicion. "Isabella surrenders no trinket so readily as that." He arched a brow at Eleanor. "I would wager that she had some encouragement in this, perhaps from you."

Eleanor sobered. "She owes you more than the value of a single silver ring," she said with that same ferocity she had shown earlier. Alexander's heart warmed that she was protective of him. To his astonishment, she eased closer and laid her other hand upon his chest. "Her folly could have seen you dead."

Alexander's heart skipped at her proximity. He felt himself beguiled once again, and for the moment, at least, he felt no trepidation. Eleanor was nigh against his chest,

her lips full and inviting. There was a slight flush upon
her cheeks and a sparkle in her eyes. He felt his pulse
quicken at the prospect of another of the lady's kisses.

"I suspect no soul in this hall would have missed me,"
he said, hoping no such thing.

Eleanor's eyes glittered and he was transfixed by this
glimpse of her passion. "You suspect wrongly, Alexander
Lammergeier," she said with resolve. "For I would have
missed you."

To his amazement, Eleanor stretched and touched her
lips to his.

HERS WAS A RATIONAL CHOICE, or so Eleanor told herself.
Indeed, she did not know why she had not thought of it
sooner.

A marriage could be annulled for two reasons alone:
common blood between man and wife, or a failure to consummate the match. She and Alexander shared no blood,
so any argument he could make to the bishop would be
based solely upon their failure to meet abed.

And that argument could be eliminated quite simply.

She had never seduced a man. Truly, she had never
wished to meet either of her husbands abed and had fulfilled her marital debt with some reluctance. Further, had
she dared to initiate an embrace with either of those men,
she would have felt the back of a hand for her wanton audacity.

Alexander not only coaxed her passion, but did not
force her to surrender to him. And neither, it proved, did
it trouble him when she showed ardor. She kissed him,

cautiously at first. She tasted his surprise, heard his incoherent murmur of pleasure, and knew she had chosen aright.

She closed her mouth over his, mimicking his earlier embrace, and touched her tongue to his lips. Alexander growled and his arm locked around her waist. Eleanor rose to her toes, she framed his face in her hands and pulled him closer. She could feel the slight stubble upon his jaw, could smell his skin, could hear him groan.

Alexander caught her buttocks in his hands and lifted her against him. Eleanor closed her eyes and kissed him again, letting desire claim her fully.

Sex had always been a matter of conquest for Eleanor, the conquest of her body by a hostile assailant. It had been about submission and surrender and the pleasure of a man, even if it came at her expense. She was unused to savoring such intimacy, but Alexander was content to kiss with leisure. To be sure, she could feel the vigor of his response, but he did not rush her. He did not hold her down and take his due.

He invited her to join him in the pursuit of pleasure.

That alone would have been sufficiently tempting, but there was also the thunder of his pulse beneath her fingertips. She could feel his heart pounding against her own; she could feel the pulse leaping in his throat; she could hear him quickly inhale when she kissed him more boldly.

She had power in this transaction, a power she had never known she possessed, a power that she would have to learn to wield. She had no doubt that Alexander would savor her every effort to do so, and the prospect made her smile beneath his kiss.

"What is amiss?" he asked, lifting his lips an increment from hers. He studied her, his eyes brilliantly blue, and her smile broadened.

"Perhaps I should have let you coax my smile with a kiss," she murmured, and he grinned.

"I seem to recall being forbidden to touch you," he mused. "Perhaps my caress is not so onerous as you feared."

"Perhaps not," she said, holding his gaze.

"And now you offer a kiss."

"I offer far more than a kiss," she whispered, delighting in the way his eyes darkened. Beneath his ardent gaze, she loosed the tie of her chemise and pulled it out of the garment. Her breasts were revealed, her nipples beading beneath his perusal and the chill of the air.

He raised a hand and cupped her breast in his palm, the silk of her kirtle gathered beneath his hand. He bent then and kissed the peak and Eleanor gasped with pleasure. She arched back and closed her eyes, letting him taste her, letting him grant her pleasure.

She knotted her fingers in his hair, pulling his lips to hers when he lifted his head. They kissed with newfound fervor and Eleanor felt his fingers loosing her braid. Her circlet fell, her veil was cast aside. She felt like the courtesan she had claimed to be, and she did not care.

"I tire of your gallantry, sir," she murmured into his ear, then kissed that ear so leisurely that he moaned. "Perhaps you merely jest with me. Perhaps you do not desire me at all."

"Perhaps you are deaf and blind," he retorted, and Eleanor laughed. He caught her up in his arms, then seated her upon the table. He braced his hands upon the wood and looked at her. "I thought you feared men."

Eleanor smiled, knowing that demon was banished in this man's presence. "I have feared men in the past." She untied the laces on the sides of her kirtle, well aware that he watched her avidly. "You would seem to have cured me of that malady." She removed the laces, then cast the silken garment aside. The chemise she had been lent was sheer, indeed, and little of her was hidden by it.

Alexander looked and swallowed.

Emboldened by his response, Eleanor removed the last ribbon that bound her hair and shook the long tresses out over her shoulders. He surveyed her, a wonder in his eyes that only emboldened her further. She shed her chemise, then leaned back upon the table, the cold wood against her bare buttocks. She wore only stockings and shoes, and felt a moment's vulnerability beneath the heat of his gaze.

He smiled then, smiled a smile that lit his eyes, and caught her nape in his hand. "Do not fear," he whispered, and her heart skipped a beat that he had glimpsed her uncertainty. "Your trust is an honor I will fulfill." She might have smiled, so reassured was she, but Alexander bent his head and kissed her fully.

His seduction was both gentle and demanding; he awaited her assent, then left her gasping for more. His fingers caressed her as he trailed kisses down her shoulder, along her collarbone. It was as if he would learn her every curve, her every mole by touch alone. Eleanor had never felt so cherished, had never been so sensuously explored. There was no violence in him and he did not restrain her. Eleanor knew that she could urge him aside with a fingertip and that was intoxicating, indeed.

Alexander showed no haste; he savored her. He captured her nipple with his lips and discovered the best combination of teeth and tongue to tease it to a pert point. He found the ticklish spot behind her knees and caressed her there until her very bones melted. He deduced somehow that a kiss beneath her ear dissolved her every inhibition. He bracketed her waist with his hands, showing that his hands could almost encircle her completely.

"Wrought for each other," he whispered, and Eleanor dared to hope that such a thing was possible.

Eventually he lifted his head, looking so tousled and mischievous that she knew he had some other feat in store. Eleanor knew she was flushed and disheveled and aroused as she had never been before. She fairly ached to feel his heat inside her.

Alexander granted her a wicked smile, locked his hands around her waist, and then his kiss turned intimate, indeed. He ducked between her thighs, the heat of his mouth landing upon the most secret place of her. Pleasure soared through Eleanor and she fell back, gasping, upon the table.

Alexander did not cease his caress and, truly, she did not want him to do so. He roused a passion she had never guessed she possessed and did so with such ease that she marveled at what she had missed. Her very flesh seemed to be afire; there might have been sparks flying from her fingers; she burned with so fiery a lust that she feared it might consume her.

She moaned his name, and he chuckled, his breath tickling her yet more. Relentless, he coaxed the inferno within her to burn more brightly. She writhed and twisted; she sought some goal she could not name. She moaned and did not care who heard her. There was nothing in all the world save Alexander's teasing kiss.

Suddenly Eleanor was engulfed with pleasure, the fire

bursting with unexpected ferocity. She shouted; she locked her knees around him; she clutched at the table. She had never felt such passion; she had never been shaken to her very core.

She stared at him in awe when the tremors ceased and he grinned, knowing full well what he had done.

"More," she whispered when she caught her breath. "I desire more."

Alexander was quick to comply. He was atop her, his chausses undone but otherwise fully garbed. There was a determination in his expression, and a wild light in his eyes that made her heart race anew. She gasped as he entered her, for he was uncommonly large, then gripped his shoulders when he waited for her.

She smiled at him, liking the heat of him well. The strength of him sated her as little else could have done— or so she thought, until his mischievous fingers found that tender place once again. He kissed her throat, that place behind her ear, and Eleanor fairly swooned with the pleasure he conjured. He caressed her even as they moved together in that ancient and intimate dance.

His eyes glittered a fearsome blue, his hair was tangled and damp with perspiration, his attention was wholly fixed upon her. Eleanor felt both potent and captive, free and ensnared. She knew that this was right, that this was how man and wife should meet abed, that this was how pleasure should be shared.

Tears rose to her eyes that he should show her such a wondrous truth. She held him fast, wanting both to make this moment last forever and also to find that spellbinding release again. The heat rose ever higher between them, her heartbeat raced, and Alexander smiled at her. They moved as one, enthralled with each other as they fed their passion; then lightning struck her very marrow.

"Alexander!" she shouted, not caring who heard.

"Eleanor!" he bellowed, and buried himself deeply within her. They shuddered together in their mutual release, then fell still. He rolled to his back, keeping her clasped against him, and lay back on the table with a moan of satisfaction. Eleanor sprawled atop him, well content, and laid her cheek upon his chest.

She put her fingertips on the pulse in Alexander's throat as she closed her eyes in exhaustion, smiling at the rhythm of their hearts beating as one.

ELEANOR WOULD KILL HIM.

That much was certain. Should Eleanor seduce him thus every day of his life, Alexander would not have to bear the burden of the lairdship of Kinfairlie for long. He was shocked that he had claimed her without even disrobing—but she had left him the chance only to unlace his chausses. He knew even as he caught his breath that he would never be able to sit at this table and labor over his accounts again without recalling this moment.

She smiled at him shyly, her flesh so rosy and her hair so tangled that he was tempted to claim her again without delay. He slid a fingertip down the side of her chin and her lashes dropped shyly. "Were you pleased?"

Her smile turned impish. "Could you not guess as much?"

"I suppose I could," he mused, much taken with the woman who filled his arms.

Whatever else Alexander might have said never made it past his lips. There was a pounding of footsteps on the stairs. Those footfalls crossed the floor outside his chamber and he had the blink of an eye to realize what was going to happen before it did.

"No!" he bellowed, just as the door of his chamber was thrown open. He rolled the lady beneath him, hiding her nudity from curious eyes.

"Alexander, are you well?" Anthony demanded.

"I heard shouting, and feared violence," Isabella said, even as she tried to peer around the castellan. Alexander braced himself over Eleanor, striving to hide her—and their intimate pose—from those two at the portal.

Anthony swore with uncharacteristic vigor and pushed the curious maiden back into the corridor. He slammed the door with force and much coughing and harrumphing carried through the wooden portal.

"God in heaven, there is no peace in this abode." Alexander groaned and dropped his forehead to Eleanor's shoulder. To his relief, the lady began to laugh.

"You have need of a lock."

"I have a lock upon that portal," he retorted, then granted her a wicked glance. "Had I known that you intended to seduce me, I would have used it."

She feigned consideration of this. "Perhaps in future, I should lock the portal when I have such a scheme."

"Perhaps you should," he agreed. They smiled at each other, then Alexander left her welcoming heat with reluctance. "You will become chilled." He shed his tabard and granted it to her. He kindled a larger fire in the brazier, then offered her the basin of water and cloth.

Anthony cleared his throat pointedly from the other

side of the wooden portal. "I trust then, my lord, that you will not be dispatching a missive to the bishop?"

Alexander glanced to Eleanor, who held his gaze. They looked as one to the missive he had so recently written, and he realized that he no longer had grounds to request an annulment.

And there were witnesses of that fact.

Eleanor became suddenly intent upon ensuring that her laces were properly tied, her very manner feeding Alexander's suspicion. She looked guilty, just as his sisters did, when one of their schemes was revealed.

"Tell me that you did not contrive this deed," he said, his voice husky.

She said nothing, merely knotted a lace more tightly. Her lips were set, though, with a stubbornness he knew well.

He stepped to her side and caught her elbow in his hand, compelling her to meet his gaze. "Did you seduce me to ensure there could be no annulment?"

"I do not have to answer you."

"Yes, you do," he said with heat. "I will have an answer, and I will have honesty between us, or we will have no match. If you cannot tell me the truth, I will find some way to put you aside, upon that you can rely."

Her eyes flashed and she lifted her chin, holding his regard boldly. "I would be wedded to you, Alexander Lammergeier. I *choose* to have you as my spouse and so, yes, I did decide to ensure that our match was consummated. I did decide to ensure that you had no grounds for annulment."

"I can still put you aside."

Her lips tightened. "It will not be so readily done."

"Did you ensure that there would be witnesses?"

Her cheeks flamed at the very notion. "No!"

Alexander believed her, in that at least. He paced the width of the chamber and shoved a hand through his hair, not liking the truth she surrendered. He stared at her from across the room. "Why?"

She grit her teeth, then regarded him warily. "Because you are not like the men I have known. Because I would seize the opportunity to be wed to a man who would treat me with dignity."

If she had pled for passion, if she had confessed love for him, it might have been easier to give her impulse credence. But Alexander studied the defiant woman before him and knew that she knew little of passion and love, that even dignity was a novelty for her.

And that made the choice for him. His heart wrenched that she had been treated so poorly, and though he knew that he could teach her to expect better, he also knew the course would not be easy. He heaved a sigh.

"Truth," he insisted gently. "We must have truth between us."

She took a breath and nodded agreement. "You shall have all the truth from me that you desire, Alexander Lammergeier. I would ask you not to blame me if you do not like its taste upon your tongue, however."

Their gazes locked and held across the span of the chamber. "Fair enough," he said, hearing a wealth of history in her words. He lifted the missive from the table and cast it into the flames of the brazier. He watched her shudder in her relief, saw the shimmer of her unshed tears.

"I thank you," she said quietly, and he was humbled by her beauty and her pride.

Eleanor would never beg for any morsel from his table, though she had no qualms in telling him that he was wrong. He respected her wits and her knowledge. Her counsel would be invaluable to him, to be sure.

He could teach her, in turn, that a lady was owed more from her spouse than her former husbands had offered to her.

Alexander smiled at Eleanor, liking the sight of his mother's ring upon her finger, liking that his heart had leapt when first he had glimpsed her. He took her hand within his and kissed her knuckles, and when she flushed, he dared to be encouraged that her wounds would heal.

Then Alexander raised his voice, not looking away from his bride. "You have guessed aright, Anthony. There will be no annulment, and Kinfairlie has a new lady on this day."

"Hoorah!" Isabella cried from the other side of the door. Eleanor and Alexander shared a smile when that maiden clapped her hands. "I will tell the others!" Isabella's feet could be heard scampering away; then the older man cleared his throat.

"Very good, my lord." Anthony lowered his voice. "Might I anticipate that you will be occupied this afternoon, my lord?"

"You might, indeed," Alexander said with a smile. "As you well know, it is imperative that I thoroughly review my accounts before year end. There are assets at Kinfairlie for which I do not as yet have a full inventory." He caught Eleanor in his arms and she began to smile, both of them forgetting Anthony's presence until that man cleared his throat.

"Very good, my lord."

"Lock that portal," Eleanor whispered when they reached the bed, and Alexander was only too glad to comply. That he surrendered the key to his lady wife with a flourish earned him a smile, one that warmed him to his very toes.

Chapter Six

〜

THE SKY WAS DARKENING when Eleanor awakened in the great bed in Kinfairlie's solar. She was confused for a moment, finding herself in an unfamiliar bed, wearing nothing but a ring that was a new weight upon her hand. Alexander dozed beside her, his hair tousled and a smile upon his lips. She indulged her impulse and pushed the thickness of his hair back from his brow, only to have his eyes open.

"It must have been the king of Jerusalem himself," he said, his eyes glinting.

Eleanor smiled. He had begun a jest this afternoon of trying to guess who her first husband had been, though his suggestions had been whimsical from the outset. Had there ever been a man so determined to make her smile?

There had, she knew, never been one so successful in that quest.

"Of course not," she said, feigning a stern manner. "There is no king of Jerusalem in these days."

"Since when? No one told me of this travesty." Alexander bent and kissed one of her nipples with diligence, as if the answer to political matters could be found upon her breast.

Eleanor laughed, then caught her breath as his tongue began to move against her flesh. The man could seduce a statue, it was clear. "It has been centuries since Saladin conquered Jerusalem."

"Truly?" Alexander slipped his fingers between her thighs, showing no great interest in the history of the Latin Kingdoms. "Someone should have told me."

"I have no doubt that you did not heed your tutor overly well."

Alexander chuckled. "True enough." Eleanor gasped when he conjured her passion anew, and did so readily. "Then perhaps your husband was the great poet Taliesin," he mused, as if he were not awakening a fire beneath her flesh.

"Dead many a century," Eleanor gasped.

"The knight Lancelot."

"He was enamored of Guinevere."

"Though the name of any wife he might have claimed is not recorded. And truly, would it not set a woman against men to be wed to a knight who so ardently courted another man's wife?"

"I trust you will not do as much."

"I intend to court only my own wife," he said, granting her a simmering glance.

"She is soundly seduced, to be sure."

Alexander grinned and stretched out beside her. His fingers still moved against her heat, making her squirm against him. He laced the fingers of his free hand with hers and held her hands over her head.

Such a pose struck terror into Eleanor's heart, but she

fought against her instinctive desire to pull away. Alexander's grip was loose, his manner was easy; indeed, he smiled at her. She struggled to control her breathing, to hide the fear that had seized her.

He watched her and she wondered what he saw, for he freed her hands without comment. His fingertips danced over the length of her, launching an army of delightful shivers in their wake, and when she smiled, his eyes began to dance anew.

That his pleasure came from granting her pleasure was a new notion to Eleanor, but one she liked well enough. She liked, too, that he granted her time to become accustomed to him.

"But my lady's heart is more elusive than her satisfaction abed," he said softly.

Eleanor caught her breath. "Her heart?"

He arched a brow. "What manner of knave would not seek his wife's undying love?"

"Love?" Eleanor eased away from his caress. "Love has no place in a marriage," she said with resolve, and his eyes narrowed.

"Do you intend to seek it outside of marriage, then?"

"No, no! But love is beyond expectation; indeed, beyond the desire of sensible men and women."

She rose from the bed then and hastily donned her chemise. Alexander remained abed, remained nude, his eyes gleaming like those of a cat on the hunt.

Eleanor straightened, feeling somewhat defended from him with the sheer linen between them. "After all, pleasure and respect should suffice," she said with a smile.

Alexander was clearly unpersuaded by this notion.

"Your husbands could not have been of much merit, if either of them persuaded you of such a notion."

"It was my father who taught me thus."

Alexander held her gaze and she knew she had found another matter about which he felt strongly. His eyes were a vibrant blue and he remained motionless. She felt the force of his will turned upon her, and knew he would not be readily convinced to change his thinking.

"It was my father who taught me that love wrought a good marriage," he said, his voice silky.

Eleanor pivoted and reached for her kirtle.

"Where do you go?"

"You must be hungry. I will fetch a repast from the kitchen."

"You need not do as much. Anthony can be summoned."

"I need also to visit the latrine," she lied. Alexander's gaze flicked to the bucket left for that purpose, but he said nothing further.

He rolled from the bed with feline grace, then came to her side. "I would suggest that you see yourself garbed properly before you show yourself in the hall," he teased, flicking a fingertip at her sides. She had fed the lace so quickly that the eyelets were not aligned and the sides of the kirtle were bunched.

Eleanor flushed, for she was never so clumsy, but Alexander smiled as he loosed the lace. He bent and touched his lips to her temple, whispering there. "It is not all bad that the prospect of abandoning your husband leaves you so discomfited."

"It is not that!"

"Is it not?" He watched her, seeing too much for Eleanor's taste.

She turned her back upon him, feeling discomfited, indeed. She combed her hair and donned her veil, but felt no more in command of the erratic pace of her heart than she had while nude. She was too aware of Alexander's strong fingers as he fastened her laces with leisure, too aware of the heat of him close by her side, too aware of the pleasure he could conjure with a touch. She dared not forget how little she knew of him as yet, dared not forget that any man could show charm for days or weeks.

Millard had been charming for the better part of a year, after all. She caught her breath when Alexander caught her waist in his hands and closed her eyes against his unholy allure.

"I expect more from marriage, Eleanor," he whispered to her. "You may have learned to expect less, but I expect more. I will win your heart, however reluctant it might be."

Eleanor swallowed, fearing that he might well succeed. And what of her then? How impotent would she be once this man held her own heart in his hands?

She could not help but raise her gaze, for she felt the full weight of his attention, though she was unprepared for the bright blue of his eyes. She stared at him wordlessly, both terrified and exhilarated by what he promised; then he suddenly grinned and snapped his fingers.

"Prester John! That must have been your spouse, for he would have granted you a taste for foreign textiles."

"He does not even exist!" Eleanor protested with an unwilling smile.

Alexander wagged a finger at her, his manner conspiratorial. "So they say, but it is all an elaborate ruse, to be sure." He sidled close to her and dropped his voice. "Tell me, did he surrender to you any secrets for the making of spare coin? I have heard that he could turn dross to gold and it must be said that I have an abundance of dross."

Though he was teasing, Eleanor knew she could be of aid in this matter.

"Charge higher tariffs upon goods coming and going," she said crisply, her manner in such sharp contrast to his that Alexander blinked. "And higher fees for the justice in your legal courts. People have no quibble paying for advantage. Host a fair, albeit one at a princely tariff to you for allowing use of the land. Charge also for the use of the bridges and roads within your demesne, as well as the right to land at your port, if you have one. Command a tax upon indulgences, from silk to ale to silver, for the rich who can afford such goods can similarly afford a few pennies for the laird's coffers."

Alexander regarded her in astonishment. "How do you know about such matters?"

"My father taught me to read and to write and to tally, the better to ensure that I would never be cheated." Eleanor straightened. "I kept the books of his household until I was wedded the first time."

"He did not do this himself?"

"He traveled much."

Alexander blinked. "But surely he had clerks?"

"He had me, and I sufficed." She met his gaze, daring him to challenge her upon this matter, but Alexander only frowned. He looked as if he would ask another question, but Eleanor pivoted. "I had best go, before the cook leaves the kitchen."

"Indeed," Alexander said, his voice thoughtful. He donned his chausses, sparing more than one piercing look in her direction. He was too thoughtful, his gaze too assessing, and Eleanor was glad to step out of his chamber before he unfurled all of her secrets.

There was no doubt about it, Alexander saw too much. That he was determined to win her heart made her quicken her pace as she ran down the stairs. There was no chance of her ever loving her husband, no matter how handsome and charming he might be. Eleanor had sworn a pledge to that effect years before and she would not permit a mere day in the company of Alexander Lammergeier to change her thinking.

She had best muster her defenses, that he not discern too many of her secrets. And she had best make herself of use, for she already wished desperately to remain in Kinfairlie and she had nothing else beyond her own merit to offer its persuasive lord.

What better time than this moment to organize her lord's hall and ensure its efficiency? She would dispatch a meal to Alexander and hope that he fell asleep before she returned to his chamber. He could have no complaint in her performing her duties, especially as they had met abed several times this day already.

Perfect.

FOR THE DURATION OF THE EVENING, Isabella had sat with her sisters, embroidering a hanging for the hall that Annelise had designed, impatient to see her mission done. How long could Alexander and Eleanor spend locked in the solar? Isabella had looked around far more than her sisters, far more than those who lingered to drink and chat in the hall.

Finally Isabella saw Eleanor step into the hall. It was the moment she had awaited and she twitched with impatience for Eleanor to go to wherever she was destined to go.

She knew that she alone spied her new sister-in-law.

Indeed, Eleanor clung to the shadows, as if she wished to avoid notice. And why not—Eleanor's shoes did not match and her cheeks were flushed. She had the look of a woman whose chemise was on backward. Isabella smiled, guessing that her brother was responsible for ruffling this woman who had appeared so unlikely to be ruffled.

Alexander had no small measure of charm, after all.

Isabella watched Eleanor covertly. As soon as Eleanor ascertained that she had not been noticed, she made for the kitchens and disappeared in the shadows of that corridor.

Of course, the new couple would both be hungry, for they had missed the evening meal. But because of his absence from the hall, there was a detail Alexander did not know about his new wife. Isabella knew that she was the one to surrender it to him, for she owed him more than one favor.

Here was her chance!

Isabella carefully slipped her needle into the tapestry and gave an elaborate yawn. "Oh, I am tired beyond belief," she said, sparing a smile for her sisters. "I think I must go to bed."

"You simply wish to cease embroidering," Elizabeth charged.

"I am tired because you snored all of last night," Isabella retorted.

"I did not!" Elizabeth said.

"You dreamed deeply, Elizabeth, for even a nudge of my foot did not silence you," Isabella said with a shake of her finger, then yawned again. "You know I have need of my sleep."

"I doubt it was a gentle nudge," Vivienne said with a smile.

Elizabeth's expression turned mutinous. "You are lazy, that is all."

"Do not be ridiculous," Annelise chided softly. "Isabella has done twice the work of you."

"It is not my fault that she is quick with a needle and I am not," Elizabeth grumbled.

"But it is your fault that you are uncommonly sour of disposition of late," Madeline commented. "What ails you, Elizabeth?"

"Nothing." The youngest sister shut her mouth with resolve and bent over her work. The other sisters exchanged glances of concern, but Elizabeth ignored them with vigor.

Isabella left the group, more intent upon her mission than Elizabeth's moods. As soon as she was out of sight of the hall, she raced up the stairs and climbed to the floor that was Alexander's own. She rapped upon his door, encouraged by the line of light showing beneath the portal. "Alexander?"

"Enter, Isabella."

"Are you decent?"

Alexander laughed, an echo of his old self. "I am garbed, if that is what you mean."

Isabella pushed open the portal and halted at the sight of her brother bent over his books. He was disheveled, to be sure, and his chemise was only partly laced, the sleeves pushed up to reveal the fading tan on his forearms. He leaned his weight upon his fists and surveyed his books with an uncommon avidity. He looked vital, as he had not in months. Isabella realized only in that moment how old and tired Alexander had looked in this past year, that he had been but a shadow of his former self.

A pang struck her as she realized the truth that Eleanor had uttered about Alexander's burden, a truth to which they had all been blind.

"Are you truly my brother?" she asked, her tone cajoling. "For I know that he does not show any such fascination with his ledgers."

Alexander grinned, the image of his old roguish self. "Eleanor granted me an idea, several ideas in fact." He laid aside his quill with undisguised satisfaction. "They are good notions, to be sure. Whatever your intent, you have found me a treasure of a wife." He then smiled at her with affection. "And are you truly my sister, Isabella? It is too early for her to consider retiring, for she is always the last to leave a celebration of any kind. Do not tell me that every soul is gone to bed so early on Christmas night?"

"Of course not." Isabella crossed the threshold, her hands knotted together. "Eleanor was right. I owe you an apology, Alexander. I never guessed the potency of what Jeannie mixed and I never asked what she did. I should have taken more care." The fear that she had felt when Eleanor told of the herb welled up within her now and her voice rose. "I never meant harm to you. You must believe me!"

Alexander immediately crossed the floor and embraced her. "I know, Isabella. There is no malice within you."

"But something dire could have happened!"

"But it did not, and so the matter rests."

"But you . . ."

"Are more hale than expected, it is clear." He held her shoulders and gave her a stern look, much as their father would have done. She knew he would hear no more of it. "Now, I understand that you surrendered your silver ring to Ceara."

Isabella fidgeted. "It seemed the least I might do to make amends."

"It was kind of you and I regret that I have no ring with which to replace it."

She touched his signet ring. "Except the one that I replaced."

Alexander shook his head. "I mean to keep it on my hand from this day forward."

"A good thing that is, for I do not have another silver ring." They shared a smile and she touched his hand again. "It was kind of you, Alexander, to ensure that they two had the chance to speak."

"Ah, well, I tired of Matthew sighing at the sky whenever I went past the mill," he said with a wink. "As did his father, to be sure. That pair only needed a nudge to set them on their course."

Characteristically, Alexander took little credit for what he had done, though he saw it as his obligation to do it.

Isabella looked down at the floor, uncertain how to begin. "I wanted you to know that Eleanor defended you boldly, just as a lady should defend her spouse, and that I regret that I never saw your side of matters."

"Did she?" Alexander regarded her with interest.

"I did not realize how fortunate we are to be so at ease at Kinfairlie, not until she told of her own fate."

His gaze sharpened. "And what was that?"

"She was wedded at twelve, against her will, to a man who had seen more than sixty summers!" Isabella could not contain her horror. "And he was cruel to her, of this I am certain."

"And wed thence to Ewen Douglas," Alexander mused. Isabella could not keep herself from grimacing. "No wonder she expects so little of men and marriage."

"She must think you too good to be true," Isabella teased, though her brother seemed to find the suggestion sobering.

"Possibly so." Alexander crossed the chamber, clearly thinking, and Isabella was loath to interrupt him. He pivoted suddenly and fixed his gaze upon her, then smiled. "I would ask a favor of you, Isabella."

"Anything!"

"Do not be quick to make a pledge without knowing what you promise," he chided, just as their father had done. Isabella had always been too impetuous with a promise, so their father had always said.

"What then?"

"What I ask of you is simple: I would ask you to tell me if there is a man who claims your heart. Or even if there is one you yearn to meet, then tell me of it, and I shall see it done."

She caught her breath. "Will you see me wed against my will?"

He regarded her, solemnity in his gaze. "You cannot remain at Kinfairlie forever," he said gently. "Nor should you desire to do so. Choose a spouse or I shall be compelled to choose one for you. It is my duty as your guardian."

Isabella nodded, understanding the fullness of what he told her. "Is there a date by which you would wish me to choose?"

Alexander spared a fleeting glance to his ledgers, a concerned glance that made Isabella's blood chill. "Of course not," he said with that easy confidence she knew so well. Once such a tone from Alexander had disguised a jest. Now she did not know what to make of it. He winked at her. "But know that you are young and lovely and men are more readily enamored of youthful virgins."

Isabella propped her hand on her hip, her ire rising in defense of her new sister-in-law. "Oh, does that mean that you will not love Eleanor, simply because she was wedded before and thus no longer virginal?"

"No!" Alexander's smile broadened and he shook his head. "No, I do not anticipate such a dire fate as that." His old humor made his eyes sparkle.

"You did not come to the hall this afternoon," she ventured.

"No, we did not." Alexander held her gaze unflinchingly.

Isabella, who had a fearsome curiosity about intimate matters, dared to ask, though her cheeks burned with her audacity. "I did not quite see what you did this morning and I was wondering what exactly . . ."

"And you should not have seen as much as you did." He tut-tutted in mock disapproval, which would have reminded her more of Anthony if his eyes had not shone with such mischief. "A maidenly gaze should not fall upon some sights, Isabella Lammergeier."

"But I am curious!"

"And your curiosity will be sated on your wedding night, as is right and good. Is that not sufficient incentive to choose a spouse?"

"You turn every detail to your objective!" Isabella said with a laugh; then they smiled at each other in understanding.

Anthony rapped on the portal, then pushed it open, halting on the threshold in surprise. He held a heavily burdened tray and his features were alight with something that might have been called joy on another face. Alexander and Isabella both fell silent.

"I beg your pardon, my lord, but I believed you to be alone."

"Even you can err on occasion, Anthony," Alexander said, and Isabella found herself smiling. Her brother winked at her, then held the door. The castellan crossed the chamber and fussed with laying out the meal, his manner indicating that he would not leave shortly.

He must have something to tell Alexander. Isabella excused herself and hastened to the chamber that the sisters shared, smiling all the while. Whatever complaints Alexander had had about his nuptials would seem to have been addressed, and his happiness ensured with Eleanor.

All Isabella had to do was consider all the men she had known, then decide which of them she wished to know better. Alexander spoke aright in one matter—there was a sole way to sate her curiosity about what happened abed between man and wife. Eleanor's comments persuaded Isabella that it was time for her to know the truth.

～

THAT OLD HARRIDAN JEANNIE WAS lurking in the kitchens, muttering aspersions, her very presence driving Eleanor to do more and more. She had not intended to remain so long, but Jeannie's comments pricked at Eleanor.

When Eleanor insisted that the last of the wine be saved for Alexander, Jeannie had cackled. "She means to have it for herself, just you wait and see." The crone had made this accusation in an undertone that had carried to every ear.

When Eleanor discussed the replacement of the strewing herbs in the hall with the maids, Jeannie had muttered, "She means to ensure that I have no plants at my disposal, but she does not know the location of half of them."

When Eleanor suggested various sauces for the venison, as the cook was clearly tired of endeavoring to fashion something new from the same ingredients, Jeannie snorted. "She will command your every gesture, just wait. We have found a harsher mistress than ever we had in a laird."

Those in the kitchens became increasingly awkward, though Eleanor chose to ignore the older woman. She knew from her own experience that it was her public challenge that irked Jeannie. She had questioned Jeannie's abilities—and rightly so, in her estimation—before the entire company. That could only lead to fewer souls at Jeannie's door begging her aid.

Fewer souls pressing coin into Jeannie's gnarled hands.

Eleanor's suspicions were proved when she reviewed the inventory with the cook. "Mind she does not meddle with your stores!" Jeannie cried. "It is treacherous, indeed, that we have one so acquainted with poisons in our laird's own bed. Will any soul who is fool enough to defy her find himself dead?"

"You should not tolerate her nonsense," the cook said gruffly.

"She is vexed and it is better that she speak of such vexation than act upon it," Eleanor said.

"Do you mean to share your counsel at Kinfairlie?" the burly cook asked.

Eleanor nodded. "Such knowledge is better shared than veiled in secrecy. This is what I was taught. I will aid whosoever asks me for assistance."

"And this is what Jeannie fears," the cook said. "Few will go to her door now that you have questioned her abilities; fewer still if you provide the same counsel without threat or mystery."

Eleanor granted him a sharp glance. "I was right to question the intent of any soul whose deeds threatened my husband's life."

The cook nodded as he fidgeted with the keys to the stores. "True enough, my lady, but I would not have old Jeannie casting her venom at my back, not for any price."

He showed her how the inventory was stored, then carefully locked the portals behind them. Eleanor was pleased to note that a number of effective herbs were kept in the keep proper, as well as a measure of spice. Once they were done, the cook offered Eleanor the keys. "These would be yours to govern now, my lady."

Eleanor accepted the ring of keys, welcoming their weight in her hands. She was Lady of Kinfairlie in truth, her administration over its household assured by her husband as was right and good. She smiled at the cook, unable to hide her pleasure.

"I hope you will be happy at Kinfairlie," he said.

"I hope as much as well," Eleanor replied, then shook her head. "Though it has seemed thus far to be a place too good to exist in truth."

"Oh, we have our share of warts in this burg!" he said with a laugh, then coaxed her back into the kitchens. Jeannie, mercifully had made herself absent, and Anthony was making the final preparations for the tray he intended to deliver to Alexander.

Eleanor hastened to the castellan's side, ensuring that there was sufficient cheese and meat, then sniffed the wine. "It has faltered since last night. Were there not a dozen cloves in the inventory? I would see its taste improved for my lord with one or two of them."

And so it was done, Eleanor taking the wine herself into the storeroom to add spices. She even mulled the wine slightly, thinking only of Alexander's pleasure, and savored how Anthony sniffed appreciatively of its aroma when he lifted the tray.

She would show herself useful to her spouse, to be sure.

ALEXANDER WONDERED WHAT MISSION kept his wife from his chamber. He had hoped that Eleanor would return with the repast, that they would share it, perhaps abed, and that he might unfurl more of her secrets. Instead, Anthony fussed over the wick of a lantern, clearly intent upon remaining in the solar.

Alexander, for his part, sat again before his ledgers, considering the merit of Eleanor's suggestions. It was true that he charged many of the fees she noted, but they had not been increased since his father had laid claim to Kinfairlie's seal. If he added a half a penny to each of these fines charged by his court, for example, the sums worked much better. He did not wish to burden his people overmuch, but perhaps there was truth in her assertion that people would pay willingly for what they perceived to be advantages.

And he liked the notion of a fair very much. It could only be good to bring merchants from afar to trade upon his lands, to leave pennies in his coffers that did not come from the hands of his own tenants. He would have to ask Eleanor for more detail of how such matters were arranged.

Anthony cleared his throat and Alexander glanced up to find his castellan beaming. That man held a lantern filled with oil and, at Alexander's nod, replaced the one before Alexander that was nigh empty. Anthony made a fuss about trimming the wick, as he never did, so that Alexander knew the older man had something to say.

"And what troubles you this evening, Anthony?"

"Nothing, sir, nothing at all." The older man smiled primly. "It is simply that I must congratulate you, my lord, upon your excellent choice of a wife."

"I thank you, Anthony, for your felicitations."

Anthony straightened, sparing a glance for the tray he had laid aside. He shook his head, as if marveling, and against all expectation, his smile broadened. "I never thought to have to ask you this, my lord, but might you put your ledgers aside, the better that I could lay out your repast?"

"Surely my lady intends to return and do as much?"

"I am not certain, my lord. She is quite busy in the kitchens."

"But the meal has been summoned. There is bread and cheese and cold meat here to suffice for any man, and certainly more than ample servings for the lady and myself."

Anthony's eyes seemed to twinkle. "Ah, but the lady seeks to bring Kinfairlie beneath her administrating hand, which is clearly a competent one."

"Truly?" Alexander was intrigued by this.

"Truly," Anthony said with satisfaction. "With a dozen kind but firmly uttered words, she has the cook contriving a new sauce for the venison, and he had been complaining just before her arrival that venison was a waste of his considerable talents. She has mustered the maids to begin a thorough removal of the strewing herbs, giving instruction this night for the task to be completed in the morning. The ostlers were yet savoring their holiday measure of ale in the hall, and she amiably persuaded them to muck your stables on the morrow to such cleanliness that one will be able to eat from the very floor."

"Mercifully, we do not have to do so, as we have tables," Alexander muttered, but his castellan did not laugh.

"The lady has a gift for lighting a fire beneath those who would do as little as possible, to be sure," Anthony asserted. "Further, the meals are planned for the remainder of the holiday season. Should you or your guests choose to hunt, my lord, there is a list in the kitchens of what could be added to any given meal, depending upon your success."

"That is well done." Alexander deliberately closed one of the books of accounts and stacked it in his trunk with such apparent concentration that he hoped the older man would leave him alone.

Anthony did no such thing. "And—though surely I

need not convince you of the lady's charms!—she has retrieved your ring, against all expectation."

Alexander found his castellan shaking a finger at him, that man's manner as admonishing as that of an affectionate grandfather. Alexander blinked, but the newly garrulous Anthony shook his head benignly.

"A man should be mindful of his treasures, my lord, that is what I have always been taught. You were careless, if I may say so, and have been fortunate, indeed, in having your ring returned. What a woman of resource you have wed!"

Anthony smiled broadly, a sight so rare that Alexander could not believe this was the grumpy castellan he knew so well.

"And further," Anthony continued, "in a mere day, the lady has convinced you to willingly spend time at your accounting. I, as you well know, have spent a year endeavoring to achieve the same ends, my lord, and can only salute the lady's persuasive abilities." The older man winked most unexpectedly. "Of course, if you do not mind me saying as much, a lady has other weapons in her arsenal against her spouse than I could ever hope to wield."

Alexander blinked. "Did you make a jest, Anthony?"

That man waggled his silver brows and winked again. "I confess, my lord, that I have not your experience with such matters, but I did indeed make an attempt at humor."

"Then the lady has wrought a considerable change in this hall, to be sure."

Anthony laughed, and Alexander was certain he had never heard the older man do as much. "She is a marvel, of that there can be no doubt. Would you care for wine, sir?"

Alexander shook his head in revulsion at the very prospect. "I have no taste for it, not after last evening."

Anthony frowned. "But it is the last measure from the cask, my lord. My lady insisted that it be saved for you, as is right and proper."

"Then it will be wasted, for I cannot so much as think of drinking it."

The older man pursed his lips and considered the pitcher. "But the lady Eleanor troubled herself mightily with seeing it spiced for your taste, my lord. I would not have you insult her efforts, however inadvertently."

"Then I shall pour it from the window and compliment her upon it. I cannot drink it, Anthony. My innards roil at the very prospect."

"Sir! To spill it would be a waste of considerable expense." Anthony looked alarmed, but Alexander shrugged. "I did not bring ale, my lord, upon my lady's instruction, but I would willingly return to the kitchens and . . ."

"There is no need, Anthony." Alexander claimed a piece of bread and yawned mightily. "In this moment, I am so tired as to have little appetite at all."

"That is a shame, my lord." Anthony frowned at the pitcher of wine in his concern, clearly vexed.

"Did you try the wine last evening, Anthony?" Alexander asked on impulse. "It is a most excellent vintage and has kept beyond expectation."

"You know, sir, that I never indulge my taste for wine."

"It is Christmas, Anthony," Alexander said kindly. "I insist that you lay claim to this pitcher and savor its contents for yourself."

"Sir! I could not so forget my obligations. I pride myself upon ensuring that no foible troubles you, my lord, and . . ."

"By your own admission, Anthony, my lady has the administration of Kinfairlie well in hand. You might allow yourself one night of respite."

The older man considered the wine, a yearning in his eyes. "I once had quite the taste for a fine wine," he said.

"Then go, I insist upon it. No one will be the wiser that you savored this delight instead of myself. You might be so kind as to advise me in the morning as to its flavor, the better that I might compliment my wife."

"Of course, sir."

"Leave the meal as it stands, Anthony. I shall either eat alone or await my lady's company. You need not trouble yourself further with me this night." Alexander stood and yawned again. "Indeed, I may be asleep before long."

Anthony wagged a finger at him. "And rightly so. I entreat you to recall, sir, that you must preserve your strength for your accounts."

Alexander laughed at that, thinking that he could grow accustomed to his newly amiable castellan.

The older man departed with the wine as if it were a trophy, and though Alexander ate a measure of the food, he did not linger long at the table. His lady did not come, and though he could not imagine what occupied so much of her time, he did not doubt that she mustered his resources in ways he had not thought possible.

He yawned again, unable to fight the exhaustion that claimed him, and returned to bed.

Still, Eleanor did not come, and the quietude of the keep began to lull Alexander to sleep. A single day in Eleanor's presence and he knew that he made great progress in dispatching the lady's fears. She might not have confided fully in him as yet, but she had defended him in his hall, retrieved his signet ring, and ensured that their marriage could not be annulled.

On the verge of sleep, Alexander smiled. His new bride liked him, he knew it well, whether she admitted as much or not. He would win her heart before spring burst upon Kinfairlie, that was beyond doubt.

ELEANOR YAWNED IN HER TURN as she climbed the stairs to the solar. It had taken some time, but she was confident that all in Kinfairlie would be more perfect on the morrow. Alexander would see her merit soon, and even if she dared not love him, he would surely perceive that she was not worthy of being put aside. She would perform every deed to perfection, so that he could find no fault with her, and perhaps he might even come to care for her.

And she would give him a son within the year, which would guarantee both his affection and a full treasury for Kinfairlie. She liked this abode well, liked its people as well as its laird.

She paused on the threshold outside the chamber shared by Alexander's sisters and smiled at the sound of their slumber. Their maid clucked over them, her shadow visible even in the darkness as she muttered to this one and that, tucking them in and keeping a vigilant eye upon the portal. Eleanor might have frightened them with her own tale, but she was as determined as Alexander to see his sisters wed happily. With some effort, it could be done.

She yawned again and began the next course of stairs, though she never reached the summit. Feet pounded behind her and she turned to find the cook's wife racing toward her. Rose was red in the face, her eyes wide with alarm.

"What is amiss?" Eleanor asked. Vera, the girls' maid, came out onto the landing, her kind face showing concern even as she pulled the portal closed behind her.

"It is Anthony! He came into the kitchen, complaining that his heart raced like a wild thing; then he fell upon the floor."

"God in heaven!" Eleanor picked up her skirts and hastened back down stairs. To her astonishment, the cook's wife put a hand upon her arm to halt her.

"I mean you no disservice, my lady, but there are those who would not have you summoned."

"What is this?"

"There were those who said that you knew too much of poison, and that Anthony looked to be poisoned."

"But why would I poison Kinfairlie's castellan?" Eleanor pushed aside the notion with impatience. "The man has been good to me, and I rely upon his counsel." She hastened down the steps, not waiting for the cook's wife to lead the way.

"But all know that Anthony drank the wine that you prepared for your lord husband," Rose said, her voice carrying with clarity.

Eleanor spun to face her and saw the condemnation in the woman's eyes. Vera stepped back, fear in her expression.

Rose lifted her chin, bracing herself for her own audacity. "Is it not whispered, my lady, that you are over-fond of burying husbands? What scheme have you for our laird Alexander?"

"None!" Eleanor replied. "What scheme have you to keep a healer from Anthony's side?" With that, she fled down the steps to be of what aid she could. She only hoped it was not too late.

ALEXANDER AWAKENED EARLY the following morning, feeling refreshed and invigorated. To his astonishment, there was no sign that Eleanor had ever come to bed. He washed and dressed with haste, surprised that Anthony had not yet brought him warm water. The sun shone and it clearly was not that early in the morn.

He smiled, thinking that his castellan must have enjoyed the wine overmuch. It was good that Eleanor was not close at hand, expecting a comment upon her spicing. Convinced that all was right, Alexander strode out of his chambers.

It was in his own hall that he discovered the fullness of his error. All was a far cry from being aright at Kinfairlie.

Chapter Seven

By MORNING'S LIGHT, Eleanor was so exhausted that she knew she saw things that were not there.

She had raced to the kitchen at Rose's summons and found Anthony writhing upon the floor. A touch at his throat revealed the worst, for his pulse was rapid and irregular. With no time to spare, she immediately thrust her fingers down his throat.

He vomited with gusto, and his offering was the deep red hue of wine. He fell back, panting from his effort, and closed his eyes, but Eleanor granted the older man no respite. She compelled him again and again and again to empty his belly, until only bile came from his lips. The household gathered around her in silence, and she could feel the weight of their anxiety.

For the moment, though, she concerned herself solely with Anthony. When it was clear that he could summon nothing more, she sat back and considered the situation.

"What ailed him?" asked the cook, his tone filled with a wariness that Eleanor knew all too well.

"The wine was poisoned," she said, allowing herself to

show no emotion. It had been destined for Alexander! And her spicing of the wine had ensured that no man would have noted the toxin within it. Would ill fortune never leave her side? "I suspect it was aconite. Do you grow monkshood here?"

The cook shrugged. "I take little interest in the inventories of medicinal herbs." He cleared his throat. "It was you, my lady, who reviewed them this very night."

And so she had. Eleanor was fairly certain that there had been aconite in the store, for it was common to possess, especially in the north. In minute quantities, the powder from its root could be soothing in a salve for painful joints and thus people were reluctant to be without it.

"What shall we do for him?" the cook asked, crouching beside her.

Eleanor considered the supine older man, whose color looked to be improving slightly. She touched her fingertips to his throat. His pulse slowed, but that could be a sign of the aconite working further. "I do not know if I came in time," she said, seeing no reason to gild the truth. "He may recover, or he may not. He should be watched and kept warm, given milk to drink when he desires it. By morning, we will know the truth."

"Not all of the truth, my lady," corrected the cook's wife. "For we will not likely know by then why the wine was tainted in the first place."

"Oh, I think there is little doubt of that," Eleanor said flatly. "Someone endeavored to kill my lord husband, but Fortune intervened."

They whispered at that and withdrew from her plain speech, but Eleanor did not care. She was innocent and she had no patience with those who would find a soul guilty with no evidence to their hands.

She ensured Anthony's comfort, and though he was not entirely aware of his surroundings, she persuaded him to sip some milk. It was fresh and sweet milk, come from goats tethered in the kitchen gardens.

She sat vigil with him all of that night, bathing his brow through the sweating induced by the herb, talking to him to encourage wakefulness when his pulse slowed overmuch. She demanded his counsel more than once and the castellan was so dutybound that he stirred himself at great effort to reply.

Eleanor was tired herself and felt bent beneath the weight of the suspicion around her. With every hour that passed, she was more encouraged that Anthony would survive.

She saw things in the midst of that long, dark night that she knew were not there. She imagined her father watching from the shadowed doorway, his lips drawn taut in displeasure that she had been so stupid as to feed doubts about herself. She imagined her loyal maid, Moira, hovering behind her, her expression one of concern and sympathy. Why had she left Moira behind? Eleanor had believed there to be a greater threat to Moira in traveling to an unknown destination than in lingering at Tivotdale, but now she wished that she had had one ally at Kinfairlie.

But when morning came, and Alexander arrived in the kitchens, Eleanor knew that she saw what was before her in truth. Her husband's brow was as dark as thunder, an expression she knew as well as her own name.

Her dawning conviction that there was no violence

within Alexander Lammergeier died a quick death and she feared him anew.

Eleanor straightened beside Anthony's pallet, her heart racing, and struggled to appear suitably demure. She was painfully aware of the red stain of the castellan's vomit upon the silk dress lent to her by her husband's sisters. She did not doubt that her carelessness would earn his ire.

As would her other deeds. The household whispered and drew back, watchful of the inevitable encounter between laird and lady. Eleanor despised their curiosity yet at the same time was glad of their presence.

Any man was less likely to raise his fists before witnesses.

"Good morning, my lord," she said with all the meekness she could summon. "I trust you slept well."

"If I slept well, it was only because the truth of what occurred within these walls was kept from mine own ears," Alexander retorted, and marched to her side. "How could I not be told of this?"

Eleanor swallowed, realizing that no one else in the kitchens would answer. "I feared to see you disturbed, my lord."

"Would you leave me slumber through the Second Coming as well?" Alexander shook his head with impatience. "Eleanor, nothing is of as great an import as the welfare of those in my household. In future, this omission will not be repeated."

Eleanor bit her lip, not thinking it timely to remind Alexander that he had been in need of his own sleep to recover from the tainted wine he had imbibed the night before. A sweat broke upon her brow, for two cups of tainted wine had been served in this hall since her arrival, and she could easily guess who would bear the blame.

She spared a glance for those souls in Alexander's household and felt sickened at the condemnation she found in their eyes. Oh, she knew this sense well, but she did not like it for all its familiarity.

Alexander meanwhile crouched beside his castellan and affection for the older man softened his expression. "How does he fare?"

"I think he will recover fully," Eleanor said, aware that Anthony himself attended their conversation. She smiled for the older man, who managed a wan smile in return. "He was most stalwart in the battle that waged during the night."

"I had a valiant defender, to be sure," Anthony whispered. He grasped Alexander's hand, and the sinews in Anthony's hand were prominent with age.

"What happened?" Alexander asked tersely.

"There was aconite in the wine sent to your chamber last night," Eleanor said, seeing no point in evasion. Alexander looked up at her. "It is a potent poison, one that kills a man with fearsome speed. I gather that Anthony took the wine, instead of you."

Alexander glanced down at his castellan and Eleanor could not see his expression. "Who prepared the wine?" he asked, his tone carefully controlled. She could not guess his thoughts, that fact feeding her fear of his response.

The kitchen was so silent that Eleanor could fairly hear the mice breathing in the cellar.

"I did," she said. She had never flinched from the truth of her deeds, whatsoever their price might be.

"And was it left unattended?"

Eleanor considered. "I do not know. It was poured before the cook and I checked the inventory in the store-rooms. I do not know who else was in the kitchens during our absence."

Alexander nodded, then impaled her with a bright glance. There were no stars in his eyes and no laughter curved his lips. He was deadly serious and she feared his judgment more than anything she had ever feared before. "And did you place the aconite in the wine, for any reason?" he asked, no accusation in his tone.

He watched her avidly and Eleanor knew that he sought evidence that she lied.

Eleanor held his gaze. "No, my lord, I did not," she said firmly. "It is true that I did not favor the smell of the wine upon our return from the inventory, when Anthony made to carry it to you. I heated it and added some cloves, for I thought a mulling would improve its flavor."

"The flavor was most exceptional," Anthony said, his determination to defend Eleanor fairly rending her heart. His grip tightened on Alexander's hand. "Do not place blame, my lord, where its presence cannot be proved."

Alexander rose to his feet and smiled thinly. That he put aside his castellan's hand with such firmness was no good portent in Eleanor's thinking. "I thank you, Anthony, for your counsel," he said gently. "And I now would counsel you to sleep and see yourself recovered." He shook a finger at the older man, his manner playful for the first time since he had entered the kitchens. "What should I do without your wise counsel?"

"You have your lady wife, my lord."

"I would have you, Anthony," Alexander said with a resolve that made Eleanor shiver.

The castellan fought against his body's determination to rest, probably thinking it discourteous to fall asleep in the presence of his laird, but lost the battle. His eyelids fluttered, looking as thin as the finest parchment. Anthony appeared much older than he had and more frail, and Eleanor did not doubt that he had come close to losing his battle.

The castellan's breathing deepened, though it was not deep enough for Eleanor's taste. She did not like his pallor, either, and bent to touch her fingertips to the pulse at his throat once more.

At least it seemed to have regained a normal pace.

Alexander's brow furrowed as he watched the castellan sleep. "What will come of this?" he asked in an undertone.

"I cannot say."

He met her gaze steadily. "You can guess."

Eleanor sighed. "He will need to rest."

Alexander considered her and she saw that he understood the import of her words. "But you anticipate a recovery?"

"I hope for one. It is a potent poison and it was in his belly longer than one would prefer."

His gaze touched upon the stain on her garb. "It did not agree with him?"

Eleanor held up two fingers. "I persuaded his belly to empty."

Alexander heaved a sigh, then studied his castellan again. "Then you saved his life. Anthony is fortunate that you were here, no less that someone thought to summon you." He took her elbow in his hand and spoke decisively. Eleanor could not help but note that his favor did not reach his eyes. "I thank you, my lady fair, for your quick wits. We shall return to our chambers now, and a hot bath will be brought for you."

"I should remain with Anthony," Eleanor said with panic. Any deed could be done behind the sturdy portal of that chamber, and a turn of the key would ensure that no soul could aid her.

Alexander shook his head. "Others can tend him in your absence. You have need of your own sleep and I will hear no protest against it." He began to lead Eleanor from the kitchen, but the cook's wife stepped into their path.

"I beg your pardon, my lord, but it must be noted that your lady prepared that wine and insisted it be taken to you!"

Alexander's eyes narrowed, his manner incisive. "My lady is above rebuke from those in my household. Any discussion upon this matter will be conducted between the lady and myself, in the privacy of our chambers."

Eleanor shivered at the portent of that.

"But . . . ," Rose protested.

"There is no reason why my lady would have wished me dead and less reason for her to desire Anthony's demise," Alexander said, his tone allowing no argument. "Instead of speculating upon nonsense, I would ask you to each consider who was in the kitchens last evening." He gestured to his brother-in-law who had followed him from the hall. "I charge Rhys FitzHenry with making a summary of your accountings."

"It shall be done," Rhys said. "You will not a one of you speak to each other before you speak alone with me."

"I will speak first," the cook said, stepping forward. "And I will offer my recollection to my laird Alexander."

"Speak with Rhys, as I have bidden you all. I have another matter before me," Alexander said with smooth assurance, his very surety making Eleanor's spirit quail. "And those of you who are not summoned immediately to Rhys, I would have you bring the lady's bath with all haste."

Eleanor understood that she was to face a reckoning from her spouse, and though she appreciated that it would not occur before his household, still she was not anxious to receive this accounting. His jaw was set and she feared that Alexander had, like her other husbands, excised his charm.

He fairly marched her toward the stairs. Eleanor felt her chest tighten with every step. She did not dare defy him, lest she provoke his anger further, but she hoped that she would have the opportunity to regain his favor.

In truth, Eleanor feared her current husband more than she had ever feared another man. Alexander was young and strong and agile. If he chose to beat her, he might well kill her. She already understood that in this hall, just as in the other halls she had occupied, no soul would raise a hand to assist her.

But Eleanor was surprised to realize the difference in herself since she had faced a man in other halls. She had a keen desire to live, and she had yet more desire to live at Kinfairlie. Although she feared Alexander's anger, a part of her dared to hope that his fury could be turned aside, that his charm could be summoned again, that Kinfairlie could prove to be the sanctuary she had initially hoped it to be.

She knew that if he granted her the slightest chance to make that dream become a reality, she would do whatsoever he demanded of her to make it so.

And that was a fearsome prospect, indeed. How had this

man gained so much power over her in so short a time that she would readily surrender her all to pacify him?

Eleanor did not know. She was uncertain whether to be more afraid of Alexander or her own desire to please him. They crossed the threshold of his chamber as one; then Alexander flicked the portal closed with his fingertips.

"It is time, my lady, for a measure of truth to fall from your lips," he said with force. Eleanor watched him, not daring to imagine how he would encourage her to confess that truth.

Then she nodded agreement, as meek as she could manage to be.

ALEXANDER HAD NOTED THE change in Eleanor's manner as soon as she had turned to face him in the kitchens. She now stood straight and tall, her emotions hidden, her body taut. It was as if they began anew, as strangers once more. He was reminded of her flight from the solar the day before, of her desperation to claim the key in that same incident, of the terror that had lit her eyes when he had incidentally held her hands over her head.

If he had not known better, he might have guessed that she was afraid, but he could not imagine his formidable wife being fearful of him.

"Are you certain of Anthony's recovery? Or is there some detail you did not wish to add before the others?"

She shook her head, then wrapped her arms around herself. There were shadows beneath her eyes, making her look both tired and hunted. "I think he will recover, but it will take time."

"What of the aconite? Do you know who added it to the wine?"

She shook her head, though she did not meet his regard.

"Could its addition not have been an accident?" he asked, hoping to encourage her confidence.

Her expression said it all. "No. Someone meant harm, to be sure. Had Anthony not vomited, and done so as quickly as he had, he would have died in painful haste."

Alexander pursed his lips and frowned. "Do you believe the tainted wine was destined for me?"

She tilted her head to regard him, her eyes narrowed. "Why do you not simply ask my intent?"

"Because you did not add the poison to the wine, of course." Alexander smiled, for Eleanor seemed so astonished by his conviction. "I know you were well pleased yesterday, Eleanor, and though you are not anxious to surrender your heart to any man, I do not believe that you wish me such ill as that. You did, after all, ensure that our nuptials could not be annulled." Her lips parted in astonishment and he found his smile broadening. "At least I am not the only one surprised to find myself defended," he teased.

She swallowed and he saw a shimmer of tears on her lashes before she blinked them away. What had he done, or not done, to make her appear so grateful?

"You have found a champion in Anthony as well, and that before this sorry incident. He was much impressed with your command of my meager resources and I am intrigued by the notion of a fair." He watched the way she glanced up and could not name the reason for her caution. He thought to encourage her with conversation. "Where did you learn to administer a household? I thought that Ewen's sister ruled in his hall."

"And so she does," Eleanor said tightly. She crossed the chamber, keeping her back to him.

"So you must have administered the hall of your first husband."

Eleanor shook her head with resolve. "Millard desired but one deed of me as his wife and it had nothing to do with administration." She turned to face him, her composure so complete that she might have been wrought of stone. "His mother reigned in his hall."

"And you?"

"Awaited him abed: supine, silent, and spread wide."

Alexander granted her a wry glance. "That is rather more than I would have preferred to know."

Eleanor smiled slightly. "It was more than I wished to know of the marital debt, you can be certain."

"Isabella said that you told of being wedded young."

She folded her arms across her chest and held his gaze, as if defying him to believe her. "I was twelve summers of age on the day of my first marriage, while Millard had seen two and sixty summers."

"Where did you meet such a man?"

"At the altar. My father said that Millard wed me on the rumor of my beauty, no more and no less." Eleanor shrugged. "He must have been pleased, for he came to me daily until his demise."

Alexander paused, knowing that he had to ask. On this morning, his thoughts were full of Alan's accusations and the lady's manner did little to dispel those harsh words. "How did Millard die?"

Eleanor held his gaze unflinchingly. "He ceased to live."

"Meaning?"

"That he ceased to breathe, and thus he died." She

seemed to be daring him to accuse her of some foul deed and that alone made Alexander reluctant to do so.

All the same, he wished for a better answer.

"There was no other contributing factor, then, save his age?"

"He retired hale, but did not awaken from that night's slumber."

"Eleanor, I would wager that you know more of this than you admit. Tell me of it."

Eleanor averted her gaze. Alexander waited, hearing the sea roll upon the shore, watching her fight some inner demon.

Finally she swallowed and spoke, her words strained. "It was rumored, of course, that his passing had not been a natural one, and this is the rumor to which Alan Douglas would allude."

"Why 'of course'?"

"Because Millard's young bride was unhappy, and known to be so by all. She was not clever enough to hide her true feelings from those who might use such detail against her." Eleanor licked her lips, awkward as Alexander had never seen her.

He found it intriguing that she spoke of her own past as if it had occurred to someone else. If it was easier for her thus, then some horrific deed must have occurred in Millard's hall. "And as you know something of poisons, the blame fell upon you," he guessed, wanting to aid her in telling her tale.

"It was not so simple as that." She turned to the window, arms yet wrapped tightly around herself. Alexander waited, granting her all the time she needed—though, in truth, he feared what she might say.

What she did say surprised him.

"It is true that I learned of plants, including the toxic ones, but not because I had any particular interest in it. It was simply due to circumstance in my father's household."

Her words were tight, as if she had to fight to loose them, and he appreciated that it was difficult for her to surrender such information about herself. He was honored that she chose to confide in him, though he could not fathom why she did so.

"When I was a child, there was a woman in my father's abode who knew much of mixing potions. She was like your Jeannie, an old crone filled with secrets, to whom few spoke unless they had need of her talents. She taught her skills to me."

"Your father arranged for such a tutor for you?" His shock made Eleanor smile thinly.

"Hardly that!" She glanced over her shoulder at him and their gazes snared for a long moment.

He could see her uncertainty and knew that she had never confided in another soul before. He lifted his hand to encourage her, but Eleanor turned her back abruptly upon him. Alexander wondered whether she sought to hide something from him, or whether she avoided the distraction of the desire between them. He was well aware of her lithe curves, well aware of the way the winter sunlight made her look both icy and fragile. Her vulnerability touched him as resoundingly as her rare passion did.

He laid his hand upon her shoulder and was startled to feel her tremble.

Perhaps she was cold. The wind was chill this morn and the shutters were drawn back from the window. He lifted her own cloak, so richly trimmed, and tucked it over her shoulders. She clutched it, her fingers bloodless.

"My father would have been shocked, had he known, and surely would have put an end to those discussions. She was merely a woman of the woods, bedraggled and passing strange, but she talked to me." She shrugged and her breath caught before she continued. "I heeded her lessons so that she would not leave me alone again."

Eleanor had been a lonely child. Alexander heard the confession she did not explicitly make. "And you kept the truth of it from your father, the better that he would not interfere."

"It was not difficult. He was gone to war most of the time."

Alexander slid his fingertip across her shoulders, nudging the silk of her hair to one side, and spoke softly. "And your mother?"

"Died in the bearing of me. We were two only, for my father never wed again."

Alexander understood a little more of the root of his lady's cool manner. She had been alone as a child, and he felt a sympathy for her. No wonder she had no regard for love in a marriage: her father must have felt none for her mother, and her husbands had shown little to Eleanor. What did she know of love? Where could she have learned of it?

Alexander was aware then of the abundance with which he had been blessed at Kinfairlie. He felt humbled that he had possessed so many gifts for so long and never appreciated their value. He had no right to complain, now that his blessings were less bountiful. "Tell me of your father," he urged, letting his fingertips trail across the bare flesh at the lady's nape.

She stared resolutely out the window at Kinfairlie village. "There is little to tell. He was a lord, like yourself, and one who took his duties most seriously."

"Even the duties of a father?"

"He saw me fed and clothed," Eleanor said tightly. "He rode to war, and saw our borders secured."

"That is a meager measure, Eleanor."

She straightened. "One takes what one is offered and makes the most of it."

"One can always wish for more."

She looked down at her hands and he felt her shoulders shake anew. "I always hoped," she said quietly, "that each time he rode out, it would be the last time he did as much, but in truth, I think he did not wish to linger at our abode. He was always restless, always anxious to be gone."

"Because of you?"

"Clearly." Eleanor turned to confront him and he ached at the loneliness in her eyes. "My mother died in the bearing of me, and I suspect that my father could not look at me without recalling his loss. He certainly did not look long or often."

Alexander frowned as several details came together in his thoughts. "Wait. Do not tell me that you administered your father's household in your mother's stead, though you were but a child?"

Eleanor shrugged. "It was some deed I could do, some way in which I could be useful to him."

"But you were wed at twelve!"

"Daughters are seldom useful to fathers as sons can be. I strove to show that there was some merit in my presence."

Alexander guessed the true root lay elsewhere. "You

did as much to gain his favor," he suggested, and she averted her gaze. "Is that why you undertook such responsibility in my hall last night? Did you mean to win my favor with your talents?"

She took a quick breath and squared her shoulders. "I have learned that men prefer to have a clean and organized hall, and to have their meals served in timely fashion, and to not be obliged to adjudicate over quibbles in the kitchen."

"And you have learned that men desire that and only one other feat from their wives, is that not so?"

She met his gaze, daring him to tell her otherwise. "What else would a man expect from a wife?"

"Companionship," Alexander said with force. "Friendship and the sharing of counsel." Eleanor looked so skeptical that he elaborated. "My father relied upon my mother's ability to understand people, for she had insight into the nature of others that far exceeded his own. Thus they ruled Kinfairlie more justly together than either could have done alone."

Eleanor said nothing. She did not move. He might not have spoken for all the reaction she showed, but Alexander sensed that Eleanor gave his words consideration. He watched her and waited, wondering what he might do to convince her to surrender more of her truth, wondering how he might persuade her of his intent, wondering if he truly could heal her wounds without knowing the malady.

"You were afraid when we left the kitchens," he said quietly. "Tell me why. Tell me what you thought I would do."

She straightened then, his warrior queen, and met his gaze with resolve. His heart thundered with pride at her valor. He did not doubt that she had endured much, but she had a fierce spirit, one that was not readily daunted.

"No more and no less than other men do."

"I have done what I was taught that men should do. I have asked your counsel," he said. "What else would you expect of me?"

Eleanor stepped out from beneath the weight of his hand and crossed the chamber with hurried steps.

"There can be no match between us without honesty," Alexander reminded her. "Though you have clearly learned to be cautious with your trust, you must confide in me, Eleanor. You must do so, or we, in truth, can never make a match."

"You are vexed with me."

"I am vexed in my attempts to make a good marriage of a poor beginning. Your reticence alone is the obstacle between us."

She watched him closely. "Not rumor?"

"I give no credence to rumor, nor to accusations made by a man like Alan Douglas. Confide in me, Eleanor."

She took a deep breath, as if steadying herself. "Then let me tell you this. Rumor was fed in the matter of Millard's death by his young widow's refusal to weep at his funeral."

Alexander chose his question with care, for there was clearly a great deal to this tale and he did not wish her to fall silent so soon. "And was rumor further encouraged by his young wife's manner toward him? Did she wish him dead?"

Eleanor nodded with vigor. "Often and with great passion." She choked on her words and Alexander recalled Isabella's surety that Eleanor's first husband had been cruel. "She could not summon any grief for his passing, only relief that he could torment her no longer." She marched the width of the chamber then, her features taut with some old fury.

"But there was no accusation made against her, was there?"

"There was rumor and there was her father's desire to ally with the Black Douglas clan. Ewen Douglas arrived with the widow's father to claim her before rumor could amount to a charge." Eleanor granted him a shrewd glance. "But that does not mean that the charge would not have come. It certainly does not mean that Millard's widow could not have been found guilty, nor that she would not have been executed for her sin."

"Her sin? You speak as if she were guilty."

Eleanor stared unseeingly across the chamber. "She did kill him, though not in the way that all believed."

Alexander started, but Eleanor did not seem aware of him, so lost was she in painful recollection.

"Millard died atop his wife, in what he called his favored place in all his demesne," she said bitterly. "He heaved atop her with his usual vigor that night, then fell still so abruptly that she was gladdened. She was gladdened that the ordeal had been of shorter duration than was his custom. Then she realized not only that he moved no more, but that he was so large a man that she could not dislodge his weight."

Alexander looked away, sickened.

But Eleanor stared at Alexander, her eyes glittering, her words hot. "And so she lay, all the night, feeling him turn cold atop her, awaiting a servant's aid to be freed. During that night, she knew herself to be filled with sin and recognized this as her punishment. She had wickedly yearned for her spouse's demise."

"That is not the same as killing him!"

"Millard had oft claimed that his wife's very presence aroused his lust to such might that he could think of little beyond bedding her. And so, as it was the lust she fed that claimed his life, it could easily be argued that she did kill him."

"I would not argue thus," Alexander said, but she ignored him.

Eleanor took a ragged breath and her words spilled in a heated rush. "And it would not be a lie to say that she oft wished in later years that the charge had been made against her, and she had been found guilty of her sins, and that her time on this earth had been ended, for then she would not have been wed to Ewen Douglas." She tipped back her head, holding Alexander's gaze, daring and defying him once more.

"Because he struck her?"

Eleanor closed her eyes, then took a breath. "Often, but always where the bruise would not be seen by another."

Alexander exhaled mightily, shaken by her confession. "But then, if she had been executed, that young widow would never have come to Kinfairlie," he said.

Eleanor nodded agreement without hesitation. "And that would have been dreadful, indeed."

"Why do you say as much?"

"Because here there is hope, and here there is sanctuary." She crossed the chamber and reached a hand to him and he saw that elusive shimmer of tears in her eyes. "For here in Kinfairlie there reigns a laird who will not treat his lady wife unjustly, a laird who puts no credence in rumor without evidence." She swallowed. "Here, I hope, reigns a laird who has no violence within him."

Alexander caught her hand in his, felt her trembling, and knotted his fingers with hers. "You are right, though I am awed that you grant me such credit so readily."

Eleanor smiled thinly. "One has only to be bitten by a dog once to see the difference between good hounds and vicious ones." She shrugged. "Though I confess that my fear of hounds and their teeth is too deep to be evaded fully."

"So now I am as complex as a hound," Alexander teased.

"I am sorry. I did not mean . . ."

"I know your meaning. I merely sought your smile." Alexander's one hand rose to cup her face. He did not know how to begin to express his admiration for her, for she had endured much in her days. He was honored that she even granted him a chance to prove that all men were not brutes. "We had best end this conversation before I take insult with its direction."

Alarm flickered across her features, despite his teasing tone, though Alexander now knew its root.

He bent and brushed his lips to hers. "You should be warned, lady mine, that when I am insulted by a lady's estimation of my nature, I feel an overwhelming urge to prove her expectations wrong." She smiled ever so fleetingly, uncertainty still lingering in her eyes; then Alexander kissed her fully.

He had to wait only a heartbeat before she softened and leaned against him. She shivered as he caught her close, but she parted her lips to his embrace. He knew that his lady fought her dragons with as much determination as he.

Alexander had no doubt that between the efforts of the two of them, those unwelcome beasts would soon be banished from the realm.

THE MAN DEFIED EXPECTATION. He was not one to use his fists, not like Ewen, which was a relief in truth. Still, Eleanor was cautious. Millard, after all, had been possessed of a smooth charm that disguised his cruelty.

She had learned early that welcoming him abed made the household more peaceful.

It was, however, far simpler to consider the merit of welcoming Alexander between her thighs. He kissed her with that seductive ease, his lips moving persuasively against hers.

Eleanor barely hesitated before she met his caress with an ardor of her own. He had not judged her. He had not struck her. He had listened to her with compassion. She did not feel stripped bare after having made her confession, and though she could not pledge to love Alexander Lammergeier, she was encouraged that honesty and trust might suit him well enough.

And a son, of course.

Their kiss heated with astonishing speed, her hands rising to tangle in his hair, his arms locking around her waist. He kissed her with such delicious abandon that Eleanor almost forgot the instruction he had given in the kitchens below.

Thus she jumped as high as Alexander when the heavy

rap came upon the portal. "Your bath, my lady!" cried some soul, then pushed the door open. Alexander beckoned and the wooden tub was rolled into the middle of the chamber. A veritable army from the kitchens followed, carrying kettles of steaming water and pouring their contents into the tub in succession.

Then Isabella appeared in the doorway. Her manner was cautious, as it had not been in Eleanor's presence thus far, though she smiled at Alexander. "I would bring you a nuptial gift," she said with a quick glance at Eleanor. She offered something in her fist, her cheeks coloring.

"And what is this?" Eleanor accepted the small glass vial, but did not know whether to loose the stopper or not. Was this a jest, or a comment upon her knowledge of herbs?

"It is for your bath," Isabella said. "I knew it would be perfect when I heard you had summoned a bath for Eleanor. Rosamunde granted it to me upon my thirteenth birthday and told me to save it for my wedding night. She said it would conjure sweetness between man and wife, though I know not what she meant. I would give it to you, as an apology and as a nuptial gift."

"Are you certain?" Eleanor asked. She had already noted that these siblings held this departed aunt in esteem. "Surely you wish to keep this gift for yourself, as you were bidden."

"I have never done what I was bidden," Isabella admitted with a laugh.

"There is truth enough," Alexander muttered with some affection.

"While I suppose that you were as innocent as all the

angels!" Isabella retorted, giving her brother a poke in the shoulder. "I will never forget that frog you left in my best slippers."

"That must have been a decade ago." Alexander grinned, unrepentant. "How can you even recall it with certainty?"

"I never did get the smell of it out of the leather," Isabella huffed. "A word of counsel to you, Eleanor. Keep a close eye upon your slippers—"

"Or your frogs," Alexander interjected.

"—for this rogue is cursed quick."

"I shall do as much," Eleanor said, unable to keep herself from smiling. Kinfairlie must have been noisy indeed with these children underfoot, all playing pranks upon each other!

Perhaps she should surrender more than one son to Alexander, the better to ensure that her children grew up amid the noise and merriment she had never known. The very prospect made Eleanor's blood heat and she found herself watching her spouse.

He spared a sparkling glance for the vial. "I thought you curious, Isabella. Do you not fear that you surrender part of the mystery, and that with it unexplored?"

"Trust you to make me regret my impulse," Isabella retorted, and Alexander laughed.

"In truth, you will receive no other trinkets from Rosamunde," he said, sobering. "If you change your thinking now, neither of us will think the worse of you."

Eleanor offered the vial in silent agreement, but Isabella shook her head. "I must surrender something of import to make this matter come aright. My error against you was not small, Alexander, and this vial is a small price to pay for your forgiveness."

"As well as a silver ring?"

"As well," Isabella said with force. Eleanor could not help but admire that these siblings had been taught to make matters right, to apologize for their errors, and to ensure that justice was preserved.

"You have my forgiveness already," Alexander said, and Isabella smiled.

"Then take it as a gift."

Alexander lifted the vial from Eleanor's grasp and viewed it with mock skepticism. "This and the silver ring," he mused, considering the vial. "Methinks, my lady, that there must be something amiss with this potion, or else this is not truly my sister Isabella."

"Truly?" Eleanor asked, lowering her voice to match his.

"Oh, she is a beauty, but is one with a keen grasp upon her possessions. It is unlike her to surrender much of merit."

"Oh, you could simply thank me!" Isabella cried.

Alexander pulled the stopper; then he and Eleanor sniffed as one.

"Lavender," Eleanor said. "With rose and honey, I would wager." She laid her hand upon Alexander's and met his twinkling gaze. "I must confess that I have always found that mingling of scents particularly beguiling."

Alexander dumped the entire contents of the vial into the steaming tub, then smiled wickedly. "Are you beguiled, my lady?"

"By more than scent, to be sure." Eleanor smiled, enjoying that they teased Isabella, but Alexander's gaze heated.

He turned abruptly upon his sister and pointed to the portal. "Time it is for you to leave."

"Oh, just as matters become interesting!" she protested good-naturedly. "I shall never know the truth of what happens between man and wife."

"All the more reason to choose a spouse with haste," Eleanor said. Alexander laughed at that, to her confusion, and Isabella cast her hands skyward.

"You even sound the same as he, and this in merely two days!" she charged, then laughed and was gone. Alexander shut the door firmly behind her and locked it with a flourish. He tossed the key into the air, caught it, then cast it to Eleanor.

She caught it, despite her surprise.

"You were afraid yesterday when I locked the portal," he said quietly, his eyes gleaming. "I do not like fear in a woman and I do not think it fitting for a lady to feel compelled to flee the chamber she should think of as her own. This key will always be in your grasp."

Eleanor smiled as she fingered the cold key. She tied it to her belt, liking that her new husband was perceptive and kind. Perhaps it was not all bad to confess a secret or two, provided such gems were surrendered to the right person.

Dare she hope that this husband was the right person?

"Such thoughtfulness is deserving of reward," she mused, then kicked off her shoes.

Alexander looked about himself in mock confusion. "Ah, but I cannot think of a single advantage lacking in my life," he said with a frown. "I have a beauteous wife, my siblings are hale, my keep is sufficiently warm."

That he could recount advantages with sincerity when

his treasury was empty warmed Eleanor's heart. She halted before him and raised a hand to touch his jaw. There was a shadow of stubble there that prickled against her fingertips. He watched her, smiling slightly, neither rushing her nor demanding of her. Eleanor stretched to her toes and touched her lips to that smile.

"I can think of one thing lacking," she whispered against his throat. The taste of him made her blood quicken and her mouth go dry. The height and breadth of him made her feel delicate and feminine. His patience made her feel potent.

"Then enlighten me," he murmured, his words stirring her hair. "For I cannot imagine what it might be."

"You do not have a son."

"True enough. But what might we do to remedy that?"

Eleanor met the merry sparkle in his eyes and pretended to consider this quandary. She liked that Alexander let her set the pace of their lovemaking, and liked even better that he was playful abed. His manner fed her confidence in her own allure and showed her much of her own desire for intimacy.

To think that she had always been called cold by her spouses. This one kindled a fire within her that could not be denied. His was a gift, one deserving of a gift in return, and Eleanor knew that the son whose birth would see Kinfairlie's treasury filled was the sole gift that would suffice.

That Alexander courted her favor in ignorance of what she could give him was the most seductive detail of all.

Chapter Eight

~

ALEXANDER WATCHED AS ELEANOR PURSED her lips and pretended to consider the conundrum of finding him a son. Her lips were so full and ruddy that he longed to kiss her, but he steeled himself to wait. It was a man's violence that made her uncertain, though already he sensed that she overcame that memory.

Had Millard struck her, as well as Ewen? Perhaps her father, too, had been abusive of her. A part of Alexander seethed that any man would see fit to injure a woman to see his will reign supreme.

That Eleanor met him abed with as little fear as she did filled him with awe and admiration. She was valiant, there was no doubt about it, though Alexander knew that full trust between himself and his wife would only come when she was certain of his intent.

So he waited, his blood boiling, and let her seduce him. It was a sweet torture he endured for the sake of marital harmony, but he could not have done anything else and been the man he was.

Eleanor let her fingertips slide down his throat in a

light caress that left a trail of fire across his flesh. Her touch paused upon the thrum of his pulse in his throat and she met his gaze as if amazed by the power of her own touch. Alexander smiled, hoping she saw the fullness of his admiration for her.

She caught her breath and her lashes fluttered downward, as if she could not bear to look upon his passion. She fanned out her hands and ran them down his chest, her touch firmer as she felt him through his garb. Alexander stood utterly still and watched her, unable to discern her response.

Her hands landed upon the buckle of his belt with purpose and he caught his breath. Then she looked up, her eyes glittering with desire and his heart clenched. "You could claim a foundling and grant him your name," she mused.

Alexander pretended to consider this. He clenched his fists at his sides, for he dared not reach for her yet and frighten her. "I could, if only I was not so proud of my lineage. Perhaps that would be more fitting for a second son, instead of my heir."

Eleanor unfastened his belt and laid it aside, then slid her hands beneath his tabard. "Doubtless you speak aright," she said as she coaxed the garment over his head. She unknotted the tie in his chemise with quick fingers. She wrinkled her nose, then cast him a playful glance. "But I have heard that your wife is cold, and does not welcome you between her thighs."

Alexander shook a finger at her. "You should not give credit to rumor!"

"Is she not frosty, then?" Eleanor opened her eyes wide, then tugged his chemise over his head and cast it aside. She swallowed as she looked upon him, then raised one hand slowly and laid it over his heart.

Alexander captured her hand within his, turned it within his grasp, and kissed her palm. She watched him, scarce seeming to breathe, and he smiled at her. "She has endured much," he said softly. "And keeps her secrets closely as a result. Any man with his wits about him would see that time is the best salve for this wound."

She pulled her hand free of his grasp, then reached for the lace of his chausses. "My father oft said that a woman has need of a babe in her arms to be truly content. Perhaps your wife could be persuaded to surrender that son to you."

Alexander was confused by her persistent references to sons. Had her failure to conceive been at the root of her former husbands' displeasure? "My father oft said that it is love that makes a woman truly content. Although I would welcome a son or even a daughter, it is not imperative that I have either."

She glanced up, clearly surprised.

Alexander smiled. "I have two younger brothers: one has no title and the other has seen his inheritance collapse into rubble. Either of them would welcome the suzerainty of Kinfairlie, should I be without heir."

"There are more of you than the sisters I have met?"

"Seven siblings do I have. Five sisters and two brothers."

"That is astonishing," she said, clearly amazed. "And your father had how many wives?"

"Only one. He loved her with such fervor that he would never have claimed another, had she died before him." Alexander cupped Eleanor's face in his hands while she marveled at this and brushed his lips across hers. "But because of my brothers, my lady wife need not fret about bearing sons. There is no concern that she must prove herself useful to remain in my affections."

Eleanor regarded him for a long moment, then her fingers eased into his chausses. She caressed him so that he caught his breath; then she smiled.

"You like this," she said, though her manner seemed so dutiful that Alexander guessed the reason behind her deed.

He laid claim to her hand, halting her fingers. "You have a beguiling touch, but I would not be embraced for duty alone." He watched her, noting her surprise. "I welcome your caress, Eleanor, only if it is one you wish to give, not if it is one you feel obliged to give."

She eyed him for a long moment; then her lips curved in a warm smile. She reached for her laces and quickly loosed her kirtle, stepping out of the ample silk folds. She untied her garters, her fingers shaking in her haste, then cast her stockings aside. She shed her chemise and shook out her hair so that it fell shimmering down her back. Her flesh gleamed in the morning's light, her nipples beaded in the chill of the chamber. She was as beauteous as a nymph, as graceful as a fairy maiden in one of Vivienne's favored tales.

But she turned and offered her hand to Alexander, her eyes uncommonly bright, a smile upon her lips. "Isabella speaks aright," she said, her voice husky. "Her potion does indeed conjure a sweetness between man and wife that knows no compare. Come, my lord, join me in my bath before it cools overmuch. You may find your life complete, but my fondest desire is to surrender to you a son. To succeed in that quest, I will have need of your aid."

Alexander laughed and took his lady's hand. He kissed her knuckles even as he shed his chausses. "I am only too glad to come to a lady's assistance," he said with gallantry, and she shook a chiding finger at him.

"You will aid only this lady in matters of creating sons," she teased, a merry glint in her eye, and Alexander was content to cede to that request as well.

This time, he resolved, the lady would be atop him, the better to encourage her confidence. The very prospect of Eleanor's surprise made Alexander smile, though it was a merry while before she discovered what so amused her lord husband.

And then she was so astonished that he laughed in truth.

IT WAS LATE AFTERNOON when Alexander descended to the hall. He called for some cold meat, for activities abed had ensured that he missed the midday meal, and joined Rhys at a table. That man looked more grim than was his custom.

"How fares Anthony?" Alexander asked.

"Well enough, I suppose. He slept this morn."

"And what tidings have you of the wine?"

Rhys rolled his eyes. "You have a busy hall, Alexander. It seems that every soul in Kinfairlie passed through your kitchens last evening. Some noted the wine and some did not; some know when they were there and others do not. All were savoring their measure of the laird's ale, so their testimony reflects as much."

"Ah. I had feared it might be so."

"It is impossible to eliminate any one person from any list of possibilities." Rhys braced his elbows upon the board and gave Alexander a steady look. "Which means, of course, that any man of sense must look at the best prospects first. Does any soul wish you dead?"

"Not as I know of it." Alexander shrugged. "But then, it would be particularly witless to tell one's victim of one's intent."

"This is no jest," Rhys said sternly.

"I meant no jest. I meant only that someone who would conjure such a scheme, the better to ensure that he or she could not be named as responsible, must be keen of wit."

"That is fairly spoken," Rhys acknowledged. He traced a circle on the wooden table and Alexander guessed that he would not welcome whatsoever his brother-in-law said next. "It must also be said that whosoever is responsible must know something of poisons." Rhys looked up then, his expression somber.

Alexander pushed aside the remainder of his bread, his hunger eliminated. "You speak of Eleanor."

Rhys took a deep breath. "I confess that I possess a wariness of healing women and those who know much of toxins, but there is much uncommon in this, Alexander." He ticked points off on his fingers. "Consider that Alan Douglas has called her a murderess. . . ."

"Alan Douglas is scarcely a man whose word is of repute!"

"Consider that he, too, alluded to some tale that she had killed her first spouse as well. . . ."

"She explained this to me. It is not of import."

"Consider that she did not confess to you her full name," Rhys said with resolve. "I do not excuse my wife and her sisters from responsibility in this ploy, but Eleanor was the sole one who knew that wedding her would pit you against your neighbors. She should have spoken of her alliances."

"She and I have discussed this matter as well."

"Aye, and if you wed a woman charged with murder, even if that is but rumor, you must wonder at the truth of it when your own life is in peril." Rhys held up two fingers. "Twice in so many days your life has hung in the balance, Alexander. What does your wife gain in your absence? Kinfairlie is a prize, to be sure."

Alexander turned away with a frown, not wanting to correct Rhys's notions of Kinfairlie's wealth. Any confession to Rhys would be certain to make its way to Madeline's ears and thence to those of all his siblings. "It is not so rich as that," he said gruffly.

Rhys snorted. "It is more than many can call to their names, to be sure. Do you not think it odd that a woman should be so anxious to wed as your lady has proved to be?"

Rhys leaned forward. "Do you not think it odd that when you proposed to annul the match, the lady not only ensured that your nuptials were consummated, but that there were witnesses of her deed? You cannot easily put her aside after that."

"I do not think she called for the witnesses," Alexander said.

"Believe what you must."

Alexander stared at the board, doubts roiling within him. "She has confessed only to wanting a son," he said quietly.

Rhys scoffed. "So with your demise, she would administer Kinfairlie as regent in that son's stead. She would not be the first woman intent upon ensuring herself affluent and powerful without the burden of a spouse."

"Rhys, you cannot know this . . . ," Alexander protested.

"No, I cannot." Rhys pushed to his feet. "It is no more than rumor and speculation, and I pray that I do not malign an innocent woman. But there were whispers in your hall, Alexander, and suspicion in the thoughts of many."

"Alan Douglas does not have a word of repute."

"Yet still his brother, Ewen, is dead, and still his lady wife came here with no more than the garb upon her back. Why else would she have fled Tivotdale upon her husband's demise, other than her own guilt?"

Alexander stared at the table, his thoughts roiling.

Rhys heaved a sigh. "We plan to depart for Caerwyn on the morrow, as you well know, though if you would have us linger at Kinfairlie, we will do this. I would not leave you in peril."

Alexander forced a smile, defending his lady wife without a second thought. "Rhys, I appreciate your counsel, but I think you make much of little. Rumor has served the lady poorly, as have her former spouses, but I know our match will prove amiable."

"Then ask her about this. That is all I request of you. At least have her explanation of what occurred at Tivotdale."

"He struck her, Rhys."

"That would not see a man dead."

Alexander wondered, for Rhys spoke justly. What had occurred at Tivotdale? Why had Eleanor fled, and done so in such fear of pursuit?

Rhys studied Alexander for a long moment, then shrugged. "I thank you for the courtesy of accepting my honest speech for what it is," he said, his tone more formal than it had been previously.

"I thank you for your counsel, Rhys."

Rhys left him then. Alexander watched as Madeline came to her spouse with a smile and Rhys bent his head toward his lady wife. His hand landed upon her belly as he attended her words and Alexander was pleased at the light in his sister's eyes.

He turned away, thinking it unseemly to watch them so openly, and considered the ale in his cup. Surely Rhys was wrong? But Eleanor had been too close at hand the night before, and she had lingered uncommonly long in the kitchens. There was no reason for her to have performed an inventory on Christmas night, to be sure. She could have brought the wine to him herself, instead of finding other labors in the kitchens.

Unless she wished to be certain that her victim was beyond aid by the time she ascended to the solar.

Alexander heaved a sigh, awkward with his own suspicions. He could not argue that her seduction of him had been deliberate, and even she had not protested that conclusion. He recalled Eleanor's capabilities with accounts, her counsel on balancing his ledgers, her competent administration of his hall. What need had such a woman of a spouse, once she had a son?

The lady had as much as admitted that she had no intent to love him. Indeed, she did not believe in love, which meant that her objectives must all be worldly ones.

Like property and power.

Could Rhys be right?

Alexander pushed to his feet, newly restless. He strode to the kitchens to assure himself that Anthony recovered.

It would be reprehensible if that man's loyalty was rewarded with malice. Alexander hoped and prayed that no one in his household paid the price for any foul intent toward himself.

THE CASTELLAN'S PALLET had been moved closer to the hearth, yet out of the way, the better to see him warm. Anthony must have been recovering, for he had braced himself on one elbow to watch the proceedings.

"You should use less saffron in the sauce," he said to the cook. "It is cursed expensive and my lord is not wrought of coin."

"If there is not sufficient saffron, the sauce will be thin and pale," the cook argued. "Which will tell every guest that his presence at the laird's table is not welcome."

"But still . . . ," Anthony argued.

"But still, the lady has ordered a saffron sauce!"

"But still . . . ," Anthony persisted.

"But still," the cook retorted, his voice rising with every word. "It is Christmas and the cost of saffron is of less import than a proper sauce!"

"Well said," Alexander interjected.

Everyone in the kitchen straightened at his words and spun to face him, for they had been unaware of his presence.

The cook bowed deeply. "Good day, my lord. Would you review the menu for the morrow?"

"Has my lady wife discussed it with you?"

"Yes, my lord."

"Then I trust all is well."

"Yes, my lord." The cook waved at his minions and they scampered back to their labors. His wife chopped scallions with a vengeance, her lips tight with disapproval.

"Is there a matter of concern, Rose?" Alexander asked, and that woman took a fortifying breath.

"I would beg your leave, my lord, to speak freely."

Alexander inclined his head. "Of course." He feared that Rose would indict Eleanor as well, but she jabbed her knife in Anthony's direction.

"If ever a man deserved another measure of what laid him low, there he be! All the day long he has counseled us upon what we know best how to do, and truly"—she waggled the blade with no small threat—"my patience thins." She drew another breath and met Alexander's gaze. "If it pleases my lord, it would also please us to have your castellan heal elsewhere."

Alexander dropped his voice to a conspiratorial tone. "My mother oft said that any man sufficiently hale to complain is sufficiently hale to rise from the sickbed."

Rose smiled with satisfaction. "I always knew your mother to be wise beyond compare, my lord. God rest her soul." And she crossed herself, that considerable blade yet in her hand.

"Use some care, Rose, or you will be bereft of a nose," Alexander teased, and the cook's wife laughed. He made his way to Anthony's side and was pleased to see that the older man's eyes gleamed and his color was good. "What say you, Anthony? Do you feel hale again?"

"I but await instruction from your lady wife, my lord, for she is beyond competent in such matters." The older man beamed, his admiration for Eleanor clearly undiminished.

"The lady Eleanor insisted that she would look upon me this evening and I pledged to await her decision at that time."

The company in the kitchens groaned as one.

"Perhaps you might be persuaded to take a respite in the great hall," Alexander suggested. "The Yule log burns there, so the hall is almost as warm as the kitchens, and you can better supervise the replacement of the strewing herbs from there."

"An excellent notion, my lord. I should not wish for your lady to find disfavor with such a simple matter."

The cook gestured and two young boys rushed to aid Anthony to rise to his feet. Alexander swallowed a smile at his impression that the castellan was being ushered out of the kitchen with haste. He winked at the cook as he accompanied the castellan, and the cook winked in return.

He knew he did not imagine the muted cheer that echoed in their wake.

"Women," Anthony expounded, "have a most admirable affection for detail and your lady wife, true to this, specified very clearly which plants should be strewn in the hall. What foresight you show, my lord, in perceiving that I wished to be present to ensure that all was as she had commanded." He heaved a sigh when he reached a bench and spared Alexander a glance. "Such a marvel of a woman, of course, must always endure jealous gossip at her own expense in her abode. It is a failure of human nature, after all, to despise those who are better than we ourselves."

"Truly?" Alexander asked. "What have you heard said against my lady wife?"

"I would not insult your ears with such petty detail, my lord."

"I bid you tell me, Anthony. I will not surrender such tales to my lady, upon this you have no fear."

The older man smiled. "You were always a most gallant man. Your father would be proud of you, my lord."

Alexander looked away, not certain he wished to speculate upon that notion.

The castellan cleared his throat. "It was Jeannie, my lord, who said the worst of it. I think her manner sour in the way of one who has been discredited. She was not present to aid me and resents the presence of one who knows as much of herbs as she does, to be sure. . . ."

"And what did Jeannie say?"

"That your lady did not save my life. Can you imagine the folly of that?" Anthony huffed in his outrage. "After your lady deigned to soil her own noble fingers—"

"But what did Jeannie mean?" Alexander interrupted him to ask.

"She said that if it had been a killing dose, I would have died regardless of what your lady did to assist me. She said that among toxins, aconite is most quick and it is fatal." He held Alexander's gaze. "You must recall, my lord, that Jeannie is aged and bitter. . . ."

"What else did she say?"

"She said that it must have been a warning, a measure inadequate to kill a man, but one solely meant to weaken him."

Alexander tented his fingers together as he considered this. Why would any person wish him to be warned? And warned of what? He could not fathom such reasoning, for surely, if a man was wanted dead, there was no justification for a half-measure.

He smiled for Anthony. "I recall also that Jeannie is oft said to be mad."

"Just so, my lord, just so." Anthony smiled, reassured that he had not given offense, and Alexander left him to harass the maids who labored in the hall.

He needed to think, and to do so in the absence of his wife. Though the evidence against Eleanor was scant or nonexistent, the possibilities were sufficiently troubling. If Rhys was correct, then Alexander planting his seed in his lady's belly might see his days numbered.

On the other hand, Rhys did not know all of Eleanor's tale. Instinct told Alexander that Eleanor had need of his trust to see the wounds of her past healed, despite how evidence might be mustered against her. For the moment, he chose to avoid his lady and her copious charms.

Fortunately, he had duties aplenty to perform.

SOMETHING WAS AMISS.

Eleanor could fairly smell it. She awakened alone in Alexander's bed, and though she lingered there until the sky darkened, he did not return to her. She washed and dressed then and descended to the hall. Every person there greeted her politely, but their gazes danced away from hers. No one stayed by her side, though their manners could not be faulted.

It was wariness she sensed and Eleanor knew the reason for it. Only Anthony greeted her with what appeared to be genuine pleasure. He expressed gratitude for her aid and attention, though was clearly glad to be given leave to return to his duties.

And then Eleanor was alone again, as she had been alone for most of her days and nights. She checked upon the various tasks she had left requests to be done, though she knew full well what she would find. Every command she had granted had been fulfilled, every detail was organized as she had seen fit. Alexander's hall was as well-managed as she could ensure, yet Alexander himself was notably absent.

She heard tell of him heading to the village, that he fulfilled some old tradition by accepting a cup of ale from the sheriff, and felt only disappointment that she had not been included. Doubtless he had not wished to awaken her, for Alexander was chivalrous to a fault, but Eleanor had a persistent sense that there was more to the tale.

His sisters invited her to share in their embroidery, but it was clear that they had each claimed a specific panel of the piece to highlight their own work. They chattered to each other of people she did not know and relations she had never met and past Yuletides that she had not shared. Eleanor knew that they did not mean to be cruel, but she was achingly aware that she was not customarily in their company.

And that as yet, she did not belong at Kinfairlie.

Vivienne's two daughters, perhaps sensing her mood, demanded of her a tale, but Eleanor could only deny them. She did not know any tales, at least none suitable for such young girls. They professed astonishment at her ignorance with such youthful candor that she could not be offended, then returned to their mother, who did know many tales.

Once again, Eleanor found herself yearning for all she had not known in her days. Her father had had no patience with fanciful tales and her tutors had not spared the time on such fripperies, at his dictate.

She paced the hall with dissatisfaction, lacking some ingredient in the recipe for her own delight. That it was one she could readily name made little difference.

That it was the presence of a man should have been more troubling than it was.

Alexander remained absent until it was well past time to retire. Eleanor would not name his departure as her malady, for that would imply that she already relied upon him. After all, they had met abed already this day in the quest for their son, so it was of little import if she did not encounter him.

So reason informed her, but still she found herself seeking a glimpse of his merry smile and glancing up whenever the portal to the bailey was opened.

Surely she could not miss her handsome husband so soon after their nuptials, so soon after they had met? Surely she had not been so beguiled by a man's charm that she had forgotten her own determination to rely on no one?

All the same, it was only after every other soul in Kinfairlie had retired that Eleanor climbed the stairs to the laird's chamber. The chamber was cold and lonely without the prospect of hearing Alexander's chuckle, though Anthony had kindled blazes in no less than three braziers. Eleanor shed her garb and climbed into the great, cold bed, listening, listening long into the night.

AN AFTERNOON, A NIGHT, and a morning without her husband's presence told Eleanor the truth. She had been judged and found guilty of trying to poison him, even by this man reputed to be just. Eleanor was disappointed, though she called herself a fool for desiring more of him.

That she would never have expected more from a spouse before meeting Alexander, that he had tainted her thoughts so quickly as this, was nigh too frightening to contemplate.

What else had he changed?

Her expectations abed, to be sure. Eleanor knew that she would never again be able to lie meekly beneath a man laboring for his own pleasure, counting the folds in the draperies upon the bed until he finished his deed.

She descended to the hall, for there were guests departing this day and she would not fail in her duties. Her heart skipped at the first sight of her spouse, who waited at the base of the stairs for her. Eleanor greedily devoured the sight of him, that his hair was yet damp against his collar, that he had changed his chemise. He wore a dark tabard and chausses, as was his custom, the orb of Kinfairlie's heraldic device fairly glowing against the dark wool of his tabard. His tall boots gleamed and a fur-lined cloak hung over his shoulders.

He looked up at her and she halted on the stairs. She noted that his color was less than it had been, that there were shadows beneath his eyes, and she dared to hope that he, too, had slept poorly alone. Alexander's grim countenance gave no encouragement to that, though, and Eleanor feared that the awe with which he had first regarded her was banished forevermore.

She was heartsick at the change in her husband, for he was merry no longer. It was worse to know that her own history was responsible. It helped little that she tingled in his very presence, that she yearned to touch him boldly again, that she wanted nothing more than his heat within her.

That was untrue. Eleanor desired Alexander's smile more than his affection abed. And she wanted to see the glimmer of starlight in his eyes.

But Alexander had no smile for her. He took her hand at the foot of the stairs and placed it within his elbow; his manners perfect, though his manner was cold.

"I trust all is well at the sheriff's abode," Eleanor said, feeling the need to exchange some words with him.

"Well enough," he acknowledged, and she ached for a jest or a wink from this formerly teasing man.

"I heard that you shared a cup with him last evening."

"It is custom."

Eleanor walked beside her spouse, wondering whether she imagined that whispers flew through the gathered company. Anna, the ostler's daughter, smirked at her, as if only biding her time before she claimed the laird's attention. Alexander did not spare Eleanor the slightest glance.

To be fair, he had defended her often, more than any other man had ever done. To be unfair, that only made the injustice of his current restraint sting all the more.

They reached the bailey, where the parties destined for Blackleith and Caerwyn waited. The horses were restless, all riders dressed both somberly and warmly.

Alexander spared a glance for the sky and Eleanor followed his gaze. It was overcast, a winter sky, but not so dark that rain or snow would fall soon. The wind was light, tinged with the salt of the sea.

She liked that Alexander was concerned for the welfare of his guests and his sisters, even when they left his hall. He was protective of those he believed himself obliged to protect, or perhaps he was protective of those who held his affections.

Eleanor yearned fiercely to be in their company.

Anthony brought the stirrup cup, a massive chalice cast in bronze and brimming with wine. He handed it to Eleanor, which confirmed her place in the household to all. He also smiled at her, the only person to do so, and Eleanor found herself grateful for his kindness. She realized then that the censure she felt from Alexander's household was a protectiveness of the laird by his vassals and tenants.

And its root was the same: these people held Alexander in affection and would not suffer any threat to his health. For that, she could scarce blame them.

Eleanor sipped of the cup's contents first, as was proper, and a familiar sweet scent assailed her. A hundred memories were conjured by the smell, each and every one of them prompting her tears. Eleanor had offered the stirrup cup for her father so many times when he rode to battle, and feared so many times that he would not return and she would be left even more alone than already she was. The scent recalled, too, the fear of her own departures, her summons to unknown men at altars far away.

The scent was bitter, or at least the memories it summoned were so.

Eleanor took a deep breath, banishing her past, and smiled for the castellan. "You have flavored it with sweet woodruff," she said graciously, and he nodded. "That is the perfect touch for sending travelers upon their way, for its scent makes a heart merry." It was a lie in her case, though she had oft heard others say as much.

Anthony did not question her assessment. Indeed, the tips of the castellan's ears turned slightly pink, as if he were flustered by her praise. "I thank you, my lady. I merely do my best."

Eleanor turned and offered the cup to Alexander. He watched her as she lifted it to his lips, his gaze so bright that she knew he had not missed her response.

"Does it make you merry?" he asked quietly.

Eleanor shook her head ever so slightly, startled yet again by his perceptiveness. "Departures cannot be merry for those left behind," she responded, her words as soft as his had been.

She pivoted before Alexander could speak and offered the cup to Rhys. That man hesitated ever so slightly before he accepted the chalice.

"Rhys!" Madeline chided in an undertone.

"Eleanor is my lady wife," Alexander said, his words cold. "And I will thank you to show her the respect due to her in our abode."

Madeline caught her breath and looked between the men, but Rhys took the cup. Eleanor knew she was not the only one who noted how his eyes had narrowed, no less how he sniffed the cup's contents before he sipped of it.

Eleanor looked away from his cool gaze, her heart thumping in her chest. Had Alexander defended her because he knew the truth? Had it been only duty that had kept him from her side? Or did he insist simply upon courtesy being shown where it was due?

She did not know and she was surprised to find herself fearful of the truth. She looked in every direction, save that of her husband, for she feared to find disapproval in his eyes, and thought she caught a glimpse of a familiar face in the jostling company. It was a face she had not expected to see again.

Moira? Moira was here?

Moira's presence would be heaven-sent in this moment!

Eleanor peered avidly into the milling company, seeking another glimpse of her faithful maid. But there were only the faces of strangers, any one of whom could have been confused for Moira with a momentary glimpse.

It was undoubtedly the sweet woodruff, the scent of memory, that conjured a familiar sight as well. Moira, after all, had oft been fast at her side when Eleanor had sipped of such a cup. But now Moira was safely at Tivotdale, where Eleanor had left her, where she would be fed and housed and would continue to serve. There was no cause to worry for a soul so competent as Moira.

Those tears mustered in Eleanor's eyes again, though she tried to blink them away. The company stood in awkward silence as Rhys passed the cup to his lady wife.

Rhys's steed nuzzled Eleanor's shoulder and in her loneliness she turned away from Rhys's wary perusal to offer her hand to the horse. The destrier nuzzled her palm and she smiled at the softness of its nose.

"My every treasure for an apple," she murmured, and looked up to find Madeline smiling at her. Madeline sipped of the cup's contents without hesitation, ignoring her husband's slight frown. Rhys's horse nibbled at Eleanor's hair to regain her attention and she smiled despite herself.

She passed the cup then to Erik and Vivienne in turn, stroking the noses of their horses as well. It had always soothed her to be with horses and she recalled how often she had ridden simply to find escape from her situation.

Inevitably she recalled a horrific incident in Millard's abode, and bile rose in her throat. She turned abruptly away from Vivienne and carried the cup back to Alexander, the pain of betrayal as raw as when it had been new.

Alexander took the chalice, then held it to her lips. "Who has left you so oft that you are yet saddened?" he asked when the wine touched her lips and she could not step away.

"It would be quicker to recount those who have not abandoned me," she said; then Father Malachy called his blessing. She sensed that her husband would have asked her more, but he had no chance to do so.

And truly, she was in no mood to protect her secrets from his scrutiny. A mere three days she had known him and that was little enough to prompt her to trust him fully. Had she lost her wits? Millard had been kind for a year!

"Ride in haste and fair weather!" Alexander cried, holding the cup high. "And return to us soon, in good health!"

"Amen!" the company cried; then the men whistled to their parties. Two dozen horses of varying hues of brown turned, their tails flicking, and cantered from the bailey. Rhys and Madeline led one party, Erik and Vivienne the other, each followed by squires and maids and palfreys loaded with trunks.

Erik's two little girls rode with their parents, the eldest cosseted in Erik's lap, the youngest with Vivienne. They waved with such vigor that they might have fallen from the saddles, had their parents not held them so fast. On another day, the sight of their enthusiasm might have made Eleanor smile.

Both parties passed through the cluster of villagers, Madeline and Vivienne accepting their good wishes; then they passed through the old walls. The sisters blew kisses to each other, then to the party before Kinfairlie's doors. Alexander waved, as did his younger sisters, who also shouted farewells. The group divided into two groups, one headed north and one south, and the horses broke into a thundering run.

Kinfairlie's household stood before that keep's portal until the last echo of hoofbeats had faded; then Alexander offered Eleanor his hand once more. His gesture was no more than one of courtesy, she could see, for caution still lurked in his eyes, but he was the husband she had and the husband she had chosen.

It was her duty to regain his trust. Eleanor knew that there were matters well worth the battle to win them and she believed that Alexander's trust was one of them. She knew that she was not without the burden of her past, and she knew it was not in her nature to trust readily.

But she was prepared to try to make a good marriage of this, even to try to create one so wondrous as the one Alexander said he sought.

Further, Eleanor knew how best to begin in seeking such a match. There was one matter, at least, that was simple between herself and Alexander, and confidences were more readily exchanged abed and in privacy.

Feeling uncommonly bold, but knowing that all was at stake, Eleanor lifted Alexander's hand and kissed his knuckles, knowing that she did not imagine how he caught his breath. It was encouraging to have that slight sign that he thought her to be possessed of some allure.

"I missed you last night, my lord," she murmured for

his ears alone, and Alexander met her gaze. "The bed was cold without your presence."

Alexander's eyes, to her dismay, narrowed. "Then perhaps you should have Anthony light another brazier for you this night," he said, his tone so even that they might have been discussing the weather, not his absence from her bed. "I have duties through the new year to attend. I trust that you will find some matter to occupy you in these days."

With no more than that, he left her. He turned crisply away, summoning Anthony and one of his squires as he strode through Kinfairlie's hall as Eleanor yearned after him.

And true to his word, Alexander did not return to the hall that night.

~

ALEXANDER DID NOT SAVOR the choice he had made, though he knew that a bitter deed oft yielded results.

That did not make the enduring of it easier.

Even the weather conspired against him and his determination to check the boundaries of Kinfairlie. It began to rain in cold, steady sheets shortly after his party left the hall and the wind from the sea turned bitter. The snow melted into a churning mess of mud and ice that made their journey even more onerous than it would have been otherwise.

The sole comfort in all of this was that he had not ridden his destrier, but chosen a smaller palfrey instead. Alexander knew that his destrier, Uriel, would have protested such indignity as this weather, and the last censure he had need of in these times was one from the ostler over risking the health of a vigorous and costly steed.

The squires accompanying him did not chatter, as was their custom, nor did the bailiff from the village. The small party checked the western and southern boundaries, some hearty villagers accompanying the party when it was closest to the village. A few mothers taught their young children the marks of the village perimeter in the old way, by boxing the child's ears when he or she reached the village boundary, the better that the line might be recalled.

The party took shelter that night at the sheriff's abode and Alexander felt the burden of exclusively male companionship. The sheriff was unwed, though hospitable. He laid a simple board, though one that Alexander complimented for its generosity. The sheriff's home seemed bereft of comfort to Alexander, who yearned for his own hall. Indeed, he longed for more than the comfort of his own bed and the heat of his own hearth and the sound of his sisters engaged in some petty argument.

He longed for the flash of his wife's eyes, for the sparkle of her wit, for the sweetness of her kisses abed. Worse, Alexander knew that the lady would have welcomed his embrace again, had he been so resolute as to remain at home.

But he sought honesty, and he had noted that Eleanor surrendered details about her history only when she felt obliged to do so. It was her nature to hold her secrets close, and given what she had endured—or what Alexander knew of what she had endured—she had good reason for that. He was impatient, though, and was prepared to compel her to tell him more of her past.

He did not put credence in Rhys's fears, to be sure, but the fact was that Eleanor wished to be wed to him, though Alexander did not know why. She had agreed to wed him on short notice, had cut her thumb to force his proposal, had ensured that their match was consummated when he threatened to have it annulled. She admitted openly that she wished for a son, though Alexander did not see why she had chosen him to grant her that child.

After all, the lady had no belief in the notion of love between man and wife. Much as it galled Alexander to admit it, she could not be smitten with him.

So why had she chosen him?

He did not know, but he did know that she surrendered tales when she believed their marriage to be in jeopardy. So, he left her at Kinfairlie, for he could not linger in her presence and feign anger with her for no reason. He still felt a knave for his choice, but Alexander was determined to oust his lady's secrets.

For he did believe in love, and further, he guessed that Eleanor could capture his heart fully. He needed to know for certain, however, that she was worthy of his trust. Alexander only hoped that this short interval bore fruit, for he knew not what else to do.

For he feared that he would not have to spend much more time in his lady's presence, witnessing her strength and her ardor and her intellect, to lose his own heart in truth.

ON THAT SAME NIGHT that Alexander tossed and turned in the sheriff's abode and Eleanor paced the solar floor,

Elizabeth dreamed a familiar dream. She tossed and turned in her sleep, but the progress of the dream was relentless. She did not want to review her part in ensuring Rosamunde's demise, but the demons of the night left her no choice. Elizabeth stirred, fighting against slumber, but to no avail.

She is with her siblings in a tavern and concern sits among their company at the board. The dream is so vivid, she might be there again. They ride in pursuit of Madeline and Rhys, and Elizabeth tastes again her exhaustion, her fear, Alexander's frustration. She watches herself save the fairy Darg from that spriggan's own affection for ale. She could not have chosen differently, she could not have let the fairy drown, but the fact is clear.

Once, she saved the spriggan's life.

The dream shifts with merciless predictability. She knows this dream and she loathes it, but it holds her fast in its clutches yet again. Elizabeth sits in the upper chamber of Ravensmuir with Vivienne. Time has passed: her hair is longer and Vivienne is more woman than she was months earlier in the tavern. Again Darg's affection for ale betrays the fairy, and again Elizabeth sees the spriggan saved from certain demise. Again she could have made no other choice; again she sees the import of her own deed.

Twice, she has saved the fairy's life.

The dream changes yet again and Elizabeth knows this to be the worst of it. She fights to awaken, but cannot. She would scream in protest but the dream condemns her to silence. She is in the labyrinth beneath Ravensmuir. She sees her aunt Rosamunde and her heart aches that she could have prevented that woman's demise. And all un-

folds precisely as it did so many months ago. Darg and Rosamunde fight, and in the ensuing struggle and confusion, the spriggan is nigh forgotten in the cold water that flows in the chasms of the labyrinth.

But Elizabeth notes Darg's absence. Elizabeth insists upon saving the spriggan. Elizabeth risks her own life to retrieve Darg.

For thrice, she had saved the spriggan's life. Three times Elizabeth had had the chance to turn away; three times she could have let the admittedly malicious spriggan die. But because she did not look away, Darg survived.

As did the spriggan's hatred for Rosamunde.

And then, just when she expected to awaken, Elizabeth's dream took a new twist.

Elizabeth is in the labyrinth of Ravensmuir, the labyrinth that cannot be entered any longer, for it has fallen to ruins. She is crawling through the rubble and she is calling for her lost aunt. Elizabeth feels the dampness of tears upon her own cheeks; she feels the heat cast by the single flickering flame of her lantern.

She knows somehow that she is in the great cavern that once marked the lowest point of the labyrinth, the chamber that had once had a high ceiling carved from the stone. From here, one could climb to the keep or walk to the hidden cove that led to the sea, the cove where a small boat could be hidden. She does not know how she knows as much, for there is only rubble and loose stone all around her and a fearsome shadow over her head.

She tastes her own bile, fearing that she has been summoned to the site of Rosamunde's demise. Indeed, she spies something in the rubble, something that could be the toe of a black leather boot.

Elizabeth prays, but she crawls closer, seemingly unable to do otherwise. Just as she reaches the boot—for that is what it is—a gust of wind extinguishes the flame of her lantern.

Elizabeth is plunged into darkness and her heart fairly stops in terror. Is she destined to die in the labyrinth as well? How will she climb to safety? How will she make her way out of the rubble without a light?

The stone begins to rumble overhead. It is shifting. Elizabeth gasps in terror. The first loose stone strikes her shoulder and she bellows in fear.

The rock begins to fall in earnest. She scrambles in the direction she thinks she has come, but her fingers land upon the leather of that boot toe. She feels a scream gathering in her throat, for she guesses that there is the foot of a corpse within that boot. She will go mad in Ravensmuir's caverns and no one will know of her fate. The scream begins to tear loose of her throat.

Then a light appears. The light is golden and welcoming, it seems to fill a portal that Elizabeth does not recall seeing before. And framed in that portal is a familiar silhouette, a woman whose very presence makes Elizabeth gasp in astonishment.

"Hasten yourself, child," Rosamunde says with some urgency. "We have not all the day and all the night to see this resolved. Hurry! Come to me immediately!"

Then all turned black.

Elizabeth awakened, a cold sweat on her back and tears upon her cheeks. The dream named the root of it: by not letting the Fates claim the spriggan each time they tried to do so, by interfering in the order of things, Elizabeth herself was responsible for Rosamunde's demise.

It was her fault that Rosamunde was dead, for it was her fault that Rosamunde had been compelled to return to Ravensmuir to sate the fairy's greed, her fault that Rosamunde had been within Ravensmuir's labyrinths when they finally collapsed. Elizabeth wept, for it was bitter that she, who loved Rosamunde so well, should have been the one responsible for that woman's death.

All the same, she had done what she had to do, for she could not have turned aside while any creature was in danger. In so doing, she had condemned the one person she loved more than any other.

Her sisters slept soundly, the echo of their even breathing infuriating their youngest sibling. What sweet dreams did they savor? Why must she be tormented by this fearsome dream, nigh every night? As Elizabeth lay there, brooding and bitter, she recalled the last, new part of her dream. She sat up, so sudden was her understanding.

She was being summoned. She did not know what her dream of Rosamunde meant, but she knew where she must go to find out.

Ravensmuir.

Alexander, of course, would never permit her to undertake such folly, and Elizabeth did not imagine that Eleanor would see her side in this endeavor, either.

Which only meant that Elizabeth had need of a scheme.

Chapter Nine

~

THE SUN ROSE with a reluctance that echoed Alexander's own uncertainties in returning to his hall. The sea was like silvered glass that morning, tranquil as Alexander was not, and the sky was clearing. There was fog along the shoreline, clustered in the nooks of the coast, but Alexander found himself studying the distant waves, gilded as they were with the first light of the sun. His party galloped along the coast, checking the boundary markers along this last stretch of Kinfairlie's borders.

The sea had always fascinated Alexander and he realized now that the root of his fascination was its change-ability. Did his fascination with his enigmatic wife have a similar root?

Was his fascination as treacherous? The sea, after all, had shown its capriciousness in claiming the lives of both of his parents a year ago. Did Eleanor have a similar fate in scheme for him? Or was the lady falsely maligned?

Their duty completed before the sun rose high, the party turned back to Kinfairlie as one. The horses began to canter, needing no encouragement to return to the comfort of Kinfairlie's stables. Alexander heard hoofbeats and thought for a moment that the passing of his own party was made greater by echoes on the walls of the homes in the village.

But no. Destriers approached. Alexander knew this with the certainty of one raised to be familiar with horses of all kinds. And they were numerous, so numerous that he feared the intent of their riders. Not for the first time, Alexander regretted that Kinfairlie's curtain wall had never been rebuilt, no less that he had no coin with which to have it rebuilt now.

"Who rides to Kinfairlie?" Alexander shouted as he rode into his own bailey, noting that his sentinels peered into the distance. They stood on what high points there were, the rubble of the ancient wall included, and more than one had his bow at the ready.

"Praise be!" one sentinel shouted in apparent relief. "The laird of Ravensmuir arrives!"

"Praise be, indeed," Alexander said with a smile of relief, then made his way to greet his younger brother.

It was Malcolm, against all expectation. What a blessing that his brother had come home to celebrate Christmas! Alexander had feared that Malcolm's duties would preclude such a journey this year, though truly Ravensmuir was not far. He waved an enthusiastic greeting.

Then Alexander's eyes narrowed at the size of Malcolm's company and his arm stilled. Something was amiss.

A veritable herd of horses formed the arriving party, though not all of them bore riders. Each and every one was a glossy steed of Ravensmuir's breeding, each one as black as the night, each one tall and proud. They stepped high and arched their necks, these beasts who had no equal in Christendom, their dark manes flowing, their nostrils flaring.

Alexander counted all eight of the destriers currently siring in Ravensmuir's stables, as well as the two dozen mares, which were none of them much smaller than the stallions. Seven foals had been born this year, he knew this from Malcolm's missives, and all seven were in this company.

With dismay, he realized that the riders accompanying Malcolm were his brother's household staff, his ostlers, and his squires.

They would all need to eat. This was Alexander's first thought and his second was a mental review of his inventories. Alexander felt cursed again by the realities of his circumstance. Every joy that came to him had to be tempered these days, it seemed.

Malcolm halted his steed before Alexander, dismounted, and doffed his gloves as Alexander did the same. Malcolm removed his helm, revealing the ebony of his hair so like Alexander's own, and his expression was uncommonly solemn.

"What is amiss?" Alexander said by way of greeting. He guessed that there was some issue at import behind Malcolm's arrival, no less with the fact that his brother was accompanied by his entire household.

Malcolm gripped Alexander's proffered hand, then met his gaze steadily. "The ravens left."

Alexander's heart sank. It could not be so! One glance at Malcolm told him that it was the truth, but still he felt obliged to argue the matter. "But they never leave Ravensmuir. You know that as well as I."

"Nonetheless, they have left."

"Surely they will return shortly, and but make a sojourn away." Alexander forced a smile. "Who can say what birds scheme? Doubtless you lose faith too soon."

Malcolm's lips set. "They never leave for even a day, you know as much. They have been gone this past week."

"But—"

Malcolm interrupted him, his manner severe. "They took flight as one, dozens of them, and flew east with nary a cry. They waited for me to witness this departure, I know it well."

"But that is madness."

"They waited for me to leave the stables, that I would see their departure. They waited to ensure that I knew the import of their choice."

Alexander laid a hand upon his brother's shoulder. He knew the import of the ravens' flight as well as his brother did, and he could understand Malcolm's bitterness. It was said that the presence of the birds at Ravensmuir endorsed the laird in power, so their absence could not be interpreted in many ways.

The Lammergeier siblings had been taught the tale of Ravensmuir's ravens from the cradle, though Alexander had always thought it whimsy. So, he had been convinced, had Malcolm, for Malcolm had always had even less patience with fanciful tales.

Alexander considered the size of the watchful company with some consternation, wondering how he would feed all of these souls for the remainder of the winter. "I think you put too much credence in this old tale," he said, hoping to reassure his brother.

"How can it be interpreted otherwise?" Malcolm demanded with anger. "Ravensmuir has crumbled to rubble, its labyrinth collapsed and the keep fallen atop the ruins. A rabbit can scarce work its way into the old hall, so collapsed is the structure. The laird himself is dead, lost in those very caverns, his body is not recovered, and his heir is yet untested. The ravens left, as the old portent recounts, because there is no true laird at Ravensmuir."

"It is but a tale, Malcolm."

"It is an ancient tale and I see now that it is a true one. The ravens do not find me worthy, thus they have abandoned me." Malcolm sighed and scowled into the distance, his voice softening. "I would prefer to discount it, Alexander. I would prefer to find no merit in old portents, but this one cannot be evaded. The birds merely echo my own convictions. I am ill-prepared for this inheritance. It is less than a single year since Uncle Tynan welcomed me to his household, and though I learned much beneath his tutelage, that is but a fraction of what I need to know to make any good of Ravensmuir, especially the ruin it has become."

Alexander considered the company, virtually all men, and found them looking as uncertain as their suzerain. "What do you mean to do?"

Malcolm glanced back to those who followed them. "We have been living in the stables since the keep's collapse, Alexander. Though these men have served me well, it is unfitting that they abide in such circumstance and with such uncertainty of their future." He met Alexander's gaze anew. "I come to ask you to take both men and steeds beneath your care at Kinfairlie. Indeed, I come to entreat you to do as much. I surrender my all to you, for you clearly are better prepared to administer a holding."

"But Kinfairlie has always looked to Ravensmuir as its suzerain."

"I would make you suzerain of both."

Alexander's chest tightened to the point that he could scarce breathe. "And what of you?"

Malcolm straightened. "I mean to seek my fortune." He heaved a sigh. "And perhaps in time, I will show myself worthy of assuming the burden of Ravensmuir again, if you see so fit as to grant it to me."

Alexander was tempted to tell his brother of the truth of Kinfairlie, but he feared that it would be too much for Malcolm to know that both holdings were in some jeopardy. "But you are already Laird of Ravensmuir, Malcolm. Is that title not sufficient for you? Think before you surrender your greatest prize."

Malcolm almost smiled, looking much older than his twenty summers. "As Ravensmuir stands, no, being its laird is not sufficient for me. I can do nothing for my holding but watch it crumble to oblivion. Our legacy deserves better, Alexander, and I intend to find the means to make Ravensmuir glorious again. In the meantime, I leave its administration in capable hands."

Alexander did not know what to say. Not only did he believe himself less than capable of succeeding in this feat, but Ravensmuir was more of a liability than an asset. It possessed no village and no fields, thus had no tithes. Its treasury had once been refilled by the trading of religious relics, but now those relics had all been sold and removed. Ravensmuir was of greater import as a legacy: it stood as a keep and piece of land to be defended for the sake of family history, but one that had little merit of its own to offer.

Especially to a laird already destitute.

Malcolm laid a hand upon Alexander's shoulder, apparently misunderstanding the reasons for his brother's reluctance to accept Ravensmuir. "Do not fear for me, Alexander. I will find the way somehow, I will return to rebuild our inheritance, and we will both know my feat to be done when the ravens land in Ravensmuir's bailey once more."

Alexander's voice rose in frustration. "Listen to yourself, Malcolm. You cannot choose your course based upon the doings of *birds*!"

Malcolm sobered and his gaze was steely. "I can and I do, for the ravens of Ravensmuir are no mere birds. You should know that as well as I do."

There was something uncanny about his brother's assertion, and Alexander regarded Malcolm with skepticism. "Surely you did not learn to speak with them, as it is said the lairds of Ravensmuir can do?"

Malcolm averted his face. "Uncle Tynan taught me much, but there is still more to learn. Will you accept Ravensmuir's seal or no?"

Alexander cursed, shoved his hand through his hair, and paced. Four dozen more men to feed. Three dozen massive, hungry horses. Miles of territory to defend, with no more coin in his coffers. His heart sank at the hope in the expressions of Malcolm's company.

But what else could he do?

"I will hold it in trust for you, no more and no less," he said with resolve. "Uncle Tynan chose you as his heir and I would stand by his choice, whether you have faith in it or not."

"Will you stable the horses as well? You are welcome

to breed them in my absence, so long as you ensure that they are not poorly treated. They, too, are part of our legacy."

"My stable is humble, but it is yours," Alexander said with resignation. "I know not how they will be fed, for we have not made provision for such a number of horses for the winter, but—"

"There is hay and straw at Ravensmuir," Malcolm interrupted firmly. "I spent the last of Ravensmuir's coin upon it, and it is yours, of course, for you are now laird." He dug in his purse, then put the seal of Ravensmuir in Alexander's hand. It seemed more weighty than Alexander might have expected.

"I thank you," Malcolm said, seemingly relieved as soon as its burden passed from his grasp. His words turned hoarse. "I knew that you would aid me, Alexander. You were always resourceful, despite your many jests, and always would give assistance where it was most needed."

"You must remain until Epiphany at least, for you cannot journey through the holy days." He managed to summon a smile of encouragement for his brother. "We might well find a solution for your woes between ourselves by that time."

Malcolm's smile turned rueful. "I doubt it, Alexander, though I welcome the prospect." He heaved a sigh, his expression a perfect echo of what Alexander's own mood had been for much of this past year. "In truth, I do not know where I should ride, I know only that I cannot remain." His smile broadened. "Perhaps I will find an heiress to wed."

"Perhaps you will find a sorceress to wed," Alexander

muttered, for he doubted that any woman's dowry could see both of these keeps rebuilt. His brother chuckled. "Come, break your fast. A problem always looks less formidable when one's belly is full."

Malcolm agreed with this, and Alexander commanded the men to take the steeds to the stable. He summoned his own ostler and ensured that that man's authority was clear to Malcolm's ostler, though it was apparent that the men would consult each other. The pair set immediately to assessing stables and steeds, and organizing the party that would return with wagons for Ravensmuir's stores.

Alexander looked at the seal, so burdened with his family's history, as Malcolm led his own stallion into the stables. He turned the seal, letting the early light play upon it, acknowledging his mixed feelings. On the one hand, it would be an honor to wield this seal, even for a short time. On the other, Ravensmuir could only sweep the last vestige of silver dust from his treasury.

He glanced skyward, perhaps hoping for divine aid, and spied movement at the window of the solar. He looked again and saw that it was Eleanor, her unbound hair stirring in the wind while she stood motionless. She watched him as he watched her and he felt a prickle of awareness beneath her gaze.

He had the curious sense that she knew what he held, that she knew what had just occurred, though she could not possibly have heard their words. And what would she make of these tidings? She began to lean out the window, as if she would hail him or congratulate him over adding to his holdings.

Alexander closed his fist over the seal and pushed it into his purse. It might be folly, but holding all of his family's legacy made him doubly determined to survive whatever intent the lady might have for him.

The simplest solution, he realized with sudden vigor, had been his first impulse. He had to win her affection in truth, for no woman would be anxious to lose the man who held her heart.

By any reckoning, he had at least nine months to do so, for it would take nine months for any son to show himself—and his gender—to the world.

Such a feat still meant that Alexander had to unveil Eleanor's many secrets first. It was fortunate indeed that he was cursed stubborn, or so his sisters had oft maintained. This was one challenge that Alexander meant to win. He spared his wife a last glance, noting that she withdrew into their chamber, then strode to the hall.

He had need of a fortifying meal to face the challenge this lady presented.

HORSES!

Eleanor awakened to the thunder of hoofbeats. She had fallen asleep atop the bed linens, still in her garb from the day before. At the sound of horses, she was on her feet and at the window. She caught her breath as the most magnificent beasts she had ever seen galloped into Kinfairlie's bailey. They were exquisite creatures, each of them with a coat of gleaming black so dark it might have been unnatural.

She had never seen their like, and Eleanor had seen many steeds. Indeed, she loved horses so that her first urge was to run to the stables to greet these beasts. They were massive but gracefully wrought, their nostrils flared and their necks arched proudly. Their tails and manes were long and silky, and as dark as ebony. They stamped with regal impatience when they were halted, as if they would have run clear to Jerusalem, given their head.

And there were so many of them. Eleanor leaned against the wall beside the window, her knees weak with the desire to ride one of these splendid beasts. She dared not leave the window, barely dared to blink, so anxious was she to feast upon the sight of them.

She noted belatedly that Alexander stood before them, his hair nigh as dark as the coats of the sleek steeds. The man who spoke with him shared his coloring and his height. They seemed to be arguing. Were they friends or family? She could not hear a word they said, and her gaze flicked between the horses and her husband.

Something was resolved, for both horses and guest turned toward the stables. Alexander glanced up, and though her impulse was to hide herself from view, Eleanor held her ground. Her heart fluttered with the hope that he would come to her, but Alexander turned away, his silent dismissal sending Eleanor's heart plummeting to her toes.

But she was no frail maiden who would hide in her chambers. If Alexander would not come to her, then she would go to him.

MALCOLM JOINED ALEXANDER in the hall, just as it began to bustle. Sentries and mercenaries broke their fast at the tables, their manner more subdued than was typical. A fire crackled merrily on the hearth, for the Yule log was scarce consumed. The smell of fresh bread filled the hall and one could hear singing in the kitchens. There was ale, though it was thin, and fresh strewing herbs upon the floor.

"Kinfairlie looks different," Malcolm said with a frown. "What has changed?"

"I married on Christmas Day," Alexander said with all the insouciance he could muster. His brother regarded him in shock. "And my lady wife takes the household beneath her command."

"You wed?" Malcolm sputtered. "Who? How? When?" He put his cup down heavily on the board. *This very week?*

"It is a shame you did not come sooner," Alexander mused, enjoying his brother's astonishment. "For Madeline and Rhys were here for Christmas Eve, as were Vivienne and Erik."

"Wait a moment. Madeline and Vivienne were here, with the husbands you arranged for them to wed without their agreement." A suspicious light dawned in Malcolm's eyes. "And they departed when, precisely?"

"Yesterday," Alexander admitted.

"And you were wed while they were resident?"

"As I said."

Malcolm began to laugh. "That was a hasty courtship, brother mine," he said, his eyes dancing. "When last we spoke, you had no intent to wed, nor were you courting any maiden's affections."

"I met the lady on the eve of Christmas . . ."

"The day before your nuptials! When Madeline and Vivienne were both present in this hall. I smell retaliation, Alexander!"

". . . though that does not change the measure of my admiration for her."

"Admit the truth," Malcolm insisted, his manner gleeful. "Madeline and Vivienne avenged themselves upon you."

Alexander nodded. "That is not to say that matters will not come aright in the end, as both of them have learned."

Malcolm sipped his ale, his gaze knowing. "The match is amiable, then?"

"Of course." Alexander had no desire to confess his misgivings to his brother, for any detail he admitted to one sibling would be immediately shared with all the others. He had protected them all from the truth of Kinfairlie's finances for so long that it was instinctive to protect them from other harsh truths. "In fact, Eleanor is most anxious to conceive a son."

"Truly?" Malcolm chewed his bread as he considered this detail. He studied Alexander as if he suspected that his brother told but half of the tale. "An amorous wife is not such a terrible fate. I salute you, Alexander, for it seems that all comes aright for you, even when our sisters scheme against you. That is a feat!"

"I do not know that all proceeds as well as that. . . ."

"You are modest! Kinfairlie is secure in your hands and at peace, you have a hall full of loyal men, a stable full of fine steeds, two sisters married well, and your own wife desirous of an heir." There was no bitterness in Malcolm's tone, for his nature had never been tinged with avarice, but Alexander felt a desire to set matters straight.

He leaned an elbow on the table, lowering his voice in confidence. "I tell you one matter that does not go aright with ease," he said, and Malcolm leaned closer. Alexander grimaced. "In truth, I forget much of courting a lady's favor. Have you any counsel for me?"

Malcolm's eyes widened. "Surely you jest."

"Surely not."

"You courted every maiden from here to London, and not without success!"

Alexander shook his head in mock dismay. "It is different to flirt with the affections of maidens than to foster love in the heart of one's wife."

"Ah, so for once in your days, you wish for more than mere pleasure abed." Malcolm grinned, his own woes forgotten. "Are you smitten, brother mine?"

Alexander only smiled.

Malcolm nodded, apparently satisfied. "I shall tell you the sole thing I know about the courtship of women, for my success in such endeavors could never begin to match your own," he said. "This counsel comes from Uncle Tynan, and I am not certain that he meant to confide it in me. He might merely have been speaking his thoughts aloud."

This was no tempting prospect, in Alexander's view, for Tynan had died unwed after rejecting the affection offered wholeheartedly by Rosamunde. "Indeed?"

Malcolm frowned. "He said that it is of import to have gifts to bestow upon a lady while courting her. He said he feared that he and Rosamunde had never found happiness together because there was nothing he could offer to her that she did not already possess."

"He could have surrendered his love to her," Alexander noted. "For she could not have had that otherwise."

Malcolm ignored this. "I think he believed that gifts soften a woman's heart and he disliked that Rosamunde had such wealth of her own. He only gave her the silver ring that our grandfather had bestowed upon his own bride."

"And Rosamunde gave it back."

Malcolm nodded. "He wore it all the time after she left his side, and he would stare at it every night in silence. I think he knew that he had forsaken his opportunity, and I think he believed that the one gift he had given her had not been the right one."

Alexander stared into his cup and considered this. There might be wisdom in it, after all. Would the right gift given to Eleanor in the right moment dissolve her determination to be rid of him? Could he prove himself to be a spouse worth the keeping?

Eleanor had an affection for horses, of that Alexander was certain. He recalled the admiration in her eyes when she had stroked the steeds of the departing parties the day before. Her features had lit as seldom they did. He could envision Eleanor upon one of the black horses of Ravensmuir, and recalled all too well how she had walked from Ewen's abode. Perhaps she had left a favored steed behind, being uncertain of her destination. Perhaps Ewen had denied her a steed of her own.

And so, what better way to persuade her that Alexander courted her affection? Further, if he gave her the means to flee him, would that not show that he had no desire to imprison her against her will? Might that not show him better than her former spouses?

A man could only try.

He fixed Malcolm with a bright gaze. "Do you fully surrender Ravensmuir's steeds unto me?"

"Of course. I know that you will see them well treated and that you know as much of breeding as do I. You lived at Ravensmuir for years, after all, while Uncle Tynan trained you for knighthood."

"Then I think I shall choose a mare for my lady wife," Alexander said, pushing to his feet with resolve.

"What a splendid wedding gift!" Malcolm agreed. "I will aid you in the choosing, for I know the nature of each horse. We can make a match to her own nature."

But the men would not have to do as much in the lady's absence. Just as they rose from the board with purpose, Alexander saw Eleanor at the foot of the stairs. She seemed hesitant to approach him, and he cursed himself for creating that hesitation.

He turned and smiled, offering his hand. "Eleanor, come and meet my brother Malcolm."

ELEANOR CROSSED THE HALL floor with deliberate steps, taking the opportunity to study this new arrival. So, this was one of the brothers who would welcome the seal of Kinfairlie, should Alexander die without an heir. He was younger than her husband, but not by much. They shared the same ebony hair and muscled build, though Malcolm had green eyes. They were far less attractive, to Eleanor's thinking, than eyes of sparkling blue.

Eleanor smiled politely even as she resolved that Malcolm would never win her husband's holding. It would pass to their son, of that she meant to be certain.

They exchanged greetings; then Malcolm smiled at Eleanor. "Do you ride often, then?" he asked, and she had the sense that she had stepped into the midst of a conversation.

"Of course, I was taught to ride, all noblewomen are," she said, sparing a glance to Alexander. He looked as innocent as an angel, a most uncommon expression for him, and one that made her wonder at his intent. "Why do you ask?"

"I have asked Alexander to ensure the care of the horses from my stable in my absence, and he proposes to grant you one as a wedding gift."

Eleanor felt the blood drain from her face at the prospect. She could not endure past horror again!

She felt her mouth work for a moment before she managed to make a sound. "I have no need of a steed of my own," she said, her voice unsteady. "Though I thank you for the thought."

"It is more than a thought," Alexander said, claiming her elbow. "It is a deed to be done. Come along and aid in the choosing."

"No!" Eleanor cried with such vigor that the entire household turned to look. "I beg of you, no. I have no desire for a horse." Her words fell with uncharacteristic haste, in her fear that the past was to be repeated. "I am content to walk, truly."

Alexander bent toward her, his eyes gleaming. "Eleanor, you make little sense in this," he said in that quiet but firm tone that brooked no argument. "You need not fear the expense," he said, mistaking the reason for her protest. "I will see my lady with a mount of her own, and that is how matters shall be."

"I will not choose one," she insisted, knowing she sounded like a fool. "I will take no part in this scheme." And then, because he looked inclined to insist, she lied. "I am afraid of horses, Alexander."

"But you said that you learned to ride young. . . ."

"And so I did, and for years I did so, despite my fear. But I have had numerous bad experiences and do not venture near steeds any longer."

"The best remedy for a fall is to climb into the saddle again," Malcolm said, his manner helpful. "And you need not fear that a Ravensmuir horse will throw you. It takes much to provoke them."

"No!" Eleanor said, too loudly. "I decline your gift!" She turned furiously upon Alexander, knowing she sounded mad, but needing to ensure that this did not occur. "Have the grace to accept my refusal! *I will have no horse!*"

The household stood in astonished silence, but Eleanor pivoted and left the hall. Once on the stairs, she ran as quickly as she could for the sanctuary of the solar. She pushed past one of Alexander's sisters on the stairs, sparing no time to answer her query. She flung herself into the solar and turned the key against the lot of them.

It was only then that Eleanor let herself weep. It was her own folly at fault, to be sure. She had betrayed Blanchefleur's memory by showing affection to the horses the day before, and now her affection would be used against her.

As it had been before.

She could not let that crime happen again, she could not—she cared not what she had to say to make it so. Let them think her mad. So long as the steeds were safe, she did not care.

~

ALEXANDER LOOKED AFTER HIS wife in undisguised astonishment.

"Most women would welcome such a rich gift, as I have heard it told," Malcolm said.

"I, too, would expect as much," Alexander said, sensing that there was more to this matter than the refusal of a gift. Eleanor had panicked. He had seen the terror in her eyes, though he could not fathom the reason for it.

"I suppose her vigor is less astonishing if one knows of her fear," Malcolm said.

"I am not certain that it is horses she fears," Alexander said, then told his brother of her response the day before. Malcolm then shared his confusion. "I think we should choose one for her, despite this incident."

"Perhaps she thinks the gift too generous," Malcolm suggested. "Or does not dare to believe it possible that she could have a steed of her own. If she is fond of them, it might seem a lofty notion."

"Indeed. She was at the window when you arrived, so she knows how fine the steeds are," Alexander agreed. "Perhaps she dares not desire one, out of fear that she will be disappointed."

"Have you disappointed your bride overmuch?" Malcolm teased.

Alexander had no chance to reply, for Isabella swept across the hall with no small indignation. "What have you done to your bride?" she demanded. "How could you make her cry so early in the day, Alexander? She is not so accustomed to your pranks as we are! And this after you have left her alone for two days and two nights. You are a churlish knave, to be sure."

"I would merely grant her a gift," he said, lifting his hands in appeal. "Is it not fitting for a man to bestow a gift upon his bride?" The company chuckled at his manner and settled back to their meal, though doubtless a good measure of the gossip in the hall was about the laird and his lady.

"She must not believe you," Isabella said with authority. "Though goodness knows how she would have discerned already that you can be merciless in teasing another soul."

"Perhaps she is uncommonly perceptive," Malcolm jested, and Isabella gasped with delight at the sight of him.

"Malcolm! I did not realize that you were home!" She hastened to give him a hug, then beamed at her brothers. "You should have told us that he was coming," she informed Alexander.

"I did not know. He has only just arrived, and I dared not send word to awaken you too soon. I suspected, after all, that you would sleep much later than this."

Isabella's affection for lingering abed was well-known and Malcolm laughed at this reminder. "Truly, are you Isabella?" he said, stepping back to study the maiden in question. "You resemble her, to be sure, but I have never seen my sister Isabella before noon."

Isabella swatted at his shoulder and missed.

"It is guilt keeping her awake," Alexander said solemnly. "For she did try to kill me Christmas Eve." Isabella gasped at this accusation and made to qualify it, but Malcolm granted her no chance to speak.

"Why did you wait so long?" he demanded of her. "We could have been rid of him years ago. It would have been so much simpler when we were younger."

They all laughed at this, though Alexander spared a glance for the stairs. Would it make matters worse to pursue Eleanor, or should he leave her be? The fact remained that she had never yet shown so much emotion as she had over the prospect of being given a horse. He had a sense that the veil over one of her secrets had been disturbed.

And the best way, he was certain, to completely reveal that secret was to proceed along the same course.

"Isabella, would you be of aid to us?" he asked. "You are as tall as Eleanor. Would you help us choose a mare for her to have as her own?"

"You mean to give her a horse?" Isabella's mouth fell open in her astonishment. Alexander would have wagered that there was no small measure of jealousy in her response. "For her very own?"

"One of Ravensmuir's mares," Malcolm contributed.

Isabella gaped at this apparent injustice. "But you have known her only a few days! You have known me for every day of my life. Alexander, you must grant a steed to me!"

"Every bride should have a nuptial gift," Alexander said mildly. "Perhaps your husband, when you choose one, will grant you a steed as well."

Isabella glowered at him. "You mean to incite me to choose a suitor hurriedly."

Alexander shrugged. "If you delay, then you cannot blame me for making your choice for you."

Isabella's eyes flashed, but suddenly she regarded him with suspicion. "It is no small gift to give a woman a horse of this ilk. You have already given her a gem."

"Every bride also has need of a ring to seal her vows," Alexander said.

"You see?" Malcolm teased. "Marriage is not without its merit."

"It is more than that." Isabella's eyes gleamed. "You *are* smitten with her!"

"I am not smitten," Alexander argued, but they both laughed at him so merrily that it seemed churlish to dispute the matter further. There was a measure of truth in it, after all, for he was at least fascinated with his lady wife. "Come along, the two of you, let us choose a steed for my lady." He made to march out of his hall, not waiting to see whether they followed him, but Anthony stepped into his course just before the portal.

"I would ask of you, my lord, whether the men in the stables would be staying for the midday meal."

Alexander kept a smile on his lips, not wanting Malcolm to realize the full import of what he had asked of his elder brother. "Of course, Anthony. In fact, the party from Ravensmuir will remain at Kinfairlie indefinitely, while Malcolm himself will linger only through Epiphany."

Anthony's shock was clear, which meant that it must be considerable. The older man was usually adept at hiding his thoughts.

Alexander spoke quickly, the better not to have Anthony's doubts expressed. "There is fodder for the horses, which will also remain, at Ravensmuir, though the ostlers intend to collect it today."

"But, my lord . . ."

"It is Christmas, Anthony, and I am certain that our guests can be ably accommodated." Alexander spoke with cheer.

The castellan drew himself up to his full height and looked Alexander in the eye. "Perhaps, my lord, you might spare a moment for the cook, that you might decide the meat to be served at the midday meal this day."

There was not sufficient of it, Alexander knew as much already. He held his castellan's gaze, relieved that the older man seemed to have understood the situation. "It is the Feast of Holy Innocents this day, is it not?" The castellan nodded minutely. "And such a holy day is a fitting one for a measure of restraint. Please instruct the cook to bake bread with brown flour and ask of him to ascertain the quantity of fish at our disposal. I shall return shortly to review matters with him."

"Of course, my lord." Anthony bowed and Alexander strode out of the hall, willing his siblings to silence.

"I hate brown bread," Isabella said with some vexation.

"It is better than none," Malcolm retorted. "I welcome any morsel after these past months at Ravensmuir. The larder has been spare, to be sure."

Isabella flushed. "You should have come sooner," she chided, taking his elbow. "There is always food aplenty at Kinfairlie, that is one matter upon which we can all rely."

Alexander said nothing. To his relief, the matter was dropped, for they arrived at the stables and the horses of Ravensmuir, as always, drove all other concerns from his sister's thoughts.

Indeed, they were magnificent beasts, and his own awe was no less considerable.

ELEANOR TOOK A SHAKING BREATH and straightened after her uncharacteristic storm of tears. She heard footsteps and voices and looked out the solar window in time to see Alexander crossing the bailey with Malcolm and one of his sisters. The fiery red of the maiden's hair and her height indicated that it was Isabella. It must have been Isabella who had passed Eleanor on the stairs. The three made their way to the stables, Alexander striding with such purpose that Eleanor was newly afraid of his intent.

She was tormented by how little she knew of him. She had trusted Millard, after all, and he had not only committed a foul crime, but had laid the blame for it at her feet. Eleanor would never forget it and so great was her revulsion that she feared the crime was to be repeated.

She needed to count the horses, now, before a single one of them could be removed from the stables.

Eleanor wiped away her tears and adjusted the circlet that held her veil fast. She straightened the sleeves of her kirtle and ensured that her garters were firmly fastened. She unlocked the portal, secured the key to her belt. She chose the edge of the stairs, where they were less likely to creak, and moved like a wraith down the stairs.

The latch upon the door to the chamber the sisters shared rattled just as Eleanor passed it. She scurried down the stairs, not wanting her mission to be witnessed. She was almost in the hall when she heard that wooden portal slam overhead, which only hastened her steps even more.

The hall was busy and she was disinclined to exchange pleasantries. She nodded and smiled at several men who bowed to her, then headed for the kitchen as if she had a duty there.

"My lady!" Anthony bowed so low at the sight of her that his brow fairly touched the floor. The cook, standing by his side, looked grim and inclined his head crisply in greeting. "Perhaps you can be of aid to us, my lady. The laird insists that the question of meat for the midday meal will be addressed when he returns from the stables."

Eleanor's heart clutched at this, though she strove to give no outward sign of her consternation.

"But the cook says the hour is late, and he would know his orders immediately if not sooner."

"Of course," Eleanor agreed, and the cook looked relieved. "I understand that we have guests this day?"

"Another twenty men arrived from Ravensmuir this very morning, including those already in the hall!" the cook said, his frustration clear. "There are only scraps of venison left. The laird has requested brown bread this day, which aids the matter mightily, but we cannot serve bread alone."

"Have you fish?"

"Two barrels of smoked fish, my lady. The laird suggested fish, but I had intended to serve these for Friday's fast."

"We shall fret about Friday on Friday," she said crisply. "And it may well be a fast in truth. We shall have the bread and the smoked fish, fried if you can manage as much, for men who have traveled favor a hot meal in their bellies."

"It can be done, my lady."

"And we shall have a stew this evening, a thin one with a great deal of gravy. Have you any kale remaining in the garden?"

The cook grimaced. "It is not as fine as once it was. . . ."

"But it is there and it will do, especially with venison gravy."

The cook beamed at this resolution. "I have a measure of butter yet, my lady, and the chives are yet growing, for

I have not cut them of late. The fish will be fare for a king, upon that you can rely."

Eleanor smiled. "I thank you, and await them with anticipation."

She turned away and Anthony was fast beside her. "I thank you, my lady, for your timely arrival and for your solution as well."

"We have need of a party to ride to hunt this afternoon, Anthony," she said, thinking only of ensuring there was sufficient meat for the board. "My laird has hunting grounds, of course?"

"Kinfairlie holds extensive lands, my lady, and its forests are abundant with wildlife."

"Excellent. A hart or another large beast would be ideal, though even a wagonload of pheasants would be welcome. Whether the laird is occupied this day or not, might you see a hunting party arranged among his guests?"

Anthony frowned. "Few are noble, my lady, so few have the right to hunt."

She granted him a stern glance. "It is a matter of seeing the board laden, Anthony. If the laird cannot lead the party, then you shall lead it. I do not care whether its members are noble or common: I care only that they return with sufficient meat for a hundred souls for at least two days."

Anthony's brow lifted. "But—"

"It is of no merit to a laird's reputation to have no morsel to offer his guests, especially in this season. I trust that you will ensure our laird's honor is upheld."

Anthony bowed. "It shall be as you decree, my lady." Whether he was surprised or pleased, Eleanor could not say, but he fixed her with a bright eye. "If I may suggest as much, my lady, it is encouraging to note that you and the laird share similar views upon this matter. Just yesterday, my lord Alexander insisted that sufficient saffron grace the sauce, regardless of the cost."

Eleanor smiled at that, and was reassured that her own advice was consistent with that of her spouse. "It is Christmas, Anthony."

"Indeed, my lady, and blessings abound at Kinfairlie."

Eleanor left the hall then and strode to the stables, the sweet scent of hay and horseflesh awakening a thousand memories. An ostler nodded to her there. He must have seen forty summers, thus must have been in a position of some authority, though Eleanor could not recall seeing him before.

"Begging your pardon, but you would be the lady of Kinfairlie, if I am not mistaken," he said, and bowed with an awkwardness that indicated that he was not accustomed to encountering noblewomen.

"That I am." A curious thrill tripped over Eleanor's flesh as she claimed her title as Alexander's wife for the first time. "I understand there are new horses arrived."

Dozens of horses peered over their stalls at the sound of voices, their ears flicking in curiosity. She could not see Alexander, though the stables were deeply shadowed in comparison to the bright morning sun.

"From Ravensmuir, my lady. I brought them." He hesitated, his heavy hands twisting in indecision when she simply stood and stared at what she could see of the beasts. They were large horses, larger than any she had ridden before, larger than she had guessed from her solar window. They were beautiful beyond belief. "Would you like to see the young ones?" he offered. "I reckon as the laird has plans for them, so you should see them sooner rather than later."

Eleanor's breath caught in fear again. "I will see them all," she said with resolve. "Though I will see the foals first, if you please."

The ostler ducked his head and turned, content to have a purpose, and led her to a large stall. "Mind your step, my lady. They have not been in the stall for long, but one never knows. And two of the mares would have no part of being separated from the young ones, so the stall is crowded, to be sure."

He opened the wooden door and Eleanor stepped just over the threshold. The foals turned, curious, their eyes gleaming in the shadows. Their tails swished and one might have stepped closer, but a massive mare interceded.

She placed herself between Eleanor and the foals with a decisive step. The mare sniffed Eleanor's hands and her hair first. It was as if the horse meant to ensure her intent, and Eleanor held her breath. The perusal seemed to take overlong, and for a moment, she feared that the mare somehow knew of her perfidy.

Did the steeds know of Blanchefleur, or worse, that Eleanor had not had the wits to save that horse?

The mare abruptly snorted and tossed her head, then bent to nibble Eleanor's hair. Eleanor, overwhelmed, felt her knees weaken at this approval. She reached to scratch the horse's nose.

At that, the foals eased closer, echoing the way the mare had sniffed her. Their coats were silken soft, their noses like the finest velvet, their haunches muscled. Even the foals were nigh as tall as she, though they must have been born the previous spring.

They were exquisitely beautiful, and though Eleanor ached to have one as her own, she dared not let any other soul witness her fondness for them. She had made that error once before and reluctantly lifted her hands away when she recalled the ostler's presence. She was here only to complete her count.

But she had no chance to do so.

"What are you doing here?" Alexander demanded before she could turn. Eleanor's heart sank like a stone. She composed her features so that none of her joy showed, then pivoted to confront him.

He stood beside the ostler, his frown surely one of confusion. "I thought you feared horses. Why would you enter the stall, then, no less do so alone?"

Eleanor met Alexander's steady gaze, and for once in all her days, she did not know what to say.

Chapter Ten

ALEXANDER HAD NOT YET SEEN Eleanor at a loss for words and he was not certain that he ever wished to witness the sight again.

He certainly did not want to be responsible for the circumstance again. She stood and stared at him with wide eyes, the color drained from her face. There was no doubt that he had given her a shock, albeit unwillingly.

"I thought you did not like horses," he repeated more gently, and she seemed to shake herself. She lifted her chin and her composure returned. He had the sense that she armed herself against him, and truly he could read no more of her thoughts than those of an opponent with his visor down.

"I do not," she said crisply. "My refusal of your gift appeared to trouble you, though, so I strove to overcome my instinct. It is the duty of a woman to see her husband pleased, after all."

It had been, on the contrary, the lady who had been troubled by the prospect of his gift. Alexander had simply been confused by her response.

Her protest might have been more plausible, had the mare not persisted in nuzzling her hair. Alexander was sufficiently familiar with horses to know that they did not show affection to those who feared or disliked them.

The horse dug its nose into the neckline of Eleanor's kirtle with some persistence. It was impossible to believe, then, that someone who disliked horses would have been deemed worthy of such a friendly assault by the mare, or, equally, that that person would have endured it. Eleanor's fingers twitched, as if she yearned to scratch the mare's nose, so Alexander did not put much faith in her words.

In fact, his blood began to simmer that she lied. How much of a fool did she believe him to be? And what was the value of her word, she who had pledged to have honesty between them?

He resolved in that moment to feign belief in her lie, the better to see how long she would insist upon it.

"You seem to make great progress," he said, as if he had not noted the conflicting evidence, as if he were not vexed, indeed. He stepped into the stall himself, granting the ostler a nod of dismissal. Eleanor stiffened and did not raise so much as a finger to the horses. The young ones jostled her, revealed that she had petted them before. "Did you ride often as a child?"

"Of course," she admitted as if she would have preferred not to do so. "My tutors ensured that I could ride with grace."

"And so they should have done," Alexander said easily. He scratched the mare's ears and the beast blew her lips in pleasure. "This is Guinevere, in the event that introductions have not been made."

"Named for Arthur's queen?" Eleanor regarded the

horse warily, though there was a telling admiration in her eyes.

Alexander nodded, biting down his rising displeasure. The woman could not have lied to save her life! She must think him witless! "Indeed, for the stallions cannot resist her allure. She foals nigh every year, despite the ostler's best efforts to ensure otherwise."

"Would you not breed her annually?"

"It has been my family's practice to breed each mare every second or even every third year, the better that she might recover from her feat." Alexander smiled thinly. "Guinevere, however, has too many ardent suitors to find that scheme fitting."

"She seems sufficiently hale."

"She is a marvel, to be sure." Alexander caught Eleanor's hand and placed it upon Guinevere's nose, covering it with his own as if she truly were fearful of steeds. He felt her fingers curve instinctively to the horse before she snatched her hand away.

"She is too large to be trusted. Look at her teeth!"

"She is as gentle as a spring rain," Alexander argued. He met Eleanor's gaze and lowered his voice so that only his wife could hear it. "You seem uncommonly familiar with horses."

She stared at him for a long moment, then dropped her gaze and spoke hurriedly. "Nonetheless, they strike a terror in my very veins," she insisted breathlessly.

Alexander stepped closer to his wife when her words faltered. She might have pushed past him and left the stall, but he caught her elbow in his hand, intent upon having the truth.

But Eleanor was shaking like a leaf in the wind. Her

vulnerability caught Alexander by surprise, and as previously, it utterly disarmed him. He urged her closer to his side before he thought twice. She stood trembling, almost within his embrace, and he marveled at her distress.

"Do not compel me to possess another steed, Alexander. Do not grant me this gift, I beg of you. If there has ever been a measure of kindness in your heart, then surrender this concession to me. And do not ask me more of this matter, I beg of you."

Alexander was astonished by this appeal, no less by the fact that Eleanor made it. It was not like her to reveal her emotions so clearly. "I meant it as a nuptial gift."

"No gift would be a better one," she said with vehemence.

Alexander held her fast, intending to ask more, but tears glistened upon his lady wife's cheeks. What had happened to so distress her?

"Would you at least look upon these steeds?" Alexander suggested gently. "They are fine beasts, and we may never see their ilk so gathered again."

Eleanor started at that, though Alexander could not imagine why, and she clutched his arm with sudden vigor. "What is your intent for the foals?" she demanded with urgency. "The ostler said you had a scheme for them?"

Alexander shrugged, not seeing the reason for her concern. "I have none as yet, though perhaps the ostler believes I do. They would fetch a fair price, to be sure, but it has not been the habit of my family to casually be rid of the steeds of Ravensmuir. We keep them until they are at least two years of age, so these foals will not be leaving our care soon."

"What then?" Her anxiety was undiminished, though he was mystified by it.

"We grant them as gifts of honor, to friends and allies whom we know to be worthy of possessing such a beast. They are treasures, and we ensure that any master who claims one will see the beast well-treated, indeed." Alexander smiled, hoping to reassure her. "There are treasures in this world with value beyond their price."

She studied him, as if uncertain whether to believe him.

"Come," Alexander suggested. "Come and meet mine own destrier. He was entrusted to my care by my uncle Tynan when I earned my spurs. I have ignored Uriel of late, and must warn you that he may well prove himself worthy of the name 'the fire of God.'"

It was meant to be a jest, but Eleanor did not laugh. She did, however, let Alexander lead her from the stall containing the foals and deeper into the stables, though her clutch upon his arm was tight.

He could make no sense of the fact that she murmured beneath her breath as they made their way through the stables. Unless he missed his guess, she was counting the horses.

But why? Did she mean to have an inventory of Ravensmuir's wealth? The dark thought was unwelcome, but not dismissed easily. Any wealth he possessed was almost entirely in these stables, to be sure, and if the horses were sold, they would fetch a high price.

Alexander knew a moment's fear. Did his wife have a scheme for his assets, one she would follow after his untimely demise? It was an unsettling prospect, but one he could not discredit easily, not when she lied to him with such vigor.

There was nothing for it: Eleanor conjured a new puzzle for each one he believed himself to have solved. And Alexander, perhaps to his own detriment, was only more intrigued with each successive mystery she revealed. Truth was what he needed from her, though he knew not how to persuade her to reveal it.

He was even less certain how he would know when he found it.

THE SAUCE MAKER PROVED to be Moira's downfall.

It was imperative that Moira confide a detail she had observed to her mistress, which meant she had to enter Kinfairlie's hall. Moira had managed to join the revels to celebrate her lady's nuptials, but had not been able to linger within the hall. That night, the merry guests had been fairly swept out to the bailey. Despite her best efforts, she had not managed to enter the keep since.

That castellan was cursed quick, to be sure.

But this scheme was ideal. It was a simple feat to pick up a load of wood and march into Kinfairlie's kitchens as if she belonged there, especially when so many others did as much. For truly, Moira *did* belong within the keep's walls, as her lady was now mistress there.

Moira's loyal heart burned at the travesty of the whispers she had heard against Lady Eleanor. Worse, there was treachery afoot in this very hall, treachery that would see her lady poorly served and that too soon. She could set matters to right, Moira could, if only she could reach her mistress.

She was relieved to note that the castellan had left the

kitchens. She followed the other women to the large pile of faggots and bent to deposit her load there, feigning familiarity with the kitchens all the while. So it was that Moira was astonished when she straightened and the plump, fair sauce maker pointed his ladle at her.

"Who are you?" he demanded, his voice loud enough that several others turned.

Moira glanced behind herself, for she knew herself to be unworthy of note.

"Nay, I mean *you*," the man insisted. "I have never seen you in this hall before. Who are you?"

Moira felt her cheeks heat. She was not accustomed to being noticed. "Do not be ridiculous." She conjured a lie with haste. "I have labored here since midsummer."

He shook his head and came closer. "I do not think so. I would have recalled you, of this I am certain. Who are you?"

"Aye, who are you?" asked the cook. He was a formidable man, and though he was not angry, his very size made Moira leery of him.

"I am merely a woman, one scarce worthy of note," Moira said with some pride, and straightened her apron. "If you will excuse me, there is wood to be brought for the fires."

"Nay, I will not excuse you, not without knowing your name," the sauce maker insisted.

Moira glared at him. "My name is not of import."

The cook began to chuckle. "She has seen your intent, Cedric, and does not welcome your attentions. Leave the woman be."

The sauce maker's ears turned crimson. "I but wish to know her name. That is the fullness of my intent."

The cook laughed harder. "The sauce has need of thickening, Cedric. Get yourself to your labor."

Cedric sputtered for a moment and gave Moira a beseeching glance. When she did not respond, he heaved a sigh. He turned to his sauce, sparing the occasional glance her way.

Glad of this reprieve, Moira turned to depart, but the cook laid a heavy finger upon her shoulder to halt her. "And still I do not know your name, nor from whence you hail," he said, his voice lowered so that the others in the kitchens turned back to their labor.

Moira shrugged. "Surely the name of a little woman is not of such import?"

The cook arched a brow. "The name of every soul in my kitchens is of import, for I will not suffer my laird's hall to be breached through my portal. Further, you have lied and done so with ease. I know that you were not here at midsummer. Indeed, Cedric speaks aright, for I know that you have not crossed this threshold before." He held her gaze, his own kindly but firm. "Who are you?"

Moira squared her shoulders, seeing nothing for it. "My name is Moira Goodall and I pledged myself to the service of Lady Eleanor Havilland, surrendering that pledge to her own mother when that lady lay at death's door."

The cook pursed his lips. "The same Lady Eleanor who wed our laird?"

Moira nodded. "The same."

"But she came with no attendant."

Moira lifted her chin. "I followed her, as is my duty."

The cook considered her for a moment. He inclined his head and Moira thought herself excused, but he laid claim to her elbow. "The truth of your tale can easily be ascertained," he said. He led her from the kitchens into the dark corridor that must lead to the hall.

It was only then that Moira's spirit quailed. Surely Lady Eleanor had not left her behind at Tivotdale for a reason? Surely her lady was not displeased with her service?

Surely her lady would not deny her?

ELEANOR WAS FLATTERED by Alexander's attentions and his determination to aid in conquering her supposed fear of steeds. It was no ordeal to have him by her side, his fingers brushing her elbow, her hand, the tip of her nose in a sequence of small gestures that left her tingling from head to toe.

The man could awaken lust in a corpse, Eleanor was certain of it. He covered his hand with hers when he showed her how to stroke a horse, he put his arm around her waist when leading her closer to one of the great steeds. There was nothing improper in his gestures, not between man and wife, but his every touch made her yearn to meet him abed again.

All the same, it was less than convenient to be the focus of his attention. She could not count the horses accurately, and a precise count was critical to her ensuring their welfare. Alexander would not be persuaded to leave her alone in the stables, which must be the warren of her fears, and Eleanor had only her own impetuous lie to blame.

So it was that her footsteps dragged when he returned to the hall and he turned upon her with laughing eyes.

"So, you are reluctant to leave the stables," he teased, his manner making her heart skip. "The antidote for your fears would seem to be half-ingested."

She wondered then if he had discerned her lie and felt churlish for ever having uttered it. "Perhaps you have dismissed my fears. You know full well that no woman with blood in her veins could resist your assurances," she retorted.

He laughed. "Then there are a cursed number of bloodless women in this vicinity, to be sure. Even you have shown yourself resistant to me."

"Hardly that!" Eleanor was certain that her attraction to him was obvious to the most casual observer and had been so from the moment that first they met. At his skeptical glance, she found herself flushing. "I yearn for your caress at the merest glimpse of you," she admitted, blushing at the truth of it. "And I ached with your absence this past night. Surely you must know as much."

"Truly?" Alexander halted between stables and hall. The sunlight danced off the last of the snow, which lingered in corners of the bailey. The sky was a clear blue, a hue that matched Alexander's eyes and made the twinkles within them seem to dance more merrily. He touched a fingertip to her arm, mischief in the curve of his lips. "What of a touch?" he mused.

Eleanor felt the weight of his fingertip and the heat of it through her chemise. "You force me to cede an advantage to you," she charged. "In your quest for truth between us."

His smile flashed and his fingertip eased up her arm. "Truth is never easily gained," he murmured. "Though this would be a welcome one."

His fingertip found her shoulder and Eleanor straightened beneath its ceaseless caress. Alexander watched his fingertip as he traced the curve of her collarbone. Even through the barrier of her garments, she was certain she could feel his touch as surely as if she had been nude before him. Her very flesh was afire, her heart pounded as if she had run a thousand miles.

"Surely you do not quail before such a quest," she said, her words uncommonly breathless. "I thought you a knight of formidable will."

He met her gaze, snaring her with that vivid blue. "Surely even the most valiant warrior should not undertake such a quest without his lady's support?"

"Do you ask for mine?"

He nodded, his manner so intent that she knew he missed no nuance of her expression.

"Then you have it," she said softly. "You have but to ask me for any deed that is within my power to surrender to you."

"What of any truth?"

Eleanor swallowed. "Yours for the asking."

He arched a dark brow, his fingertip reaching the hollow of her throat, which was bare to his touch. Eleanor caught her breath as he traced a circle there. "Did you surrender as much to your other husbands?"

Eleanor swallowed and held his gaze determinedly, willing him to understand. "Neither asked me for truth. Neither treated me with courtesy." She caught his hand in hers, lifting it from her flesh, and pressed a kiss into his palm. "Neither tempted me to indecency before the entire household." She smiled then, guessing him to be surprised by her candor. "How fares your taste for truth, husband?"

His eyes glinted with what might have been satisfaction. "I did not know that I tempted you to indecency."

Eleanor felt her smile broaden. "You awaken my desire apurpose, my lord. Have the honor to confess to some truth of your own."

Alexander grinned. "I attempt to conjure your desire, to be sure, though it is not for me to say how well I succeed."

"Yet surely you must know that you do." She laid his hand against her throat, letting him feel the thunder of her pulse. His eyes widened slightly; then she took the sole step between them. She placed her lips against his own throat and whispered against his very flesh. "Know, my lord, that I yearn for a sweet morsel this midday, a sweeter one than will be served at the board."

Alexander chuckled. "I think I should have asked for honesty sooner," he teased, catching her shoulders in his hands. "But why such ardor, Eleanor? It is my understanding that such heated desire is uncommon for women."

She studied him for a long moment, then granted him the truth he desired. "And so it was always for me," she admitted quietly. "I have never savored meetings abed, Alexander. I have only endured the touch of my husbands, until you."

He looked skeptical.

"Is it not part of every tale that the champion's kiss awakens the passion lurking in his lady's heart?"

Alexander smiled. "Now you sound like my sister Vivienne, although she would likely have said that the champion's kiss melted the frost about his lady's heart. She would insist that the lady's true love was the sole man who could awaken the love slumbering within her, and that his deed in so doing would show the lady his merit."

"You speak of love again."

"I salute its merit."

"I speak of desire and pleasure abed, and the fact that I have missed your caress these past two nights."

"That is well and good, though I warn you that I seek more."

Eleanor turned away from him, making her way to the hall. Her innards churned, for she understood what he asked of her and knew she could not surrender it to him.

She pivoted to face him and let the words spill before she thought better. "Here is truth, Alexander. Love between man and wife leads only to bitterness and unhappiness. Love may be a marvel, but it is one of short duration and one destined to turn against the lovers. I vowed young that I would never love a man, that I would never love my husband, and so I uphold that pledge. I lust for you, as I have never lusted for any man. Let that suffice."

"It will not," he said with soft conviction. He strode toward her, catching her hand when she might have left him. "Love and honesty and truth and justice were what I was raised to expect, and expect them I do."

"Do not compel me to lie to you!"

"I do not," he said with such force. "Though you choose to do so."

Eleanor flushed and looked away from him, fearful that he would spurn her for her lie, more fearful that her suspicions might prove true.

"Tell me about Ewen Douglas," he said softly, and

Eleanor's gaze flew to his in alarm. "Alan charged that you killed him, and though I put no credit in that man's word, still I wonder why you left Tivotdale in such haste, in the midst of the night."

Eleanor straightened. The gleam in Alexander's eye told her that all rested upon her answer to this. "I warned you once that you might not savor the taste of truth."

He inclined his head slightly. "And yet I ask for it all the same."

Eleanor licked her lips. Her heart raced, so fearful was she that Alexander would put her aside, that this fragile dream would be shattered so soon.

But there was nothing for it. She lifted her chin. "Alan spoke aright. I did kill Ewen Douglas, and that was why I fled Tivotdale. But that is not the worst of it."

"Tell me," he urged, his manner intent.

"I do not regret the deed, and I know that I never will." Eleanor held his gaze defiantly, then pivoted to march toward the hall. She thought he would not follow her; she thought that all she had hoped to gain in Kinfairlie was laid to waste.

Then Alexander's hand closed around her elbow as he matched his steps to hers.

"You do not abandon me," she said, knowing astonishment echoed in her tone.

"I already know of one good reason you had to see Ewen dead, and I do not doubt that there are others," he said with such conviction that Eleanor's mouth fell open in her surprise. She looked up, fearful that he jested with her, but Alexander merely winked at her. "I thank you for your confidence, Eleanor. This bodes well for our marriage, indeed."

Eleanor blinked as they closed the distance to the hall. No man had ever granted her the benefit of the doubt. No man had ever suggested that she might have had cause for her deeds.

"I would ask you to reconsider the merit of your youthful pledge against love," Alexander said as they neared the threshold. "It was, after all, made without the fullness of all you now know to be true."

She stared at him, astonished to find herself considering that very prospect. This was the danger of this man, with his handsome visage and his smooth charm. He could persuade her that day was night or that night was day. He could make her wonder whether love had any merit at all; he could make her burn to meet him abed; he could tempt her to conjure for him a son; he could persuade her to offer her very heart to him.

And what would befall her after Alexander had a son? Then he would learn of her father's bequest; then he would have coin aplenty for Kinfairlie; then he would have no need of a lady by his side who refused to open her heart to him.

But would it not be worse to be cast aside then if she had opened her heart and come to love him? Eleanor stared at him, not knowing what to say, and Alexander smiled.

"It is a fool who imagines that the prize of a lady's heart can be won with ease, for what is readily surrendered is seldom of any value at all."

Eleanor did not challenge his assertion, for she was beginning to fear that he spoke the truth. What that would mean for her, she could not begin to guess.

～

ELEANOR HAD LITTLE CHANCE to consider the matter further, for Anthony met them at the portal to the hall. The cook stood beside him and between the two men was the last woman Eleanor had ever expected to see again.

And worse, the maid looked frightened.

"Moira!" she exclaimed. "Whatever are you doing at Kinfairlie?"

Moira bowed and the two men exchanged a glance. "I followed you, my lady, for I was certain that you had not meant to leave me behind at Tivotdale and I could not break my pledge to your own mother, made as it was upon her deathbed."

Typically, words fell with haste from Moira's lips. The maid had never been valued for her discretion, but for her loyalty. In this moment, Eleanor wished the maid would fall silent.

"I did not wish to endanger you, Moira. I knew not where I would find sanctuary or even if I would find it." Eleanor smiled. "Such an uncertain fate seemed a poor reward for your years of service. I had thought that you might find a place at Tivotdale."

Moira snorted. "I would not linger willingly in that hall! The foul words they utter about you are beyond belief!" She spared a sidelong glance to Anthony. "Would you linger beneath the authority of any soul who saw fit to defame your laird?"

Anthony opened his mouth and closed it again, for he was not averse to criticizing his own laird himself. Eleanor saw Alexander bite back a smile.

"It is improper, and it is wrong," Moira declared. "No maid should so much as whisper against her lady. I told them, I did, that it might look bad for you, my lady, but that we must have seen only half the tale. My laird Ewen might well have deserved to have died for the deeds he committed against you, but that is not the same as certainty that you saw him dead with your own hand." Moira took a deep breath.

"That is sufficient, Moira," Eleanor interjected, trying to halt the torrent of the maid's words.

Her attempt failed utterly.

"Nay, it is far from the same, though that is not to say that he would not have deserved as much, the drunken sot." Moira spat on the ground. "There is no man worth his salt who treats a lady so poorly as he treated you—"

"Moira, enough!"

"Taking the gem from your mother on the night of your nuptials!" Moira shook a finger at the castellan, then at the cook, and both men took a step back in their discomfiture. "A man who would not show honor to his lady on such a night is a knave and a cur and a shameless rogue, to be sure. I would not wipe my feet to attend his funeral!"

"What gem?" Alexander asked softly, and Eleanor knew he would not cease until he had the full tale.

"It was a sentimental piece, and scarce worthy of note," she said hastily, doubting that she could limit his curiosity. The man was cursedly determined in pursuit of a secret! "Moira found his gesture discourteous, no more than that."

"Yet again, Ewen showed his measure," Alexander murmured.

"I beg your pardon, my lady, but there was much more than that!" Moira cried. "My lady gives credit where it is not due, if I may be so bold as to say as much."

"Would that not be a *criticism* of your lady?" Anthony murmured, but Moira ignored him.

She appealed instead to Alexander. "This was a gem from my lady's own mother, the sole token that she had remaining of that great lady, a lady I served from the time I was ten summers of age. I was there when Lady Eleanor was born; I was there when Lady Yolanda breathed her last; I was there when the laird himself rent his hair and wept like a child."

"Moira," Eleanor said. Hers was a token protest, for she knew that the full tale would spill now and there was nothing she could do about it.

Moira took a ragged breath and jabbed her thumb into her own chest. "I was there when the great lady Yolanda took the crucifix from her own neck and pressed it into mine own humble hand and bade me swear that I would see to the welfare of her babe, the child whose birthing would claim her own life, and that I would ensure that her newly born daughter would have that gem for her own."

Moira shook that finger at Alexander. "And I protected that gem with my life and I secured it for my lady, and my lady Eleanor's father saw fit to let me—me!—hang it around her neck when she first celebrated the miracle of the Eucharist." She took a shaking breath and wiped away a tear. "He was a hard man, was your father, my lady Eleanor, but his heart was good."

"Moira, I believe you have said enough," Eleanor said so firmly that the maid blushed.

"On the contrary," Alexander said. "I would hear more of this gem." Eleanor would have protested, but his grip tightened on her hand. He granted her a piercing look. "If

I am not mistaken, it would be the one you wished you wore at our nuptials."

Eleanor nodded and averted her gaze.

"Rightly so, my lord, for it is a gem that should adorn any bride in my lady Eleanor's lineage. So, the great lady Yolanda told me and so I saw with mine own eyes, and that more than once." Moira fell abruptly silent. The maid's gaze danced between laird and lady, for she finally understood Eleanor's manner.

"Moira?" Alexander prompted. Eleanor nodded minutely, for the harm was done, and the maid smiled.

"It was a crucifix, my lord, one that had been in Lady Yolanda's family for generations, or so she told me. The women in her family wore it openly upon their nuptial day and beneath their garb otherwise, lest it attract avaricious eyes, and so Lady Eleanor wore it on the day of her nuptials with Laird Ewen, just as she had when she wedded my lord Millard."

"And what was it like?" Alexander prompted.

"It was wrought of rubies set in gold, my lord, as long and as broad as my hand, as brilliant as the sun in the summer sky. It was a treasure, to be sure, and one that fiendish Laird Ewen stole from my lady fair."

"A treasure, perhaps, with a value beyond its price," Alexander mused. Eleanor felt Alexander's gaze upon her, as well as the attention of both cook and castellan, but she stared at the tips of her shoes. Her entire being roiled at the injustice she had been served at Ewen's hand, and though a part of her longed to tell Alexander all of it, another part of her feared that he would not take that particular truth well.

"Indeed!" Moira agreed with gusto.

"And you never retrieved it?" Alexander asked Eleanor quietly.

She had been so certain that he would ask another question, one less mild, that she glanced up. There was consideration in his gaze, a consideration that told her that his larger questions would be asked in privacy.

There was much to be said for a man who treated her with courtesy before his household. Eleanor released the breath she did not realize she had been holding and forced a small smile. "It was to be returned to me when I bore him a son, but I never rounded with child in Ewen's household." She shrugged as if the matter were of less import than it was.

"Drunken sot," Moira muttered.

Alexander ignored the comment. "And you did not retrieve it when you left?"

"I could not find it on the night I departed from Tivotdale," Eleanor said with a smoothness that belied her panicked search of Ewen's chamber. "Though truly I was disappointed to lose so precious a reminder of my mother."

"As any thinking soul would have been," Alexander said with resolve. "I welcome you, Moira, to Kinfairlie. Should your lady desire your continued service in her chamber, I have no objection, or if not, there will be a place for you in my hall in gratitude for your loyalty to my lady wife."

"I thank you, my lord," Moira said with a deep bow, then looked expectantly at Eleanor. The cook bowed and returned to the kitchens.

"I thank you, my lord, for this courtesy," Eleanor said. "And I would counsel Moira upon what must be done, with your indulgence."

"Of course." Alexander kissed her fingertips in parting, granting her a significant glance that Eleanor did not doubt was a portent of the questions he would ask later. He looked determined, did her spouse, as he had not before in her presence.

He would ask about Ewen and she could only hope for his mercy.

Eleanor urged Moira aside as Alexander progressed into the hall. "I would have you make your way to the stables," she whispered to the maid. "Without any noting your passage." The maid nodded vigorously. "And there would have you count the steeds. They are numerous, as many have arrived this very day. . . ."

"I saw them! Such marvelous beasts . . ."

"Moira!" Eleanor chided in a whisper, wishing there were another soul she might ask to do this errand. "I beg you, let no soul see you enter or leave the stables. Come to me before the evening meal with your tally. The laird's chamber is two flights up from the hall: I shall ensure that your passage is not impeded."

"Yes, my lady." Moira bowed, then gave her mistress a shy smile. "I am gladdened to find you hale, my lady."

Eleanor smiled in return. "And I, you, Moira."

"And I offer congratulations, my lady. There is not a foul word to be heard about the laird of Kinfairlie."

Eleanor nodded, hoping rumor proved true in this circumstance.

"But there is something I must confess to you, my lady."

"I thank you for your tidings, Moira, but they will wait until later." Eleanor shook her head, knowing the maid would chatter the day away. "Make haste upon my errand!"

ALEXANDER WAS JUBILANT. Eleanor had confided in him, and better, she had surrendered a truth that could not have been easy to confess.

He was untroubled that she had killed Ewen Douglas. He knew well enough that a woman could strike back in the midst of abuse and see her abuser felled. That Ewen drank with such gusto only lent credence to such a notion.

Alexander did not mourn Ewen's passing, and he could not blame his lady wife for not so doing. This confession of hers, though, vastly encouraged him. If she could tell him this, then she trusted him, in truth.

And that could only be a good omen for their future together.

To Alexander's further delight, the cook had no need of his counsel. Eleanor had already resolved the questions about the menu for the midday meal. He could well become accustomed to such assistance as she so adroitly offered—indeed, it made the weight of responsibility seem less onerous to have it shared.

Alexander turned toward the hall with a lightened step, content to let Eleanor dictate to Moira's actions as well. He was yet mulling upon the details offered by the garrulous Moira when Anthony cleared his throat portentously.

"Is that not the sum of it, Anthony?"

"I am afraid not, my lord. My lady has made the most excellent suggestion that a party ride to hunt this afternoon, better to provide meat for tomorrow's board. A hunt would provide entertainment for your guests, as well as see their bellies full."

Alexander, bold with recent revelations, could not help but tease his stern castellan. "And it is a fine idea, Anthony." He sighed and frowned, just as Eleanor rejoined them.

"Is there a problem, my lord?" she asked.

He shook his head, as if sorely burdened. "Only that my responsibilities tear me both one way and another. I intended to spend the better part of this day with my accounts, the better to ensure that they were resolved by year end, but your suggestion that we hunt this day is a good one."

"You meant to labor again at your accounts?" Anthony demanded, fighting unsuccessfully to hide his delight. "Willingly, my lord?"

"Of course, *willingly*, Anthony. A laird cannot neglect his duties, and I should not have to tell you that balancing the ledgers is a duty of considerable import."

"Certainly, my lord. You will find no argument from me upon this matter."

"Ah, but the meat." Alexander shook his head and let his brow furrow anew. "Is it a greater duty to see one's guests entertained and well-fed, or to know the status of one's holding?"

Eleanor came to his side; the way that she fought a smile revealed that she had overheard their words. "Perhaps another could lead the hunt. Your brother, perhaps?"

"But he has ridden already this day and it is not his duty." Alexander spared his lady a mischievous glance, deciding that it would not hurt to tease her, either. "And I could not ask you to take a hawk upon your fist and lead the party, not given your fear of horses."

To her credit, Eleanor flushed and looked away.

Anthony appeared to be genuinely concerned. "But, my lord, surely the ledgers could wait until the morrow?"

"Anthony! I am shocked to hear you suggest such a course! How many times have you told me that leaving a deed until the morrow only encourages a man to leave it to the morrow again and so on, next to next, until the deed is never done?"

Anthony flushed and averted his gaze in turn.

Alexander placed a hand over his heart. "Ah, my beloved ledgers. Duty calls and I shall have to put them aside for the fickle pleasures of the hunt. Such is but one of the burdens laid upon me." He began to walk to the board, leaving them both with something to consider.

To his surprise, Eleanor stepped after him. "I could labor upon the accounts in your stead, my lord."

Alexander pivoted.

Anthony's eyes had widened in his own surprise. "My lady, such skill is not typically among the talents of a noblewoman."

She lifted her chin. "My father taught me to read and to write, as well as how to balance an account, the better to ensure that I not be cheated."

The men exchanged a glance, but Alexander recalled her earlier assertions about her duties in her father's hall and, indeed, her sage counsel regarding tithes and fees.

All the same, her offer came in a moment that made him wonder. Why would she wish to see the ledgers of Kinfairlie? Did she mean to have a better assessment of the weight of his purse? Did she not believe his protests of his estate's poverty?

Or did she merely mean to be of assistance? He looked upon her—her chin held high, her gaze steady—and wanted to trust her.

He looked upon the fullness of her lips, their ruddy

hue, their delicious curve. He recalled her own confession that he easily kindled her ardor, and thought about partaking of another feast than the one being laid in the hall.

But that pleasure would have to wait.

"I could not ask such a deed of you, not when you already do so much," he said with gallantry. "Come, let us make merry at the midday meal; then I shall take our guests to hunt." He pulled her close to his side as they stepped toward the high table and lowered his voice so that only she could hear his words. "I warn you, though, that I will have a fancy for a sweet this night, after we retire to our chambers."

"How sad," she murmured, "for I have a taste for just such a sweet, though I yearn for it now." Then she spared him a sparkling glance, one that brought his very blood to a simmer and made him wonder how quickly his party might fell a buck or two.

In the end, it was not a buck that was felled.

Uriel, true to his name and Alexander's recent inattention, was in a fearsome fury as soon as he was led from the stables. The steed scarcely calmed, even when Alexander himself seized the beast's bridle. The entire household watched, and Alexander had no intent of being bested by a feisty steed.

From the corner of his eye, he saw Eleanor's maid, Moira, slip from the stables. She made her way to her mistress's side, then murmured something to Eleanor. Eleanor nodded, her gaze unswerving from Alexander.

Alexander had little time to wonder about this oddity, for Uriel commanded his full attention.

"Calm yourself," he bade the steed, his words stern and low. He held the reins fast. "I am not so unfamiliar to you as that." The stallion blew out his lips, his ears quivering, and there was a fearsome light in his eye. "Has any foul deed befallen him, Owen?" he asked the ostler, unable to account for the stallion's mood.

"Not as I know, my lord. He has been brushed and turned into the fields daily, as is our routine. Perhaps he takes insult that you have not ridden him of late." Kinfairlie's ostler smiled. "He is a cursed proud steed."

Alexander chuckled in his turn. "That is true enough." He scratched the steed's ear. "Have you been neglected of late, Your Highness?"

Uriel snorted and tossed his head anew. It was not uncommon for Uriel to make his feelings known, though it was uncommon for him to pursue the matter unduly. The steed oft made a token protest, but always surrendered to Alexander's command.

This time, he protested at length. Alexander could not fathom why. The stallion exhaled mightily. His eyes flashed even as Alexander spoke soothingly to him. His back hoof stamped the ground in fury.

"I will brush him before I ride, for that soothes him," Alexander said.

"He has been groomed, my lord."

"All the same, a familiar touch can be reassuring." At Alexander's word, a groom fetched the brush. Alexander brushed the horse, liking the rhythm of this task. Tynan had always told him to make acquaintance with a horse before riding it, to win its trust each time with attention.

So, oblivious to the watchful household, he spoke to Uriel of nonsensical matters, then took to the saddle with resolve.

Uriel reared.

The stallion fought the bit, he whinnied in a fury such as Alexander had never witnessed in him. The ostler swore and made to seize the reins, but failed, the company backed away.

Uriel kicked, tossed his head, fairly spat in his indignation. He took every effort to throw Alexander from the saddle. It was as if another horse, a demon steed, had been substituted for the beast Alexander knew and loved so well.

He fought to command the horse, but the steed might never have borne a saddle. It was shocking, for Uriel had shown spirit, but he had never fought Alexander as he did in this moment.

Uriel bolted, leaving the astonished company of Kinfairlie far behind. He ran like the wind, desperate to escape some torment that Alexander could not name. Alexander heard the company shout and the hunting party give chase; he heard the familiar bellow of his ostler, but he merely hung on.

He feared that Uriel would run clear to London or drop of exhaustion en route, but the beast would not heed any command to halt. Alexander's choices were few: he could allow himself to be thrown, or he could hang on. He gripped his knees tightly and hunkered low, working with Uriel's rhythm, hoping the beast would tire himself. He spoke constantly to the horse, hoping the low murmur of his words would reassure him.

Uriel showed no signs of being reassured. Alexander

used his knees to urge the steed to curve his course toward the sea, thinking that the stallion would halt when the way before him was not flat.

At first, it seemed the horse would defy his command, but his training ran too deep and he could not deny the command in the pressure of Alexander's knee against his right side. Uriel turned, the coast rose ever closer; Alexander urged the beast down a point that jutted into the sea, just north of Kinfairlie proper.

If the horse did not stop on this point, they would both be sorely injured.

Alexander took the gamble, though feared its import when Uriel did not slow his pace. The crest of rocks on the lip of the point drew closer and closer, and yet closer again. Alexander's heart leapt in fear that they would soon be in the sea.

Then Uriel stopped cold, planted his hooves against the ground, and ducked his head. Alexander, unprepared for this move, was cast over the steed's head.

He flew head over heels. He endeavored to land upon his feet, but all happened too quickly.

Instead, Alexander landed upon his buttocks and roared in pain. He then hit his head and both elbows on the rocks, bouncing as if he were no more substantial than a figure wrought of husks.

Finally he fell still. Alexander lay back and groaned. He would be black-and-blue, to be sure. He was not anxious to rise and assess the damage to his person.

At least he was out of Uriel's saddle and was not quite dead. The horse snorted at close proximity, uninjured. That, he supposed, was the best that could be made of this matter.

Much worse, it would prove, could come of this event.

Chapter Eleven

OWEN'S DISMAY KNEW NO BOUNDS, for his laird and master had been injured by a steed beneath Owen's care. He was somehow responsible for Uriel's foul deed, of that Owen was certain. So it was that Kinfairlie's ostler reached Laird Alexander first.

Owen fell upon his knees beside his fallen laird and said a prayer when his laird opened his eyes and winked at him.

"It is clear that I have forgotten all that ever I knew of steeds, Owen," the laird jested, making it clear that he did not blame the ostler for events. He was uncommonly kind in that way, this son of the old laird, and his graciousness only redoubled Owen's determination to see this mystery solved.

"It was a clever ploy to lead him here, my lord. I feared he would run the length of Christendom and tire himself to death."

"As did I, Owen." The laird moved tentatively and winced. He then grinned at the ostler, his charm and good humor clearly unaffected by his fall. "Though I do not think my concern for his welfare was repaid in kind."

Owen did not smile. "It is not like Uriel, my lord. I cannot think of what came over him."

"True enough. It has been decades since I have been tossed from a saddle, and never has Uriel taken such exception to me." The laird frowned. "Did he flee?"

"He lingers, my lord, stamping his feet and shaking his head. He is in a sweat, to be sure, and trembles mightily. He perhaps is too tired to flee farther."

"Then go to him, Owen, and see if your touch soothes him. You have a way about you that a restless beast oft welcomes." The laird's mischievous smile flashed again. "I believe I will remain here for the moment. The view is most fine."

How like the laird to tempt the smile of others while he himself clearly felt pain! It was no wonder that men served him with such fervor.

Owen bowed and rose to his feet, then approached the black stallion with caution. Uriel stamped and exhaled noisily, his temper riled as it had not been when Owen himself saddled him. What ailed the beast? Owen knew horses and he knew this one and he knew there had to be a reason for Uriel's manner.

Then he saw the blood. Three streams of ruby red blood stained the stallion's side.

Owen pivoted in terror, but his laird did not obviously bleed, and such a quantity of blood as this would have stained his garb.

Uriel was injured! How could this be?

The rest of the party arrived noisily, their cries making the stallion dance away from them. Owen shouted for the ostler from Ravensmuir to aid him, as well as the three stoutest grooms in his service. They enclosed the stallion in a tightening circle; then Ravensmuir's ostler seized the reins. He held the reins fast and the boys stilled the horse with their hands as Owen hastily unbuckled the saddle and lifted it away.

Uriel shuddered from head to tail at its removal, and Owen immediately saw why. Three thorns were there, each as long and nigh as broad as the last digit of his thumb. Owen had never seen the like of them.

The blood ran cleanly and the wounds were not as deep as they could have been, but still it was a horror to look upon Uriel's damaged flesh. The underside of the saddle had been cut to accommodate the base of each thorn, leaving the point exposed.

"When Laird Alexander took the saddle, the points of the thorns were driven into Uriel's flesh," Ravensmuir's ostler said, his expression that of a man sickened by what he saw.

Owen lifted his gaze to meet that of his peer. "But I saddled Uriel myself, and I swear by the grace of God that these thorns were not there." His bile rose at the injury done to the horse. "I would never have committed such wickedness. I would never have seen a steed willfully injured, you must all know as much!"

Uriel bent and nibbled at Owen's hair, perhaps sensing the ostler's consternation, perhaps grateful that the ostler had removed the thorns.

Ravensmuir's ostler smiled, the expression softening the harsh lines of his face. "The horse absolves you, Owen, though that leaves us no closer to knowing who did the deed."

"Alexander!" The cry of the laird's new lady wife

echoed over the company. She cast herself from the saddle of a palfrey with the ease of one accustomed to riding, flung her reins aside, and ran to her husband.

"I thought she feared horses," muttered one of the grooms.

"She rides with the ease of one who has ridden all of her life," said Ravensmuir's ostler.

"And her maid was in the stables," said another boy. The other four looked to him in surprise. "I saw her. She said she came to see the fabled horses of Ravensmuir, but she went from one stall to the next with great diligence, as if she sought a particular horse."

"And the laird showed the lady his own steed before the midday meal," mused Ravensmuir's ostler, before meeting Owen's gaze.

"And I left the laird's horse alone once he was saddled, cursed fool that I am, for I fetched Uriel an apple." Owen rubbed the beast's nose as the five frowned in unison. "Would that you could tell us what you had witnessed, my friend."

"The laird must know of this," declared Ravensmuir's ostler.

Owen watched the lady exclaim over the laird's wounds and wondered if he was the sole one who recalled the charges of Alan Douglas in this moment. What scheme had the lady? What shadow in her heart was eclipsed by her bright beauty?

ELEANOR FELT THE ABSENCE of goodwill in her husband's household the very moment that it was rescinded.

Alexander, to her relief, was not sorely injured, though she had feared greatly for him.

"I am sufficiently cocky to withstand such a blow to my pride," he jested as his brother aided him to his feet. Eleanor did not miss how he winced when he put his weight upon his foot, or how he stretched his back with a grimace, but at least none of his bones were broken.

"It is not your cock that I fear for," she retorted, wanting only to see his smile.

"No? I thought you yearned for a son."

Eleanor flushed at that and Alexander laughed. Then he sobered suddenly, granting her a stern look. "How did you come to be here so quickly as this? Surely you did not ride?"

And Eleanor realized her error. She had not thought of her earlier lie, she had thought only of pursuing Alexander, of trying to ensure his welfare. She straightened, not knowing what to say, and found suspicion in every face turned toward her.

Alexander alone watched her with a knowing gleam in his eye, as if he were not surprised by these tidings. He stepped closer, unable to stifle a wince, though he raised a hand to ward off her assistance.

Eleanor knew she would have little chance to repair her mistake. "I lied to you," she admitted softly, and Alexander's expression hardened.

"I know." His tone was cold. He arched a brow, his gaze unswerving. "And this after you pledged honesty to me."

Eleanor felt the blood drain from her face. She found only anger in Alexander's stony expression and knew that she stood before a judge who had no reason to grant her mercy. She had lied to him; she had deceived him; she had sheltered him from the truth simply because it was ugly. Now her efforts to ensure that this marriage had a chance to find its footing would destroy that marriage.

Unless she could persuade Alexander to grant her a hearing. She recalled belatedly that his most furious response had been to the revelation that he had been the victim of a lie and knew her position to be perilous.

She might well have lost his support forever in this choice, though she knew she could not have done otherwise. She thought again of Blanchefleur and was sickened by the persistent taste of her own dark past.

Kinfairlie's ostler came to Alexander in that moment, three bloody thorns upon his palm and accusation in his expression. "These were beneath the saddle, my lord. They were not there when I saddled Uriel, but I left him before your arrival to fetch him an apple. Thomas declares that my lady's maid, the one newly arrived, was in the stables then, and that she checked each stall as if seeking a specific steed."

Alexander's expression was grim. "What do you say, Owen? I bid you speak your thoughts clearly."

"I make no accusation, my lord, for I have no evidence, but it seems that matters add together in a most cunning way. You introduced your lady to your steed before the midday meal, and her maid was found seeking a steed at the time that thorns were placed beneath your steed's saddle." The ostler squared his shoulders. "You might have been cast to your death, my lord, for these are massive thorns, and thus I cannot help but recall the charge made by Alan Douglas on Christmas Day in our own chapel."

Alexander's features might have been set to stone. He

spoke with quiet heat. "Then surely you recall that he, too, could offer no evidence to support his charge against the lady."

Eleanor felt her lips part. Did he defend her?

Owen's expression turned grim. "You are a kind laird, and one who has been good to me, and thus, sir, I would be so bold as to continue to speak my thoughts, though you may not welcome them. I fear for your survival. Your lady wife admits herself to knowing of poisons and there have been two poisonings in our hall since her arrival. She admits herself to having buried two husbands and rumor would have one believe that at least one of them died before his time. And though it is true that there is no proof of this, the lady shows herself a liar by her own deed." He pointed to the palfrey Eleanor had ridden. "I heard her tell you this very morn that she feared horses, yet she rode with uncommon ease just moments past."

"Perhaps my laird is uncommonly persuasive in easing my fears," Eleanor dared to suggest.

"Perhaps my lady told a falsehood," the ostler retorted, his gaze hard and his words sharp. "No one learns to ride as you just did in a matter of hours. You have ridden from the time you could reach the stirrup, upon this I would wager my very soul, and there is not a scrap of fear within you for horses, upon that I would also wager."

"You overstep yourself, Owen," Alexander said softly.

"I mean no impertinence, my lord—"

"Yet you are impertinent."

"I would only see you warned, my lord, if you cannot see the portent yourself. Is it not the duty of a man sworn to a laird's service to repay that laird's goodness with tidings, even if they be ill?"

"If it is so, then such tidings should not be surrendered before the entire company," Alexander said quietly. "I respect your intent, Owen, but it is churlish to speak ill of the lady of a keep before all those who serve her. Had you proof of your charge, that would be another matter, but in this, you repeat only rumor and innuendo."

"Forgive my so saying, my lord, but it is more than rumor." With that, Owen placed the three thorns in Alexander's hand. "With your forgiveness, my lord, I would tend Uriel's injury."

Alexander inclined his head and Owen spared Eleanor a cold glance before he turned away. Alexander, she noted, turned the bloody thorns in his hand and his expression became grim.

"Owen," he said quietly, and the ostler halted, though he turned only after a pause. "Do not imagine that I do not welcome your tidings, even if they be ill. My father taught me simply that no laird or lady should be condemned in his or her own hall. There have been unconventional choices made by my kin and rumors aplenty of their intent, though not a one of them has had a black heart. Matters are not always what they seem, this was my father's counsel."

Owen would have spoken, but Alexander held up a finger for silence. "This matter will be resolved, upon that you may rely, and if there are charges and if there is evidence, then we shall hear all of it in Kinfairlie's court. Until that time, I counsel you and your fellows to speak of my lady with respect."

Owen seemed to fight his urge to argue the matter. His gaze flicked between laird and lady, then he inclined his head. "As you say, so shall it be, my lord."

Alexander nodded crisply, then turned to his castellan. "We shall return to Kinfairlie, Anthony, and I shall retire to my chambers for the remainder of the day."

"Very good. I shall send for a physician, my lord."

"There is no need, Anthony. I am sufficiently hale to survive." Alexander gave Eleanor a look so cold that she was chilled to her very marrow, then turned away.

Her marriage was over, unless she set matters aright.

"No!" Eleanor cried when they might have abandoned her there. "No. This matter cannot be left as it stands. It is true that I lied to you about my fear of horses, but I would surrender the truth to all of you. I would do it now."

The ostlers and squires paused and turned, clearly incredulous. Alexander watched Eleanor, his expression inscrutable, and she knew that all hung in the balance.

The sooner she made her confession, the better.

"Surely this can wait, my lady," Anthony suggested. "I would see my lord made comfortable."

"And I would see the truth granted its hearing," Eleanor argued. "It is late for me to confess as much, and I know it, but I would redress the matter now, before you all, before another moment passes." She took a shuddering breath. "I hope for nothing more than that you all stand witness to the fact that my suspicions are groundless."

"Suspicions?" Anthony echoed in confusion. "What suspicions have you of us?"

Eleanor squared her shoulders. "Let me tell you of it."

ALEXANDER WATCHED HIS LADY with mingled awe and pride. She stood as straight as a finely wrought blade, her chin high and her bearing regal. She spoke clearly and with conviction, her words carrying over the company with ease. The sunlight glinted on the gold of her hair, for her veil had been lost in her pursuit of him, and burnished her finely wrought features. She was beautiful and pained, and his heart ached at her courage.

"Once there was a woman whose father saw her wedded to a man many years her senior," she said. Alexander knew full well who that woman was, and saw that others in the company had also guessed as much. "She was twelve summers of age, while he had seen two and sixty summers. He was a corpulent man, enamored of the pleasures of the table and one disinclined to deny himself any indulgence. He was rumored to be cruel, albeit in a cunning way, but he was a comrade of the maiden's father and she chose to believe that he could not be guilty of what was whispered of him."

She nodded slightly. "And truly, the evidence seemed to support her faith in him, for he was kind to her. She had brought a palfrey of her own with her when she joined his household, a steed of chestnut hue with a white star upon her brow. As a young girl, she had thought the mark looked more like a flower and so she had called the horse Blanchefleur. The steed was treated well in her lord husband's stables, though he oft teased her that she loved the beast more than she loved him."

Eleanor looked down at her slippers for a moment. "She denied this, though she feared that he had discerned her secret. It would have been uncommon, indeed, for such a young woman to have held such a man as he in her most ardent affections." She swallowed and looked over the company. "And so it was that the maiden was relieved beyond belief when she learned that she bore her husband's child. He had made it known that he wished for nothing more than a son, and she hoped that she might fulfill his desire."

Alexander frowned at this reference to a son. Was this where Eleanor had learned her insistence upon a babe of that gender?

"But Fortune did not smile upon the maiden. The babe was only five months in her womb when her water broke. She fought against her labor, not wanting to surrender the prize her husband sought, but the babe came all the same. It was small; it was wizened and red; it was dead." She licked her lips. "And it was a boy."

The ostlers fidgeted at this unwelcome detail, and Alexander noted that sympathy lit the gaze of more than one of them. He waited, for he guessed the loss of the child, even so late in her pregnancy, was not the origin of whatever scar Eleanor retained of those events.

"The maiden feared the reprisal of her spouse, but he was charming. He was solicitous and sympathetic. He urged her to lie abed, to recover, to eat tempting morsels. He coaxed her smile when she felt she had no reason to smile. Indeed, he proved himself to be more gallant than she had ever imagined, and she faulted herself for not having seen his merit. Three days after this sorry loss of their child, he announced that he had prepared a feast in his wife's honor."

There was a murmur in the company at this. Eleanor looked over the sea, her eyes narrowed, though still she recounted her tale. "No expense was spared, to the maiden's astonishment, for she could not understand why her deed was so worthy of celebration. The hall was filled to bursting with nobles and neighbors, all in their finest garb. The board groaned with the quantity of food prepared and her husband insisted that all drink to the maiden's health. She was grateful for his understanding and newly determined to provide him with his son.

"Then the great dish was served at the husband's dictate, a stew that the maiden was told had been wrought for her own pleasure. It was laid before her with a flourish on the finest silver plate in their home. Her husband insisted that she eat first of it, that she eat heartily of it, for she would have need of her strength. Indeed, no one could eat a morsel of it before she had eaten all she could bear to consume."

Eleanor's teeth visibly set on edge. "It was strange stew, the like of which the maiden had never eaten. It was redolent with spices, for no expense had been spared in its preparation, yet the meat was odd."

Owen, the ostler, turned away, his expression sickened.

"It was silky on the tongue, unctuous even, and the maiden had little taste for it. Her husband insisted, though; indeed, he filled her trencher and stood beside her until she ate it all. And when she sat gorged with a meal she had not desired, he laughed and his was not a pleasant laugh. He grasped her elbows with force when he whispered in her ear, ensuring that she could not escape whatsoever he told her.

"'We have each lost what we loved best this week, which is a kind of justice,' he said, and she did not understand his import. 'You lost my son and the price to you is Blanchefleur.' It was then that the maiden knew what she had eaten, what meat had wrought that stew."

The ostlers roared at this travesty. "Barbarian!" cried the ostler from Ravensmuir.

"Death is too good for such a villain," declared Owen.

Eleanor straightened. "And the maiden ran to the stables, even as her husband laughed at her dismay, for she could not believe that any soul could be so wicked. But Blanchefleur was gone and the ostler told her the truth of it. She vomited all that day and all that night as she wept in the stall that her beloved steed had occupied." Eleanor lifted her chin, even as the tears streamed down her cheeks. "And so she resolved that she should never love another steed, the better that she could not cast that beast's life in peril."

She turned to Alexander, her cheeks wet. "I am sorry, for I lied to you. But the cook said there was need of meat, and that you would resolve the menu upon your return from the stables, and the ostler said you had a scheme for the foals and"—she took a choking breath—"and you insisted that you must make me a gift of one of these wondrous horses and I was afraid as I have never been afraid." She ran a hand over her brow. "I am sorry, for I have the wits to know that no man would serve you so loyally as these men do, if you were of the ilk of Millard."

"It was not your wits that fed your fear," Alexander said quietly. He went to her side and took her hand within his, lowering his voice. "It was love and fear of its loss. It was your heart, Eleanor, the heart that you would feign not to possess."

She stared at him, weeping yet still proud, and he kissed her palm, even as she trembled before him. He folded her fingers over his salute, then pulled her fast against his side. He could see how difficult this confession had been for her—and indeed, it was a horrific one. What kind of man would do such a deed? Alexander could not think upon it.

He respected not only that Eleanor had faced her fear in surrendering a secret she held fast, but that she had done so for the sake of his trust.

"We return to Kinfairlie," he said. "My lady and I will ride the palfrey she rode here and Uriel will be led."

Owen, the ostler, stepped into their path, his manner contrite. "My lady, I beg your forgiveness for the charges I made against you this day. There is no person who could both feel such pain as you did in the loss of your palfrey and commit such a crime as that committed against Uriel."

"Appearances were against me, Owen," Eleanor said quietly. She clung to Alexander's side, seemingly weakened by the tumult of her tale. "I appreciate as much and hope that you never cease to surrender such good counsel to my lord husband."

"Never!" Owen bowed. "I would ask a boon of you, my lady."

Alexander sensed his wife's confusion, though he guessed what the ostler would ask. "Your request cannot be filled unless it is shared," he said when the ostler did not speak.

Owen spared a glance for Uriel, then cleared his throat. "It is said that a healer's talents can be used for a horse as well as a man. Is there a salve you might make to see Uriel healed more quickly? I would not see him suffer unduly for some soul's cruelty."

Eleanor caught her breath and Alexander smiled. The

other ostler and the squires stood and watched, approval in their eyes.

"You would trust me with this?" she asked, awed.

Owen nodded, his manner gruff.

"I would be honored," Eleanor said, her words husky. "I would be proud to aid such a magnificent steed." Owen smiled and bowed, then hastened away. Uriel meanwhile tossed his head, seemingly in agreement with this sentiment, and snorted with vigor.

Alexander smiled down at his wife, well pleased with what she had achieved this day.

"You have made a conquest of every man in my stables," he teased beneath his breath. "And that with a single tale. I shall have to pray that you are sated with the attentions of one man alone."

Eleanor turned her shining gaze upon him. "I can only hope that he will prove to be attentive, indeed. Tell me, my lord husband, is there time for a *sweet* before the evening meal?"

SHE LOVED HIM.

It was as simple as matters could be and Eleanor marveled that she had not guessed the truth sooner. Eleanor loved Alexander, with his conviction that all was good, with his surety that honesty and good humor would make all come aright, with his determination to hear the whole of the tale before he rendered a judgment.

Alexander was fair, he was just, he was kind. She loved that those in his household served him with unswerving loyalty; she loved that he was protective of every creature, big or small, human or horse, who relied upon him.

She loved that he could be pensive or playful, that he was clever and unafraid to show his feelings. She loved that he cherished truth and honesty above all, and that he rewarded their surrender to him.

And that was but a smattering of what he offered to her. She loved that Alexander gave her the benefit of the doubt, as no soul ever had done, that he assumed that she had a reason for any deed she had committed. Alexander gave her choice, gave her time, treated her with honor and dignity.

He had persuaded her that the merit of what was offered by loving him far outweighed any risk. It was not an easy lesson for Eleanor and she did not doubt that she would err again in his company, but she knew that Alexander would always grant her the chance to remedy any misstep.

It was a weighty boon he offered to her and one she welcomed. With ardent pursuit of her secrets, he had broken the last shield protecting her battered heart.

She wanted to show him as much, in the best way that she knew.

Moira met them at the base of the stairs, but Eleanor smilingly turned the maid away. "There is no need for your tally now," she said, tugging at her husband's hand.

Alexander followed her, only limping slightly, his eyes fairly glowing at her enthusiasm. "You are anxious to reach our chambers," he teased. "It must be the lure of my ledgers."

Eleanor laughed. "I am anxious to have your company to myself," she retorted, not caring what any person made of her bold words.

Alexander grinned. "But I am injured . . ."

"And I know the best tonic to see you healed."

Alexander sobered slightly. "You should know that I am not so determined to have a son as other men have been. Sons and daughters may come in their own time or they may not—their presence or absence changes nothing in a good marriage."

"It is not solely a son for which I would strive!"

Moira wrung her hands at the base of the steps, not sharing the pair's merry mood. "But, my lady, there is another detail I would confide in you!"

"Later, Moira, later will serve well enough."

"But . . ."

Deaf to the maid's entreaties, Eleanor tugged her husband's hand until he stood on the step immediately below her. She framed Alexander's face in her hands, ran her thumb across his smiling lips, then kissed him fully.

She heard him catch his breath at her show of affection; then his arms were around her waist. He pulled her closer, even as he opened his mouth beneath her assault. He let her take what she would have of him and Eleanor reveled in the awareness that she was not alone in responding to their embrace.

She broke their kiss reluctantly, only to find his eyes awash with stars. "You look so merry," she whispered with wonder.

"How could a man not be merry, when his wife looks at him as you are looking at me?"

"How am I looking at you?"

His smile turned mischievous. "As if you mean to surrender more to me than a mere smile."

Eleanor laughed. "I challenge you, sir, to take upon yourself another quest."

"Another? Surely my lady's esteem is well-earned?"

Eleanor made a mock frown. "But not her smile. You said once that a courtesan's smile could be encouraged with an intimate tickle abed. I doubt that you can see the matter done."

She saw only the flash of his eyes before he caught her in his arms; then he took the remaining stairs three at a time. He kicked the door to their chamber closed behind them and kissed her with lingering abandon, holding her fast against his chest. Eleanor reveled in his embrace, in the complete banishment of her fear, and knew with utter surety that Fortune finally smiled upon her.

When they finally parted, she lifted the key from her belt and turned it in the lock with satisfaction. "I shall not loose you from this chamber before you succeed in your quest," she teased, then granted him a wicked smile.

"Then we had best begin," he said with enthusiasm, "for I cannot imagine that such a goal would be readily won."

WHEN ELEANOR LOCKED THE door of the solar behind them, her smile was both shy and bold. She held Alexander's gaze, her own eyes bright, even as her cheeks flushed with her audacity.

The lady was a marvel. Alexander loved the complexity of Eleanor, loved that she could be as regal as a warrior queen or as vulnerable as a new chick. She could defend him with the ferocity of a mother wolf, yet she surrendered to his kiss as softly as a blossom opens to the summer sun. He would never tire of her many moods, her quick wits, her ferocious defense of all she held dear.

She crossed the floor to him, reached up, and cupped

his chin in her hand. Her eyes were a clear, brilliant green, devoid of shadows and mysteries. She regarded Alexander as if he were the marvel, then touched her lips to his.

Her kiss was both languid and impassioned. She coaxed his response with the slightest touch and offered him a caress that made his blood simmer. It was the first time that she had initiated an embrace that Alexander did not wonder whether she sought to distract him, that he had not feared, at least a little, that she gave of herself in body to keep the secrets of her thoughts from his perusal.

They crossed the floor toward the bed as if in a dance, moving as one with nary a word exchanged. They feasted upon each other's lips, tasting and teasing, their hands running ceaselessly over each other. It was as if they met for the first time, as if they each mated for the first time in their days. Alexander was fairly deafened by the thunder of his pulse, and he felt a similar urgency in Eleanor's heartbeat.

He undid the laces of her kirtle as she urged aside his tabard, kissing hungrily all the while. He shed his chemise while she kicked off her slippers; he loosed her chemise while she unlaced his chausses. He broke their kiss only to pull off his boots, watching as Eleanor shook out her hair.

She came to him, wearing naught but a smile, and pushed him back onto the mattress. She climbed atop him and kissed him fully, holding his hair as if she imagined he might try to evade her. The very notion would have made him laugh, had Alexander not had better deeds to do with his mouth.

Eleanor surrendered her all to Alexander, and did so with abandon. He could not believe the difference in her manner; he would never have believed that she had so much more to grant to him. Telling the tale of Blanchefleur and finding sympathy in his household, perhaps the first compassion she had ever been shown, seemed to have softened Eleanor. She opened herself to Alexander and gave of the feast that only she could offer.

And he was smitten, in truth. He was in awe of his lady wife, of her strength and her ability to heal. He marveled that she had any shred of tenderness left within her, that she could even acknowledge the possibility that a man could offer more to her than all of the other men in her life had done.

He pleasured her as he had before and savored her eventual shout of release. She rolled atop him then, straddling him with her legs, her hair spilling around them like a curtain of gold. He caught her around the waist and lifted her above him, guiding her to sit atop him, in truth.

Eleanor laughed, clearly delighted with this pose. "You are my captive now," she teased, her eyes dancing, as he wished they always had done.

"And a willing one, to be sure."

She moved, making him catch his breath. "I may never release you," she threatened.

"No man of wit would yearn for release from such captivity."

Eleanor laughed. She moved with deliberation, quickly discerning what best enflamed him. She leaned down and kissed him again, her tongue dancing within his mouth. She caught his nape in her hand, holding him beneath her kiss as she rocked her weight atop him. Alexander caught her buttocks in one hand, then slipped his fingers between them.

"Together this time," he told her between kisses, and she caught her breath as he caressed her. They fitted together as if they truly had been wrought for each other; they moved together as if they had been created to dance solely with each other. Alexander watched passion put sparkles in his lady's eyes, watched her cheeks flush as her arousal reached its peak. He himself was on the threshold of pleasure—for what seemed a thousand years—as he waited for her to join him there.

She caught her breath suddenly and her eyes widened in pleasure. Her lips parted, her face flushed crimson, and before she could cry out, Alexander allowed himself to leap over that threshold alongside his lady wife. They shouted as one and clutched each other tightly; then in the wake of their release, she began to laugh.

"Surely my effort was not deserving of laughter," he teased in a growl, and she laughed all the louder.

"Not that! Anthony will be certain that you find uncommon pleasure with your ledgers," she said.

Alexander chuckled, then kissed her slowly. He knew an uncommon conviction that all would be aright between them, that they would only learn more about each other in the years they were to share, that their match would only grow better with each passing day.

And that was prize enough for any man.

ELIZABETH FINALLY CORNERED Malcolm in the hall after the midday meal, and managed to have him to herself. He was the one who could aid in her quest, and she wanted the chance to persuade him to her side without Alexander's counsel.

"Malcolm," she murmured after they had exchanged pleasantries. "I have a boon to ask of you."

Malcolm smiled. "Surely any boon should be asked of Alexander. I have nothing to my name, save my own self, thus can grant little to a lady."

Elizabeth gripped the cup of ale, which she did not desire. "I want to go to Ravensmuir." Malcolm started, but she hastened onward. "I must go to Ravensmuir. I must seek out Rosamunde and see to her welfare. . . ."

Malcolm laid a hand upon her arm. "Elizabeth, Rosamunde is dead," he said gently.

"No, no, it cannot be thus. How can you know? We have never found her corpse, nor that of Tynan. They could be alive still, in the rubble, awaiting our aid. . . ."

"Elizabeth!" Malcolm spoke so firmly that Elizabeth fell silent. "No soul could survive the collapse of Ravensmuir's labyrinth, much less do so for months. Further, it would be foolhardy to venture into the rubble, for one cannot tell how it might shift."

Elizabeth sat back on the bench and regarded her brother unhappily. "You will not take me there."

"Do not even imagine that you should go there alone."

Elizabeth frowned and looked away, fighting against her tears of disappointment. "I thought you would want to retrieve Uncle Tynan's body, to know for certain of his demise, to see him buried with honor if necessary."

Malcolm reached across the table and seized her hands, compelling her to look at him. "Why do you desire to do this? What do you think to find? It has been months since their disappearance, Elizabeth."

She sighed and studied their interlocked hands. There was nothing to be lost in confessing all of the truth. "I dream of Rosamunde, all the time. She is in the labyrinth and it is collapsing and she is summoning me to her aid." She dared to meet Malcolm's gaze, which was compassionate. "I have to go. I have to try to aid her."

He shook his head and held fast to her hands. The warmth of him was reassuring. "It would be folly, Elizabeth, and you would not find what you would seek."

"How can you know?"

"They are dead, though it is not easy to believe as much." Malcolm sighed. "I did not tell any of you this, but I dreamed of Maman and Papa after their demise at sea. I dreamed that they were calling for my aid, and I dreamed that I failed them. I must have had this dream two hundred times." He met her gaze steadily. "Uncle Tynan found out, because I awakened shouting more than once. He told me that it was grief that wrought a tale in my thoughts. He told me that it would pass as I grew accustomed to my new truth."

"And did it?" Elizabeth's mouth was dry, for she did not like his counsel.

"It did. I do not have this dream any longer." He forced a smile and squeezed her hands tightly. "I shall make you a wager, sister mine. I shall depart at Epiphany to find my fortune, and if, by the time I return, you are still plagued by this dream, then I shall take you to Ravensmuir."

"Promise?"

"I promise." Malcolm touched his cup to hers and Elizabeth drank with him. It was not what she had wanted of her brother, but as it was the best offer she was likely to have, Malcolm's would have to suffice.

She hoped with vigor that Malcolm would not take overlong to find his fortune.

ALEXANDER AND ELEANOR COUPLED thrice before they dozed, exhausted, within the shadows of the great bed. It had fallen dark outside and the first stars could be seen through the window.

Eleanor's fair hair was cast across Alexander's chest and her legs were entangled with his. Her hand was curled within his own, both hands over his heartbeat, and he felt the sweet rhythm of her breath against his flesh. The great bed smelled lustily of the pleasure they had conjured and shared. Although he was hungry, Alexander was so fatigued that he could see no compelling reason to stir . . . until Eleanor shivered.

She nestled closer to him and he made to pull up the bedclothes. She yawned and made to sit up. "It is so late. I should fetch a morsel from the kitchens before all retire."

"Do not be ridiculous. If you are hungry, I will go."

"No, you are injured," she said, her tone allowing no argument. She pushed him back, her hand in the midst of his chest, and he fell back as if boneless.

"I am not so injured as that." He caught her around the waist and pulled her atop him. "And it would not be chivalrous to let you fetch a meal."

"You have need of your strength," she chided. "I want that son." Alexander shook his head, marveling at her insistence upon this single matter, even as she shivered. "And you are beneath my care, as I am the healer in this chamber," she said, scolding him with a wag of her finger.

She would have looked more solemn—and less endearing—if her hair had not been so disheveled and her bare breast had not been so pert in the chill. Alexander caught the weight of her breast in his hand, then ran his thumb across the turgid peak. She shivered.

"You are too cold. It is my noble intent to warm you," he said, then kissed her nipple.

Eleanor caught her breath and stretched like a cat beneath his caress. "It is your noble intent to meet abed yet again."

"I will see you well-pleased."

"And so you already have!" she protested with a laugh. "We must have a morsel in our bellies, Alexander. You remain here, but you had best don some garb. It is cursed cold in this chamber and my father oft said that it takes heat to conjure a son."

"Anthony has not been able to light the braziers with the portal locked against him," Alexander said, impatient with her repeated references to sons. "Eleanor, understand that there is no need for haste in creating a child. Children will come in their time."

"There is every need for haste," she corrected. "Especially if you mean to grant your sisters the choice of whom they wed." She rose from the bed, her pale flesh fairly glowing in the darkness, and scampered toward the pile of clothing they had cast on the floor.

"What is this?" Alexander was confused, but she did not say more. "What do you mean about my sisters' nuptials? What can our having a son possibly have to do with that matter?"

Eleanor searched through the garb as the gooseflesh rose on her skin. She danced a little, for the floor was probably cold. "Oh, I shall be wrought of ice before I find my stockings!"

"It cannot matter what you wear."

She gave him a look. "It always matters what the laird's wife wears."

"Women!" Alexander rose, but did not don the chemise she offered to him. "Wear whatsoever comes to hand!"

"No!" She regarded him with dancing eyes. "They still talk in the kitchens about me coming into the hall with slippers that did not match after our vows were consummated."

Alexander grinned. "Your laces were bunched as well. I recall fixing them."

"How could you not have told me?"

"It was not your slippers I noticed."

She granted him a glare that would have been more fearsome if her eyes had not twinkled so. "Then be of aid to me, lest all of Kinfairlie laugh at the laird's smitten wife."

He reached for her boots. "Don these first."

She shook her head, her teeth fairly chattering. "Not those."

"Whyever not? You are cold!"

"Because it is not proper to wear boots in the hall. I will wear slippers, if I can find them. Here is one stocking at least." She rummaged without so much as a tinder lit to aid her in her task. He cursed, not for the first time, at the notions of women and their garb.

"You will wear slippers and be cold rather than breach some foolish convention?" He sat down on the trunk there, pulled her onto his lap, and made to pull one boot onto her foot. "Eleanor, this is folly" was all he managed to say before she cried out in pain.

He pulled off her boot and peered into it. There was something dark lurking in the fur lining. Eleanor sat silent on his knee, rubbing the base of her foot as he inverted her boot.

Two thorns spilled into his hand, thorns as large and as fearsome as those that had pierced Uriel's hide. He glanced across the chamber, but the three Owen had surrendered to him still rested on the opposite table.

This additional pair lurked in her boot—the boot she had not wished to don—as if hidden there. The key to the chamber glinted upon her belt, discarded in a coil by his very feet.

Eleanor gasped and Alexander met her gaze. Days past he might have taken her expression as one of guilt, as if some dark scheme had been discovered. "I suppose I am to think that you had too many thorns for your purpose this day, that you saved some for a similar feat on another day," he mused, and she caught her breath. "You did not, after all, wish to don your boots. A man could believe that you knew the thorns to be hidden there."

Eleanor scarce breathed while Alexander rolled the thorns across his palm. But if she had known about these thorns, if she had been the one to injure Uriel, then she had not only tried to kill him—perhaps twice—but had lied to him over and over again.

It could not be so.

Alexander wanted the marriage he had tasted this very afternoon. He wanted the match they had only begun to share—and that meant that he must trust his lady wife, just as she had shown that she trusted him.

He held the thorns before his ashen wife. "Have you a better explanation?"

Eleanor rose to her feet, looking small and fragile. Her gaze fell on the key tied to her own belt. Then she looked at him, fear in her eyes. "I have none," she whispered. "I know nothing of them, certainly not from whence they came."

Alexander rose to his feet. "Then we must find who in the household seeks to see you blamed for what you have not done."

Eleanor's features lit with such pleasure that he knew he had chosen aright. She cast herself toward him, but he had no chance to savor her embrace.

For the sentries blew their horns with force in that moment, and men shouted in the bailey. "Kinfairlie is besieged!" roared one man, and Alexander hastened to the window.

It was true. A veritable army rode toward the keep, the moonlight glinting off their armor and their unsheathed blades. They were numerous and fully armed, their company stretching into the distance. Alexander's heart sank, for he doubted their force could be turned aside.

"Unlock the portal!" he cried to Eleanor. "We are attacked." He donned his chemise, his chausses, and threw open the trunk containing his mail as he donned his boots. He heard a shout at the gates and knew he had no time to arm himself properly.

"But it is the peace of Christmas—"

"Our assailants seem not to care." Alexander shrugged into his tabard and snatched up his blade. Eleanor meanwhile unlocked the portal, her eyes wide with fear. "Find some garb to cover yourself, gather with my sisters, and see this portal barred against all assailants," he bade her, and she nodded understanding.

Then she seized his sleeve. "But surely you will be triumphant?"

"Surely it is only good sense to be cautious. Secure yourself with my sisters," he said, then caught her nape in his hand. He kissed her deeply, lingeringly, then departed the solar in haste.

Alexander, despite his injured leg, lunged down the stairs, taking them three at a time, sparing only a moment to hammer on the door of the chamber his sisters shared. "Lock yourselves, all of you, in the solar," he bade Vera, then made haste to the hall.

There was already the clash of steel against steel and the smell of blood in his own hall. Alexander was not the only one to have been surprised. Kinfairlie could be defended by few men, but only if the attackers did not manage to enter the hall. This battle, he feared, would be decided quickly and not in his favor.

He leapt into the fray, swinging his blade at a mercenary. He had done his best for Kinfairlie, he would do his best until his dying breath, but he feared in this moment that his best had not been enough.

This battle would be the reckoning that he had long expected, and Alexander Lammergeier hoped that he would be the only one to pay the price for his own failure.

Chapter Twelve

~

ELEANOR HAD NO INTENTION of waiting meekly in the solar while her husband faced certain slaughter in the hall below. There had to be some deed that could be done to aid him.

Whosoever attacked was a villain, to be sure, for no man violated the injunction against battle on the holy days of the year. Eleanor feared that she knew who that villain might be, for she had lived closely with a family of villains, one of whom had already shown himself to be interested in her fortunes.

Alan Douglas.

Annelise and Elizabeth and Isabella arrived in the solar in their chemises, with their hair unbound, chattering all the while. They each carried some trinket or another, as well as their own cloaks and boots. Their eyes were wide with fear. Vera came behind them with an armload of sturdy woolen kirtles, muttering as she gathered them like wayward chicks. Moira, Eleanor hoped, had found refuge in the kitchens.

"Lock the portal, my lady," Vera instructed as she dumped the clothing onto a trunk. "We are all here now, and there is little else to be done. I would have you maidens don your kirtles and boots, the better that you be prepared for whatever occurs."

"But what could occur?" Annelise asked with a shiver.

"Garb yourself," Isabella said tersely. "If Alexander does not win, this night will not be an amusing one for us."

Vera's lips tightened at that.

"Let us move the trunks against the portal," Eleanor suggested. "The better that it cannot be forced open."

The sisters followed her dictate, and she was pleased to see that they were not fragile maidens with no strength beyond that necessary to thread a needle.

"We must be able to defend ourselves," Elizabeth said, looking about the chamber.

"What weaponry has Alexander?" asked Isabella. They showed a familiarity with their brother's possessions that surprised Eleanor, but then she had never had any sibling with whom to share. In moments, they had rummaged through his trunk of weapons and each sister held a blade more fearsome than her own eating knife.

"I say we should join the battle," Elizabeth said. "Alexander has need of every blade he can muster on this night."

"No, no, no!" Vera cried. "There will be no maidens under my care in a hall filled with fighting men."

"Or there will be no maidens at all in the morn," Eleanor concluded. The maid nodded, but the sisters caught their breath as one. Isabella parted her lips to ask a question, but Eleanor glared at her. "A rape is no way to learn of matters abed," she said with resolve, and that sister fell silent.

Annelise crossed herself and sat down, pale with fear.

The sounds of swordplay grew louder, and more men shouted. Torches could be seen burning in the bailey, and to Eleanor's amazement, a group of people marched toward the keep from Kinfairlie village. They carried scythes and knives, clubs and hoes, and their expressions were grim.

"There is the miller and his son, Matthew," said Annelise, her tone indicating that she shared Eleanor's surprise.

"The tanner and his apprentice, and the blacksmith," said Isabella, forcing her way closer to the window.

"God in heaven," Vera whispered.

"Look! There is Father Malachy!" Elizabeth said, pointing as she did so. The maid snatched back the maiden's hand, lest her presence at the darkened window be discerned. "And the baker and the shepherd and even the silversmith."

"But it is neither their right nor their duty to fight," Eleanor said. "Such is the order of men: those who work, those who pray, and those who fight."

Vera granted her a wry glance. "Such is the order in some realms, to be sure. Can a man not be expected to raise a blade in defense, regardless of his calling, when his own abode is at risk?"

"They will be slaughtered," Eleanor whispered. "Such tools are no match to the swords and blades of knights. They have no training and they have no armor, either."

"Alexander has no armor, either," Elizabeth retorted. "This battle is unfair in every way. I am glad the town comes to our aid."

"They have their love of Kinfairlie," Annelise said softly. "And that is no small weapon."

Eleanor hoped she was right.

A man shouted below and Eleanor knew that the villagers had been spied by Kinfairlie's assailants. A dozen armed men turned upon the approaching group, laughing at the sight of them.

"We cannot simply wait here!" Isabella protested. "We must do something!"

Eleanor leaned out the window as scythe and sword clashed, hoping to see better how the villagers fared. She could not imagine them dying in the defense of Kinfairlie, but at the same time, she could well understand their loyalty to Alexander. She too would do any deed to see him and Kinfairlie secured. She stretched farther and saw a familiar horse, the insignia on its caparisons fairly stopping her heart.

It was Alan Douglas.

She could stop this carnage. The realization came suddenly. Alan Douglas wanted only her, or more accurately, he desired only the legacy she would bring to him with the delivery of a son.

If she surrendered to Alan, the assault upon Kinfairlie would halt. As soon as Eleanor realized the truth, her choice was made. She pivoted and lifted the key from her belt. She unlocked the portal, Alexander's sisters clustered about her in their excitement.

"What are we going to do?" Elizabeth demanded, her grip fierce upon her borrowed blade.

"You are going to remain here, as you have been bidden to do," Eleanor said firmly. She placed the key within the maid's hand and closed Vera's fingers surely over it. "And you will lock the portal behind me. Open it only to Alexander."

"But where are you going?" Isabella asked.

"To end this madness, for once and for all," Eleanor said with resolve, then stepped out of the chamber. She waited on the landing until she heard the key turn in the lock, listened for a moment to the unanimous protest of the three maidens, then marched down to the hall.

Alexander, Kinfairlie, and all the people pledged to serve both had need of the sacrifice only she could make. Eleanor would not regret making it, not for a moment, for she believed it would see this haven and its laird saved from certain destruction.

That would be a sufficiently potent legacy for any woman.

THE HALL WAS THICK WITH SMOKE. Someone had dropped a torch into the strewing herbs upon the floor, but they were so freshly cut that they smoked rather than burned. Only a few other torches burned, so the hall was full of shadows. Malcolm peered through the tangle of men and tried to make sense of who was who.

One matter was for certain: only those who attacked wore armor, for no man in Kinfairlie had had time to don his mail. Malcolm saw his brother come down the stairs and, with characteristic confidence, step directly into the fray. Alexander had dispatched two men and rounded upon another by the time Malcolm reached his side. They fought, more or less back-to-back, cutting a swath through the hall.

"I trust you slept well," Alexander said to Malcolm, as if they rose on a peaceful morn to break bread together.

He grunted as he drove his sword into the gut of a mercenary.

"Quite well," Malcolm replied, his tone genial. "Though I must admit, I did hear some ruckus in the midst of the night." He swung his blade at a mercenary's knees, and that man fell. He rounded quickly and jabbed the point of his sword into the eye of a man who had tried to sneak up beside him.

"Rats," Alexander said, as if confiding a sorry secret of his hall. "We are besieged by them at the most uncommon times."

He whistled a warning to his brother, who understood the signal as no others did. Not for nothing had these two brothers sparred together for years!

Malcolm ducked in the nick of time as Alexander's blade slashed over his head, then struck an assailant's elbow. That man howled and dropped his blade. Malcolm picked it up, then tossed it to Alexander, who was more adept at fighting with both hands.

Alexander circled another mercenary, both blades swinging, as he continued in a most conversational tone. "Like all vermin, they must be diligently hunted and excised."

"Ah, so that was why I heard swordplay," Malcolm said. He parried the thrust of another man, their blades locking so that their wrists almost touched. "Oh, look there!" Malcolm said to his opponent, who was fool enough to do so. Malcolm dispatched him with a blow while he was so distracted.

"We are plagued by particularly large and vile vermin this year," Alexander said with a shake of his head. He and his assailant met in a furious clash of steel on steel.

Alexander grunted and jabbed, and cast the man's corpse aside. "I only apologize that such necessities interrupted the slumber of a guest."

"And there is the largest vermin of them all," Malcolm said, nodding toward the gates. Alan Douglas had just crossed beneath the portcullis. He pushed up his visor, his strangely pale features seeming to glow in the shadows, and looked over the company. His gaze fell on Alexander and he smiled his cruel smile, apparently in anticipation of an easy victory.

"The king of the rats himself," Alexander muttered, and strode to confront his attacker. "He will not steal the finest morsel from my table so readily as that."

The two leapt at each other and Malcolm valiantly tried to defend Alexander's back. His brother moved quickly to engage with Alan, though, so quickly that Malcolm was snared by a mercenary determined to see him dead.

The mercenary struck a fierce blow that took Malcolm to his knees. Malcolm feigned greater injury than he felt, then slashed upward. His opponent was caught by surprise and the blade slipped beneath the bottom of his jerkin. Malcolm plunged the blade deep, then pulled it out and kicked the man's corpse aside.

By that time, Alexander was surrounded by three men as well as Alan. It was not a fair fight, and though Alexander was a competent swordsman, Malcolm could see the sweat on his brother's brow.

Malcolm leapt into the skirmish with a bellow and distracted the men sufficiently that Alexander felled one with a telling strike.

"One rat less in my abode," Alexander said through

gritted teeth, then parried the blow of another assailant. Alan struck in that moment, taking advantage of the fact that Alexander was engaged, but Alexander still had the second blade in his left hand. He swung it, even as he drove his own sword into the mercenary's throat, and Alan yelled as he retreated.

Blood ran from Alan's ear, Malcolm noted with a quick glance. He was busy himself, for the fourth man who had been attacking Alexander turned upon Malcolm. They fought with ferocity; then the mercenary pivoted abruptly to swing his blade at Alexander. Malcolm whistled, his brother ducked, and the heavy blade swept over Alexander's head to strike down his opponent.

"That was neatly done," Alexander said with a grin. He nodded to the mercenary still before Malcolm. "I thank you for your timely contribution."

The mercenary roared in fury and lunged at Alexander, who halted that man's bloody blade with his own. They struggled back and forth, neither gaining any quarter against the other; then Alan stepped out of the shadows.

He smiled and Malcolm began to shout a warning, but too late. Alan's swinging blade struck Alexander on the back of the head.

Alexander's eyes widened briefly; then he fell so hard that Malcolm feared the worst. Blood pooled around Alexander's body with alarming haste.

"No!" Malcolm cried, but the mercenary turned upon him, a deadly gleam in his eye. Malcolm ducked his blow, then stepped closer to the man. The man's eyes widened, so startled was he by Malcolm's proximity, but his eyes widened more when he felt Malcolm's knife blade slide into his throat.

It was a trick that Alexander had taught Malcolm, to step inside the swing of a blow, and though it was a marvel to see it work in a desperate situation, Malcolm wished his brother might have witnessed its success. He turned upon Alan, intent upon seeing that man dead, but in that same moment, a woman shouted.

"No!" she cried. "Cease your assault!"

Alan looked toward the stairs, a knowing smile upon his face. He lifted his hand and called for the fighting to halt, as calmly as if he called for more salt at the board.

Malcolm turned, followed Alan's gaze, and saw Alexander's wife, Eleanor, standing on the third-to-last stair. She looked out of place, her garb so perfect that she might have been appearing at the king's court for dinner, not stepping into the midst of a bloody battle. Her poise was also perfect, her stance regal, her composure complete.

Only her pallor revealed her distress.

She descended the last of the stairs from the solar without hesitation. She walked through the hall, as fair as a wraith, as unexpected as an angel. She paid no heed to whatsoever was strewn beneath her feet and she did not stumble.

The men fell back to grant her passage, seemingly so astonished by her presence that they let their blades fall by their sides. Malcolm did not doubt that her manner was a greater power than Alan's command.

Her footsteps only faltered when she neared the red pool of blood surrounding Alexander. She halted as the first fissure showed in her composure. She made a little sound, a gasp of pain, and her head bowed as if to hide her tears. She stood between Malcolm and his fallen brother.

Malcolm did not doubt that Alexander's wound was fatal, but Eleanor would have stepped into the blood. She would have gone to Alexander's side, but Alan shouted at her. "Do not touch him. His fate is sealed, as is yours."

Eleanor hesitated for a moment and Malcolm could see how she found her urge to defy the other man's command.

"What do you think you can do to me now?" she asked softly.

Alan chuckled though it was not amiable.

Eleanor exhaled, the steel leaving her shoulders with that breath. "I am sorry, beloved," she whispered to Alexander, her words uneven. Malcolm could not imagine for what she apologized, for the blame for this assault could not be laid at her feet.

Or could it?

To Malcolm's astonishment, she then addressed him, though she faced Alan. "I would ask you, Malcolm, to inform that witch Jeannie that if she does not see her laird healed from this malady, she will have me to fear." Her words were uttered with such conviction that Malcolm did not doubt she would be vengeful indeed. "Whether I find her in this world or the next, my vengeance for any incompetence she shows in this matter will be so fierce as to make her wish she never drew breath. I fear that it is too late, but she must try, as never she has tried before."

Malcolm nodded. "I will so do."

Eleanor looked down at Alexander and Malcolm saw a glisten of tears upon her cheek when she turned to face Alan. "Alexander ensnared me with a kiss," she said, her words husky, "while this man would capture me with a blade." Eleanor granted Malcolm a glance, her eyes so vivid and piercing a green that he caught his breath. "A wise man knows which is the more formidable weapon."

"Do you bow to the inevitable, then?" Alan demanded, raising his voice so that all could hear him.

"I will accompany you, if that is your meaning, but only so long as your men sheath their blades immediately," Eleanor said, as if she had something with which to wager. "You will depart from Kinfairlie and not a one of you will ever cast a shadow across her lands again. These are my terms for accompanying you."

Alan nodded. "Agreed." He sheathed his blade, sparing a condescending glance to the man fallen before him. "Though we could have taken all we desired by force."

"Only because you cheated," Eleanor said with some heat. "On a level field, you would not have won an advantage so readily."

"You speak boldly, for one who surrenders herself to my power," Alan said with a scowl.

Eleanor smiled coolly. "I am only of worth to you so long as I live. We both understand that. You may claim my body, but you will never claim my heart, and you cannot silence my words."

To Malcolm's astonishment, Alan did not dispute this. Eleanor reached for Malcolm then, her hand closing around his wrist with vigor. "Be with him," she counseled with quiet vigor. "No soul should pass through the veil without a familiar hand upon their shoulder."

When Malcolm moved to do her bidding, he felt her push something hard and heavy into his hand. Instinctively, he grasped it, without knowing what it was.

"Because your brother taught me that there are treasures with a value far beyond their price," Eleanor murmured to him, ensuring that her words could not be overheard.

Malcolm guessed that none realized she had given him any token and closed his hand over it as if he held nothing at all.

She crossed the floor to a smirking Alan then, and Malcolm knew that he did not imagine that the lady shivered as she drew close to that villain's side. She did not flinch from what had to be done, though, and true to Alan's word, his men filed peacefully out of Kinfairlie's hall behind him.

When they were gone and Malcolm finally opened his hand, he found a ring within his grasp. The emerald gem that his mother had worn as a sign of her nuptial pledge to his father, the gem that Alexander had used to seal his own vows, glinted back at him within his own palm.

And Malcolm understood then that Eleanor had surrendered herself to ensure Kinfairlie's security, though still he did not understand why Alan should content himself with solely the lady as his prize.

ALEXANDER AWAKENED in his own hall, a sea of faces crowded around him. One face was notably absent. His head throbbed with unholy vigor. His sisters were clustered around him, and Isabella burst into tears when his eyes opened. Someone washed the back of his head with a pungent concoction, the gestures rough but not unkind. He could smell the herbs within the solution and winced at the pain.

"I am not dead yet," he said with feigned irritation,

though it took much effort to do so. "Unless you mean to see that situation changed."

"Praise be!" cried Rose, the cook's wife. "The laird speaks!"

The people of Alexander's household pushed closer then, their faces alight with relief. Elizabeth cheered and Annelise smiled through her tears; Isabella hugged Alexander so hard that it hurt, but he did not complain.

"I thought you would have preferred me dead," he teased Elizabeth, and she flushed.

"You are not *that* bad," she acknowledged. "At least not as yet."

"There is no one better than a sister to ensure that a man's vanity is kept within limits," he muttered, then winked at her when she flushed crimson. She made to swat him, then thought better of her impulse and pulled back her hand. Alexander caught her hand and kissed her knuckles, appreciating her concern however it was expressed.

The effort left him dizzy, though still he lay upon the floor, and he knew he had been wounded, indeed. He closed his eyes and lay back, and the nausea lessened. He recalled only facing Alan's man, then an explosion of pain in the back of his head.

Then nothing. He looked again, but Eleanor was not yet in the company. Her absence had him rising, ignoring the pain that accompanied his movement.

A gnarled hand planted firmly on his chest and pushed him back toward the floor. "Alan Douglas is gone, my lord," Jeannie said, mistaking the reason for his urgency. "There is naught to fear, save your own welfare."

"It is not Alan I would seek, but my lady wife."

Alexander made to rise again, but was no more successful. Indeed, it was galling that the ancient midwife could halt his intent with a single, albeit strong, hand. "What ails me?" he asked her quietly.

"A wound to the back of your head, my lord, and one that shed a great deal of blood. It looks to be worse than it is, though you will ache mightily for a few days even with my care." She gave him a shrewd glance. "You do not look so hale, my lord."

"I must seek my lady wife," he said, seizing her hand with resolve and putting it aside.

"You need not trouble yourself, my lord. She, too, is gone from Kinfairlie," Jeannie said with no small satisfaction.

Alexander rose unsteadily to his feet, despite the midwife's protest. The hall swayed slightly when he did so, but Malcolm stepped to his side and claimed his elbow with a firm grip. Alexander seized his brother's shoulder and fought to quell the protest of his very innards.

"Be warned, Jeannie," Malcolm said. "The lady vowed to see you injured if her lord husband was not tended well and healed."

Jeannie snorted. "She can scarce raise a hand against me while with Alan Douglas." She smiled up at Alexander, her eyes glinting. "If no one will tell you the truth of it, my lord, then I will. Your faithless wife chose Alan Douglas over you, and that without a backward glance."

"She did no such thing!" Malcolm protested.

"What do you know of women, particularly those who scheme to see their own advantage? Did she not leave willingly, her hand upon his arm?" Jeannie demanded. "I saw no shackles. I witnessed no struggle."

"It was not as you would imply," Malcolm insisted, his voice rising. "She sacrificed her own welfare for our own."

Those in the hall began to murmur, even as they gathered closer to hear the details of this dispute. Alexander did not know what to think of Eleanor's choice. Why had she accompanied Alan, after refusing to do as much just days past? She had said that he wished to wed her in Ewen's stead, and Alexander had been certain that she did not share that desire.

"She abandoned her laird for what she saw as a better spouse," Jeannie retorted. "Did she not put my lord's ring in your custody?" The old healer cackled at Malcolm's start of surprise. "I see more than most would believe possible, and now you know it to be true."

"She meant only to see the gem safe," Malcolm said, his defense of Eleanor warming Alexander's heart. "She did not wish Alan to claim the ring." His lips set and he held Alexander's gaze. "She said there were treasures with a value beyond their price."

Alexander's hope surged at that echo of his own words. In truth, it was difficult to believe that Jeannie named the matter right, not after the mating he and Eleanor had shared the day before. He had been certain that she had been on the verge of surrendering her heart to him.

He intended to ensure that she had that chance.

"She thought you dead or close to it," Malcolm said, stoic in his defense of Alexander's bride. "She said she was sorry, though I know not for what, and she called you her beloved." His jaw set. "Do not discredit a noble gesture, Jeannie, just because it was not your own."

The old midwife propped a hand upon her hip. "So, now Jeannie is not to be believed, even though this woman who would call herself a healer could not discern that my lord yet breathed." She sneered. "Or do you suggest that I brought him back from death with the sorcery of my potion? Is that how you would be rid of old Jeannie?"

"We have no desire to be rid of you," Alexander said, though that was not entirely true.

"Alan forbade her to approach Alexander," Malcolm said with force. "No healer could see all at a distance in the smoke-infested darkness of this hall! Grant credit where it is due!"

Jeannie snorted again. "And grant fault where it is due," she cried. "Did she not leave with Alan Douglas? Did she not abandon our laird in his own blood? Did she not pull the ring that sealed her nuptial vows from her own finger?"

"Did Alan Douglas not leave Kinfairlie when she did so?" Malcolm asked, his voice falling low. "Did her deed not ensure that we all lived to see the morn?" The assembly caught their breath and Alexander watched his brother look over them. "Did she not extract a promise from Alan to honor our borders and leave Kinfairlie unscathed if she accompanied him? The lady surrendered herself to him to save us, this much is clear."

"She is not what you would think her to be." Jeannie pulled herself up to her full height. "Was the laird himself not poisoned on the night she arrived?"

"By your concoction, Jeannie," Malcolm argued.

The old healer snorted. "A concoction that would have done him no injury, had he eaten of the meal, instead of chasing her across the snow!" Glances were exchanged over this, seemingly emboldening the older woman. "I tried to warn her, that I did, by granting her a taste of her own treatment, but she managed to evade the lesson."

Alexander frowned. "What is this you say? What warning did you grant?"

"The last of the wine that she said she claimed for you." Jeannie snorted. "I knew she meant to savor it herself, and so I spiced it that she might have a taste of her own—"

"You mean the wine that Anthony drank?" Alexander asked with dawning fury.

"You mean that you meant to see our lady fall ill?" Anthony himself demanded in outrage.

"It was a lesson," Jeannie insisted. "And one that would not have killed any soul." She shook a finger at Anthony. "She did not save you from any fate. You would have been healed all the same, with or without her deed."

"Out!" Alexander roared. "Out of my hall! Jeannie, you will never cross the threshold of Kinfairlie's keep again!"

There was a rumbling of assent through the hall, and nods were exchanged. A passageway was made for Jeannie, who did not seemingly believe that she was being cast out. Helping hands urged her toward the portal, and she began to mutter.

As soon as she was out the portal, all gazes turned to Alexander. "My lady has been unjustly maligned," he said.

"And she has sacrificed herself to see us all safe from Alan Douglas," Malcolm said.

"Such valor must have its reward," Alexander agreed with surety. "We will ride in pursuit of the lady."

The men in the hall grunted agreement. Alexander could not reply, so loud and numerous were the avowals of assent. Indeed, he was having trouble remaining on his feet and his vision was clouding. This injury would need time to heal before he could be of much aid to Eleanor.

"You will not ride soon," Malcolm said quietly, evidently seeing his brother's malaise.

Alexander wavered on his feet and Malcolm seized his elbow once more. "No, not soon," he said, embarrassed by how much he had to rely upon his brother's support. He raised his voice with an effort. "We will ride forth, upon that you may rely, though the time will remain to be decided. Indeed, we must wait until the twelve days of Christmas are past so that war can be conducted honorably." He smiled for his company with his customary bravado. "By then, I assure you, I will not only be hale but will have a scheme."

The company roared approval of this notion, but the hall swirled around Alexander in a drunken dance. He felt himself falling, felt shadows closing around him with frightening speed; then he knew no more.

"Determined fool," he heard Anthony mutter, the castellan's tone both scolding and affectionate. "He should not have been upon his feet with an injury like this. How can a man so clever prove himself such a fool?"

Fool. That single word gave Alexander an idea before the encroaching darkness swallowed him completely.

ELEANOR WAS NIGH SICK with her fear. She did not like the line of Alan's mouth or the set of his jaw. She did not like how he grasped her upper arm as soon as they were outside Kinfairlie's hall and dragged her after him so roughly that she tripped.

His manner was too reminiscent of that of his brother.

But Alan was not drunk, as Ewen so frequently had been. Alan's blow would not miss, he would not misjudge its target. He would not stumble. He would not fall into a stupor before he could injure her severely.

She saw Matthew on the ground, blood flowing from his arm and his face pale. His father leaned over him with concern, all the villagers appearing dazed.

"You must bind the wound," Eleanor said, without a second thought. "Take a length of linen and tie it around his arm. Keep your fingers upon it and the flow of blood will stop."

They looked up at her, so shaken that they did not understand her.

"A length of cloth!" Eleanor said, then reached for her own hem. "Here, I will give you one—"

"You will do no such thing," Alan snarled, and tightened his grasp. His grip was so tight that she cried out in pain, but he only dragged her toward his horse.

"My lady!" cried the miller.

"I will be well enough," Eleanor said in haste, not wanting them to endure further injury. "Tend to Matthew. Bind his wound, then take him to Ceara. He will be well if you tend him quickly."

"What do you care for the health of an ignorant peasant?" Alan asked, his manner mocking. "Or was he the one you meant to wed next?"

Alan and his men found this comment amusing beyond expectation, though Eleanor did not share their humor. She was fairly tossed into a saddle, her heart sinking when Alan put his foot into the stirrup of the same saddle. She sat sideways, her knees pressed firmly together, for she feared his intent.

"I can ride alone," she said with haste. "I have the skill."

"And you will flee at first chance," Alan said with a skeptical roll of his eyes. "I am not so witless as that."

"I give you my word that I will not."

"And what is a woman's pledge worth?" Alan did not wait for a reply, but pulled himself up into the saddle behind her. He caught her fast against him and closed his gloved fist over her breast without any effort to hide the crude gesture from his men. Eleanor caught her breath at his unexpected familiarity and he tightened his grip upon her breast so that she knew she would be bruised.

"I beg you, do not injure me," she whispered.

Alan laughed. He gave her breast one final squeeze of such vigor that it brought tears to her eyes, then spurred his horse onward. "Ride on!" he bellowed. "There is a welcoming heat to be savored in our own hall."

The mercenaries laughed and Eleanor did not doubt that Alan made a lewd expression. She was glad not to be able to see him and feared his intent anew. Would the mercenaries each sample her in their turn? It was clear to her that several relished the prospect.

"I thought you desired my legacy," she said, hoping that she was successful in making her voice sound calm.

"What man would be fool enough not to desire it?" Alan asked.

"The father of any son I bear must also be my legal husband to gain the legacy," Eleanor said. "Though I am certain that you are aware of that detail."

"Verily, I am. You have buried another spouse in your determination to flaunt the will of men, but you will not be rid of this one so readily."

"You are not my spouse, but my jailer."

"As yet." He tore the laces from the side of her kirtle with sudden force, ripping the eyelets. He forced his gloved hand through the opening and grasped her crotch with crude force. Eleanor gasped and jumped, for his grip was painful. "This, too, shall be mine," he rasped in her ear, and her heart galloped in fear.

Though she knew it to be inevitable that she meet Alan abed, she had to think of some way to delay that horror.

"Surely you would want no doubt cast upon any claim you might make," Eleanor said, her words rushed.

"And what is that to mean?"

"That I have lain with the laird of Kinfairlie, my lord husband, and should his seed bear fruit, my legacy shall be paid to his heir, regardless of who my husband might be."

Alan loosed his grip upon her in his dismay. "You cannot do that!"

"I most surely can." Eleanor strove to sound bold. "Do you imagine that my guardian will discredit my testimony as to which man is the father of my child?" Eleanor knew that Reinhard von Heigel, her father's confidant and her guardian, would do precisely that, without a moment's remorse. Like Alan, Reinhard believed the word of a woman to have no merit. She lied and she knew it, but she did not regret it.

Alan growled in dissatisfaction. "I will kill his heir, then."

"And break your own pledge to leave Kinfairlie untroubled, with no guarantee that the coin will then come to you. The Lammergeier are plentiful and are said to have dark powers as well. Do you mean to engage them all in war?"

"I could beat any child out of you."

"And readily kill me as well." Eleanor shook her head, striving to appear as if she had a choice and was confident in it. "I will wed you after I next bleed and not one day before. There will then be no doubt cast on the rightful recipient of my legacy, should I bear a child."

Alan heaved a sigh and it seemed to Eleanor that the horse galloped over many miles before he replied. "I cede to you in this, but solely because it suits my own ends." He tightened his grip upon her again so that she winced and his voice fell to a growl in her ear. "But if you deceive me, understand that you will pay for your perfidy. I will have an obedient wife, even if she has to be trussed and beaten to keep her so. A woman can be bruised in places that do not affect the fruitfulness of her womb. Are we understood?"

Eleanor nodded, her mouth dry. She knew then that as soon as she bore a son, as soon as Alan had her legacy, her life would be over. He might guard his blows until that day, but afterward, when he had no need of her, he would kill her.

Tivotdale's shadow rose before the company and Eleanor was so terrified by the sight that she had to remind herself to breathe. What she had endured in this place was not easily forgotten!

There was no denying that she had done a good deed for Kinfairlie and its people, for Alan's men had left without further violence to those residents.

Though truly they had already done their worst. Her

tears rose with the certainty that Alexander must be dead. She would have liked to have laid her fingers against his throat to be certain. She would have liked to have leaned her ear against his chest to dispel the last of her doubts.

But to be honest, she did not want to know for certain that Alexander Lammergeier was dead. She wanted to nurse a faint, if futile, hope that he would live, that he would be healed against the odds, that he would laugh and make a jest at his sisters' expense once more. She wanted to believe that Kinfairlie would not be bereft of its protective laird, that Alexander would witness the wedding vows of Matthew and Ceara, that that holding would remain the tranquil sanctuary she had known it to be. Even if Alexander forgot about her, or chose not to pursue her, Eleanor would like to believe that he yet drew breath and found cause for merriment.

Eleanor knew that her hope was folly, for she could close her eyes and see that fearsome puddle of blood. She also knew it was her fault alone that Kinfairlie had been cursed to feel the weight of Alan's hand. She should never have fled there. She should never have lingered. She should never have loved its laird, for it had been Alexander and her unexpected love for him that had persuaded Eleanor that she might hope.

They rode beneath Tivotdale's portcullis and Eleanor knew a dreadful certainty that she would never leave this keep again alive.

Yet, though the loss of the man she loved hurt more than Eleanor had feared, against all expectation, she had only one regret. She did not regret having loved Alexander: she regretted that she had not told him that he had succeeded in his quest to win her heart. She knew how much value he had placed in love and she knew that he would have been triumphant at the tidings of his success. She had not told him, not even when she knew of it, not even when she had had the chance.

And now, she never would have that chance again.

Eleanor would pray, she resolved, that she and Alexander might meet again in heaven, solely that she might have the chance to redress her error. She wanted to see satisfaction curve his lips; she wanted to see stars light his eyes. She wanted to hear him laugh at his triumph, a triumph that surely he had never doubted would be his own.

Alan swung out of the saddle, then reached up for her with a rough gesture that filled her with foreboding. He resembled Ewen so much in this moment that Eleanor's spirit quailed.

She suspected that she might meet Alexander soon, indeed.

FOUR DAYS PASSED and still Alexander lay abed. Malcolm found himself standing vigil at the portal to the solar, fretful as he had not been before in all his days. Alexander had been pale when they carried him to his own bed and his flesh had been strangely cold. Anthony had stanched the blood flowing from his wound, and in these past days, that wound had begun to heal.

But still Alexander slept. A large bump had arisen behind the healing wound, though it no longer seemed to grow larger. On those few occasions when Alexander awakened, he asked for Eleanor, no matter how many times he was told that she was gone. He had vomited so often the first few days that Matthew had thought any malady would be easier to endure than this.

He had been wrong. His brother's unnatural sleep was far more difficult to watch. They had debated the merits of summoning Jeannie, but Malcolm was set against it, and truly, no one knew where the old healer had gone.

"Well?" Isabella asked from sudden proximity and Malcolm jumped.

"The same as yesterday," he said, forcing a smile for her. "Perhaps he recovers in his dreams."

Isabella grimaced. "That sounds like something Jeannie would say, and we all know that she concocted half of what she insisted was truth. Eleanor would know the truth."

Malcolm could not argue with that. They turned as one and watched the rhythmic rise and fall of Alexander's chest. "Does he still ask for her?" Isabella asked in a whisper.

"Every time he awakens," Malcolm said. "Her name is the only thing he murmurs in his sleep."

Isabella smiled, though it was a sad smile. "Perhaps he dreams that she tends him."

"Perhaps."

Annelise ascended the stairs and came to a halt beside them, her manner subdued. She asked after Alexander and was no less pleased by the tidings than Isabella and Malcolm had been.

Something glinted in her hand as she hesitated beside them and Malcolm frowned as he tried to discern what it was. "What do you have?"

Annelise blushed. "It is a vial of scent, given to me by Rosamunde."

"For your wedding night!" Isabella guessed. Annelise nodded, her cheeks aflame, and Isabella turned to Malcolm. "I gave mine to Eleanor and Alexander, and Eleanor poured it into the bath she had summoned."

"Rosamunde said it would conjure sweetness between man and wife," Annelise said, her manner cautious.

"I do not know what occurred"—Isabella paused for a moment, but Malcolm said nothing—"though it was long before they came back to the hall."

Annelise held the vial out, like an offering. "I thought it might help."

"But Alexander does not mean to take a bath on this night," Malcolm said.

"I know that." Annelise smiled sadly. "But Maman once said that scent is a potent summons, and I knew what Isabella had done with her vial, and I thought . . ."

"That it might call him back," Isabella concluded with satisfaction. "I think it a good idea." She took the vial from Annelise and marched into the solar.

"Let me see what you do!" Annelise complained, and ran after her.

Malcolm followed the pair to watch. They paused beside the bed, and Malcolm suspected, not for the first time, that his sisters shared a secret language, one that needed no words. They exchanged a glance; then Isabella opened the vial.

Malcolm smelled flowers. He thought of summer, though he could not name the precise scents that assaulted his nostrils. He closed his eyes and envisioned himself within a garden of blossoms, the air fairly buzzing with bees, the sun spilling gold over all.

Annelise had brought a napkin wrought of linen. She poured the merest drop of the oil onto the linen; then Isabella stoppered the vial again. Annelise waved the linen beneath Alexander's nose and they waited, breathless, for some response.

There was none.

Annelise waved the cloth again and Malcolm was struck by his brother's pallor. Alexander's skin was the hue of snow, and faint blue circles of exhaustion were visible beneath his eyes despite how much he had slept. He had lost weight, for his face was leaner, and his hair seemed to have lost its gloss. Malcolm looked away, unable to face the prospect of losing the brother he had admired every day of his life, and his vision veiled with tears.

"I must talk to the laird," said a woman at the portal.

Malcolm seized the chance to do something to aid his ailing brother. "You cannot come into the solar. He must have his rest."

"But he must know what I know. I tried to tell him, and the lady Eleanor, before the keep was attacked, but they would not hear of it, and look what happened!" The older maid threw up her hands, though Malcolm was not certain who she was. "And now I have spent every day and every night trying to come up these stairs to tell the laird what he has need of knowing, and I only face obstacle after obstacle."

"There must be guards posted to defend the laird, for there have been assaults upon his life," Malcolm said. He did not welcome this woman's criticism, as he himself had commanded the sentries to defend the stairs.

"Would you defend him from the truth?" the maid demanded. "Would you defend him from knowledge of a spy in his own hall? Have you no desire to know what threats you face?" She jabbed her finger into her own chest. "I know far more than any of you, and though I try to share my tidings, you will not hear of it. It is a kind of pride, a sinful kind, that keeps men of wit from listening to the counsel of those they think beneath themselves, to be sure."

She paused for a breath and Malcolm took the opportunity to speak. "Who are you?"

She drew herself taller. "I am Moira Goodall, the maid of my lady Eleanor by sworn word to her dying mother, the lady Yolanda." Moira shook a finger at Malcolm. "And there was a great lady, a lady who relied upon the counsel of those in her household and never shirked from hearing a truth, however painful it might be. . . ."

"What truth would you tell, Moira?"

"I followed Lady Eleanor from Tivotdale, so devoted is my service to her, and your brother the laird welcomed me to Kinfairlie with the grace of a king. My gratitude is not small in this matter because he could have readily turned me from his gates and I would have had no place to go, but Laird Alexander allowed me to remain and fulfill my pledge to my lady's mother—"

"These are not dire tidings, Moira," Malcolm said with resolve. "Though I applaud my brother's goodwill in granting you the chance to continue your service, this tale hardly demands to be told. There are many who have been welcomed at Kinfairlie."

Moira blinked. "But that is precisely my point, and that is what the laird needs to know."

Malcolm shook his head and would have dismissed the woman, but Moira caught at his sleeve. He looked at her and saw the fear in her eyes.

"I regret only that I did not notice the intruder sooner; for then, much wickedness could have been avoided."

"What is this?" Malcolm's interest was piqued.

"There is a man in service here, a mercenary, whom I recognize from Tivotdale. He must have come with the party that rode in pursuit of Lady Eleanor on Christmas Day, just as I did, and he must have lingered here apurpose, just as I did." Moira shook her head. "But unlike me, my lord, I would wager that this man remained at Laird Alan's command and that his intent was not to grant faithful service to Laird Alexander."

"Is he still here?"

Moira nodded with conviction and Malcolm's hand fell to the hilt of his blade.

"Lock this portal behind me," he said to them, then hastened after the maid. "What do you think he has done?"

Moira licked her lips. "Far be it for me to speak ill of a man without evidence against him, sir, but this one is known for his cunning and his malice. Alan Douglas oft relies upon him to see to the disappearance of any man who irks him overmuch."

"You mean that this man kills?"

Moira nodded and looked about herself before lowering her voice. "Those thorns, the ones found beneath my lord's saddle, the ones that the ostler Owen has spoken of?"

"They are large, larger than any I have seen."

"I have seen them." The maid held his gaze with conviction. "They grow upon the briars at Tivotdale."

So intent was Malcolm upon the capture of the dangerous intruder in his brother's hall that he did not give note to his sisters' cry of delight behind him.

Nor did he hear his brother ask for his lady wife.

Chapter Thirteen

THERE WERE WORSE THINGS than being sole porter at Tivotdale on Epiphany. The man left to that task was certain of it, though his conviction waned as the sound of merrymaking within Tivotdale's hall grew steadily louder. The night was cold and dark and the skies threatened rain or snow. The wind over the moors had a bite, to be sure, and he felt somewhat sorry for himself at being excluded from the festivities of the night.

He always managed to choose the short straw. There were others patrolling the perimeter of the village, to be sure, but he did not doubt that they would be invited to share the warmth of one hearth or another, and they were easily forgotten as he could not see them. He stamped his feet and paced behind the closed portcullis, and strove to entertain himself with the prospect of what those worse things might be.

He could be fed to wolves, one piece at a time. That surely would be worse than being porter for a night. Laughter carried from the hall beyond and he could discern music. He sighed and huddled in his cloak and paced.

He could be flayed alive, or drawn and quartered, neither of which appeared to be particularly amusing ways to pass an evening. Surely that would be worse than spending a night in the cold, even if it was the sole night upon which this particular Douglas laird showed any generosity.

He turned and looked toward the hall wistfully. They were drinking ale, he knew it, and at the laird's expense, too. He had seen the venison, both the roast haunches and the thick, rich stew, when he had claimed a meal in the kitchens before reporting for his duty. He had seen and smelled the fresh bread, the eggs in red wine, the hare in pepper sauce, the boar in mustard sauce, rows of pigeon pies and roasted ducks. He salivated even at the recollection and his belly grumbled.

When he had gone to the kitchens, they had given him a bowl of thin soup, wrought of the leavings of the day before, a piece of cold bread, and bade him stay out of the way.

He could draw the short length next Epiphany as well as this one. That would be not only worse but also cursed fortune, indeed.

He pivoted, intending to pace the width of the gate once more, and straightened at the sight of a small party on the road leading to his very feet. They were a motley band, dressed in all manner of garb, and they cavorted rather than walked. They had no steeds, but seemed amiable enough.

Indeed, they were singing. He strained his ears and only barely heard the words:

> *"With a rink tink tink,*
> *for sup or drink,*
> *we will make the old bell sound.*

A merry Christmas to you all,
and may happiness abound."

The porter smiled despite himself, for he had a fondness for a performance of any kind. He wondered from whence this group had come, and assumed them to be from the village. They seemed to have appeared from the twist the road made around that distant copse of trees, though there was no destination close enough for walking along that road.

They must have wandered the long way from the village, the better that their arrival not be anticipated.

Perhaps the laird had commanded their presence, for he was well-known to be uncommonly pleased this year. His own nuptials would be celebrated on the morrow, hence the bounty on the board this night. Only a man more dim-witted than this porter would suggest that there was aught amiss in a man wedding his brother's widow, and that within a month of that brother's demise.

There was a worse fate. The porter could have been sharing Tivotdale's dungeon with the priest who had refused to perform the nuptial ceremony on those very grounds.

Certainly, the approaching company was drunk. They laughed and fell over each other's feet, tumbling and staggering along the road. One of them had a bell, but the rhythm of its ringing was not steady. Their singing was tuneful, though, and tempted the porter's foot to tap in time.

He watched them draw ever nearer, oblivious to all else. Indeed, it was such a quiet night that he already knew there to be naught else to watch. There must have been thirty of them or so, and they were of every height and size. They were a carefree lot, but harmless to be sure. There were several who looked to be maidens, but the porter knew that these must be young boys, in truth.

Whether he had ordered it or not, the laird would be pleased to savor their entertainment this night. After all, it was an invitation to bad fortune to deny such performers a chance to dance and beg in one's own abode. The porter was not prepared to court any such fate.

The company halted a half-dozen paces away and one stepped cockily forward. His face was blacked, probably with soot, as were the faces of all in his company. He wore a length of red cloth wound around his head, as the porter had heard the infidels were wont to do. His boots were mired, though they were uncommonly tall, and his tabard was of myriad colors, with silver bells hanging upon its hem. He carried naught more worrisome than a broom and several wineskins, the contents of which were undoubtedly responsible for the little company's joyful mood.

He made an elaborate bow, then winked at the porter before he sang:

"Open the door and we will enter in,
whether we lose or whether we win.
If ever we rise, we will stand or fall,
but we will do our duty to please you all."

The company applauded him, the man with the bell rang it merrily; then they all looked expectantly at the porter.

"Aye, your company will be welcomed here this night," he said as he reached for the rope. "The laird's own wedding is to be celebrated on the morrow, after all, and doubtless more largesse will fall from his hand this night than is customary."

The company exchanged glances among themselves, undoubtedly pleased by this prospect. No sooner had the porter cranked up the gate, than they had all slipped beneath it.

He turned, but they were as quick as eels, and just as difficult to catch. They flitted around him like shadows and he did not manage to land a hand upon a single one of them.

"Hoy!" he shouted. "Wait!" The rules demanded that he check every soul who entered the gates for weapons and he knew a moment's fear when the company merely laughed at him.

They repeated their song, half a dozen of them dancing around him in a circle as the others darted toward the hall.

"This is forbidden!" the porter cried. "You cannot do this thing! I must ensure that you bear no weapons."

A large member of the company caught him in a tight hug from the side before he could say more. The porter was momentarily confused. All performers in all places were men, by tradition, but he felt a pair of enormous breasts press against his arm.

"Do you not have a kiss for me?" The words came in a feminine falsetto, the barest breath against his ear. The porter's interest was kindled, for it had been a long and lonely autumn.

He closed his eyes and turned his face ever so slightly. His affectionate assailant kissed him soundly on the lips and the porter was more than a little aroused by her ardent embrace.

She was gone, dancing down the corridor with her fellows, before he realized that he had also felt the tickle of a considerable mustache.

Then he knew without doubt what was worse than being left alone as porter at Tivotdale's gates on Epiphany. He scrubbed at his lips with his gloved hand and hoped no soul had noticed how much he had enjoyed that kiss.

ELEANOR PUSHED THE MEAT from her side of the trencher to Alan's side. He ate it with undisguised enthusiasm, seemingly oblivious to her discontent.

But then, she had not expected any other response from him. He saw the prospect of wealth in her, a curve of breast that meant the task of getting a son upon her would not be so onerous, and little else.

No one had troubled to tempt her smile. No one in Tivotdale had even taken note of her unhappiness. No one cared what she thought, what she felt, whether she felt welcomed or at home. Five years ago, when she had sat at this same table at Ewen's side, she had never felt the lack, but now Eleanor felt it keenly.

She missed Kinfairlie and its easy camaraderie, the affection between its people and its ruling family. She missed the Lammergeier sisters, their compassion for a stranger and their willingness to make her feel one of their family. And she missed Alexander with a painful vigor, his confidence, his laughter, his attention to her.

She was convinced that she would never see the stars from Tivotdale, not in the eyes of any man, not in the gaze of any maiden, confident and merry, not even in the sky above.

There was singing suddenly, carrying from the short corridor outside the great hall. The sound was so delightful that Eleanor thought she imagined it, for such merriment could not belong at Tivotdale.

> *"With a rink tink tink,*
> *for sup or drink,*
> *we will make the old bell sound.*
> *A merry Christmas to you all,*
> *and may happiness abound."*

A bell sounded suddenly, drawing the attention of all, even the most drunken mercenary in the great hall. A man with a red turban, tall boots, and a blackened face stepped confidently into the chamber. There were bells on the hem of his tabard, but they were not the source of the ringing sound. He stood with an expectant manner while his fellows—evidently still outside the chamber—sang the verse again.

There was something familiar in his cocksure stance, though Eleanor did not dare to name it.

The company gathered at Tivotdale began to nudge each other at this prospect of entertainment, and even Alan sat back with a cup of ale and smiled. He beckoned to the man, who bowed low with such grace that Eleanor's heart skipped a beat.

It could not be Alexander, not truly. She bit her lip and fought to appear indifferent, even as she studied the man.

The new arrival brandished his broom with authority and began to sweep the hall as he sang his verse:

> *"Room, room, gentlemen, room do I obtain,*
> *for after me steps Galgacus and all his royal train.*
> *A battle you will soon see of fearsome might,*

between Galgacus and the Black Knight.
If you do not believe what I now say,
step in, Galgacus, and clear the way."

He stepped to one side, tucking his broom under his elbow with a jaunty gesture, and threw out his hand to indicate the portal. A man stepped through the doorway and looked from one side to the other with a fearsome scowl. His armor was wrought of kitchen pots tied together, their bottoms blacked with use, which made the company of mercenaries laugh. His face, too, was blackened, but Eleanor scarce breathed.

It was Malcolm. She knew it well.

She forced herself to appear only mildly interested in the proceedings, though her heart had begun to race. Alexander not only lived, but he had come for her! She could not guess his scheme, but there was a good chance of success, given the drunken state of Alan's mercenaries.

Why, though, did he attack within the holy days? It was forbidden, and though she was glad he had come, she feared for his immortal soul in making such a choice.

She picked at her meat, as if desultory.

"You should watch," Alan chided. "This will cost me good coin, in the end."

Eleanor shrugged. "I do not care for such follies."

Alan shook his head and turned back to the pair on the floor, apparently fascinated.

The Black Knight then sang:

"In I come, I am the Black Knight,
come to this land to wage a good fight.

I will fight Galgacus on this spot,
that valiant man of courage bold.
Let his blood be ever so hot,
I will shortly see it cold."

Alexander then feigned surprise, and sang:

"Galgacus? Galgacus stands outside the door!
He will see this braggart dead on the floor."

A man bounded through the portal, a pot on his head
for a helmet, but chain mail on his chest. He brandished
a weapon that looked genuine enough to Eleanor's eyes.
She had to peer at his blackened face, but she was fairly
certain that it was Kinfairlie's miller, who sang:

"Galgacus am I, and in I stride,
a noble champion and bold.
With my loyal blade by my side,
I won three crowns of gold.
'Twas I that killed the infidels
and brought dozens of them to slaughter.
'Tis I that by this fight
mean to win the king's own daughter."

A familiar figure stepped into the room and fluttered
his lashes. It was the ostler Owen, those two loaves of
bread in his chemise once more. He bowed and one leapt
free, compelling him to crawl after it under the benches.

Alan's men laughed heartily and Malcolm sang again:

"Galgacus calls himself a champion,

I think myself as good.
Before I surrender to him,
I will lose my precious blood."

He lifted his sword and the two would-be combatants sang in unison:

"Battle, battle, I will cry,
To see which on the ground shall lie!"

They lunged at each other and their blades clashed. Their swordplay took them back and forth across the hall, their every gesture exaggerated. Though the mercenaries laughed at their antics, Eleanor saw skill in their battle, particularly from Malcolm. He stumbled and rolled, scrambled out of the way of the miller's assault with the agility of a cat. He hid behind a serving wench and must have pinched her buttocks, for she squealed and struck him. His astonished expression made the mercenaries howl with laughter.

He fell then, before his opponent's blade was even close to him, and the miller froze. "You were not supposed to fall as yet," he whispered, then spared a glance to the watchful company.

Malcolm sat up. "Just strike me dead now then," he whispered, his words loud enough for all to hear. "No one will notice."

"They cannot even show the competence to feign a fight," Alan muttered with a shake of his head. He drained his cup.

The miller looked around in apparent despair, then bent low. "But where is the bladder? How will they know you to be dead if you do not bleed?"

Malcolm looked suddenly dismayed. He searched under the myriad pots of his armor, then held up something that looked like a stuffed sausage. Both men's faces lit with triumph.

Malcolm leapt to his feet and they battled again, apparently repeating the part that they had done incorrectly.

Galgacus stabbed his blade into the sausage, missed, and his blade clanged on a pot. The Black Knight fell all the same, despite having no injury, then pointed insistently to the sausage perched on his chest. Galgacus stabbed again and this time pierced the sausage, which spurted something red all over the floor.

The company cheered, as much at the illusion of a genuine wound as the fact that they had gotten it right. Galgacus then bent his head beside his fallen opponent, apparently filled with remorse at his accomplishment.

"Gentlemen all, see what I have done,
I have cut the Black Knight down!
Is there a sorcerer that can be found?
To cure this noble knight on the ground?"

He turned and appealed to the hall, and every man there looked about himself. A cloaked figure stepped into the hall then and raised his hands. Even his blackened features could not disguise Father Malachy from Eleanor's detection. He spun as he sang, his cloak swirling in a great arc as he crossed the floor.

"There is a sorcerer to be found
to cure this noble knight on the ground."

He stopped beside the fallen Black Knight and looked upon him in apparent surprise. Alexander stepped forward.

"But what can you cure, o sorcerer?"

Father Malachy nodded confidentially to the crowd.

"I can cure all diseases you hear about.
I can cure the hitch, the stitch, the palsy, and the gout.
Raging pain both inside and out.
If a devil is in a man, I can fetch him out."

Alexander and the miller nodded appreciatively at this and Father Malachy sang on:

"Give me an old woman four score and ten
and I will make young and plump again."

"I have need of that talent!" a bold man in the company cried, and the others laughed.

"Take my wife, then," shouted another, to the amusement of all. Alexander raised his voice again:

"But how will you cure him, sorcerer?"

Father Malachy lifted a finger.

"I have a hundred potions,
and spells three times three.
But I shall confess to thee:
there is no better cure

than potent eau-de-vie,
especially that from Sicily."

He pulled out a wineskin with a triumphant gesture, tipped it, and squirted a measure of it into his own mouth. He shook his head, as if impressed by its potency, then squirted it at the fallen knight. He missed that man's mouth, which left the "dead" man groping for his cure like a fish cast out of water.

The company roared, no less when the Black Knight bounced to his feet hale again. Instead of that cured man singing his lines, the sorcerer sang his last verse again:

"I have a hundred potions,
and spells three times three.
But I shall confess to thee:
there is no better cure
than potent eau-de-vie,
especially that from Sicily."

And he squirted a measure of eau-de-vie at the mercenary at the closest table. That man caught the liquid in his mouth; then his face lit with pleasure.

"It is eau-de-vie, in truth!" he bellowed, opening his mouth for more.

The sorcerer obliged and soon the hall was clamoring for the expensive and uncommon liquor.

"I have need of a cure!" shouted a man on the other side of the hall.

"As do I!"

The company of entertainers seemed prepared to share their rare libation. More characters with blackened faces strode into the hall, each singing a ditty of introduction, which was lost in the noise of the hall.

Meanwhile, Alexander passed out wineskins to his companions and soon there were arches of potent liquor flying through the air in all directions. In moments, Alan's mercenaries had eau-de-vie all over their faces and their tabards, but not a one of them cared. Alexander's men had brought a lot of the liquor, which told Eleanor that her husband had a scheme.

Eleanor noticed that a great deal of the eau-de-vie was spilled on the linens upon the tables in the same moment that she heard the bell in Tivotdale's church striking the hour.

One, two, three, four.

"Enough!" Alan roared as chaos claimed his hall. Alexander pivoted and sent a long stream of liquor directly at Alan's mouth, silencing any protest with a gurgle. Eleanor stifled her smile, for it was a poor move to laugh at the expense of this man, just as it had been to find amusement at his brother's expense.

Five, six, seven, eight.

There were nigh thirty performers in Tivotdale's hall now, making a broad circle in the midst of the hall. At least half had moved around the perimeter of the hall unnoticed, for the attention of every man in the hall was focused on the unexpected bounty of liquor.

Nine, ten.

"Something is amiss," Alan said abruptly, rising to his feet. Eleanor feared that any scheme was doomed, for he laid his hand upon the hilt of his blade.

Eleven, twelve. At the last ring, Eleanor realized the truth. The holy days were over. The injunction against warfare no longer applied.

As the last strike sounded, Alexander stepped forward. He emptied his wineskin upon Alan, making no effort to aim for that man's mouth. Alan sputtered in indignation to find himself sodden with liquor, but before he could speak, Alexander winked.

Eleanor caught her skirts in her hands and prepared to move, knowing she had been warned. In the same moment, those of Alexander's company around the perimeter seized the wall sconces and cast the flaming torches onto the tables.

The flames devoured the liquor-soaked cloth and burned high with fearsome speed. Alan roared in fury. He snatched for Eleanor, but she had already leapt over the high table.

Alexander caught her and shoved her behind him. "How could I not love such a clever woman?" he mused, and she fairly glowed with pleasure.

In one smooth gesture, Alexander pulled his sword from the scabbard hidden in his high boots and faced Alan. Eleanor looked around to find every member of the apparently besotted group of performers armed and steely-eyed. There were not just villagers from Kinfairlie in their company, but a number of mercenaries from Kinfairlie's hall. Those in Alan's employ who did not find their garb afire roared and leapt into battle.

"You again," Alan said, then pulled his own blade. "I have killed you once and I will kill you twice."

"In a fair fight?" Alexander shook his head. "I think not."

Alan laughed. "An injured man is easily laid low again. You took a killing blow when last we met. It will not take much to see you dead, in truth." He waved the tip of his sword at Eleanor. "And this time, you need not expect such kindness from me as you have seen thus far."

"You know nothing of kindness," she said; then Alan leapt from the high table.

His blade struck resoundingly against Alexander's own, nearly sending that man stumbling. Alexander freed his blade and struck quickly, before Alan completed his swing. Alan swore and blood stained his sleeve where the blade had bitten.

"A nick, no more and no less," Alan snarled. "Though you shall have more than equal compense for that deed."

Their blades clashed again and Alexander pushed Eleanor out of harm's way. Malcolm fought his way to defend his brother's back, though he spared her a smile of encouragement. She found herself surrounded by the miller, the ostler, Father Malachy, and the miller's son, Matthew, who must have been in the company. The circle of men defended her vigorously, slowly making a steady course toward the portal.

A mercenary lunged at them unexpectedly and injured Father Malachy. That man cried out and the little company faltered for a moment, so unaccustomed were they to battle. Two of Kinfairlie's mercenaries joined their circle, their blows fearsome.

Eleanor reached past the priest and seized a torch that burned atop one of the trestle tables. She pivoted and jabbed it at the mercenary. His tabard flamed with alarming speed, for he had been soaked by the liquor, and even his beard lit. He fell back in horror and pain. Eleanor spun with the burning torch fast in her grip, determined to do her part.

"My lord needs our aid!" Matthew cried suddenly.

They looked as one to see that Tivotdale's surviving

mercenaries had made a barrier between Alexander and Malcolm and the portal. Those two men fought with such vigor that they had not noticed their quandary.

"They mean to ensure that there is no escape, even if Alan falls," Eleanor said, hating Alan Douglas and all who served him.

"What shall we do?" the miller asked.

"We have to thwart them," Eleanor said. She lit another torch and passed it to Matthew. "Fire is our best weapon, but pray that it does not see to our demise as well."

"I would gladly die in defense of my laird," Matthew said with resolve. The men nodded their accord and the little company turned as one to assault the mercenaries closest to them. The others from Kinfairlie saw their deeds and echoed them. Within moments, they had turned the men to a wall of flame. Men fell, men screamed, men rolled on the ground.

Eleanor stamped out a flame on the priest's shoulder with the flat of her hand and the others took to watching each other. Those souls from Kinfairlie around the edges of the room echoed their scheme of attack and soon Eleanor had to brace herself against the scent of burning flesh. The hall was becoming smoky and so hot that her own flesh seemed to sizzle.

She wondered whether they would even be able to make the portal. They reached Alexander and Malcolm and she saw that the cloth wrapped around Alexander's head had fallen aside. There was a red scar at the base of his skull and a lump beneath it.

He should not have been on his feet, much less doing battle! His hair was dark with sweat and his teeth were gritted, but he gave Alan no quarter.

Until suddenly and unexpectedly, Alexander faltered. Eleanor caught her breath in fear. Alan stepped forward with a gleam in his eye, intent upon his kill. He raised his blade in triumph and made to bring it down upon Alexander's head.

"No!" Eleanor screamed, though her cry was swallowed by the din of the hall.

Just as Alan began his killing stroke, Alexander drove his blade upward and into Alan's belly. Alan choked, his own sword fell, and he staggered backward. Alexander drove his blade ever higher, until Eleanor was certain Alan could taste it. That man's eyes gaped.

"Did you not heed our performance, Alan?" Alexander asked, then tsk-tsked. "The truth that the dead will rise was before your very eyes. You should have had the wits to be warned." He pulled his blade out of Alan's chest, the length of it stained with blood, then kicked Alan backward. Alan fell and the flames claimed him in their fiery embrace, his tabard burning with a crackle.

Alexander pivoted and seized Eleanor's hand. Their task complete, the company fled the carnage in Tivotdale's burning hall.

And Eleanor knew there was one last thing she must confess to Alexander, though it might well cost her every prize she had won thus far. The man had asked for honesty, and it was past time to surrender it to him.

All of it, no matter how ugly it was.

～

THE PORTCULLIS WAS OPEN, to Alexander's relief. His head pounded with painful vigor, but there was no ease to be savored before they were safely within Kinfairlie's walls.

A trio of shadows separated themselves from the wall and he braced himself, but it was his sisters, still beneath the fretful eye of Eleanor's maid, Moira. Isabella and Elizabeth matched their steps to that of the company, and Elizabeth spared him a nod that told of her success.

Alexander winked at her, well-pleased. He had been fearful for the success of her scheme, even for his sisters' survival, but they had made an argument he had not been able to protest. He could scarce think for the pain between his ears, much less summon a clever comment, but he dared not indulge his urge to halt now.

"You let your sisters accompany you?" Eleanor demanded of him in outrage. "How could you so endanger maidens beneath your care? I thought you were a man well aware of his responsibilities!"

His wife had much to learn about his willful sisters, though Alexander had no chance to tell her as much.

"He could not have left us behind," Isabella said grimly. "Even if he had locked us in our chamber, we would have found a way to follow and be of aid."

"Annelise remained at Kinfairlie," Elizabeth confided. "But only with reluctance. She acts as regent in your and Alexander's absence."

"And if they were coming, then so was I, my lady," Moira said. "I have as stout a heart as any and I would not be left standing aside while you were retrieved from the clutches of this lot."

"But there were many come to my aid," Eleanor argued. She granted Alexander a quelling glance. "You should not have put your sisters in peril." Her lips tightened. "Nor should you have imperiled yourself by this feat. How do you mean to walk all the way to Kinfairlie?

I see that scar upon your flesh, Alexander Lammergeier, and I am enough of a healer to know that you risk much in this pursuit."

"I risked all," he said, granting her a quick kiss that left her blushing and silent. He held her gaze. "And regret none of it."

She blinked back tears and tightened her grip upon his hand, her first outward sign of relief. Alexander quickened his pace, for they were not free of Tivotdale's boundaries as yet.

"We could not have surrendered you to Alan Douglas!" Isabella grimaced and shuddered. "He was never a man of merit."

"Besides," Elizabeth said with some confidence, "I am the only one who can pick a lock. Alexander could not have left me behind."

"And I had to keep Elizabeth out of trouble," Isabella added.

Eleanor blinked, clearly unaware of the import of this, then a fearsome groan filled the air behind them. Alexander looked back in time to see Tivotdale's roof crumble, shifting so that its considerable weight fell into the great hall. Smoke rose from the fissures in the roof and the dull orange of the flames could be seen on the stone.

The last of the sentries—who must have been sleeping— bellowed at the sight. They shouted to each other, then roared when they spied the fleeing party.

"Run!" Alexander cried, for it did not matter if they were overheard now. An arrow buried itself in the ground beside him. "Run!"

The entire company took to their heels, fleeing as quickly as they could. A hail of arrows buried themselves in the ground on their every side, and Alexander heard one grunt of pain. One of the villagers held fast to his shoulder, which now bled, but ran grimly onward.

Alexander felt his grasp of his surroundings faltering. Alan had fought more vigorously than he had expected; though in the moment, Alexander had not been aware of his own weakness. Now he felt the full impact of his former injury.

He felt Malcolm take one of his elbows and knew that Eleanor held fast to the other.

"We will never make it," Eleanor muttered.

"Of course, we will," Malcolm replied.

"You have little faith in the Lammergeier," Alexander teased, his voice weak. Eleanor spared him a glance filled with concern; then the welcome pound of hoofbeats filled the air. "You see? Aid is nigh upon us."

Eleanor turned, a frown drawing her brows together, for in the blackness of the night, it was easier to hear the horses than to see them.

"Destriers," she whispered, and Alexander smiled.

"*Our* destriers," he confirmed.

The ground rumbled with the steeds' approach and the small company cheered. Alexander saw the horses of Ravensmuir, a great herd of them, bearing down upon the group. Their ebony necks were arched, their manes and tails, as dark as midnight, gleamed in the wind. Their hoofbeats were sure and resolute, their approach made the very earth tremble. Their saddles were empty, save for a mere trio of them.

The beaming face of the ostler of Ravensmuir became visible, for he rode the foremost steed. Two of his boys rode the horses on the flanks, but the beasts were so disciplined—or perhaps so clever—that they seemed to know their destination without being told.

They surrounded the small company as it came out of the range of the archers, pacing and prancing, and Uriel bent to nuzzle Alexander. Owen and Malcolm fairly heaved Alexander into his destrier's saddle, and he felt Eleanor's concerned gaze upon him.

"I will ride with him," she said to Owen, who shook his head.

"No, my lady." Owen seized the reins of a large mare and offered Eleanor his hand that she might climb to the stirrup. "It is more fitting that you ride your own steed."

It was a moment that Alexander savored and he knew he would recall it a thousand times. His wife looked between the ostler and the horse, seemingly lost for words. She looked then to Alexander, tears welling in those magnificent green eyes.

"Guinevere insisted," he said lightly, feeling better now that he was in the saddle. "I told you that she had no care for our counsel, but then, I have an affection for females with thoughts of their own."

"I cannot . . . I should not . . . ," Eleanor said, her very incoherence a sign of her pleasure. She stroked the mare's nose, clearly overwhelmed.

"Of course you should!" Isabella chided. "You are the lady of Kinfairlie and family as well. It is only fitting."

"Make haste, my lady," Owen said, glancing back to burning Tivotdale.

Eleanor needed no further encouragement. She shook her head and swung into the saddle, her grace that of one well accustomed to riding. The light of her features told Alexander the truth of how pleased she was.

"You must give me a ride," Isabella insisted to Eleanor. "It is likely the closest I shall ever come to having a Ravensmuir steed for my very own." She granted Alexander an arch look, which he ignored. Elizabeth, meanwhile, rode a smaller mare, with Moira riding behind her, that maid fairly trembling at the size of the steed.

The company turned as one and the horses began to canter toward Kinfairlie. Eleanor rode upon Alexander's left, Malcolm upon his right, and his sisters' two steeds to Eleanor's left. Tivotdale fell behind them, becoming a dull red gleam in the distance. By morning, there would be nothing left of the brothers who had so abused his lady wife, and not much more of their abode.

Alexander believed that most fitting.

"MY LADY, I did not realize that you blamed yourself for Ewen's death," Moira said when they had passed the copse of trees where the horses had been hidden, and Tivotdale was lost to view.

Eleanor started. "Of course I did. How could I not do so?"

"What happened?" Alexander asked, knowing full well what Moira knew that his lady did not.

Eleanor met his gaze steadily. "He came drunken to our chamber, as was his custom. He locked the portal. He shed his garb. He insisted that we would lie together, and when I declined, because he was besotted, he raised his hand to strike me as so oft he had before." She swallowed. "And I did not deign to be struck again."

Her words sat in the air between them all, the group listening intently. Alexander understood why she had feared him at first, why she had panicked when he had locked the door to the portal. "Did he always strike you?"

"Only after the first year, though he was always rough. It was when I did not conceive a son, and that despite his efforts, that he was so angered with me."

Again this demand for sons. Alexander supposed her expectation that he would demand boys from her came from her experience of men. He reached for her hand and she clutched at his, even as she sat straighter in the saddle. "And so, you did not deign to be struck again," he said, encouraging her to continue.

"No. And so I struck him back," she confessed. "Indeed, I hit Ewen before he managed to hit me, so drunken was he. He fell. He moved no more." Her throat worked. "I knew that my life was as good as over if they tried me at Tivotdale for his murder; so in terror I fled, in the midst of the night."

She looked to Alexander again, a plea in her eyes. "And so I happened to come to Kinfairlie, a rare sanctuary if ever there was one, as if someone guided my path. And so I surrender this truth to its laird, because I know he favors truth, even if it is condemning, and I plead for his mercy."

"You have no need of his mercy," Alexander said quietly. "For your truth is but a measure of the full truth."

Eleanor blinked in her astonishment. She frowned at Alexander and he indicated Moira, who cleared her throat portentously.

"I came to your chamber that morning, my lady, and found you gone. I found my lord Ewen fallen upon the floor as well, and I thought at first that he but slumbered there. God knows but the man had fallen into a drunken stupor far from his bed a thousand times before. He was snoring, though there was a bump upon his head, and truly I felt much sympathy for you that you should have to endure such a boar of a spouse."

"Snoring?" Eleanor exclaimed. "How could he have been snoring?"

"Aye, my lady, he snored. He was alive. I went to fetch my lord Alan, for I knew it would take at least one man to heave Ewen into his own bed. I thought merely that you had risen and gone down to the hall or the kitchens."

Moira took a deep breath. "I brought Alan to your chamber, and he bent over his brother, who had ceased to snore by this time. Alan paused in a way that prompted me to look closer. He asked where you were and I confessed that I did not know. He noted that your cloak and boots were gone, as if you had departed. I could not explain this. I looked about the chamber seeking some reason why your garb should be gone, and had I taken longer about it, I would not have seen the truth of what he did."

Eleanor's fingers tightened on Alexander's own.

"I saw the knife," Moira said. "I saw the blade flash in the morning sunlight; I saw him bury it in his own brother's throat. I heard the gurgle of Ewen's death, though I had my wits about me and feigned to seek your stockings. And Alan rose, as calm as ever a man could be, and he turned, and he looked me in the eye and he informed me that my lady had stabbed her lord husband to death. He said that his brother had been murdered, that his brother's widow was a murderess and that he would have to assume the burden of the lairdship of Tivotdale."

"But Ewen never allowed me to carry a knife!" Eleanor exclaimed. "With what would I have stabbed him?"

"I was not the only one to note that detail, my lady, though I said nothing. Those who argued with Alan Douglas found themselves savoring the hospitality of his dungeons."

Eleanor's mouth worked in her surprise, but Alexander merely held fast to her hand.

"Just as another man finds himself in Kinfairlie's dungeon," Elizabeth said with gusto.

"Who?" Eleanor asked, looking between them all.

"One of Alan's mercenaries, left behind when that army sought you at Kinfairlie on Christmas Day," Alexander said.

"He put the thorns beneath Uriel's saddle," Malcolm said with disdain.

"And I spied him in the hall," Moira said. "I recognized him well, though at first I could not fathom his reason for being at Kinfairlie, his scheme was soon clear enough." She nodded with satisfaction. "The laird Alexander saw him rightfully condemned for his attempt to see the laird of the abode laid low."

"What will happen to him?" Eleanor asked Alexander.

He shrugged, but spoke with resolve. "A fate that befits his crime. In several months, a scent will doubtless rise from Kinfairlie's dungeon. We shall see the dungeon cleaned, as is fitting for all of the keep in the spring." He met her gaze. "Perhaps we will find something in the dungeons that we have forgotten."

Eleanor held his gaze unflinchingly. "It is fitting that he suffer," she said with vigor. "He will have time to repent of his sins." Then she frowned. "But what of the potion that felled Anthony?"

"It was of Jeannie's concoction," Elizabeth confided.

"Jeannie?"

"She meant it for you," Alexander said. "As a warning that you not discount her talents." Eleanor's lips thinned, but Alexander granted her no chance to speak. "I would be pleased if my lady wife would take the care and welfare of those at Kinfairlie beneath her hand, as our former healer has seen fit to depart."

Eleanor smiled and her grip tightened upon his. "I would be delighted."

Alexander smiled at his lady wife. He turned and saw Kinfairlie's silhouette rising before them, the tower outlined against the silver of the sea, and felt a surge of pride at the sight of his abode.

Their abode. It was not affluent, but it was a handsome home, and with Eleanor by his side, he felt certain that his fortunes had changed for the better.

Somehow, they would see Kinfairlie prosper again.

"THERE IS SOMETHING ELSE you should have," Elizabeth said when Eleanor thought there could be nothing else to be confessed. The girl fumbled with something she had knotted to her belt, then offered a bundle wrapped in cloth to Eleanor. "Alan was so predictable," she said with a scornful shake of her head. "It was right in the top of his treasury."

The weight of the bundle was so familiar, so precious, that Eleanor dared to hope. "Was that the lock you picked?" she guessed.

Elizabeth smiled with pride. "The very same. Rosamunde taught me that skill on one of her visits when there was little else to do and neither of us had an appetite for embroidery. I never thought to use it, though."

"Be careful, sister mine," Alexander warned, his teasing tone not hiding the fact that he was much more pale than he had been. "You shall become the unusual woman in our family."

"I do not care if I am!" Elizabeth said with a jut of her chin.

Before she could argue more, Isabella interjected. "Open it," she urged.

Eleanor closed her hand around the cloth-bound bundle and her heart leapt at the familiarity of the shape hidden within it. Her mouth went dry and she felt her heart pound. "I never thought to see this again," she said, her voice thick.

The others waited, patient with her even as she sat overwhelmed. Did they appreciate the magnitude of the gifts they offered to her? Eleanor could not believe herself deserving of such bounty—or else, they were more generous than any souls she had ever known.

She unwrapped the gem with care, half-fearing that she had guessed wrong, that the promise of this gift would again be snatched away before her eyes.

But no. Alexander never disappointed her. The rubies in her mother's crucifix gleamed in the starlight, the gem glinting in her palm.

Eleanor's tears began to fall in her joy. "I thank you," she whispered, looking to each of them in turn. "I thank you, all. It was the sole memento I had of my mother, though I am astonished that you would risk your life to see it returned. Thank you!" Alexander laid his hand atop hers and she took a shuddering breath, her hand trembling atop the gem.

"Don it!" Elizabeth urged.

Eleanor needed no more encouragement to put the golden chain over her head. The gem fell just below her collarbone, its weight welcome beyond belief. She smiled at Alexander, who watched her with bright eyes. "You have given me gifts beyond expectation," she whispered.

"I grant you no more and no less than what you deserve," he said, then kissed her knuckles. The others turned to speak to each other, granting the pair a moment of privacy.

"I wish I had had this to wear on our nuptial day," Eleanor said, stroking the crucifix. "It was said to bring good fortune."

"Considering the fortune you had in the two marriages for which you did wear it, I am rather glad that you did not have it then," Alexander said with a grin. "You can wear it from this day forward."

"Indeed, I will, for I find this marriage a fortunate one, indeed."

"Guinevere, too, is your nuptial gift, although belatedly given," Alexander said. "I hope you will ride her long and in good health, as I hope our marriage will endure long in good health."

Eleanor smiled, feeling lighter and more blessed than ever she had. "I thank you, though I regret that I have but one gift that I can surrender to you in this moment."

Alexander arched a brow. "Indeed?"

"Indeed." She held fast to his hand. "My lord husband has succeeded in his quest to make my heart his very own, and so I surrender it to your care. I love you, Alexander Lammergeier." She smiled at him. "I am told with good authority that this is the foundation of all marriages of merit."

"That was always my understanding," he said with a wink.

They entered the bailey, the horses stamping and snorting. Squires came running from the stables and villagers clustered about the company, anxious to hear details of their adventure. Anthony strode from the hall, shouting commands, and ensuring that the wounded had prompt care.

But Eleanor had eyes only for her husband. He was more pale than she would have preferred, though still he moved with vigor. Alexander dismounted, then lifted her from her saddle.

"You should not have fetched me, not until your wound was healed," she chided, unable to halt herself.

He grinned, holding her so that her feet were just above the ground, as if he meant to put her back in the saddle. "Shall I return you to Tivotdale, and come for you later?" he asked, his manner playful, and she laughed aloud.

"You know what I mean," she said, putting her arms around his neck. "I love you. I am pleased beyond all to be by your side, but I care for your welfare."

He bent and kissed her brow. "As I care for yours." His voice caught as he held her closer. "There was no choice, Eleanor. I love you too much to abandon you to such a fate." His arms surrounded her, his embrace all that she would ever need. "Know that I shall treasure the gift of your love always," he said. "Though you should be aware that you hold my heart hostage in return."

"I vow to protect it as it so rightly deserves." She reached up and eased some of the soot from his face, then held up that finger in accusation. "You, sir, have need of a bath."

"And shall I bathe alone?"

"Never again!"

Alexander laughed and Eleanor was happy as she had never known herself to be. Anthony cleared his throat at close proximity, then offered something to his laird, which he had kept hidden in his hand. "You might be desirous of this, my lord," he said, then smiled at Eleanor. "Welcome home, my lady."

"Home," Eleanor repeated, and felt those tears rise again.

Alexander opened his hand to reveal his mother's emerald ring and his eyes lit. "This would belong on this finger," he said, lifting her left hand and holding the ring above her hand. He arched a brow at her and Eleanor pushed her ring finger through the circle of gold, accepting once again what he offered her.

"You, sir, have need of a son," she said with force.

"I have need of my lady's healing caress," he said, then claimed her lips in a possessive kiss. Eleanor met his embrace with a passion of her own, not caring who witnessed their ardor. As always, his touch set her to simmering and she found herself anxious to retire to the solar and that great bed.

The assembly cheered all around them, and when Alexander finally lifted his head, Eleanor realized that her hand gently rested upon the bump on the back of his head.

It was not large, but neither was it small.

She frowned at him in mock consternation. "A fortnight abed, my lord, and not one moment less. That is what will see you cured."

"A man of honor can only cede to his lady's every command," Alexander said, his eyes alight with a wicked gleam.

Eleanor laughed, then stretched to her toes to kiss him fully, liking well how Alexander responded to her caress. His conquest of her reluctant heart was a victory to be celebrated, indeed.

Epilogue

⁓

It was October at Kinfairlie and Alexander knew there was mischief afoot in his hall.

Kinfairlie had hosted its first fall fair just the month before, and this with Eleanor's sage counsel. Although there were matters that could be improved in the future, he considered it to have been a success. His borders were secure and there were a few coins in his coffers. There had been seed at Tivotdale that they had claimed in the spring and the weather had been perfect. The harvest had been a good one.

Alexander was sufficiently content that he did not trouble himself over some measure of mischief. His three younger sisters were smug, and he caught them giggling at some secret they would not confess. Even Eleanor, ripe and round with his child, seemed to hold some detail from him. He did not beg after the tale; indeed, he feigned obliviousness of their many hints, for he knew these portents well.

There was a jest in the offing, and he was to be the butt of that jest. He did not fear that it was a foul trick, for his wife was clearly engaged in this mischief. Indeed, so secretive was her manner that she might have been its instigator, and this possibility lightened his heart. The lady had fairly blossomed since they had wed, and Alexander knew it was her true nature that revealed itself. That she trusted him sufficiently to make a jest, even one at his expense, was merry news, indeed.

Alexander only hoped that the four women would spare a measure of his pride, though he doubted it would be done.

ALEXANDER FORGOT ALL about his suspicions on the day that Eleanor began her labor. The babe came earlier than expected and the entire household was set to scrambling when her water broke. Alexander found himself grateful that Jeannie had not been seen since her departure from his hall, for he would not have trusted her to aid Eleanor in the birth of their child.

Women raced hither and yon, kettles of steaming water were carried to the solar, and a runner was dispatched to a midwife. Eleanor was led to the great bed in the solar, Annelise supporting her, and Vera and Moira took joint charge of the proceedings.

Only Alexander was left with no deed to fulfill. Indeed, he was forbidden by those two maids to so much as enter his own chamber.

"I must be by my lady's side," he argued, knowing full well that his case was lost.

"It is no place for a man, my lord," insisted Moira.

"It is oft said that the man who attends the birth of his

own child will never regard his wife the same way," counseled Vera.

Eleanor screamed then, all three of them wincing as one. "We have a long day ahead of us, my lord," Moira said with false cheer.

"The first babe always takes the longest," agreed Vera. The two smiled at Alexander with a pert confidence he could not bring himself to share. Elizabeth and Isabella arrived then, breathless from running, and the maids ushered them into the chamber with a nod. "My lady will appreciate your comfort," Vera said.

"But . . . ," Alexander protested, reaching for the latch.

"We shall summon you, my lord, though it will not likely be soon," Moira said with crisp authority. Then the women ducked into the solar and closed the portal firmly in Alexander's face.

He stomped down to his hall in poor temper. Eleanor screamed again, her last cry ending with a gasp that made him shudder.

"Her cries are not close together as yet, my lord," Anthony counseled, offering his laird a cup of ale. "The babe will not arrive soon."

Alexander spared his castellan a telling glance, accepted the ale, and drank half of it in one swallow.

But there was no lie in either prediction. The day stretched long and Alexander paced the hall so diligently that he swore he would wear a trough in the floor. Eleanor cried out at intervals, her cries becoming ever louder and more close together. When night began to darken the hall and the child had not yet arrived, Alexander wondered how his father had endured this ordeal eight times—no less how his mother had done so.

"It has not been so long as that, sir, though truly it seems as much." Anthony placed another cup of ale upon the board before his master, along with a slice of bread and some cheese.

"The better part of a day is long enough!" Alexander protested.

"There are those women who labor for several days and nights before the child sees fit to emerge," Anthony asserted with an acceptance of that fact that Alexander found galling. "I do not doubt that your lady feels the passage of time even more onerously than you."

"I do not doubt as much myself, Anthony." Alexander drank some of the ale, then began to pace the hall again. He was restless beyond all.

"You seek a task in this," his castellan said. "But truly, my lord, your part in this quest was completed many months ago."

"I thank you for reminding me that I am responsible for my lady's anguish," Alexander said, and the castellan shook his head.

"It is natural, my lord, and Lady Eleanor is both young and hale," he said. "From my understanding, there is little to fear before the second day."

Alexander straightened. "Thank you, Anthony. I shall pray that the lady's ordeal ends soon."

Eleanor punctuated that comment with a bellow both louder and longer than any previous. There was a cheer from the solar and the murmur of encouraging voices.

"The babe," Anthony whispered.

"I cannot bear it," Alexander said as his wife cried out again, and did so even more loudly. The women cloistered with Eleanor cried encouragement and he could not linger in the hall any longer.

There was a bustle at the portal to the hall, but Alexander did not care. He made for the stairs with purpose, knowing that two older women would not halt him this time, despite their convictions.

Anthony cleared his throat with sudden volume. "You have a visitor, my lord."

"He or she can wait until the morrow," Alexander said tersely, not sparing a backward glance. "Please ensure that our guest is made comfortable, but I have neither time nor patience to entertain on this day."

"You may think otherwise once you know who I am," an unfamiliar voice said with some humor.

Alexander turned partway up the stairs to find an older man standing in his hall. That man had a bright eye and stood with an expectant manner. He was not young, his hair a thick mane of white, his garb was most expensive. Rings adorned most of his fingers, his tabard was richly embellished with golden embroidery, and a fur-lined cloak in lavish black spilled over his shoulders. Four pages hovered behind him, their manner attentive and their garb echoing the man's colors.

Alexander forced a thin smile. "I doubt as much," he said politely. "As you may have ascertained, my wife labors to deliver our child and she is my sole concern on this evening." He gestured to Anthony. "All the same, I bid you welcome to Kinfairlie and anticipate that we shall become better acquainted on the morrow. Until then, my abode is as yours."

Eleanor cried out again and Alexander spared a nod

for guest and castellan. He had barely taken a step before another cry carried to his ears.

It was the cry of a baby.

The women cheered above him and Alexander took the remaining stairs three at a time. He burst into his own chamber, and saw to his relief that Eleanor yet lived. He went directly to her side and kissed her hand, then her brow. "How do you fare?"

"I am glad to see this task complete," she said, smiling at him through her exhaustion. Her brow was damp with perspiration and the linens were soaked with blood, but she was alive and flushed in the face.

"As am I."

"Tell me, Alexander, are you committed to having eight children, as your parents did?" she asked, her eyes sparkling.

"One will suffice," he said with vigor, uncertain whether he could endure more days like this one.

"Surely you have need of a son?" Eleanor teased. Her eyes sparkled with uncommon humor, though Alexander did not comprehend her jest.

"A son or daughter will suit me well," he said. "So long as my lady is hale."

Eleanor smiled. "Fool man," she whispered, no censure in her voice. "A son is what you need, even more than most men do."

Isabella eased to Alexander's side, a plump bundle in her arms. "Look!" she said with such pride that the child might have been her own. She offered the babe to Alexander and he smiled at its ruddy-faced indignation. He accepted its burden with care and it promptly bellowed with greater gusto.

He had no time to ask its gender, much less why his lady wife was so insistent upon having a son, before the women gasped in collective dismay.

"Who are you?" Vera cried. "And what makes you imagine you have a place in this chamber?"

"You will not look upon my lady in this state," Moira exclaimed, and cast a clean linen sheet across Eleanor's knees.

"Sir!" Alexander stood at the sight of his guest in this chamber at this time. The older man looked about himself with some interest, as if assessing Alexander's very worth by his furnishings. "You go too far in this! It is scarcely the place of a guest to look upon my lady in such a state." He and Vera made to block that man's passage, but the older man only arched a brow at this obstacle.

He peered over their shoulders and smiled thinly. "Good evening, Eleanor," he said crisply.

Eleanor, to Alexander's shock, sat up, straightened her chemise, and smoothed her hair. "Good afternoon, my lord Reinhard."

"You know him?" Alexander asked in an undertone.

Eleanor nodded. "I invited him to Kinfairlie, that he might arrive for this day as our guest."

Reinhard tut-tutted. "Though your summons should have been more urgently stated. You told me, in fact, that the child would not arrive for at least another week. You are early in bringing this child forth into the world, Eleanor, and very nearly lost all in so doing."

"I am sorry, my lord." Eleanor dropped her gaze demurely.

"It is not her fault, my lord," Moira said, standing beside Eleanor as if she meant to protect her. "A babe will come in its own time."

"And there are witnesses aplenty, should you have arrived later," Elizabeth noted. She moved to stand by Eleanor's side, as if defending her. Alexander watched Annelise stand beside Elizabeth, while Isabella straightened beside him.

"What does this mean?" Alexander asked. "What is the import of this?"

They ignored him.

"I scarce made it here in time to witness the deed, and no matter what you believe, it is critical that I do witness the babe's arrival," Reinhard huffed.

"Is the child not hale?" Alexander demanded, fearful now of what they meant. He looked down at the bundle in his arms.

Eleanor grasped his hand. "The babe is fine."

Alexander looked between the pair in confusion.

Reinhard snapped his fingers and one of his pages—all of whom had also followed him into the solar, to the dismay of Moira and Vera—surrendered a feathered quill to him. Reinhard snapped his finger again and was given a scroll of vellum adorned with an impressive number of ribbons. He unfurled it, revealing the many red wax seals upon it, and cleared his throat.

Then he eased aside the sheet over Eleanor's knees with the tip of the quill.

"What folly is this?" Alexander roared. "I protest this indignity shown to my wife!"

"It must be done," Eleanor said.

"Let him do what he must," Isabella counseled, putting a restraining hand upon Alexander's elbow. They had both been struck mad, Alexander was certain of it, not to find this man's very manner offensive.

"It appears that you have indeed borne a child very recently, Eleanor," Reinhard said with some approval.

"Indeed, I have, my lord."

"It would have been ideal, of course, for me to have witnessed the birth and thus to have ensured there to be no doubt that this child came from your womb, but one must make do with one's opportunities, I suppose."

"I apologize again, my lord."

Reinhard harrumphed and made a notation upon his parchment, then looked about the chamber. His gaze fell upon the child in Alexander's arms and he crossed the room. "And this would be the infant in question?"

"Of course," the women replied in unison.

"What is the reason for this madness?" Alexander asked, but Eleanor hushed him with a fingertip upon his elbow.

"Trust me," she whispered. Her eyes sparkled so merrily that he was more reassured by her manner than any words she might have uttered.

Reinhard, who was clearly not enamored of small children, used the feathered tip of his quill to push aside the swaddling. His lip curled slightly, though he persisted. The babe's small penis was soon revealed, though the boy protested this intimacy with another wail.

"A boy," Reinhard said, then nodded approval at Eleanor. "Well done."

"I strove to ensure as much, my lord," she said, sparing a smile for Alexander. She squeezed his hand, her eyes dancing with such delight that he was both charmed and confused.

"But what is the meaning of this?" he demanded. "Who are you?"

Reinhard straightened, insulted at this question. "You do not know?"

Alexander shook his head. His sisters giggled and nudged each other.

The older man looked at Eleanor. "You did not tell him?"

She flushed. "He wed me for my own merit."

"Truly?" Reinhard blinked. He looked between the wedded pair with some astonishment, then shook his head. "And they say the world is not full of marvels in these days," he mused.

"I take exception to that. My lady is a marvel in and of herself. . . ."

Reinhard waved Alexander to silence. "I do not argue that, sir. My point is simply that a man who looks beyond the weight of his own purse is a marvel." He fixed Alexander with a bright eye. "And you would be the father of this child?"

"I am."

"Beyond doubt?"

Alexander bridled, but Eleanor silenced him with a touch. "Be not insulted," she counseled. "For there is much at stake." Then she spoke to Reinhard. "We were wedded on Christmas Day, my lord, and I have known no other man since that time."

"That would be more than ten months past. Excellent." Reinhard made another notation, his quill pausing above the vellum. "And your full name and title, sir, would be?"

"Alexander Lammergeier, Laird of Kinfairlie," Eleanor supplied when Alexander might have argued this man's familiarity.

"Excellent." Reinhard marked his vellum with a flourish, then snapped his fingers again. He surrendered both vellum and quill to his squires, then sent them all scampering with a murmured command. Then he folded his hands together and returned Alexander's glance, saying nothing at all.

The chamber filled with expectant silence. After a moment, Reinhard returned to his survey of the solar's contents. Alexander frowned as the guest peered at a stool, as if finding it lacking some attribute, but Eleanor shook her head minutely.

The boys returned momentarily, bearing chests that were small but obviously weighty. "And where would you like the coin to be secured, Laird Alexander?" Reinhard asked. Four pages and an elderly man turned their expectant gazes upon him.

"What coin?" Alexander asked.

Reinhard, against expectation, smiled thinly. "You truly did not know. Allow me to introduce myself properly."

Alexander did not comment that such an introduction was past due.

"I am Reinhard von Heigel, the friend and confidant of the late Étienne Havilland, Baron of Breton. Étienne, of course, was the father of your wife, and appointed me to execute his will." Every soul in the chamber crossed herself and Reinhard nodded acknowledgment of the courtesy.

He then continued. "Étienne insisted that his legacy could only pass to a male heir and thus, when he knew himself to be possessed solely of a daughter, he stipulated that his estate would remain in trust until his daughter, Eleanor, gave birth to a son. Étienne decreed that the father of that son would be his heir and that I, should he depart this world before me, should act as trustee of those funds."

Reinhard cleared his throat and gave Eleanor a stern glance. "I must confess that I had hoped that Eleanor would deliver of a son much sooner than this. The burden of managing Étienne's considerable wealth has been onerous. In truth, I feared that I would meet my own demise before an heir had been produced." He smiled tightly. "I congratulate you both on ensuring that prospect was never realized."

"Wealth?" Alexander echoed, eyeing the chests with new certainty of their contents.

"Wealth aplenty," Reinhard declared. He flicked open each trunk, revealing each one to be filled with coins. One held gold coins, the other three were filled with silver ones. "Which was why, sir, I asked where you would see your inheritance secured."

Anthony coughed delicately, drawing every eye, including Alexander's, for he had not realized that his castellan had joined the growing company in the solar. "I would suggest, my lord, that the coin be counted before it is accepted in Kinfairlie's treasury, the better to ensure that all has been delivered as anticipated."

"A most prudent notion," Reinhard said. They looked to Alexander once again. His sisters were grinning, waiting to see how he would accept this extraordinary fortune.

"You knew of this," he said to Eleanor.

"Why do you think that men have desired so ardently to wed me?" she asked, and he shook his head.

"I can think of a thousand reasons beyond this one."

The lady's answering smile was all the reward he could have hoped to win. He perched on the side of their bed and she caressed the cheek of their son. Alexander wanted nothing more than to explore the child's marvels with Eleanor.

"Look at his tiny fingers and toes," Isabella whispered with awe.

"He is perfect," Annelise whispered in her turn.

"As is his mother," Alexander said, and Eleanor flushed crimson.

Anthony cleared his throat pointedly. "My lord?"

"On the floor above this one, Anthony, we will use the chamber with three windows as our counting room," Alexander said decisively without glancing up. "Please ensure that the windows are secured from the inside and that a guard is placed upon the portal. Only you or I shall be admitted once the coin has been secured, and once that coin is secured, I would bid you offer my finest hospitality to our esteemed guest, Lord Reinhard."

"Very good, my lord." With Anthony's bow, the men finally left the solar.

"Praise be," Vera muttered. "I thought they would never leave!"

"Men in the birthing room," Moira clucked. "It is shocking."

"Strangers even," Vera agreed with no small measure of indignation. She then patted the boy's cheek with a fingertip. "You are a clever one, lad, seeing yourself in an affluent household from the first!" The babe gurgled, seemingly content to be cosseted by his father now. "We can expect much from this one, to be sure."

"His presence is sufficient," Eleanor declared.

"You should have seen your face!" Elizabeth said, poking Alexander in the arm. She then mimicked the fierce scowl that Alexander had presumably shown moments before. "I thought you might cast him out the window!"

"It is good that you did not, for he might have taken insult," Annelise said.

"Think of all that coin, Alexander," Isabella whispered. "Think of what might be done with it."

Alexander looked down at his smiling wife and held her gaze. He knew full well what he would do with it and he imagined that their thoughts were as one. Kinfairlie had some debt, to be sure, but nothing to match the sum of coin Eleanor had brought to his coffers.

"Strangely," he mused, "I find myself envisioning three weddings that will be the talk of all of Christendom, so beauteous will be the brides at each of them."

His sisters roared outrage as one and Alexander laughed at them.

"Of course, each maiden will choose the man she loves best to be her spouse," Eleanor interjected. "And will do so in her own time."

Alexander claimed his wife's hand with his own. "And until that moment and beyond it, Kinfairlie will be secured."

Eleanor sighed contentment and the pair shared a smile that fairly heated the chamber. "Begone all of you," Alexander roared with mock outrage. "I would have a moment with my lady wife." They all left, complaining as they did, and once the portal was firmly closed, he bent toward Eleanor. "For it is she and no other who is the crown jewel of Kinfairlie," he murmured before his lips closed over hers.

The lady did not seem inclined to argue with that.

More
Claire Delacroix!

Please turn this page
to see how the trilogy began with

The Beauty Bride

and continued with

The Rose Red Bride.

The
Beauty Bride

Chapter One

~

THE AUCTION OF RAVENSMUIR'S relics promised to be the event of the decade. Madeline and her sisters had spent the short interval between the announcement and the event ensuring that they would look their best. Uncle Tynan had declared it imperative that they appear to not need the coin, and his nieces did their best to comply.

It was beyond convenient that they could pass kirtles from one to the next, though inevitably there were alterations to be made. They might be sisters, but they were scarcely of the same shape! Hems had to be taken up or let down, seams gathered tighter or let out, and bits of embroidery were required to make each garment "new" for its latest recipient.

There were disagreements invariably between each one and her younger sibling, for their taste in ornamentation varied enormously. Madeline preferred her garments plain, while Vivienne savored lavish embroidery upon the hems, preferably of golden thread. These two did not argue any longer—though once they had done so heatedly, for Madeline sorely disliked to embroider and had been convinced as a young girl that it was unfair for her to endure a hateful task simply to please her sister.

Now, they bent their heads together to make Madeline's discarded kirtles better suit Vivienne, while Vivienne's quick needle made short work of any new garb destined for Madeline. Vivienne was also taller than Madeline, even though she was younger, so the hems had to be let out.

Annelise was shorter even than Madeline, so those hems had to be double-folded when a kirtle passed to her. This often meant that the finest embroidery was hidden from view, though this suited Annelise's more austere taste. Isabella, sadly, was nigh as tall as Vivienne, but could not abide golden embroidery. Her hair was the brightest hue of red of all the sisters and she was convinced that the gold of the thread made her hair appear unattractively fiery. When kirtles passed to her, the sisters would couch the gold with silver and other hues, and the kirtles would be resplendent indeed.

Finally, Elizabeth had the last wearing of each kirtle. This had never been an issue, for she seemed wrought to match the height of Isabella perfectly and was not overly particular of taste. Elizabeth was a girl inclined to dreaming, and was oft teased that she gave more merit to what she could not see than what was directly before her.

But there was a new challenge this year, for Elizabeth was twelve summers of age and her courses had begun. With her courses, her figure had changed radically. Suddenly, she had a much more generous bust than her elder sisters—which meant that she turned crimson when any male so much as glanced her way, as well as that Isabella's kirtles did not begin to fit her. There proved to be insufficient fabric even with the laces let out fully to grant Elizabeth an appearance of grace.

Tears ensued, until Madeline and Vivienne contrived an embroidered panel that could be added down each side of the kirtles in question. Isabella, who was the most clever with a needle, embroidered patterns along their length that so matched the embroidery already on the hem that the panel appeared to have been a part of the kirtle all along.

Shoes and stockings and girdles took their own time to be arranged, but by the time the sisters arrived at Ravensmuir and were summoned to the chamber of the auction, no one could have faulted their splendor. They had even wrought new tabards for their brothers, with Alexander's bearing the glowing orb of Kinfairlie's crest on its front, as was now his right.

SO THEY RODE BENEATH THE GATES OF RAVENSMUIR, attired in their finest garb. A rider came fast behind them, a single man upon a dappled destrier. He was darkly garbed and his hood was drawn over his helm. Madeline noted him, because he rode a knight's horse but had no squire. He did not appear to be as rough as a mercenary.

Oddly, Rosamunde answered some summons sent by him into the hall. She cried a greeting to this mysterious arrival, then leaned close to hear whatsoever he murmured. Madeline was curious, for she could not imagine what messenger would seek her aunt here, no less what manner of messenger would ride a destrier instead of a horse more fleet of foot. He had but a dog as companion.

"The colors of Kinfairlie suit you well," Vivienne said, giving Alexander's tabard an affectionate tug.

"This work is a marvel!" Alexander declared, sparing his sisters a bright smile. "You all spoil me overmuch, by sharing the labors of your needles." He kissed each of them on both cheeks, behaving more like an elderly gentleman than the rogue they knew and loved. His fulsome manner left the sisters discomfited and suspicious.

"You were not so thrilled at Kinfairlie, when we granted it to you," Vivienne noted.

"But here there are many to appreciate the rare skills of my beauteous sisters."

Years of pranks played by this very brother made all five sisters look over their shoulders.

"I thought you would tickle us," Elizabeth complained.

"Or make faces," Isabella added.

"Or tell us that we had erred in some detail of the insignia," Annelise contributed.

"To grant compliments is most unlike you," Vivienne concluded.

Alexander smiled like an angel. "How could I complain when you have been so blessedly kind?" The sisters stepped back as one, all of them prepared for the worst.

"Do not trust him," Madeline counselled. The two elder sisters shared a nod.

"Alexander is only so merry at the expense of another," Vivienne agreed.

"Me?" Alexander asked, all false innocence and charm.

"Well, at least you are not garbed like a duchess," Malcolm complained. He gestured to the embroidery on his tabard. "This is too lavish for a man training to be a knight."

"At least you do have not to wear this horrendous green," Ross said, shaking his own tabard. "I would not venture to name this hue."

"It matches your eyes, fool," Annelise informed him archly.

"We spent days choosing the perfect cloth," Isabella added.

"I surrendered this length of wool for you, Ross," Vivienne said. "And I will not take kindly to any suggestion now that it would make a finer kirtle than a tabard."

Ross grimaced and tugged at the hem of his tabard, looking as if he itched to cast it aside. "The other squires at Inverfyre will mock me for garbing myself more prettily than any vain maiden." He tugged at the tabard in vexation. "What if the Hawk will not take me to his court?"

"You need fear nothing. Our uncle is most fair, and Tynan has sent him a missive already," Madeline said soothingly. Her gaze followed the stranger and Rosamunde as they entered the keep, her curiosity unsated by what she had seen.

"A maiden might take note of you, Ross, if you look your best," Elizabeth suggested shyly. Ross flushed scarlet, which did little to flatter the fiery hue of his hair.

"Our fingers are bleeding, our eyes are aching," Vivienne said with a toss of her tresses. "And this is the gratitude we receive! I expected a boon from my grateful brothers."

"A rose in winter," Annelise demanded.

"There is no such thing!" Malcolm scoffed.

"You should pledge to depart on a quest," Elizabeth suggested. "A pledge to seek a treasure for each of us."

"Sisters," Ross said with a roll of his eyes, then marched toward the nearest ostler.

Madeline had no further time to wonder about the stranger who had summoned Rosamunde. There was the usual bustle of arrival, of horses to be stabled and ostlers running, of squires and pages underfoot, of introductions being made and acquaintances being renewed. The stirrup cup had to be passed, sisters had to dress, and the company had to be gathered.

Soon, the moment would be upon them. The auction that all awaited, the auction that made the very air tingle at Ravensmuir!

"EVERY SOUL IN CHRISTENDOM MUST BE HERE!" Vivienne whispered to Madeline as they entered the chamber behind Alexander. Dozens of men watched their entry, standing politely aside as the family proceeded to the front of the chamber.

"Not quite so many souls as that," Madeline said. She had felt awkward since their arrival, for men seemed to be taking an uncommon interest in her.

"Perhaps you will find a husband here," Vivienne said with a merry wink. "Alexander is most determined that you choose soon."

"I shall choose in my own time and not before," Madeline said mildly, then knew a way to distract her sister. "Perhaps Nicholas Sinclair will be here," she added, her tone teasing.

Vivienne tossed her hair at the mention of her former suitor. "*Him*! He has not the coin for this."

Alexander stood aside and gestured that Madeline and Vivienne should precede him. He seemed stiff, and uncommonly serious.

"Smile, brother," Madeline whispered to him as she passed. "You will never catch the eye of a merry maid with so sour a countenance."

"The Laird of Kinfairlie must have need of an heir!" Vivienne teased with a laugh.

Alexander only averted his gaze.

"He never remains somber for long," Vivienne said as they sat upon the bench. "Look! There is Reginald Neville."

Madeline spared no more than a glance to the vain boy who imagined himself to be besotted with her. As usual, his garb was not only very fine, but he labored overhard to ensure that all noticed it. Even as he waved to her, he held his cloak open with his other hand, the better that its embroidery might be admired.

"I have only rejected him a dozen times." Madeline's tone was wry. "There might yet be hope for his suit."

"What a nightmare his wife's life will be!"

"And what will he do once he has exhausted the treasury he has inherited?"

"You are always so practical, Madeline." Vivienne edged closer, her voice dropping to a conspiratorial whisper. "There is Gerald of York." The elder sisters exchanged a glance, for that somber and steady man's endless tales put them both to sleep without fail.

"His bride will be well-rested, that much is beyond doubt."

Vivienne giggled. "Oh, you are too wicked."

"Am I? Alexander will turn his gaze upon you next, and demand that you wed soon."

"Not before you, surely?"

"Whyever not? He seems determined to wed all of us in haste."

Vivienne nibbled her lip, her merry mood dispelled. "There is Andrew, that ally of our uncle."

"He is nigh as old as the Hawk of Inverfyre, as well."

"Ancient!" Vivienne agreed with horror. She jabbed her elbow into Madeline's side. "You might be widowed soon, if you wed him though."

"That is hardly an attribute one should seek in a spouse. And I will wed none of them, at any rate."

The Red Douglas men and the Black Douglas men arrived and took to opposite sides of the hall, all the better to glower at each other from a distance. Madeline knew that Alexander preferred to ally with the Black Douglases, as their father had done, but she could not bear the sight of Alan Douglas, their sole remaining unwed get. He was so fair as to be unnatural. He fairly leered at her, the rogue, and she averted her gaze. Roger Douglas, on the other side of the hall, as swarthy as his cousin was fair, found this amusing and granted her a courtly bow.

Madeline glanced away from both of them. Her heart leapt when she found the steady gaze of a man in the corner fixed upon her. He was tall and tanned, quiet of manner and heavily armed. His hair was dark, as were his eyes. He stood so motionless that her eye could have easily danced past him.

But now that she had looked, Madeline could not readily tear her gaze away. He was the stranger from the bailey, she was certain of it.

And he was watching her. Madeline's mouth went dry.

His hair looked damp, for it curled against his brow, as if he had ridden hard to arrive here. He leaned against the wall, his garb so dark that she could not tell where his cloak ended and the shadows began. His gaze darted over the company at intervals, missing no detail and returning always to her. He stood and watched the proceedings, his stillness making Madeline think of a predator at hunt. The sole bright spot upon his garb was the red dragon rampant emblazoned across the chest of his tabard.

She felt his gaze upon her as surely as a touch and she knew her color rose.

"Look!" Elizabeth said, suddenly between Madeline and Vivienne. "There is a little person!"

"The chamber is full of persons of all size," Madeline said, glad of some diversion to make her look away from the dark stranger.

"No, a very small person." Elizabeth dropped her voice. "Like a fairy, almost."

Vivienne shook her head. "Elizabeth, you are too fanciful. There are fairies only in old tales."

"There is one in this chamber," Elizabeth insisted with rare vigor. "It is sitting on Madeline's shoulder."

Madeline glanced from one shoulder to the other, both of which were devoid of fairies, then smiled at her youngest sister. "Are you not becoming too old to believe in such tales?" she asked.

"It is there," Elizabeth said hotly. "It is there, and it is giggling, though not in a very nice way."

The elder sisters exchanged a glance. "What else is it doing?" Vivienne asked, evidently intent upon humoring Elizabeth.

"It is tying a ribbon." Elizabeth glanced across the chamber, as if she truly did see something that the others did not. "There is a golden ribbon, Madeline, one all unfurled around you, though I do not remember that we put it upon your kirtle."

"We did not," Vivienne whispered, dropping her voice as their Uncle Tynan raised his hand for silence. "Madeline does not like gold ribbons on her kirtle."

Elizabeth frowned. "It is twining the golden ribbon with a silver one," she said, her manner dreamy. "Spinning the two ribbons together so that they make a spiral, a spiral that is gold on one side and silver on the other."

"Ladies and gentlemen, knights and dukes, duchesses and maidens," Tynan began.

"A silver ribbon?" Madeline asked softly.

Elizabeth nodded and pointed across the chamber. "It comes from him."

Madeline followed her sister's gesture and found her gaze locking with that of the man in the shadows again. Her heart thumped in a most uncommon fashion, though she knew nothing of him.

"You should not speak nonsense, Elizabeth," she counselled quietly, then turned her attention to her uncle. Elizabeth made a sound of disgust and Madeline's heart pounded with the conviction that the stranger watched her even as she turned away.

"As all of you are aware, the majority of the treasures will be auctioned on the morrow," Tynan said after he had extended greetings and introduced the family. Rosamunde stood at his side, radiant in her rich garb. "You will have the opportunity in the morning to examine such items as are of interest to you, before the bidding begins at noon. Of course, there will be many more arrivals in the morning." The company stirred restlessly and the sisters exchanged a glance of confusion. "You gentlemen have been specifically invited this night for a special auction, an auction of the Jewel of Kinfairlie."

"I did not know there was a Jewel of Kinfairlie," Vivienne whispered with a frown.

"Nor did I." Madeline looked at Alexander, who steadfastly ignored them both.

"I thank you, Uncle," he said, clearly uncomfortable with the weight of the company's attention upon him. "As you all have doubtless ascertained, the Jewel of Kinfairlie is flawless."

"Where is it?" Vivienne demanded and Madeline shrugged that she did not know. A few men leered and she began to have a foul feeling in the pit of her belly.

How could there be such a gem and the sisters know nothing of it?

Alexander turned to face Madeline, and gestured toward her. "A beauty beyond compromise, a character beyond complaint, a lineage impeccable, my sister Madeline will grace the hall of whichever nobleman is so fortunate as to claim her hand this night."

Vivienne gasped. Madeline felt the color drain from her face. The sisters clutched each other's hands.

Alexander turned to the company, and Madeline suspected he could not hold her gaze any longer. "I urge you gentlemen, selected with care and gathered this night, to consider the merits of the Jewel of Kinfairlie and bid accordingly."

"Surely this is but one of his pranks," Vivienne whispered.

Madeline felt cold beyond cold, however. If this was a prank, it required the complicity of many souls. If this was a mere jest, it was difficult to see how it would not compromise Alexander's repute with his neighbors.

But it was beyond belief that he would truly auction her.

To Madeline's dismay, Reginald made the first bid with undisguised enthusiasm.

"Alexander!" Madeline cried in horror.

But her brother granted her a glance so cool as to chill her blood, then nodded to the company that the bidding should continue. He stood so straight that Madeline knew he would not rescind his words.

But to sell her? Madeline's gaze flicked over the company in terror. What if one of these men actually bought her hand?

They seemed intent upon trying to do so. Reginald countered every bid, raising the price with such reckless abandon that his purse must be fat indeed.

The bidding was heated, so heated that it was not long before Gerald of York bowed to Madeline and stepped back into the assembly, flushed with his embarrassment that he could not continue. Madeline sat like a woman struck to stone, shocked at her brother's deed.

Reginald Neville bid again with gusto. Was there a man within this company who could match Neville's wealth? The older Andrew grimaced, bid again, then was swiftly countered by Reginald.

He glared at the boy and shook his head.

"Is that the sum of it?" Reginald cried, clearly savoring this moment. He spun in place, his embroidered cloak flaring out behind him. "Will none of you pay a penny more for this fair prize of a bride?"

The men shuffled their feet, but not a one raised his voice.

"Reginald Neville," Vivienne whispered, her tone incredulous. Her cold fingers gave Madeline's a tight squeeze of sympathy. Madeline still could not believe that this madness was occurring.

"Last chance to bid, gentlemen!" Alexander cried. "Or the Jewel will be wed to Reginald Neville."

Madeline had to do something! She rose to her feet and every man turned to face her. "This would be the moment in which you declare your jest to be what it is, Alexander." She spoke with a calm grace that did not come easily, for her heart was racing.

"It would have been," Alexander said, "had this been a mere jest. I assure you that it is not."

Madeline's heart sank to her very toes, then anger flooded through her with new vigor. She straightened, knowing her anger showed, and saw the dark stranger smile slightly. There was something secretive and alluring about his smile, something that made her pulse quicken and heat rise in her cheeks. "How dare you show me such dishonor! You will not shame our family like this for no good reason!"

Alexander met her gaze and she saw now the steel in his resolve. "I have good reason. You had the choice to wed of your own volition and you refused to take it. Your own caprice brings us to this deed."

"I asked only for time!"

"I do not have it to grant."

"This is beyond belief! This is an outrage!"

"You will learn to do as you must, just as I have learned to do as I must." Alexander lowered his voice. "It will not be so arduous a fate, Madeline, you will see."

But Madeline was not reassured. She would be wed to the highest bidder, like a milk cow at the Wednesday market. Worse, they all found it to be merry entertainment.

Worse again, the highest bidder was Reginald Neville.

Madeline could not decide whether she would prefer to murder her brother or her ardent suitor.

She swore with inelegant vigor, thinking it might dissuade Reginald, but the men in the company only laughed. "You are all barbarians!" she cried.

"Oh, I like a woman with spirit," said Alan Douglas, fingering his coins. He offered another bid which was swiftly countered by Reginald.

"No marriage of merit will be wrought of this travesty!" Madeline declared, but not a one of them heeded her. The bidding rose higher even as she stood, trembling with anger. She could hear Vivienne praying softly beside her, for doubtless Vivienne feared that she would face a similar scene soon.

Could matters be worse?

Reginald bid again, to Madeline's dismay. She felt the weight of the stranger's gaze upon her and her very flesh seemed to prickle with that awareness.

No matter who bid, Reginald countered every offer. He urged the price higher with giddy abandon and as the company became slower to respond, he began to wink boldly at Madeline.

"You are worth every *denier* to me, Madeline," he cried. "Fear not, my beloved, I shall be stalwart to the end."

"So long as victory can be achieved with his father's coin," Vivienne said softly.

There were but five men bidding now, the counterbids coming more slowly each time. Madeline could scarce take a breath.

"Out of coin?" Reginald demanded cheerfully as one man reddened and bowed his head, leaving the fray.

Four men. Madeline's mouth was as dry as salted fish.

Roger Douglas thumbed his purse, then outbid Reginald.

Reginald pivoted and upped the bid, fairly daring Roger to counter. That man bowed his head in defeat.

Three men. Reginald's manner became effusive, his gestures more sweeping as he became persuaded of his certain victory. "Come now," he cried. "Is there not a one of you willing to pay such a paltry sum for the Jewel of Kinfairlie?"

Then two men were left, only Reginald and the uncommonly pale Alan Douglas. As much as she loathed Reginald, it was a sign of her desperation that Madeline began to wish that Reginald would triumph. At least Reginald did not frighten her, as Alan did.

Every bid Alan made, Reginald defeated with gusto. He did so quickly, flamboyantly, clearly not caring how much he paid.

But then, Vivienne had spoken aright. It was his father's coin and though there would be no more once it was spent, Reginald showed no restraint in ridding himself of its burden.

Alan frowned, stepped forward and bid again. The company held its collective breath.

Reginald laughed, then topped the bid, his tone triumphant.

There was a heavy pause. Alan glared at Reginald, then his shoulders dropped. He stepped away in defeat, his pose saying all that needed to be said.

"I win! I win, I win, I win!" Reginald shouted like a young boy who had won at draughts. He skipped around the floor, hugging himself with delight.

Madeline watched him with disgust. This was the man she would be compelled to wed.

There had to be some means of escape from Alexander's mad scheme.

Reginald chortled. "Me, me, *me*! I win!"

"You have not won yet," a man said, his voice low and filled with a seductive rhythm. "The winner can only claim his prize when the auction is complete."

Madeline's heart fairly stopped as the dark stranger stepped out of the shadows. Though he was not much older than Alexander, he seemed experienced in a way that Madeline's brother was not. She did not doubt that he would win any duel, that his blade had tasted blood. He moved with a warrior's confidence and the other men created a path for him, as if they could do nothing else.

"He is a fool to wear such an insignia openly," muttered one man.

"Who is he?" Madeline asked. She jumped when Rosamunde spoke from behind her. Her aunt had moved while Madeline had been distracted by the auction.

"The King of England has set a price upon his head for treason," Rosamunde said. "Every bounty hunter in England knows the name of Rhys FitzHenry."

"I daresay every man in Christendom knows of me, Rosamunde," the man in question said with confidence. "Grant credit where it is deserved, at least." He spared Madeline a glance, as if daring her to show fear of him. She held his gaze deliberately, though her heart fluttered like a caged bird.

Rhys then doubled Reginald's bid with an ease that indicated he had coin and to spare.

THE LADY MADELINE WAS PERFECT.

She was the proper age to be the surviving child of

Rhys's cousin Madeline Arundel. She shared her mother's coloring and her mother's name. Her supposed family were so anxious to be rid of her without a dowry that they resorted to this vulgar practice of an auction, something no man would do to his blood sister.

And Rhys had to admit that he liked the fire in this Madeline's eyes. She was tall and slender, though not without womanly curves. Her hair was as dark as ebony and hung unbound over her shoulders, her eyes flashed with fury. Rhys had seen many women, but he had never seen one as beguiling as this angry beauty.

A single glimpse of her had been all it had taken to persuade Rhys that buying Madeline's hand was the most effective solution to his woes.

After all, with Caerwyn beneath his authority, he would have need of a bride to have an heir. And wedding this woman, if she indeed proved to be Madeline's daughter and the sole competing heir for Caerwyn, would ensure that no one could challenge his claim to the holding. He did not fool himself that he had sufficient charm to win the hand of such a bride any other way. Rhys had no qualms about wedding his cousin's daughter, if Madeline proved to be that woman. In Wales, it was not uncommon for cousins to wed, so he barely spared the prospect of their common blood a thought.

Indeed, she would be compelled to wed some man this night, and Rhys doubted that any would grant her the even-handed wager that he was prepared to offer to his bride. Rhys had to believe that he could grant a woman a better life than that offered by her family or this irksome boy, Reginald.

Marriage was a perfect solution for both of them.

And so he bid.

And so the chamber fell silent.

It was as simple as that. Madeline would be his.

Rhys strode forward to pay his due, well content with what he had wrought.

The young Laird of Kinfairlie responsible for this foolery spoke finally with vigor. "I protest your bid. You were not invited to this auction and I will not surrender my sister to your hand."

Before Rhys could argue, Tynan granted the younger man a poisonous glance. "Did I not warn you that matters might not proceed as you had schemed, Alexander?"

Alexander flushed. "But still . . ."

"The matter has passed from your grasp," Tynan said with finality. Rhys knew that Tynan would indeed have cast him out if Rosamunde had not vouched for his character. The lady Madeline had some souls concerned for her future, at least.

"You cannot claim her!" Alexander cried. "I will not permit it."

Rhys smiled a chilly smile and let his gaze drift over the younger man. "You cannot stop me. And you cannot afford to exceed my bid."

The young laird flushed crimson and stepped back with a murmured apology to his sister, which Rhys thought long overdue.

Rhys then turned to the huffing Reginald Neville. "Have you no more coin?"

Reginald's face turned red and he threw his gloves onto the floor. "You cannot have that much coin!"

Rhys arched a brow. "Because you do not?"

Anger flashed in the boy's eyes. "Show your coin before we continue. I insist upon it!" Reginald flung out his hands and turned to the assembly. "Can we trust a man of such poor repute to honor his debts?"

A murmur passed through the company and Rhys shrugged. He sauntered to the high table, removing a chamois sack from within his leather jerkin. The lady caught her breath when he paused beside her and Rhys studied her for a heartbeat. Her eyes were wide, a glorious simmering blue, and though he sensed her uncertainty of him, she held her ground.

It was not all bad that she was as aware of him as this. He liked the glitter of intelligence in her eyes, as well as the fact that she had tried to halt this folly. He was accustomed to women who spoke their minds and a bride who did as much would suit him well.

He smiled slightly at her, hoping to reassure her, and she swallowed visibly. His gaze lingered upon the ruddy fullness of her lips and he thought of tasting her, knowing then how he would seal their agreement.

But first, the agreement had to be confirmed.

"You need not fear, sir," Rhys said coolly. "I will owe no debt for the lady's hand." There were more than enough gold coins in his sack, but Rhys was not anxious to flaunt his wealth. He cautiously removed only the amount necessary, and stacked the coins upon the board with care. Tynan bent and bit each one of them to test their quality, then nodded approval.

"Then, have her!" Reginald spat in the rushes with poor grace and stormed from the room. His gallantry, in Rhys's opinion, was somewhat lacking.

There was utter silence in the chamber as Rhys reached out and laid claim to Madeline's hand, such silence that he heard her catch her breath. His hand was much larger than hers and her fingers trembled within his grasp.

But she did not pull her hand from his and she held his gaze steadily. Again, he admired that she was stalwart in standing by the terms of agreement. He bent and brushed his lips across her knuckles, feeling her shiver slightly.

Alexander placed a hand upon Rhys's arm. "I do not care for convention or broken agreements. You cannot wed my sister—you are charged with treason!"

Rhys spoke softly, not relinquishing the lady's hand. "Do not tell me that the Laird of Kinfairlie is not a man of his word?"

Alexander flushed scarlet. His gaze fell upon the stack of coins and Rhys knew that he had desperate need of those funds.

He leaned closer to the boy, the lady's hand yet firmly clasped in his own, and dared the new heir of Kinfairlie. He would show the lady, at least, what manner of man her brother was. "I will grant you a chance to rescind your offer, though it is more than you deserve. Reject my coin, but solely upon the condition that the lady shall not be sold to *any* man."

It was clear that the younger man struggled with this decision. He appealed to his sister with a glance. "Madeline, you must know that I would not do this without cause."

And he reached for the coin.

"Cur!" she cried, her scorn matching Rhys's own. Rhys turned to her, his breath catching at the fury that lit her expression. "Take it then, Alexander! Take it, for whatever debts you have, and reject whatsoever loyalty Papa might have thought you owed to your siblings."

Alexander's hand shook slightly as he claimed the coins. "Madeline, you do not understand. I must think of the others . . ."

"I understand as much as I need to understand," she said, her words as cold as ice. "God save my sisters if you think of them as you have thought of me."

"Madeline!"

But the lady turned her back upon her sibling, her bearing as regal as that of a queen, her gaze locking with Rhys's own. He saw the hurt that she fought to hide and felt a kinship with her, for he too had been betrayed by those he had believed held him in regard.

"I believe there is a meal laid to celebrate our pending nuptials, sir," she said, her words carrying clearly over the hall.

Aye, this bride would suit him well. Rhys lifted her hand in his grip and bent to brush his lips across her knuckles in salute. She shivered and he smiled, knowing their nuptial night would be a lusty one.

"Well done, my lady," he murmured, liking that she was not readily daunted. "Perhaps our agreement should be sealed in a more fitting way."

A beguiling flush launched over the lady's face and her lips parted as if in invitation. Rhys gave her hand a minute tug as the company hooted, and she took a pace closer. He could fairly feel the heat of her breath upon his cheek and her cheeks flushed. Still she did not look away, though her breath came quickly in her uncertainty.

Rhys entwined their fingers, then lifted his other hand to her face. He moved slowly, so as not to alarm her, well aware of her uncertainty. She would be a maiden, without doubt. It would not do to make her fearful of his touch. Rhys tipped Madeline's chin upward with his fingertip. Her flesh was soft beyond belief, her valor admirable. He smiled slightly, saw a spark in her eyes that reassured him as little else might have done. This was no fragile maiden who would fear her own shadow.

Rhys bent and captured Madeline's sweet lips beneath his own. To his satisfaction, the lady did not flinch, nor did she pull away.

Aye, this was a wife who would suit him well.

The
Rose Red Bride

Chapter One

Kinfairlie, Scotland

VIVIENNE WAS POSSESSED of a new restlessness since their
return from Caerwyn. It was more than the rigor of routine
after the adventure of pursuing Madeline and Rhys clear
across England. It was more than missing Madeline, though
they two had shared more secrets with each other than with
their other sisters.

It was that smile that Madeline had gained upon her journey that was at root of Vivienne's dissatisfaction. It was a curious smile, both content and teasing, a smile that Madeline
bestowed upon her husband in the most unexpected moments, a smile that claimed Madeline's lips when her hand
stole over the curve of her belly, a smile that turned mysterious when Vivienne asked about matters abed.

It was a smile that haunted Vivienne, long after she was
no longer in her sister's presence. Madeline knew something—
and Vivienne had a fair guess what that something involved—

something that Vivienne did not. That created a gulf between the sisters wider than the distance that separated them.

Vivienne ached with the certainty of it. She had never been one to take well to mysteries or matters left undiscussed. She had never been able to keep a secret and seldom failed to surprise her siblings with some clever prank, for she could not keep from sharing it. And she had never had any capacity for patience.

She wanted to know what Madeline knew and she wanted to know immediately, if not sooner.

Vivienne was aware that Alexander wished to see her wed, as well, and she was willing to make vows before the altar. She wanted, however, to pledge herself to a man she loved with all her heart, for she suspected that Madeline's secret was not shared by every couple in Christendom.

There were not so many women who smiled as Madeline did. Vivienne aimed to be one of them. She attended every social event of which she heard tell, she begged Alexander to accompany her to York and to Edinburgh and to Newcastle, she met every eligible man with optimism and her best smile.

To no avail. Not a one of them made her yearn to know more about him. Indeed, Vivienne felt little but desperation. She knew that Alexander would not be patient forever—after all, she had already seen twenty-one summers. Time, and the right to choose, was slipping away from her, like sand flowing through a glass.

Surely she, who loved tales so well, could not be destined to live her days unhappily?

It seemed, though, that the gods would have their jest with her.

AS A RESULT OF THIS FRETTING, Vivienne had so little appetite at the board on Friday night that her mood did not escape notice.

"Do you not want your fish?" Isabella demanded. Already as tall as Vivienne, Isabella had begun to grow with vigor, and her appetite showed similar might. "The sauce is quite delicious. I could eat another piece, if you intend to waste it."

Vivienne pushed her trencher toward her sister. "Consider it your own." Isabella attacked the fish with such enthusiasm that she might not have eaten for a week.

"Did you not like it?" quiet Annelise asked, her concern evident. "I suggested to Cook that she use dill in the sauce, as it would be a change. It was not my intent to displease you."

"The sauce is delicious, as Isabella said," Vivienne said with a smile. "I am not hungry this evening, that is all."

"Are you ill?" Elizabeth, the youngest sister, asked.

Vivienne fought her frustration as every soul in the hall turned a compassionate gaze upon her. Nothing escaped comment in this household! "I am well enough." She shrugged, knowing they would not look away until she granted a reason for her mood. "I simply miss Madeline."

The sisters sighed as one.

"Perhaps you have need of a tale," Alexander said with such heartiness that Vivienne was immediately suspicious. Their eldest brother, now Laird of Kinfairlie, had played so many pranks upon his sisters over the years that any gesture of goodwill from him prompted wariness.

"What do you desire of me, that you would so court my favor?" Vivienne asked and Alexander laughed.

"I desire only to see you smile again, Vivienne. I am not the only one who has noted your sadness in recent weeks."

"Doubtless you are the only one who thinks a babe in her belly and a ring upon her finger would see the matter resolved," Isabella said. The three younger sisters rolled their eyes at this absurd notion, their response only making Vivienne feel more alone.

She was, after all, the only one who thought Alexander's scheme had some merit.

"You know how much I love a tale," she said to Alexander, sensing that perhaps their motives were as one. "Though I cannot imagine that you know one I do not."

"Ah, but I do, and it is a tale about Kinfairlie itself."

"What is this? And you never told it afore?" Vivienne cried in mock outrage.

Alexander laughed anew. "I but heard it this week, in the village, and have awaited the right moment to share it." He cleared his throat and pushed away his trencher.

He was a finely wrought man, this brother of theirs, and already Vivienne saw the effect of his recent responsibility upon his manner. Alexander thought now before he spoke, and he spoke with new care, considering his words before he cast them among the company. He treated the servants fairly, and his authority was respected. His courts were reputed to be among the most just in the area, his reputation already rivaling that of their father.

It had been no small challenge Alexander had faced since the sudden demise of their parents, and Vivienne felt a sudden fierce pride in her brother's achievement. She did not doubt that there was much he had resolved or shouldered without ever sharing the fullness of the truth with his siblings.

"You all know the tower that faces the sea, no less the chamber at its summit," Alexander began. "Though you may not know the reason why it stands empty, save for the cobwebs and the wind."

"It has always been empty," Vivienne said. "Maman refused to cross its threshold."

"And Papa had the portal barred," Alexander agreed. "I have only the barest recollection of ever seeing that door open in my childhood. I fancy, given the details of this tale, that it was secured after Madeline's birth, when I was only two summers of age."

The sisters leaned toward Alexander as one. Elizabeth's eyes were shining, for she loved a tale nigh as well as Vivienne. Isabella, who had made short work of the second piece of fish, wiped her lips upon her napkin and laid the linen aside. Annelise sat with her hands folded in her lap, characteristically quiet, though her avid gaze revealed her interest. Even the servants hovered in the shadows, heeding Alexander's tale.

Alexander propped his elbows on the table, and surveyed his sisters, his eyes twinkling merrily. "Perhaps I should not share the tale with you. It concerns a threat to innocent maidens . . ."

"You must tell us!" Isabella cried.

"Do not tease us with a part of the tale!" Vivienne said.

"What manner of threat, Alexander?" Elizabeth asked. "Surely it is our right to know?"

Alexander feigned concern, and frowned sternly at them. "Perhaps you demand the tale because you are not all such innocent maidens as I believe . . ."

"Oh!" The sisters shouted in unison and Alexander grinned. Annelise, who sat on one side of him, swatted him repeatedly on one arm. Elizabeth, on his other side, struck him in the shoulder with such force that he winced. Isabella cast a chunk of bread at him, and it hit him in the brow. Alexander cried out for mercy, laughing all the while.

Vivienne could not help but laugh. "You should know better than to cast such aspersions upon us!" She wagged a finger at him. "And you should know better than to tease us with the promise of a tale."

"I cede. I cede!" Alexander shouted. He straightened his tabard and shoved a hand through his hair, then took a restorative sip of wine.

"You linger overlong in beginning," Elizabeth accused.

"Impatient wenches," Alexander teased, then he began. "You all know that Kinfairlie was razed to the ground in our great-grandmother's youth." He pinched Elizabeth's cheek and that sister blushed crimson. "You were named for our interpid forebear, Mary Elise of Kinfairlie."

"And the holding was returned by the crown to Ysabella, who had wed Merlyn Lammergeier, Laird of Ravensmuir," Vivienne prompted, for she knew this bit of their history. "Roland, our father, was the son of Merlyn and Ysabella, and the brother of Tynan, their elder son who now rules Ravensmuir. Our grandfather Merlyn rebuilt Kinfairlie from the very ground, so that Roland could become its laird when he was of age." She rolled her eyes. "Tell us some detail we do not know!"

Alexander only smiled.

"And so the seal passed to Alexander, Roland's eldest son, when Roland and his wife, our mother Catherine, abandoned this earth," Annelise added quietly. The siblings and the servants all crossed themselves in silence and more than one soul studied the floor in recollection of their recent grief.

"My tale concerns happier times," Alexander said. "For it seems that when Roland and Catherine came to Kinfairlie newly wedded, there were already tales told about that chamber. Though Merlyn and Ysabella had not lived overmuch in this hall, there were servants within the walls and a castellan who saw to its administration in their absence.

"And so it was that the castellan had a daughter, a lovely maiden who was most curious. Since there were only servants in the keep, since it was resolved that she could not find much mischief in a place so newly wrought, and since—it must be said—she was possessed of no small measure of charm which she used to win her way, this damsel was permitted to wander wheresoever she desired within the walls.

"And so it was that she explored the chamber at the top of the tower. There are three windows in that chamber, from what I have been told, and all of them look toward the sea."

"You can see three windows from the sentry post below," Vivienne said.

Alexander nodded. "Though the view is fine, the chamber is cursed cold, for the openings were wrought too large for glass and the wooden shutters pose no barrier to the wind, especially when a storm is rising. That was why no one had spent much time in the room. This maiden, however, had done so and she had noted that one window did not grant the view that it should have done.

"Clouds crossed the sky in that window, but never were framed by the others. Uncommon birds could be spied only in the one window, and the sea never quite seemed to be the same viewed through that window as the others. The difference was subtle, and a passing glance would not reveal any discrepancy, but the maiden became convinced that this third window was magical. She wondered whether it looked into the past, or into the future, or into the realm of fairy, or into some other place altogether.

"And so she resolved that she would discover the truth."

Vivienne eased forward on the bench, enthralled by Alexander's tale. "What happened?"

"No one knows for certain. She slept there for several nights and when she was asked what she had seen, she only smiled. She insisted that she had seen nothing, but her smile, her smile hinted at a thousand mysteries."

Vivienne's attention was seized, for she suspected she knew how that maiden had smiled.

Alexander continued. "And on the morning after she had slept in that chamber for three nights, the damsel could not be found."

"What is this?" Isabella asked.

"She did not come to the board." Alexander shrugged. "The castellan's wife was certain that the girl lingered overlong abed, so she marched up the stairs to chastise her daughter. She found the portal to the chamber closed, and when she opened it, the wind was bitterly cold. She feared then that the girl had become too cold, but she was gone. There was not a sign of her in the chamber. The mother went to each window in turn and peered down, fearing that her daughter had fallen to her death, but there was no sign of the girl.

"And on the sill of one window—I suspect I know which one it was—the castellan's wife found a single rose. It appeared to be red, as red as blood, but as soon as she lifted it in her hands, it began to pale. By the time she carried it to the hall, the rose was white, and no sooner had the castellan seen it, than it began to melt. It was wrought of ice, and in a matter of moments, it was no more than a puddle of water upon the floor."

Alexander rose from his seat and strode to the middle of the hall. He pointed to a spot on the floor, a mark that Vivienne had not noted before. It shimmered, as if stained by some substance that none could have named.

"It was here that the water fell," Alexander said softly. "And when an old woman working in the kitchens spied the mark and heard the tale of the rose, she cried out in dismay. It seems that in Kinfairlie, there is an old tale of fairy lovers claiming mortal brides, that these amorous fairy men find portals between their world and our own when they glimpse a mortal maiden who captures their heart."

He smiled at his sisters. "And the bride price they leave is a single red, red rose, a rose that is not truly a rose, but a fairy rose wrought of ice." He scuffed the floor with his toe. "Though its form does not endure, the mark of its magic is never truly lost."

Silence reigned in the hall for a moment, the light from the candles making the mark on the floor appear to glimmer more brightly.

Alexander shrugged. "I cannot imagine that Papa believed the tale, but doubtless once he had a daughter, he had no desire to have her traded for a rose wrought of ice."

"Someone should discover the truth," Isabella said with resolve.

Annelise shivered. "But what if the tale is true? Who knows where the maiden went? Who would take such a risk as to follow her?"

Vivienne clenched her hands together and held her

tongue with an effort. She knew who would take such a risk. She knew, with eerie certainty, that this tale had come to light now because it was a message to her. A fairy spouse would suit her well, of that she had no doubt, no less the adventure of a life in another realm.

Vivienne would sleep in the tower chamber on this night.

She only had to figure out how the feat could be done, and done without rousing the suspicions of her siblings.